Waves Upon the Shore

By the same author

Dreams of Other Days
A Man Made to Measure

For David, my children and grandchildren, Yvette my editor and Agnes and Jack Toohey who lived in Annilaun

Part One

1847

Chapter One

They still had the look about them of people who had suffered a terrible ordeal, Katy O'Hara thought as she watched from the trap her husband Jamsie help the children up the step and in. The Hunger had left its mark. It was there to see in how Jamsie's old coat hung slackly on him, in the hollows at his wrists and the dark hollows beneath his eyes.

Bridget's yellow hair, once glossy as a buttercup, had lost its sheen and her cheeks their roundness and brightness. And poor Thomas was as pale as new milk and Mary Kate the same colour. As for herself, Katy had no idea how she looked for it was months since the sliver of mirror fell from the shelf and smashed in smithereens. Only by the flat slackness of her once-firm breasts and the fit of her skirt did she know that from her, too, the flesh had melted.

Father Bolger whose trap it was and who was taking them to Kinsale, tried to make the leaving of their little home less tragic. 'Wipe away your tears, Katy. America will be the salvation of you all, please God. Ireland is finished, Kilgoran is finished. You're the last to go. Only Carey left below at the Cross, with not a customer to come in for a glass of porter. Don't be crying now, all you're doing is upsetting the children. Even if you had money, or the potatoes were to flourish again – what life would you have here?'

'I know, Father, only 'tis hard when you know the leaving is forever.'

'America will be the making of you. Think of the children – they'll grow up free men and women. They'll never again know hunger. And in no time, Jamsie with a bit of work and a decent morsel of food will be your laughing black-haired boy. And who's to say that you mightn't run into Peader and his wife over there. Wouldn't that be the grand thing, now? You'd soon create your own little Kilgoran in America. And mightn't I myself one day take the notion to cross the water.'

Katy swallowed the lump in her throat as the priest closed the trap door. Prince, the dog she had reared from a pup, loving him like a child and was now deserting, pleaded with his eyes. She looked away unable to bear his sorrowful gaze, her heart breaking as the trap moved off, leaving the dog and her little cottage behind. She kept her head turned, and the tears ran down her face as she thought how never again would she walk down the boreen, never again smell the wild woodbine and see the fuchsia's hanging bells. Never again, never again so many things.

They stopped at Carey's public house to say goodbye. Carey wished them luck in America and Father Bolger in his new parish in Limerick. As they were about to leave Cary said, 'I nearly forgot the letter.'

'A letter, for me?' asked the priest.

Never a great lover of the clergy since Father Matthew had tried to stamp out drinking, Carey replied with a smug air, ' 'Tis not, it's for Jamsie. It came a while back and didn't I forget all about it till this very minute.'

Jamsie looked incredulous as the letter was handed over. Never before in his life had he received one. He handled it as you would a fragile thing. Cautiously fingering it, hesitantly opening it, taking out the notepaper and finding the money. 'A sovereign – a golden sovereign!' he exclaimed. 'Would you believe it – a whole sovereign.'

'Who sent it?' asked Katy. 'Look at the letter – who's it from?'

'Here Father,' said Jamsie, handing him the letter. 'You read it for us.'

With a shaking hand he passed the note to Father Bolger. Then he and Katy waited with impatience while Father Bolger searched his pockets for his spectacles. Once they were on, he scanned the top and bottom of the page and announced, 'Two weeks ago it was written and in Liverpool and it's from Peader.'

'God bless his generous heart,' said Katy and then the priest read the letter.

Dear Jamsie and Katy,

By the time you get this we'll be on our way to America. We missed the boat from Cork and came over here, afraid to delay in case Charlotte's father came after us. Once I arrive and get settled I'll write again. I hope you are all in good health, and that the few shillings will be a help. Remember me to everyone, and tell Father Bolger I'll not forget to write to him. Mind yourself and Katy.

Peader

'God send them all the blessings in the world and comfort poor Miss Charlotte,' said Katy, and thought – like myself she's going far from her home. Going for the love of her man. Going against all she was brought up to be. Putting the ocean between her and her father, not knowing

4

that he's no longer here to bar her love for Peader. Lord have mercy on his soul. The good, kind man and master that he was. 'Poor Lord Kilgoran dying like that,' she continued. 'Such a terrible end and Miss Charlotte not knowing that at the very minute she was running away to be married her father was breathing his last.'

'The Lord have mercy on him,' said the priest and Katy, Jamsie and Carey blessed themselves and repeated the prayer.

'May he rest in peace. He was a good landlord – the best. If more had been like him we'd not have known the hunger, the fever, the deaths and the thousands like yourselves having to leave your native land. May he be in Heaven.'

'Amen,' responded the others.

'And now,' said Father Bolger, 'we had better make a move.' Again they said goodbye to Carey and went on their way, the children waving until they could see the Cross no more.

Kilgoran House came into view. From the distance of the road it looked as it always had – a pale stone mansion flanked on either side by curving wings. From this far away its dilapidation wasn't visible. But Jamsie, Katy and Father Bolger had seen at close quarters its shattered window panes, the grass and nettles growing between the flagged terrace stones. Katy knew that behind the pale façade, mildew mottled the walls, rats nested behind the wainscotting and spiders' webs festooned the high, beautifully moulded ceilings. She knew that the great range in the kitchen was cold, the furniture and carpets, the books from the library, the silver and china, all the precious things were gone. The house was an empty shell.

And more precious than the things, the people, the people she had known and loved or respected all of her life, they too were gone. Lord Kilgoran and his daughters, the servants, all gone. Some were dead and others scattered. All were gone.

'God be with the times there were before the potatoes failed,' Father Bolger said, 'and may He be with us in the times ahead.' For a while then no one spoke, each adult mourning and remembering. For mile after mile the horse and trap went on passing the devastated potato fields, the deserted cottages from which whole families had fled either to America or England or, having died of hunger or fever, been unceremoniously dumped on carts and taken to communal graves.

They were nearing the port. Soon, Katy thought, there'll be another goodbye. She would never see Father Bolger again. His earlier remark

5

that one day he might cross the ocean was no more than a way of taking her mind off her sorrows, of giving her heart. He was getting old and infirm, his rheumatics had him crippled. She hoped his new parishioners would take as kindly to him as had the people of Kilgoran. Love him as they had.

Danny stirred in her arms, opened his eyes and looked up at her, smiling sleepily. She held him closer, the warmth of his little body comforting her. Rocking and rhythmically patting his back, bending her face low over him she let her tears fall on his dark hair as she thought of this last parting, of never again seeing the priest who had influenced her life so much. Almost from the day ten years ago when he arrived in Kilgoran. A girl she was then, eighteen years of age. Promised to marry Peader. Her mother delighted at the prospect of her marrying the son of a comfortable farmer with a fine stone house and thirty acres of a fine farm. But she fell in love with Jamsie, her blue-eyed black-haired boy and there was ructions when her mother knew. But Father Bolger knew how to handle her mother, Lord have mercy on her.

Ten years ago and sometimes it only seemed like yesterday. Miss Charlotte was a child then. Miss Catherine getting ready to marry her Captain and Miss Olivia, the beauty of the family, throwing her tantrums. Poor Miss Olivia . . . wasn't it as well you couldn't see into the future – the terrible end that was in store for her. And Master Charles careering and sowing seeds for other tragedies.

Her own lovely children born during the years and God taking two of them. Hannah in charge of the Big House kitchen, kind gentle Hannah wrapping up the parcels of leftovers for her to bring home for the children. Kind, gentle Hannah – where was she now? And Jamsie's brother Padraig transported for a crime he didn't commit and Johnny the other brother . . . where were they all? Where had Master Charles finished up – and did Miss Catherine go back to India?

The dead she hoped were in Heaven, her children and her parents. And Statia, surely Statia was in Heaven with God and His Mother and all the holy saints. Statia who had traipsed the village delivering babies, sitting with the dying and laying them out when they died, who made cures for ailments, charms for lovers and potions for them that were barren. Always there to scold or comfort, whichever she thought you needed or deserved. Statia with a heart too big for her body – who had handed over her burial money for me and mine to go far away to the west in America. Ah, yes, surely Statia had found her place in Heaven.

And so would Father Bolger, her other deliverer from trouble. 'Twas he who had put things right for her and Jamsie – and for Peader and

Charlotte when they fell in love. For Lord Kilgoran, too, Charlotte's father, when he died. Father Bolger was a saint. Only sometimes, when grief for her dead twin daughters overwhelmed her, did Katy question what he had once done. The sermon he had preached – his voice thundering from the altar, his words painting a picture of Hell as clearly as if she had opened a door and looked into its heart. Was he right then to ask mothers to make such a sacrifice?

She told herself she should never think such a thing – it was a sin to question him. Now above all when she was about to take her leave of him. 'God, forgive me for it and for all my bad thoughts. But You know I don't ask for them to come into my head.' Silently she now prayed in the way she often did. Speaking to Him in her own words, asking advice, explaining her thoughts or actions. Always with the hope that He was more kind and forgiving than she had been led to believe.

'Well, this is where I'll leave you,' said Father Bolger as they entered the port. 'Get yourself a night's shelter and first thing in the morning a few provisions for the journey.'

'But didn't you say, Father, that they'd feed us on the ship?' asked Katy, a worried look on her face as she contemplated having to dip into her reserve of money which was to give them a start in America.

'I did, 'tis what the agent who sold me the passages said. But I'd never rely on an agent's promise. Three pounds sixteen shillings a head for you and Jamsie, and half each for the children would have been the cost had you gone from a bigger port. Haven't you saved the difference?'

'We have, Father, and the sovereign besides,' Jamsie said with great optimism.

They got down from the trap. The cobbles were hard and cold beneath Katy's bare feet, but the children didn't seem to notice the discomfort of hard stones after the grassy tracks their feet were used to.

'Goodbye now and may God guard you every step of the way to America. I'll remember you always in my prayers, and you pray for me, too.' Father Bolger then shook Katy and Jamsie's hands and touched the children affectionately. Thomas he signalled out. 'Thomas,' he said, 'you're the fine boy and you're off to America. So listen to me now. Never forget that you are a Catholic and Irish. I hope that America will be kind to you but never forget why you had to go. Will you promise me that now?'

Thomas, embarrassed by the attention, went red in the face and hung his head.

'Look at me Thomas – you're eight or nearly, old enough anyway to understand why you are going away. Always remember you had no

7

choice – you had to go or die of starvation. Never forget that. Never forget the terrible wrongs done to your people. One day it will be righted. But only if the young keep alive the memory. So now like the good boy you are, give me your promise.' And Thomas raised his head and made his promise.

Chapter Two

'Go down, you and the children. I want to see the last of it,' Katy said when they had boarded the ship. 'Secure them in a berth, will you do that for me.'

'All right, so,' Jamsie said, 'but don't stay too long.'

All round her other people were taking their last farewells of Ireland, watching the green hills fade into the distance. Some cried loudly, lamenting their loss, others were praying and some like Katy just staring while the tears washed their faces. Crew members were ordering them below, but were ignored until their commands became harsher so that eventually only a few remained. Still Katy stayed until she heard Jamsie's voice pleading, 'Aghoille, come down now there's no more to see.' His arm was round her and she let him lead her from the rail. Wiping her eyes as she went, putting on a brave face for the children's sakes. No more tears. The children needed all her courage. For their sakes she had to keep up, do her sorrowing in private. They were setting out for a new life. A good life. One where they'd not know want, where they'd all be happy.

By the time she reached the steps leading to the hold there was a smile on her face. A wave of foetid air came up the stairs to meet her and her smile was replaced by an expression of disgust. The boat was rolling slightly but enough, combined with the foul stench, to make her want to vomit. Shakily she went down the last few steps and into the semi-darkness of the hold. As her eyes became accustomed to the poor light she saw where they were to spend two – maybe three – months.

Picking her way through the narrow aisle, banging her shins against barrels, bundles and boxes so that there was less than a foot of space to walk in, she was appalled at what she saw. Rough partitions enclosing spaces not quarter the size of her little kitchen lined the passage. In them narrow planks in tiers of two and three were fixed to the sides.

'Sacred Heart of Jesus is this where we're to sleep? I didn't expect luxury, but how could I, never mind a man the size of you, stretch out on one of them? A coffin is wider.'

' 'Tis bad alright,' Jamsie said, 'but our space is better, it's at the end

9

and nearer the privy. Though I'd say you'd have to be up early in the morning – there's only the one. There'll be ructions there.'

Katy, from the time she had left her mother's home where there were two commodes, one for her father and one for the women, had used the field behind the cottage, squatting behind a bush. Appalled at first by the experience. Necessity had accustomed her to it and eventually she found – at least when the weather was reasonable – that easing your bowels or emptying your bladder in the fresh air was preferable to commodes. And now she must use a privy, stand in line for a turn. And what about the children? Mary Kate, who couldn't hold her water for a minute. Thomas, who got short notice when he had to go. She was pondering these questions and stumbling and banging her shins and trying to remember to keep her head lowered.

'A sin against God it is. Cattle travel better,' Jamsie was saying. 'Look at them hatches. On a rough sea the water will wash in on top of us. And only the one privy for a hundred and fifty-six men, women and children.'

Katy's courage drained – it ran cold in her blood. She could feel the coldness all through her, draining the blood from her heart. I'm going back, she thought. I'd rather die by the road than stay a night in this hole of darkness that smells of rotten things, of rats and too many people, sick and old and dirty, God help them through no fault of their own.

She could hear women's voices, lamenting, protesting, echoing her own feelings about the conditions. But lamenting more than protesting, for they had realised what she for the moment had forgotten. They were far from the shore. There was no going back. They might starve, suffocate, drown, be eaten alive by rats or with God's help arrive in America – but go back they could not.

Katy heard another voice – one that didn't keen, saying resolutely, 'Keening and crying won't alter anything. Save your breath and energy to change what can be changed.'

'That's all very well,' Katy heard someone reply, then ask, 'But what about young girls travelling on their own – having to share berths with men? And husbands and wives who haven't enough children to fill up their space, strangers in on top of them. 'Tisn't natural nor Christian.'

'Listen,' said the practical woman whose accent Katy thought was Dublin, 'we'll get all the single girls to bunk together – and the fellas do the same. But as for the married couples who have to share, there's nothing you can do. I feel sorry for the poor women. Lack of privacy won't take a feather out of their husbands – they won't go without their rights.'

In that instant Katy made a decision – Jamsie whether he liked it or not would learn what the lack of privacy meant. She might be penned like a cow but she wouldn't behave like one.

When they reached where Jamsie had left the children minding the corner berth, they were huddled in the aisle crying. Bridget was nursing Danny and Mary Kate clinging to Thomas. 'What ails you?' Katy asked, alarmed at the sight of her children. 'Mammy, I want to go home,' Mary Kate wailed. 'It's too dark and I'm afraid.'

'It was him, him there,' Bridget said, turning her head and looking in the direction of their bunk space. 'We were minding the place and he threw us out. He pucked me and Thomas as well.'

'And me, too,' Mary Kate added.

Katy took a long look at him there. And saw a youth maybe sixteen or seventeen and a younger boy with him. She stared and the older one stared back. Anger surged through her. Rage that anyone should lay a finger on one of her children. She could kill him. Her passionate rage propelled her towards him. 'You,' she said, 'you hit my little childeren.' Jamsie caught hold of her, she shook off his restraining arm. 'You dared to hit one of mine. You big lump of a coward. If I'd been here you'd have got more than you bargained for. Now pick up your belongings and get from this place.'

She was close to him now and could see his ugly face, his dirty ginger hair and through the parted lips blackened broken teeth. She kept staring at him, her eyes daring him to defy her. As many times she did when confronting Thomas, only Thomas though stubborn was a child and this one not far short of a grown man.

'And you're going to make me shift, ma'am?' There was an insolent smile on his ugly face.

'I'm going to make you. Drag you by the scruff of the neck if I have to. Get out of here immediately.' She could sense Jamsie behind her – moving in on her. In a minute he'd be calling her off. Making peace because it was too much trouble to do otherwise and in the process losing the spot where they might rest in tolerable comfort. 'Now this minute. You bully. You big hulking brute hitting little children.'

While she berated him thoughts went through her mind. Supposing he had a father bigger than Jamsie, a mother bigger or stronger than her, a couple of brothers. But nothing showed on her resolute face. And she saw the boy lower his eyes and look away. It was, she knew, the beginnings of victory unless assistance came to him. Having gained ground she didn't want to lose it. 'Go on, off you go and take your

11

belongings with you.' When he bent to gather his things she saw that his bare splawed feet were bleeding and she felt sorry for him. Imagining what hardships he had suffered. Maybe he was an orphan, maybe he had had the fever. Maybe. Stop maybeing, she told herself. From now on stop pitying everyone. You needn't rob or kill or lose every shred of decency – but if you want you and your family to survive, to get to America, forget that once you tried to live by putting others before yourself. Forget nice manners. Remember the twins: remember the poor oul dog. Harden your heart the way you had to then. You have to for the sake of your family. Otherwise you might just as well have laid down in the cottage, let the hunger make you drowsy and fallen into the long sleep.

The youth humped his pack, said something to the boy with him and went looking for another berth.

'God bless us, you gave him a fine going over. Like a tinker you were. Supposing he comes back with a father twice the size of me,' said Jamsie.

'Then save your breath for the fight the pair of you will have. And don't laugh. If you only knew what that took out of me. I was shaking inside, doing it all with my eyes, with my will.'

'Didn't you have me behind you. Wouldn't I have put him through the hull had he looked crooked at you.'

'You might as easily have said I was creating about nothing and sure what difference did it make – wasn't one place the same as another.' Her tone was light and bantering. Nothing was to be gained by using a different one. 'Keep an eye on the children while I arrange our things,' she said.

She arranged their few possessions in the small space. All round her people were doing the same. Thin haggard men and women nervous and apprehensive-looking, talking to each other in whispers. Everyone aware that every action, every torn ragged garment they unpacked was open to the scrutiny of all. Katy talked as she worked. 'We'll have to sleep in our clothes. And Jamsie, the few shillings we've left – don't let them out of your hand for a minute. And don't you, Bridget nor Thomas, move from here. In all the nooks and crannies you could be lost. Where will we sit at all?'

'There's half a barrel that's empty and a wooden box there at the end of the passage – I could get them,' Jamsie said.

'Do then,' said Katy, 'for we can't stand all day.'

Thomas complained about being hungry. Katy smiled and said,

12

'That's what having the bit in your belly lately does for you.' He looked at her uncomprehendingly and she explained. 'Until Statia gave me her burial money you were starving. Gone beyond wanting food. Lord have mercy on her the few pounds bought our steamship tickets and enough food to put strength back into you. New life into you, the life that was nearly gone making you too weak to even look or ask for food. That's what I meant. And if you let me finish what I'm doing I'll feed you now in a minute.'

It didn't take long to arrange her space. When it was done she sat on the half-barrel and Jamsie on the box with their backs to the aisle so as not to appear curious about their neighbours. But Danny breaking free from Bridget's hold wandered into the passage and the woman in the opposite space spoke. Saying what a fine child, he was, God bless and spare him. And Katy turned round and acknowledged the blessing and compliment.

'Aren't the conditions desperate, ma'am,' the woman said.

'Terrible indeed,' replied Katy. She saw that the woman had a little girl with her and thought it was a grandchild, for the woman appeared too old to be her mother. Then Katy reminded herself that the thin inoffensive, lined face could be the after-effects of the Hunger or sickness. And that for all she knew, the woman might not be a day older than herself. She hadn't seen her own face this many a day and a sorry sight she could very well look.

The woman was gentle mannered and soft-spoken, and Katy took a liking to her. She told her she came from a village called Kilgoran and the woman said she had heard tell of it. Wasn't there a fine Big House there. In her own village in the north of Cork there wasn't one. She had often thought having the gentry in the village might have been a grand thing. Her name was Mary Callinan and the child was her daughter, Kathleen.

'Is it just the two of you going to America, please God?'

'It is. Kathleen's all I've left now. I had a fine family, another daughter, two sons and a husband. All gone now, the Lord have mercy on them. One after the other in the space of a week.'

'The fever?' asked Katy.

' 'Twas hard to tell – between the Hunger and disease sure how would you know? Tell me now, what sort of a place was Kilgoran?'

'Only a small village but as lovely as you could wish to see.'

'One day I'd love to hear you tell of it, maybe the telling could put in an hour of our time.'

'Maybe so,' said Katy, and wondered what sort of a woman was Mary

Callinan – a fool or what – sitting on a splintered box in the dirt and the semi-darkness, one minute relating about the loss of her family and with the next breath wanting stories of a place she knew nothing about.

Mary smiled at her, her worn face almost childlike-looking with the eagerness shining out of her eyes. 'I love a good story – it does take your mind off things.'

'It does,' Katy agreed. One day perhaps she would tell Mary about Kilgoran. But not now. For were she to let her mind go back to her home – to the way life was before the Hunger – in the telling and thinking she would surely lose her mind. The past was over – the present she must get through, minute by minute – all her hopes were pinned on the future. Only when that was as secure as anyone's future could be would she be able to face the past.

She asked Mary who was sharing her berth and Mary told her two girls, nice girls and their old grandmother – not one of them with a word of the English – but nice all the same. They were gone, she supposed, to gossip with others who had the Irish. And then Mary said she wondered what it would be like in America. Katy replied that from all she had heard there was full and plenty and oceans of land for the taking.

'So it is said,' Mary nodded. 'I never heard of one that went who wasn't content. But sure it was all in letters. They were grand to get and read and have the dollars. Many's the time a neighbour who couldn't read brought them to me and I'd be reading about New York and Boston and them places. Grand it all sounded but 'tis a different thing reading a letter by your own fireside and letting your mind imagine the great living and then being homeless and on your way to America.'

'Have you anyone there belonging to you?'

'Two cousins who used to send the dollars – saving them I was for a passage. Lord rest them they both died and the money went during the Hunger except a bit I kept in the thatch which paid for me and Kathleen. And yourself – will you be met?'

'No,' said Katy. 'I know of two people from the village. I heard from them the day they were sailing to America. They had gone to take passage from Liverpool, from there the letter was sent. But where they are now I don't know.'

Jamsie interrupted the conversation to say, 'I was thinking I'd take Daniel up on deck. He's getting cranky – the fresh air might soothe him.' Katy watched him go and was sorry for feeling irritable towards him earlier. She loved him and would sorely miss his love in the time ahead. Silently she said a little prayer for the journey to soon pass and they be in a place of their own.

14

Mary and Katy had hardly resumed their conversation when Thomas said, 'Daddy's coming back.' Katy saw Jamsie and when he came near asked, 'What brought you back before you were there a minute?'

'You're not allowed on the deck,' said Jamsie.

'Oh, and who says so?'

'One of the crew. Steerage passengers aren't allowed up. I went to go closer to him and he held up a hand and said, "No farther. Stay where you are." "Why so?" said I. "Because I don't want no bloody fever, that's why." '

'I thought we'd left all that behind. All the fear and shunning. Ma'am, that was the terrible thing when my family died, the way we were shunned, shunned by them I'd thought were friends and neighbours.'

Katy remembered her own fear of the sickness, her terror that someone could bring it to her family. She said nothing of it to the woman. But turned instead to Jamsie and told him to go back again and tell the man that you couldn't herd people below deck as if they were cattle. 'Tell him we paid our passage and if we're not entitled to much we're entitled to breathe fresh air. Go on,' she said when he made no move.

'I won't. For one thing it won't do any good. And if he pulled away from me again the way he did I'd hit him through the wall.' She saw from the set of his mouth that he meant it, so she went herself. Handing Daniel to Bridget. Ignoring the people who asked her to stop traipsing about.

The crewman watched her climbing the stairs. A tall, fair-headed woman, thin but with a good shape still on her. He eyed her appreciatively as she approached, noticing her clear skin and rosy mouth, her clean clothes. She was the finest and the prettiest woman who had boarded. And he knew, for he had watched them all, thinking of the long nights ahead and the favours he hoped to get in return for a few privileges granted. He put out an arm to bar her way, but smiled.

'I want to go out on the deck,' Katy said in a pleasant way. There was no point in inviting trouble, so she smiled at the man.

'You can't – Captain's orders. No steerage passengers allowed on deck except to collect the water ration.'

'The water ration?'

'Yeah,' said the sailor. 'Once a day you'll come up for that, otherwise you have to stay below until we dock.'

'But that's terrible. I can't breathe below. I'm stifled. I've a baby, three little children. Surely no one would do that to us.'

The seaman shrugged. 'That's the Captain's orders.'

'You must have got it wrong.' Katy's voice lost its pleading note. She became agitated, her heart beating so that she was aware of it. She could feel the colour surging up her neck and her face flaming. 'No one can do that. We've got tickets, we paid our passage, we – I want to see someone else.' She became incoherent. Rage and exhaustion, hunger and the earlier encounter with the red-headed youth and now this terrible aggravation brought her close to breaking down. But she mustn't do that. She mustn't grovel before this man.

'You look nice in a temper,' the crewman said and smiled at her. 'It's not my fault, love. I have to obey orders. But listen,' he moved closer to her, his fear of the fever less than his desire for this raging woman. 'I could fix it for you to come up when it gets dark, you know.'

She wanted to spit in his face. But something warned her not to. This man could be a bad enemy – with the power to make the weeks ahead into a nightmare. The splaw-footed boy was one thing – this one was a different kettle of fish. Her thoughts had given her a breathing space so that when she spoke her voice was calmer. 'I'm a married woman with a husband – what would I be doing up on deck in the dark?'

'That'd be up to you. Let me know if you change your mind.'

The pleasure it would have given her to have spat at him. To have seen Jamsie thrash him. Though that was a forlorn hope. This man was bigger than Jamsie and hunger hadn't weakened his constitution. Muscles bulged on his arms, his face was well-fleshed and tanned from the wind and sun. And above all he was part of authority. Even for spitting at him she could bring the law on herself – maybe ruin their chances of landing in America.

'I mean it – lots could come out of a stroll on deck.'

'Thanks very much,' Katy replied in what she hoped was a contemptuous manner and pulled her shawl's edges together, for the man's glance made her feel naked. She walked away and the sailor called after her, 'I won't go away.'

Chapter Three

The red-headed youth, whose name was Terence McCabe, watched Katy coming back down the stairs from the corner he had found for himself and his brother Mikey. He had followed her up and got the gist of the conversation between her and the crewman before returning to his place. No sexual desire stirred in him at the sight of Katy. She was an 'oul wan', a skinny oul wan who had thwarted him, made little of him, bested him. He hated her. One day he would get his own back. If he waited for a thousand and one days he would get his own back.

'I'm hungry. When will I get my food?' asked his brother.

'In a minute, don't ask again.'

The boy, who was four years younger than Terence and a bit simple, settled back against the wall and was quiet. Terence was his mother and father. Terence had nursed him when he had the fever from which their parents had died. Carried him on his back when his legs were too weak to support him. Warned him if he didn't stop crying for his mother and father he would put him by the side of the road and leave him. He had watched Terence strip people they found dead by the wayside and rob them of their rags, search their pockets and if there was money, take it. Terence had hidden him in ditches while he robbed nests and stole milk from the cows of strong farmers.

He was with Terence the night he killed the old man. It was lashing rain when from the brow of a hill they saw a cottage. 'We'll shelter there for the night,' Terence had said. 'It'll be empty, they'll have died or gone to America, come on.' Mikey followed him down the narrow rutted track where the grass grew so high on either side a man could walk through it and not be seen. 'It's empty, all right. Not a puff of smoke going up from the chimney and plenty of turf by the gable wall. We'll stay till morning.'

The door was fastened. 'To America they've gone. If they'd died of the fever no one would have bothered to lock up.' He put his shoulder to the door and pushed. It moved slightly but held. 'It's bolted from the inside – that's queer!' He banged on the door then put his ear close to it. 'Not a stir,' he said after banging again. The heaviness of the rain increased.

17

'Will we go on?' whimpered Mikey. Terence ignored him. 'Will we?' asked his brother again.

'Shut up, you little bastard. I've got to find something to force the door.' After searching and finding nothing he picked up a big stone. 'I'm going to smash the window then in you go.' Through each of the panes he banged the stone then beat at the wooden frames which cracked and were forced apart. 'Listen,' he told his brother. 'The house is the same as at home – in at the window, turn and open the door.' He repeated his instructions.

'Terry, don't make me I'm . . .'

'*In*,' hissed Terence.

He heard the bolt being drawn then Mikey's scream as the door opened. 'Someone touched me, there's someone here.'

Terence pushed him out of the way. 'A coat brushed against your face, that's all.'

' 'T'wasn't a coat, a hand it was.'

'Stop whinging or I'll give you something to whinge for!' Terence pushed him into the room. It was pitch dark.

'Listen, there they are. I'm afraid, Terry.'

Terence heard the breathing, chesty breathing coming from where the fireplace was. 'Rats,' he said, 'or maybe a bird in the chimney,' and walked to where the noise was. It was only a few paces to the hearth. The breathing was louder now. Then a voice cracked and hoarse said, 'Get out whoever you are.'

'We only want a shelter for the night. We won't harm you. Light the candle.'

'A candle! Where would I get a candle? The candles and rush-lights are gone this long time. Go on away now. Leave me alone, I'm a sick old man.'

Terry's groping hands found the man and dug into his bony shoulders. He could smell his sour breath and hear the wheezing chest. 'We'll sleep here and leave when it's light. Is there a palliasse?'

'Only the one where I was sleeping till the window went and nearly killed me with the fright.'

'Lead us to it.'

The old man whimpered and moaned as Terry's grip on him tightened. ' 'Tis there, to your left.'

'Right so. Commere Mikey, feel your way and throw yourself down. And you,' he said letting go the old man, 'sleep in the chair. We'll be gone in the morning.'

★

18

He woke with the first light. Through half-open eyes he saw that the man was very old and feeble. Watching, he saw him rise, go to a corner near the chimney piece, bend then kneel and begin clawing at the earthen floor. He then lifted out a small pouch which hung heavily from its drawstring.

Money! Guineas! A passage for him and Mikey to America. With difficulty the man arose and with his foot smoothed the disturbed earth. He looked towards the palliasse. Terry snored loudly while still observing through slit eyes. Hesitantly the old man made his way towards the door.

'Going out to piss and find a new hiding place,' Terry said under his breath, as he got up and followed the old man. Quietly, careful not to make a sound he dogged the man. There were stones, plenty of them, stones like the one with which he had broken the window. He bent and picked one up. A bang of it would fell the oul fella. He'd drop like an ox being slaughtered. Then he'd grab the bag and they'd be a long way gone before he came to.

He was close to him with his hand raised when the man looked round. He opened his mouth, toothless with a coated tongue, his breath foul on Terry's face. He brought the stone down on the scantily-covered head and again when the man didn't drop immediately. Untwined the pouch from his fingers and ran to the house. Shaking Mikey, he shouted: 'Get up quick – I've done for him. Look,' he held up the bag, 'enough for America – a bag of sovereigns, enough for America.' He kept talking. 'It'll be weeks, months before he's found. And nowadays no one looks too close at the dead – afraid of the fever. *Get up.*'

They met no one for miles, by which time the sun was well up. There was little heat in its autumn rays, but soon a wind rose and dried their sodden clothes on them. 'Keep going,' Terry urged when Mikey lagged. 'Keep going till we reach the next place – then we'll eat and ask about boats.'

Bundles of straw were issued to passengers who like Katy hadn't brought a feather mattress aboard. The straw was damp and mouldy-smelling and all over the hold people could be heard sneezing, as they spread it on the shelf-like banks that were to be their beds.

Mary in the opposite berth carried on a conversation while the two women arranged the straw. 'There is a woman I was talking to who has a grand book – the *Emigrant's Guide*. Anything you ever wanted to know is in it. We'll be well-fed according to it. Twenty-one quarts of water, two pounds of biscuits, one pound of wheat flour, five pounds of oatmeal and two pounds of molasses.'

'Indeed,' said Katy. 'And where will we cook it?'

'I never thought of that. I must have another read of the book. Wait now till I do,' said Mary, leaving her bed-making and going to find the woman with the *Emigrant's Guide*.

'In some ships,' she said when she returned, 'there's provisions for cooking on the deck. And all the amounts of food I mentioned is per man, woman and children. Won't we be the well-fed people? Only a man who was there when I read the book said it mightn't be so on this ship. Them regulations – the ones in the *Guide* are for the British ships. But God is good and maybe we'll get the same.'

Katy said she hoped so. She had made the bunk spaces as comfortable as possible. Everyone would have to sleep in their clothes for there wasn't enough otherwise to cover them. And had there been, modesty would have forbidden her to undress in sight of so many.

Food was brought to the hold – its arrival announced by a seaman banging two tin lids together and shouting for the passengers to come and get it. Some had no utensils in which to receive the greasy pork stew and in desperation they cupped their hands and had it ladled into them, most of the stew seeping through before it reached their mouths.

'Goodnight and God bless you,' Katy said to Jamsie as she wearily got onto her wooden plank and he onto his. He reached and held her hand. She knew his wants and felt sorry for him and knew that on many a night he would climb in beside her, onto a space not wide enough for one and try persuasion. Poor Jamsie, she gave him back his hand and closed her eyes.

She said her prayers, ones of thanks for being on the ship, ones for a safe journey and arrival in America and then her long litany for the dead . . . 'Lord, have mercy on my mother and father and Jamsie's parents. On Statia who brought all my children into the world and gave me the money for this passage, on the Master and Miss Olivia. And Sacred Heart of Jesus take care of my little girls, my Peg and Nora that in Your wisdom You took to Heaven. May they and the souls of the faithful departed rest in peace, amen.'

She lay and listened to the sound of the ship. The flapping of sails and the creaking of timbers, mice and rats scratching, but as one after another of the passengers fell asleep little was to be heard but a crescendo of snores. Short ones like the grunts of a pig. Strangled ones, where the snorer reached a high note then gasped and gurgled before emitting a whistle and the big snore began again. I'll not be able to close my eyes, she thought, but before she knew it she fell asleep and dreamed.

20

And she dreamed she was back in Kilgoran on a lovely summer's morning, in the Widow Murphy's cottage where she went to live after being married. She was expecting Bridget and yet the queer thing in the dream was that her younger children were also there and she couldn't understand how this could be when Bridget was her eldest. Peg and Nora's red hair was glinting like copper in the sunlight. And she was glad that they hadn't died. That had only been a bad dream. She called their names and they ran towards her. They ran and ran and still they never reached her and she scolded them: 'Stop play-acting and come here at once,' for she wanted to touch them, to hold them close. They ran faster and still they didn't reach her.

Then she felt a sickness in her stomach. It was, she told herself, because of the child she was carrying. Though that was the strange thing, for Bridget was there in the distance with the other children and running towards her, the distance narrowing but Peg and Nora were as far away as ever. Her stomach lurched, wakening her. Only she didn't waken but knew she had slipped into a nightmare for she was in some strange place, with strange noises and in front of her was a tiny blue light that as she watched it rose up and up in the air until its blue flame almost disappeared. She became aware of the noises, the snoring and the sound of retching and remembered the ship and that she was on it. And the blue light was the soot-covered small lamp hanging from a beam and it was the ship that was rising, not the lamp. Up and up it was borne and then it stopped, hovered for a few moments before plunging in a fall she was certain would take her and the ship to the bottom of the ocean. She screamed, all round her there were screams, 'Jamsie, Jamsie,' she cried. 'Jamsie, we're sinking. Jamsie, we'll be drowned!'

'It's all right, it's all right,' he told her, climbing in beside her and squashing her against the wall. 'It's only the Atlantic rollers – we're well away from land and feeling their force. Many a seagoing man told me about the Atlantic rollers.' His hand caressed her. 'There's no storm, no danger. The only danger is that I'll be pitched out on top of my head. The divil fire whoever thought a man could take his ease on one of these boards.' His hand was urgent in its caressing and her body was responding – she wanted him so much. Wanted to feel his strength, the comfort of his weight covering her. To move with him as if they were one being, gently at first and then, oh then, she wanted that so much. But even more than her desire she was aware of the noises that surrounded them, all the ones she had heard before she went to sleep – and others – the men and women who weren't letting the Atlantic rollers or lack of privacy interfere with their married life, and their

21

grunts mingled with the grunt-like snoring. So Katy stilled Jamsie's hand in its wanderings, holding it captive, whispering to him that she was sorry, sorry for both of them but especially for him, but that she couldn't and wouldn't – not until they had landed and had four walls around them.

In the beginning the weather was good with a brisk wind before which the ship made good headway – and the wind also found its way through the rotten hull timbers and freshened the air slightly. As the days passed the passengers tried to give some normality to their lives. Acquaintances were formed, the women gossiped and prayed and talked about what they had left behind in Ireland but mostly they speculated on what America, please God, when they got there held for them.

On board there were cranky people, quarrelsome ones, sickly women and frail old men, young bachelors and spinsters and some that weren't so young. But the majority were families like Jamsie and Katy, making the best of things, finding ways of passing the long dreary days below decks. A man and his son had a fiddle and a melodeon which they sometimes played and to which people sometimes sang and even on occasions attempted step-dancing to, in the narrow aisles.

They talked often about food, complaining of the quality and quantities they received. 'I suppose,' said Mary one day after a meal of watery soup scummed with grease and scraps of meat and gristle, 'they think we should be grateful for anything because for so long we had nothing. 'Tis people not saints we are. And this isn't Ireland with the potatoes rotting. We were led to believe we'd be well-fed and handed over our money. I was that looking forward to pounds of flour and oatmeal. Thinking of the stirabout and brown cakes I'd make.'

'Without a fire to cook on flour and meal wouldn't have been palatable,' said Katy, and went on picking weevils out of the bread.

'I suppose you're right, all the same they're daylight robbers.'

'Indeed,' said Katy. 'Do you know what, Mary? From this minute I'm digging out no more of these little brown insects. They've been baked, so little harm they'll do us. Far less anyway than the amount of bread I'm wasting. 'Twas only me noticed them – Jamsie and the children devour anything without giving it a glance.'

' 'Twas you drew my atttention to them – I thought it was the grain in the flour,' said Mary. 'But now that I know what they are I couldn't let one pass my lips nor Kathleen's either. I'll keep on with the picking.'

Collecting the water ration allowed the steerage passengers a brief glimpse of the sea and a breath of fresh air. A glimpse and a breath was all it was, for the doling out of the water was arranged so that no fewer than six people at a time came on deck, were quickly served and as quickly had to return below. So that when they had been at sea for a week and it was announced that they were to be allowed up for half an hour once a week if the weather wasn't stormy a cheer went up. Everyone prayed for calm seas.

It was a fine bright day when they went on deck for the first half-hour period. The sunlight dazzled their eyes. They gulped in the fresh air. They straightened their backs and walked tall.

'If only,' said Katy, 'we had half an hour here every day. Look at the sea, look at the sky. I'd come up whatever the weather was like. Isn't it well for the cabin passengers, who have the freedom to go on deck when they like? Wouldn't it be grand if we could do the same. Maybe we will. Maybe the Captain will change his mind and let us do the same.'

'Don't torment yourself with wishing. Half an hour once a week – that's all we'll get,' said Jamsie.

On that first time on deck, Katy made friends with a woman from Dublin. Her name was Eileen O'Flaherty and she and Katy took an instant liking to each other. Katy thought she had a lovely face. A longish thin one, full of expression. Smiles and frowns danced across it. Her hair was dark and long and she wore it loose. It flew back in the breeze and streamed behind her head. 'I was thinking,' she said now, 'we could wash out things up here. You know them half-barrels, well, if your husband brought up a couple we could leave them to catch water – what do you think?'

'That's a grand idea,' said Katy and sent Jamsie to fetch two. While she and Eileen continued talking the crewman passed, glanced at Katy in what she considered a too-familiar way, making her blush. Eileen shouted something after him.

'What was that you said?' she asked.

'That I hope the weather keeps up.'

'Do you know him them?'

'Larry – of course I do.'

'That didn't take you long and you got to know his name quick.'

Eileen laughed. 'That's not all I got to know.'

Before they knew it it was time to go below again. Back into the dark and dirt, back to bending their backs and stooping their heads. But at least, Katy thought as she descended the steps, she had a new friend. One who in their short time on deck had made her laugh. It was a relief to have someone other than Mary, who looked on the black side of everything.

On fine days when word was given that they could go on deck the children and men left whatever they were doing and raced to the stairs, while the women collected the younger children and the clothes they were to wash. There were a few men and women, mostly elderly, who wouldn't leave the hold. One old woman that Katy tried to coax up explained her fear. 'Daughter,' she said, 'down here in the dark it's bad enough, but if I shut my eyes and say my beads I can forget I'm on the water. When I went above last week I saw the sea – everywhere my eye would stretch water like mountains and every drop of it coming towards the ship.'

'But the fresh air would do you good,' coaxed Katy.

'The old woman shook her head. 'Nothing will do me good until I set foot on firm land. Go you now and get the fresh air and God bless you for your kindness.'

The half-barrels had collected water but mostly salt water, washed up in waves. A few of the women had brought bars of soap with them but not all their slapping, banging and rubbing would lather their changes.

The men separated themselves from the women and walked up and down in the restricted space. Once a boy spotted a school of porpoises – not knowing what they were, he shouted that there were people out there splashing and swimming and maybe drowning. A man who had been a sailor gave a name to the porpoises and everyone left what they were doing to come and lean over the rail and watch.

Sometimes the women quarrelled over the makeshift lines they had strung. On occasions pucks were exchanged, hair pulled and names called – but overall the atmosphere on deck was a happy though sometimes boisterous one. The women sang while they washed, looked up at the sky, breathed deeply of the air and reminded each other that every mile the ship sailed was a mile nearer America.

The three friends spent hours on their upturned barrels and boxes gossiping. One day Eileen told them the story of how she came to be on her way to America. 'I'm from Dublin, as you know. There we weren't depending on the potato so it wasn't the Hunger that drove me out.'

Mary, a woman with a curious nature, was impatient for details of why Eileen had left and interrupted to ask, 'What was it, so?'

'A man, what else. Isn't it always a man?'

Mary was all ears, her head leaning forward and a look of anticipation in her eyes.

'I used to sing in a drinking tavern off Dame Street. One night a man in the audience sent me a note asking me if I'd have supper with him.'

'Did a thing like that often happen?'

'Now and then, Mary. Sometimes I'd go and sometimes I wouldn't. It all depended – more often than not they were oul fellas. But this one didn't look too bad and anyway that night I was ravenous with the hunger – a mutton chop I thought will go down nicely. So I agreed to go and he took me to this eating house and we're sitting in this booth with red velvet curtains hanging on brass poles and I'm thinking I've landed on my feet and that the minute I'd had my fill I'd make an excuse to go to the jakes, then out through the back door. But then your man tells me he's from London and in the stage business and in all his born days he's never heard a voice like mine before. Beautiful, melodious, full of expression, them's the kind of things he said. Wasted I was in a singing tavern.

' "On the London stage, that's where you should be. You'd make a fortune and have gentlemen beating a path backstage and the stage itself knee-deep in flowers that would be showered on you at the end of every performance."

'Well, I needn't tell you I was ten foot high. "Me?" I said to him. "You're having me on." "Having you on?" said he and he looked offended and I thought, now maybe you've spoiled your chances with your big mouth. So I was all apologies. He took a few minutes to get over his huff – the oul shite. "My dear girl," says he, "I told you nothing but the truth. I was going to make you a business proposition, but of course if you're not interested . . ."

'I needn't tell I lost no time convincing him I was. And he said he understood how a girl couldn't be too careful and all he wanted to do was help me get on. There was no hurry to decide anything. If I liked we could meet again and talk things over. He was in town for a week.

'So for nearly a week he took me to supper every night and all the time his praise of my voice and my prospects in London grew in leaps and bounds. Jesus – I must have been an awful eejit all the same. But d'ye see he gave me no cause to suspect him – never once did he say a word out of place or try to make free. I agreed to give London a try, anyway.

'He was catching the early boat. Would I have trouble getting a cab at that hour, he wanted to know.

' "Not with the cab but I might with my mother who'd think it queer me up at the crack of dawn. I think she sleeps with her eyes open my mother," I told him. "Well then," said he, "here's what you'll do – that's if you're in earnest about wanting to come to London. Bring your things to the tavern, I'll collect you and you shall have a room in my hotel which is only a stone's throw from the boat" '

'And you went – to the man's hotel and not a word to your mother!' said Mary.

'Like a gobshite I did – me that thought I knew the ropes. Went I did. And what d'ye think happened when we got to the hotel? Didn't he only have the one room booked with a double bed in it the size of the Phoenix Park. It didn't take me long to see what his game was.'

'The blackguard!' said Mary, her eyes gleaming. 'And what happened then?'

'When he wouldn't take no for an answer I upped with my knee and left him gasping. Then I was down the stairs in two leps and him roaring and shouting, "Stop thief!" With my breath in my fist I never stopped running until I reached Ringsend and went headlong into this man. Only for him catching hold of me in his two arms I'd have been on my mouth and nose. Larry it was.'

'Larry? Larry from the ship?'

'The very same. I was crying and shaking with fright thinking the polis would be after me, for who'd take my word against that oul shite with his "Stop thief!" I told Larry the whole thing, a man I'd never seen before in my life, a black stranger as the saying goes. There was a cab coming so he bundled us into it and home I went in style. That's how I first met Larry. I met him a few times after that. He was very understanding when I told him how since my hopes were raised and dashed I'd got discontented with the singing tavern. Larry had jumped ship in Dublin. He was waiting for news of one sailing to America. He suggested me going there, too. "For all you know," he said, "your man might have been serious about your voice being that good. So give America a try." And I did and here I am.'

'Oh, I see,' said Katy, hoping nothing in her expression gave away the surprise at hearing that Eileen and Larry had known each other for a while. Putting two and two together she now knew where Eileen went every night, often returning on legs that weren't steady though the sea was calm. Sometimes coming to where she lay, whispering her name, bending over her smelling of drink and pressing into her hands an apple, a piece of fresh bread or some treat, saying, 'For the children.'

Eileen and Larry, Katy thought and jealousy stirred in her and she asked herself – why? Larry was nothing to her. He shouldn't be. He was nothing but a free-making cur. Insulting her with his suggestion and whenever she passed him giving her the eye. The nerve of him. And all the while he had Eileen. The cheek of him.

26

Eileen was answering Mary's questions while Katy pursued her thoughts, trying to make sense of why she should be jealous. It was a fault of hers, she well knew. Once long ago she had almost lost her mind through it. But that was different – that was when she knew Peader was marrying Miss Charlotte. When even though she was already married to Jamsie the thought of Peader and another woman nearly sent her crazy. But was it so different really? Didn't it stem from the same thing – her vanity. Peader had loved her, found her attractive and then someone else took his affections. Her vanity was wounded just as it was now. She had believed that the crewman found her attractive and she was pleased that a man other than Jamsie did so, even a scut like Larry. Sick in my soul I am and sick in my head, she decided. God forgive me and let me put thoughts of jealousy out of my mind. I wouldn't have Larry not if he was handed to me on a plate and him decked in flowers. Nor do I really begrudge him Eileen nor her him. She's my friend and I'm glad he makes her happy.

Mary was still questioning Eileen. 'You'll never know now if all the things the blackguard said were true – about the flowers and the young gentlemen, will you?'

'Not about London, Mary, but there's still New York.'

Mary said that tomorrow it would be Katy's turn to tell a story, tell what it had been like with having a Big House and seeing the gentry. And Katy said, 'What about yourself – haven't you anything to tell us?'

'Nothing at all,' replied Mary. 'For nothing ever happened where I lived. One day was like the next. Seldom a stranger came to the place. Though before the Hunger that was nice enough. Contentment like, with one day following another. Waking in the morning and thanking God for a new day you'd lived to see. It wasn't a bad life – but seldom was there much excitement. But Kilgoran – now that would have been altogether different so you won't disappoint me, Katy.'

And Katy promised that she wouldn't.

Eileen was popular, always in demand to hear this or that piece of information the passengers had come by, called to give her view on the subject, so she missed the first instalment of Katy's story about Kilgoran. Mary settled herself as comfortably as was possible on a half-barrel and coaxed Katy to do likewise and tell the story. 'Do,' she said, 'while the children are quiet and the child asleep.' Katy sighed, for she wasn't in the humour for story-telling but Mary was waiting with a look of expectancy about her face.

'It was a lovely place. I was born there and had I thought about it

27

would have said that as sure as the sun rises and the tide comes in would have died there. But I was young and little thought I gave to death. Little thought to anything but being alive. Everything I could wish for was there in the village, doting parents and do you see we were comfortable, for my father was Lord Kilgoran's coachman and we had the house at the lodge gates – bigger and better than any labourer's cottage.

'My father earned money. And you know yourself how few did – little farmers and labourers never handling a penny that wasn't already spoken for to pay the rent. We didn't live on potatoes and buttermilk. My mother could buy meat and fish and having been in service she knew how to cook more than a cake of brown bread. I had the happiest childhood with full and plenty. And God forgive me, I put on airs and graces. For didn't I play with the Master's children, and didn't my mother that was clever with the needle copy many a dress that she'd seen on Miss Catherine or Miss Olivia – and clothes they grew out of came down for me. Oh, indeed I considered myself a cut above the others in the village. So did my mother, Lord rest her.'

Mary interrupted her to say, ' 'Twas a failing of many that worked for the quality, harmless when it wasn't taken too far. Only trying to copy what they thought was an improvement. Tell me about the Big House and what the young ladies and their mother was like.'

'My mother spoke highly of her. A lady she said she was, in more than name. She died when I was only a child so I don't remember her. There were four children, Master Charles, Miss Catherine, Olivia and Charlotte. It was on her Lady Kilgoran died, Lord have mercy on her soul. Miss Catherine was the eldest, quiet and gentle, kind to the tenants, a sweet good creature. Now her sister, Miss Olivia, was the very opposite – fair and a beauty, daring, more like a boy in her nature. You wouldn't warm to her like Miss Catherine – though in the long run she showed her true metal. Master Charles was spoiled while his mother was alive and grew up terrible wild – no one could get good of him, and Miss Charlotte . . . well, she was younger than me and I loved her like I would have a little sister.'

Here she paused and Mary asked had Lord Kilgoran been a good landlord and what about the balls and parties – was there plenty of them and did Katy see all the grand people that would come from afar for them?

'The best, the kindest, caring landlord you could meet, broken-hearted by the loss of his wife and beggared in the long run by the carousing of his son. When I think of how it all turned out. The lovely happy peaceful life in Kilgoran that seemed as if it would go on for ever and ever. The kind neighbours, my poor mother and father. The place, the little village near the sea and the little hills above it and on the summer's day the cottages white against the green fields and the smell of the sweet turf smoke going up from every chimney.'

'And all of it was Lord Kilgoran's?'

'Every inch of the place, Mary, the strand and the fields, the hills and the cottages and the river that ran through it. Every bit of it except the bog that was cleared a long time ago and owned by a landlord no one had ever seen, and terrible conditions there were there for the people living on it.'

'You never told me about the parties and that.'

Katy was sorry she had started reminiscing – the memories were too painful. Too many terrible things had happened in Kilgoran. Too many wonderful things that shouldn't be recalled here in this stinking, rat-infested hold. Shouldn't be recalled for many a long day – for how would she make a go of her life in America if forever her mind was somewhere else. The past was gone, no use was served by dwelling on it.

'Go on,' urged Mary. 'Tell me about all the great goings-on.'

Katy sighed for she had no heart for telling stories about balls or parties, but Mary was insistent. And so she related some of the happenings at Kilgoran but with such little enthusiasm that Mary became bored and her usual mournful expression returned to her face. Katy cut the stories short and they sat in silence until Mary asked. 'Do you know anyone in America?'

'Only them that I mentioned before – the ones we had a letter from on the day we were leaving for Kinsale.'

'Ah,' Mary said wearily, 'I'm that afraid. There's that much to be wary of if you've no one to claim you when you land . . . Touts that fleece you. Offering to carry your few things. Demanding to carry them, snatching them out of your hand and that's the last you see of them or your belongings. And all of the scoundrels are Irish, so I believe.'

Katy could hear Eileen laughing somewhere down the passage – and the happy excited voices of men playing cards – playing as hard for buttons and fragments of wood as if the stakes were golden guineas. Everyone making the best of things except Mary, who couldn't let a day pass without meeting trouble halfway.

Her voice was droning on. 'Then there's the bondsmen wanting money to guarantee you won't become an encumbrance on the Government. It's all in the *Emigrant's Guide*.'

'You should stop reading that – it does nothing but worry you,' Katy said. When she had risen that morning her spirit was as easy as it would ever be until they landed. Mary's moaning and complaining had lowered it and she thought of the peril they were in . . . nothing between them and the deep ocean, only this little wooden vessel packed with people, carrying cows and ducks and heavy baggage belonging to wealthy farmers who were taking plenty with them to America. Such a fragile little ship carrying all the things and people and tons of sails and masts. Only the hand of God protected it and them.

'But what puts the fear of God in me, Katy, is the thought that me or Kathleen should be taken with the fever. Were we both to die that would be God's Will – but supposing only one of us gets it when we are nearly in America. The doctors come on board, poking at you, feeling your joints and looking at your tongue. One sign or symptom and you're carted off to a place called Staten Island. Imagine that. Separated one from the other. Me in the fever hospital and my poor child thrown to the winds of the world.'

At the mention of fever Katy made the Sign of the Cross. Terrible memories of the affliction came flooding back. She had had the fever and survived. Maybe you didn't get it a second time. But Jamsie and the children! Supposing they got it and like Peg and Nora died. She was sunk in the depths of despair. Imagining Jamsie and her children dead, their bodies thrown into the sea. Only herself left. She couldn't bear that. In after them she would jump. In Heaven they'd be together. Scene by appalling scene she tortured herself until the final moment when she committed suicide. Suicide! A mortal sin. A sin which would bar her from ever seeing the faces of those in Heaven.

'Katy, you're miles away,' Mary's voice brought her back to the present and seeing her poor woebegone face Katy pushed her own fears aside.

'Mary, listen. You are driving yourself and me mad. First, before bondsmen or touts will bother us we have to get to America and all we can do about the fever is pray for God's protection. Meeting trouble halfway never solved anything.' And as she gave Mary advice she took it herself.

Today they were in their health – today the sea was calm, today they'd have the bit of food and ration of water. Today they'd go on deck for half an hour. She could look at the sea stretching all the way on every side to meet the sky, breathe deeply the fresh air and look up at the sky. You couldn't, you mustn't ask for more than that.

Where minutes before her heart raced with apprehension and her mind was in a turmoil of fears, now a feeling of peace spread through her so that her heart slowed its frantic beat and distraught thoughts no longer chased one another through her mind. She gave a long sigh of relief and looked at Mary. By Mary's face she could tell she was still tormented by fears real or imagined and she took pity on her. 'Will I tell you more about Kilgoran?' she asked. Mary said yes, but with little enthusiasm.

'I could tell you about the man and his wife who wrote to us from America.'

'Do,' said Mary, her voice and expression unchanged. Katy felt that a good shake was what she needed but knew that the bit of information she was about to impart would have Mary sitting up and begging for more.

'Their marriage caused a great stir in Kilgoran.'

Mary moved her seat closer to Katy and the dawn of curiosity was in her eyes. 'How was that? Was someone against the match?'

'They were indeed, but it's a long story and I'll begin at the beginning and you'll have to be patient.' Mary eagerly nodded her agreement and Katy began.

'The man's name was Peader Daly and a fine, handsome, fair-haired man he was. There wasn't a mother in Kilgoran who wouldn't have given the two eyes out of her head to have Peader Daly as a son-in-law. For not only was he the only son of a strong farmer, but wasn't he as well a great scholar, kind and generous, not over-fond of the drink and well up in the politics of the day. A great follower of the Liberator.'

Mary listened as if in a trance, not stirring, not blinking, not seeming to draw breath. Katy continued. 'The Liberator was his hero. Daniel O'Connell never had a follower more worshipful than Peader. Not one of the Monster Meetings did he miss. From end to end of the country Peader went to hear Dan do peaceful battle for Catholic Emancipation.'

Mary broke her silence to say fervently, 'God bless him and may he rest in peace. The saint of a man who without shedding a drop of blood gave back to the Irish nation its dignity. Go on with the story do, Katy. And tell us about his wife and what was the cause of the stir when they married.'

Katy, not to be diverted from her way of telling, continued about Peader. 'He was at the Clontarf Meeting that the Government proscribed. We were all waiting for him to come back with what we thought would be great news. For that's how it was – back to the village – to my cottage for I was a married woman by then and 'twas easier for the people to come to me so the children slept safely and wait for Peader

31

and the news of the meetings. Jamsie was with him that night and you never saw two more down-hearted men when they returned from Clontarf. And I needn't tell you there wasn't a dry eye in the cottage when we heard that the Liberator had been arrested.'

'The poor man. Poor Dan, he never overed it. But what about the girl Peader married. Who was she? Where was she from? Did you know her, Katy?'

'From the time she was a child. Sure, didn't I help rear her. She was the Master's youngest daughter, Miss Charlotte.'

Mary gasped. 'The daughter of a Lord and she married a farmer's son and a Catholic into the bargain. No wonder the match caused a stir. But how did such a thing come about?' Without giving Katy time to answer Mary continued, 'I suppose she was a great beauty – was that it? And did the poor young man lose his head and run off with her?'

'You're a terrible woman, do you want me to tell you the story at all?'

'Oh girl, I do and not another word of interruption will there be.'

'Poor Miss Charlotte was let run wild, spending more time with the servants than she ought. Forever in the kitchen with Hannah who was the cook. There was always talk of a nurse being engaged but it never came to anything.

'And you were right, Miss Charlotte *was* a lovely-looking girl. Slight and dainty with a tiny heart-shaped face and a cloud of brown hair that grew wild around her. The years passed and the other two girls got married. The House wasn't what it was any more. Times were hard for the Master and there weren't the parties and balls there used to be. Sometimes as Miss Charlotte grew up I used to wonder where was she, buried alive in the country, to find a husband. Little thinking that she had already found the man. It turned out they'd been seeing each other for a long time and eventually Jamsie and myself were the go-betweens.'

Unable to resist butting in Mary said, 'God bless you to help the pair of lovers.'

And bitter memories came flooding into Katy's mind so that she had to make an excuse for going to the stinking closet that was used as a lavatory and when she came back pleaded a headache and promised that another time she would finish the story. Poor Mary's face fell but she had the manners not to annoy Katy with a request to go on with the story that had her all agog.

Two old men, an old woman and a child died. Fear gripped every passenger – was there fever on board? Families kept close to each other, some refusing to use the same water closets, preferring to hold on until

32

the time each day when they were allowed on deck to collect their water ration, leaving the waves which washed over the decks to take into the sea the emptying of their bowels and bladders. Others moved into dark corners and used those. The deaths were declared to be of natural causes in the case of the old people, and the child's though not from fever, remained unexplained.

The gossiping and card playing, the wagers as to how long the ship would take to reach New York took place again. Katy noticed that Terence took part in any game where money or possessions were wagered. She also noticed that he no longer went barefooted but had won or cheated himself a pair of boots. Whenever he was in her vicinity he regarded her with a malign expression. He was evil, she felt instinctively.

The Atlantic rollers seemed bigger than ever, then the wind rose and screeched like someone demented. Passengers were thrown from one side of the ship to the other. The waves, whipped up to gigantic heights by the wind, crashed onto the decks and poured into the steerage section. Pieces of clothing floated in water inches deep. The water found its way into the nooks and crannies where people had relieved themselves. Excrement washed up on people's legs and feet. As the ship heaved so did the passengers' stomachs, pools of vomit adding their stink to all the other appalling smells. Terror gripped the hearts of all but the dim-witted, for it seemed that at any minute the ship must be smashed to smithereens. Terrified cries, screams and prayers filled the air. For three days the storm raged and for three nights few slept, terrified to do so lest while they did they drowned.

When it seemed that they were to be tossed and thrown forever, vomit when there was nothing to vomit and their insides were sore from retching, sit or lie in sodden clothes holding anything for support the motion of the vessel altered. There were pauses between one lurching roll and the next, pauses that became longer and gradually the sound of the wind changed. Its screeching became a moan that grew weaker and weaker until it died.

'Blessed be God the storm is over and we've been saved,' said Mary and immediately said prayers of thanksgiving for their deliverance.

Jamsie collapsed on the sodden straw bunk and was asleep in a minute. 'Men,' said Katy, 'isn't it well for them,' as with pieces of rags she attempted to clean the filth that had accumulated during the storm.

Chapter Four

It seemed as if no sooner had Katy allayed Mary's fears over one thing than she found another to take its place – and from her usual source –the woman with the *Emigrant's Guide*. Bad cess to her and it, Katy said to herself as she waited for Mary's latest tale of woe. Before coming to the point Mary did a lot of sighing and uttered interjections for God to assist her.

'For the Lord's sake, Mary, will you tell me what ails you now and don't take all day about it.'

Mary looked offended – it was unusual for Katy to be short with her, and instead of coming to the point she began a rambling defence as to why she was upset, eventually revealing that she'd heard the ship was going to Canada and not America. This news took the wind out of Katy's sails and left her looking as shocked and worried as Mary.

'But why? Why would they do that? America, they said. America we paid for. Are you sure, Mary?' Her earlier confident, impatient tone was now an anxious one.

'I'm sure all right. 'Tis because this is a small vessel and the health regulations aren't right. And if they're not right the Americans won't let us in. It's the law – a new one since February. What'll become of us? I know nothing about Canada. Where is it, Katy?'

Katy said she didn't know. She'd heard tell of it once or twice, but knew neither where it was nor anything about it. Mary was inconsolable. Her hopes of salvation were pinned on America. Hadn't dozens of girls from her village gone over the years, dozens of them, she repeated in between sobbing and wailing and wiping her eyes and nose with the hem of her skirt. 'Plenty of dollars they sent back, too. Dollars that paid the passage for a brother or sister. You'd hear the talk – so and so was going, and the names, Philadelphia, New York, Boston, Chicago. I got to know them well, but Canada I never heard of. What'll we do, girl?'

'I don't know,' said Katy despondently. And she thought how if she went to Canada Peader and Miss Charlotte would never find them, for Canada might be nowhere near America.

Other women, hearing Mary crying, came to ask what ailed her and she told them the bad news. Men joined the group, some hazarding guesses as to where Canada was. The one who had been a sailor and named the porpoises said it wasn't too far from America, though he'd never been there. He was ignored. One man knew for a fact that the sun never shone there so it was always night and another thought it was near France and they'd be lost with not knowing the French tongue. A woman suggested going to see the Captain. She was laughed at and told that the Captain, even if he saw her, would divulge nothing. And if she created a commotion he could have her shot.

'Just a few of us asking a question, how could he have us shot for that?' asked the woman.

'Couldn't he say you were inciting a mutiny? On his ship he has more power than a landlord at home even,' someone replied and no more was said about a deputation for they knew all about the power of the landlord.

'Commere for a minute,' said Eileen, who had stood silent while the debate about Canada went to and fro. 'Don't be jumping to conclusions. You've only that oul wan's word for it that we're going to Canada.' Eileen had forgotten or didn't care that the oul wan was in the crowd.

'You mind who you're calling an oul wan, you Dublin rossy. You could give me a few years any day. And what's more, my information's here in black and white – read it if you know how,' said the woman, pushing the *Emigrant's Guide* under Eileen's nose.

'Wipe your arse with it, ma'am. I get my information from the horse's mouth.'

'It's more than that and all you get – you cheeky bitch.'

Ignoring the remark, Eileen led Mary and Katy to her bunk and told them not to worry. Tonight she would find out from Larry where Canada was, what sort of place it was, and was the ship sailing to there or America.

Katy lay in the dark worrying that the ship might be sailing for Canada. Wondering, what sort of a place was it? How would they live in perpetual darkness? How would they make themselves understood if no one spoke English? Earlier she'd mentioned her fears to Jamsie. 'There's nothing we can do to alter where the Captain sails his ship – Canada or Timbuctoo, wherever he does we'll land up. So go to sleep now like a good woman.'

Already he was snoring – though if she'd told him to come into the bunk it would have been a different story. Out like a hare he'd have lepped with sleep far from his mind. Men, she thought, hadn't they the great ability to not dwell on anything troublesome, to fall asleep like a child. Asleep or awake, Jamsie had the gift of not looking further than his nose. A comfortable way it was if you were made like that. Believing that you went wherever the wind took you. Not able to alter course, or have a say in your life, or make a plan. Taking life easy, never thinking about tomorrow. But tomorrow always came and though sometimes the worry that was on you was less in the new day often it wasn't. Something had to be got, or said or done – and the doing and saying or getting was always left to her.

About whether they went to Canada or not he was right – nothing could alter the Captain's course, so all she was doing was tormenting herself. But she couldn't help it. She wouldn't be able to close her eyes until Eileen came back from Larry and told her one way or the other. Please God, she prayed, let it be America.

Then she wondered where Eileen and Larry spent their time together. She supposed in his bunk – one that would be wider than a coffin – or maybe up on the deck – making love with the stars looking down. Once, only once in her life had that happened to her. She'd never forget that as long as she lived. Opening her eyes and looking up at the sky and the bright stars shining. It seemed so long ago now, that night when she and Jamsie had made love under the stars.

The ship rose and fell on a gentle swell, and the motion wasn't unpleasant. Like the rocking of a cradle, Katy thought, it could lull you to sleep if it wasn't for the noises in the hold and her ears straining for the sound of Eileen returning. She yawned and rubbed her eyes. She mustn't drop off in case Eileen wouldn't waken her with what news Larry had of where the ship was going. But despite herself she did, for the next thing she knew Eileen was bending over her whispering. She could smell drink, lavender water and the powder Eileen used when she went to Larry. Eileen was giggling and squeezing her arm and saying, 'Canada's lovely. And it's not always dark. Larry says it's a great place. A grand place.'

Katy's heart sank. 'So it's there then we're headed?'

'Where?' asked Eileen.

'Canada,' said Katy. 'The woman with the guide book was right after all.'

'That oul shite,' laughed Eileen. 'As far out as the wind that blew her first shirt. America, that's where we're going. She was right about the law – it was passed but it's not in yet. America, me oul segosia, that's where we're going. You'll sleep easy now, won't you, Katy?' she hiccupped. 'Ah Katy, I love you, you're like the sister I never had.'

'God bless you Eileen, God bless you astoir. Will you be steady on your feet or will I walk with you?'

'I'm as steady as a rock,' replied Eileen rising from Katy's bunk, swaying.

'You'll sleep all right?'

'Fall into it,' Eileen said and staggered away.

In the morning Katy told Jamsie and then Mary the good news and in no time Mary had put everyone's mind at rest as to their destination. And afterwards she said to Katy, 'In future I'll take your advice and never go next nor near that woman and her *Emigrant's Guide*.'

The ship was becalmed. Motionless she sat in the water, her sails hanging limply. At first the cessation of motion was greeted with relief. 'It's like as if we were on firm ground again,' Jamsie said. And Katy agreed it was grand.

'Grand it is to stand upright and not be walking like a drunken man.' But the wind that had bellied the sails and propelled the ship had also found its way through the hull's rotten timbers and however slightly, freshened the air.

Some people began to complain. They couldn't breathe. They were too hot, too clammy. And how would they dry their few rags? And if the ship didn't move how would they get to America? Maybe the wind would never rise again and forever and ever they would be there, an old woman who constantly foresaw doom in every situation said. And wished as she frequently and loudly did that she had never left her home. 'Wouldn't it have been a better thing to stay where I was, to have died there and not smother here. Food I hadn't nor money either, but I had God's sweet fresh air to breathe.'

'That oul cow, one of these days I'll brain her,' Eileen threatened. For she was as irritable as everyone else. The air was oppressive – the smells disgusting. People with the strongest stomachs who during the storm had eaten everything before them and anything others couldn't because of seasickness, were now nauseated by the revolting mess of soups, porridges and weevily biscuits. Tempers got shorter. Husbands and wives quarrelled. Friends fell out over trivialities. Fractious children drove their mothers to breaking point. Hands lashed out and slapped faces and boxed ears and the children's crying made conditions more unbearable.

Jamsie's thoughts turned to sex. His demands became more

insistent. No sooner was Katy drifting towards sleep and a brief escape from her misery than Jamsie was in her bunk, wheedling and when that failed making accusations. Telling her she had no heart, no love, she didn't understand what it was like being a man.

'Nor have I,' she snapped one night. 'And what's more, if you waken me again I'll go up on deck and throw myself over the side. I've told you and I'll not tell you again – you'll have to wait till we get to America!'

The wind returned and the ship sailed on her way. One day Mary told Katy that there was a lot of talk about Larry.

'Talk, what sort of talk?' asked Katy.

'He's a terrible man for making free with the women. Not one can pass him without a comment or him throwing his eye at them.'

'Is that a fact now?' asked Katy, all innocence for sometimes she liked to tease Mary. 'And tell me now has he been throwing his eye your way?'

'I wouldn't encourage such a thing,' Mary replied indignantly. 'I only know what the women do tell me – and their men don't like his freemaking . . . Larry'd want to be careful.'

'Larry means no harm. You must be the only one he doesn't cod. I've seen him at it with girls of seventeen and women of seventy. And every one of them delighted, blushing and all of a flutter, though sometimes they let on to be insulted. It's his way – it means nothing. Larry has his own woman.'

'The less said about that the better,' Mary retorted with a prim expression on her face. 'If I was her I'd give him a word of warning.'

'Warning about what?' asked Katy.

'What I've been telling you. Women are the queer creatures. Larry's attentions make them wish they got a bit more of that and less of the other from their husbands.'

'I don't know what you mean.'

'Ah, Katy, of course you do. A bit of codding, a laugh, a smile, a soft word. Don't we all want that. And all we get is no more than the cow with a bull.'

Katy wanted to contradict, to say, 'Well speak for yourself, Mary,' but said nothing, for she never talked about her private life with Jamsie.

Mary continued, 'Wasn't I married, don't I know all about it. Lord have mercy on them that's dead, but it's little time or thought he gave me in that department once his ends were seen to. Women turn sour when that happens to them – and it happens to most of them. To them that's all a flutter when Larry's giving them the eye. It's him they'll be thinking about when the other fella's jumping on them in the bunk. Lying there enduring it and thinking about Larry and her above in the moonlight, but especially about Larry. It makes them bitter and bitter women are dangerous.'

Kathleen came to Mary then and demanded her attention, and while she was giving it Katy thought with amazement of the conversation she and Mary had just had. Such things for her to say! Who'd have thought Mary capable of thinking such things, let alone putting them into words. Did she lie awake at night thinking about Larry and Eileen up on the deck? And what did she mean about bitter women being dangerous? When Kathleen's needs were attended to, Katy asked Mary, 'What did you mean about bitter women being dangerous?'

'Dangerous, that's what I mean. Wakening up in the morning. Worn out from their husband's demands during the night. The children looking up in their face for food. "What's the matter with you?" asks the husband. "Your face is like a fiddle." She lets on not to hear him for peace sake, there's the children to see to and the water ration to get. So up on deck she goes nursing her grievance and there's Larry maybe stripped to the waist, whistling and giving her the eye. And her mind is working while she waits for the water – making comparisons between him and her man. Imagining the difference. Her humour's worse when she goes below and her husband's worse still. He turns on her, asking what kept her. Why has she still a puss on her. And she pours out her heart about the freemaking sailor – the cur that can't let a woman pass without making comment. Venting the spleen meant for her husband on Larry.'

'Well, isn't it you that's the wise woman,' said Katy, surprised and impressed by Mary's explanation.

' 'Tisn't wisdom at all. Amn't I listening to the stories every day. There's bad feelings towards the sailor. If I were you I'd tell Eileen to warn him. Maybe you're right. Maybe there's no harm in him but that's not how the husbands see it.'

'I will,' said Katy. 'I'll take your advice and have a word with Eileen,' and she intended to.

But neither the warning nor the conversation took place. For when Katy went looking for Eileen she found her shivering and shaking, her lovely face flushed, sweat pouring off her one minute and the next complaining of the cold. Oh dear God, Katy silently prayed, don't let Eileen be sick, don't let her have the fever. She was torn between pity for her friend and fear that she had the sickness. Mary's warning about Larry left her mind as she struggled with her pity and terror. In a hoarse voice Eileen whispered, 'I know what it is. I've had it before. It's malaria, honest to God. I'll be all right. It's not the fever.' Katy made her as comfortable as possible and nursed her in the following days.

One morning while Eileen lay in her delirium there was a terrible commotion. A young girl had been raped during the night. She had struggled, she said, but the man was powerful strong. When she tried to scream he put a hand over her mouth. She was hysterical, crying that she was destroyed, her life ruined, her prospects of marriage gone for ever.

'The poor child, the unfortunate little girl,' keened the old woman who delighted in tragedy. 'What's the world coming to when girls leave Ireland virgin as the driven snow and land in America with a baby in their belly and no man to claim it.'

The girl was young, a likeable person, never given to drawing attention to herself. An orphan travelling alone, she shared her berth with an old woman who was deaf and had slept through the rape.

Everyone looking at the girl, at her blotched face and swollen eyes red from crying and an ugly bruise by her mouth, felt pity for her and a fury against the man who had raped her. The women questioned her gently. 'Did you see nothing at all?'

'How could I,' she replied, 'for wasn't it pitch dark?'

'But think child, wasn't there anything at all – a beard, a moustache, a bald head?'

'I bit him, he'll have a sore finger, it was a good bite. I tasted his blood.'

'Ah,' the women crowed. They had something, a clue. A man with a sore finger, a finger wrapped in a rag.

Later in the day Mary got Katy on her own and told her, 'I said so, didn't I? Didn't I say Larry should mend his ways? He has a sore finger, it has been noticed wrapped up in a rag. The women are talking and plotting. Their men are angry about the rape. The women, they are saying, must be protected.'

'Oh, Mary, you've had no part in the talking, I hope. You haven't been spreading gossip,' Katy asked anxiously.

'Me?' Mary said. 'That I have not – only to you. But I listen. There's something afoot that I don't like. Did you tell Eileen?'

'Don't you know well she's been at death's door for days.'

' 'Twas a pity you couldn't. Whether he did it or not suspicion will fall on him. The women are remembering the nods and winks and the men the women's complaints. 'Tis as if a madness has taken hold of them. They want blood.'

40

'Don't Mary, don't say such things. Don't listen any more. Don't tell me any more.'

'There's no more to tell. Larry's wearing a bloodstained rag – he's been judged. Watch how the women are huddling in groups whispering and the men silent-seeming – but it's all decided.'

'What'll we do?'

'Nothing, nothing at all,' said Mary.

When Katy asked Jamsie's advice his answer was the same as Mary's. 'There must be something,' she insisted.

'Like what, be an informer?'

'Oh no, not that, never that.'

'Then put it out of your mind.'

That she couldn't do. Fear of what might happen to Larry haunted her, though nothing happened for the next few days. And for brief moments she hoped that Mary had let her imagination run away with her. The only one to whom she could have talked was Eileen and she was still too ill. Another few days passed and Katy's hopes that she had been worrying herself for nothing were high. All talk of the rape had died down and the young girl had stopped breaking into floods of tears any time she was spoken to. Please God, Katy thought, she wouldn't be pregnant – it could all blow over.

With a light heart she went up on deck to wash the clothes. There was nothing to distinguish this day from another. As usual the women were scrubbing and rubbing and complaining that the soap some had brought on board wasn't a bit of good. Katy's few things were soon washed. She draped them over a makeshift line and was about to return to the women when she saw Larry leaning over the rail, coiling in a rope. Towards him walked three men, men not so young, men who when there were discussions amongst the passengers took the lead – hard men, decisive men, leaders. Instinctively she knew something terrible was about to take place. She stood transfixed, wanting to shout a warning to Larry, scream, create a commotion, do something, anything that might avert the awful thing about to take place. Then realising she was helpless to alter anything she moved back to where the women were washing their clothes, talking in low voices, now and then covertly glancing towards Larry and the three men approaching him.

Larry seemed unaware of them and continued reeling in the rope. The men leant over the rail, to all intents and purpose apparently just looking at the sea. Watching, Katy saw them once or twice look round and guessed they were checking that no other crewman had come on deck. Then suddenly they moved in on Larry, so suddenly that Katy

41

wondered then and many times afterwards had she really witnessed Larry being grabbed hold of and thrown over the side, or had she imagined it and the beginnings of his scream that was quickly lost beneath the loud singing into which the other Irishmen burst forth. Only the furtive glances of the women, their eyes darting to the rail, to the hatch door from whence at any moment another sailor might appear, and their accompanying of the singing men convinced her that Larry had indeed been thrown overboard. No one uttered a word, no one said aloud, *'Lord have mercy on his soul.'* Nothing out of the ordinary had happened. No one had seen or heard anything.

Eileen, Eileen, poor Eileen, poor Larry, God rest him. Poor Eileen, what am I going to tell her, Katy kept thinking as she staggered down into the hold, found Jamsie and told him what had happened. She wondered again what she should tell Eileen.

'Nothing,' Jamsie said. 'Nothing. You saw nor heard nothing.'

'But Jamsie – you know why they did it. They think he raped the girl. And he didn't – I'm sure he didn't. And there they were singing their hearts out while he, poor man, was being drowned.'

'Commere to me,' said Jamsie. 'Commere and dry your eyes. It was a terrible thing to happen to Larry but it's done and can't be undone. For our sakes, for everyone's sake forget it ever happened.'

'But what about the real culprit? There he is, walking around like a milk-white lamb, only we don't know who it is. And couldn't he do the same thing to another woman.'

'No,' said Jamsie. 'He got away with it once. He won't chance his luck again, not on this ship anyway.'

'That God's curse may fall upon him, the cur,' Katy said, drying her eyes.

'Remember, not a word to Eileen. Tell her all the lies you like, but not a word of what you witnessed. In her sorrow she might forget that even when a wrong is done you don't tell the authorities.'

The seaman wasn't missed until later in the day. The steerage passengers were assembled and questioned. Faces remained inscrutable as they answered, 'Yes sir,' and 'No sir, I saw nothing, sir. I heard nothing, sir. That's the truth, sir.' The mate stared at them and sullenly they stared back. Afterwards he told the Master, 'How would you ever know anything about them? How would you know if they spoke the truth? Even when they do talk they say nothing. Words and words, blessings called down on you, prate and more prate and at the bottom of it all – nothing. You'd have to catch them red-handed to prove anything. They "yes sirred" and "no sirred" me and talked and talked and said nothing.'

'It's unlikely that the seaman fell overboard – the weather was fine,' the Captain said.

'It was,' the mate agreed.

'Curtail their rations for a few days – make life uncomfortable and in future see there's more than one crew member on deck when they are let up.'

'Aye, aye, sir.'

Eileen never for a minute accepted that Larry had fallen overboard. Once she was up and about she questioned anyone who would let her and though no one admitted to what had happened Mary let slip that Larry had been suspected of raping the girl.

'But why him? Larry wasn't like that,' Eileen said.

'I'm only telling you what I heard the others say.' Mary wished she had kept her mouth shut, for Eileen's face that had been ravaged with grief was now livid with rage.

'What did they say? Go on Mary, you seem to know it all, go on and tell me.'

'About his sore finger. The girl that was interfered with bit the man and Larry was seen to be wearing a rag on his finger.'

'Jesus, oh Sweet Jesus!' Eileen screamed. 'Was that why they killed him? Was that why they did it? Oh Jesus – my poor Larry.'

Alarmed by Eileen's outburst and afraid of more questions, Mary mumbled something about cramps in her bowels and clutching her stomach went off in the direction of the privy.

'Did she have anything to do with it? Was she one of them that threw suspicion on him? Tell me, Katy! Tell me the truth! I'll kill her if she did.'

'No, Eileen, no. Mary wouldn't harm a soul. You mustn't think like that.'

'Oh Katy, what am I going to do? Oh Katy, Katy.' She rocked herself to and fro, her anger gone, and cried and cried. 'It was never him. He'd never take a woman that wasn't willing. He didn't have to. He had a way with him, a way of looking at you that women like – you know yourself –I've seen him give you the eye many a time. Having a woman was as natural to him as a drink of water – but not raping them. Never that.

'I loved him, so I did. My lovely man. He was that gentle. And the skin on him as soft and smooth as a young girl's belly. That's why he

43

was wearing a rag on his finger. He was always wearing rags. His poor hands, something always ailed them – like his body the skin was delicate and never got used to the ropes and salt water. And for that they killed him. My lovely man, my beautiful lovely man.'

'Hush now,' Katy took Eileen in her arms. She was shocked by her grief, by the outpouring of her heart, never having thought that Eileen regarded Larry as more than a man who gave her a good time. 'Don't cry any more. Hush now and don't be upsetting yourself.'

'He said he'd marry me – one day he'd finish sailing and marry me. Why did they do it? Katy, why him? Why my lovely man?'

'There now, there now,' Katy kept saying, not knowing what else to say or do that would comfort Eileen. Gradually she was getting control of herself, anger again taking the place of grief, so that she cursed all responsible for Larry's death. 'God blast them that did it and them that first put the finger on him.' She wished all the afflictions and maledictions to befall them and hoped they would never see Heaven. Eventually her anger subsided and in a weary voice she said, 'What's done is done and they'll have to answer before God for it. I know you'll bear with me in the days to come when I won't be so brave.'

'Indeed I will,' Katy promised.

The next day Katy came face to face with Terence. Whenever possible she avoided him. But today he had a card-school going up on deck and to reach the spot where the water ration was being doled out it was necessary to step over him. He was dealing a hand of cards awkwardly, she noticed and being jeered by the waiting players. A kithog, they called him – a left-handed man. She knew he wasn't, for other times she had seen him deal like lightning. She stared and at the same moment he looked up and their eyes regarded each other. Such malevolence shone out of his that Katy turned away, but not before noticing the reason for his right hand being out of action. Around his index finger he wore a filthy blood and pus-stained rag. Her own blood ran cold, her legs became weak so that she felt she might faint and staggered to the ship's rail where she leant over and pretended interest in the sea until the weakness passed.

Great plumes of spray cascaded against the ship's sides, falling to wash behind her like yards of silk rolled out, and as Katy watched she heard again the cut-short scream of Larry and the men singing. And she remembered something else, how in one of her sidelong glances she had seen Terence amongst them, singing with fervour.

She had no doubt now but that he was the one who had raped the girl and stood by singing while Larry was thrown over the side. Could she do anything about it, she wondered. Who could she tell? Not the authorities – you could never do that. In any case, they wouldn't be interested. But what about Eileen, didn't she have a right to know? She collected the water and went back to the hold where Jamsie was dozing on the bunk. She roused him and in whispers told him what she had learned and how she thought that Eileen should know the truth. 'It's only right,' she said. 'I'd want to know if it was me.'

'You wouldn't,' he said, sitting up and scratching himself, 'for what good would it do?'

'Wouldn't it give her something definite to go on, to blame and hate, to clear Larry's name.'

'Musha,' he said, 'it's not much sense you have. Clear Larry's name? It would do no such thing. Whatever Terence can be accused of, it's not making free with the women. I think myself he has a dislike for them – though that's not to say he wouldn't have a need of them from time to time. I don't doubt for a minute that he raped the girl. But who else would believe it – and they're not going to drown the second man. The Captain's not a fool altogether. So let poor Eileen spread her hate about, that way it's watered down. Better she should suspect everyone than know for certain the one, and not be able to do a thing about it.'

'It's a terrible thing to be blamed in the wrong.'

'It is,' said Jamsie. 'Didn't it happen to my own brother.'

'He didn't lose his life, though.'

'Fourteen years transportation – he mightn't have appreciated the difference.'

There were days and nights of brisk wind when the ship made good progress and hope rose in the people's hearts that soon the wearisome voyage would end and firm earth once more be beneath their feet. But once periods of calm set in they were again thrown into despair and then niggling, quarrelling and pettiness reigned.

Eileen sought Katy's company more than ever. The bloom from love and the extra food given her by the seaman was gone. Her face was as gaunt and hollow-eyed as a sick old woman. Sometimes she wanted to say nothing, only sit by Katy while her eyes swam with tears. At other times she asked questions. 'You didn't see anything on the day?' and Katy would lie, 'I wasn't there – I had been and saw Larry busy reeling in a rope. Then I finished the bit of washing and went below.'

'What else was happening while you were there?' Eileen inquired as she had many times before.

45

'Nothing out of the ordinary. The women were washing and complaining and laughing and singing.'

'And the men, what about the men?'

'The same as always I suppose – I saw nothing out of the usual.'

'Katy,' Eileen said, 'may God bless you for your patience. I'm a terrible nuisance.'

'Indeed then you are not. Talk away if it gives you any comfort.'

'I still can't believe it. Every minute I'm on deck I'm expecting to see him. I do think to myself I'll tell Larry so and so or I'll ask Larry when I see him tonight. And then the realisation comes over me that I'll never see him again. Ah Katy, you couldn't understand, nobody could unless you'd lost someone yourself.'

Katy didn't say that she knew exactly the feeling but let Eileen continue. 'Then I do think if he'd died with the fever I could have accepted that. Anyone can get fever, no man has a hand in it. I'd console myself that it was God's will. But to know that he was murdered!'

'You don't know that, Eileen. Don't be tormenting yourself.'

'I know it as surely as if I'd seen it. Larry wouldn't jump overboard nor fall over either. No, it was murder all right. Someone did it, someone planned it.

'My poor lost love. Did he know d'ye think when they laid hands on him that his last hour had come? Did he let out a scream? Murdered he was by them that got rid of him and murdered by whoever it was that raped the girl. And he's walking round, passing me by, laughing up his sleeve. Maybe I talk to him, smile at him. Isn't that a terrible thing?'

Katy couldn't bear to look at Eileen, afraid that in the face of her grief she would break down and confess what she knew. So she moved to sit beside her on the upturned box and put an arm round her. 'Don't cry any more, you'll make yourself sick. Dry your eyes astoir, come on now there's a good girl. And try not to think of him whoever he is. He'll never have an hour's luck, of that you can be sure.' And with all her heart she hoped for it to be true.

An old man sickened and the fever was diagnosed. Within hours there were more cases. Eileen nursed those who had no one to help them. Bringing water, cleaning them, comforting them while they were still conscious and sitting by them while they died.

Katy watched anxiously for signs of the sickness in Jamsie and the children. At night she lay sleepless, reliving the time when Peg and Nora were stricken. The time before that. Seeing them as if they stood before her with the sun shining on their red-gold hair. Two handfuls of mischief from the minute they were born. Never still for a minute. Pulling Prince by the tail, making a horse out of him and he like a lamb letting them ride on his back.

She saw them running down from the field, their mouths stained with blackberry juice, long bramble scratches on their arms, little beads of blood standing out against their pale freckled flesh. Her bold, unbiddable children running and calling. Telling her to come quickly for there was a terrible smell in the potato patch. Not taking no for an answer, dragging her to the field by the hands. And the smell was terrible. Such a terrible smell it made her want to be sick. She made Jamsie go in among the green haulms, sure that some dead thing lay there, an animal or a man of the road who had collapsed and died before reaching the cottage to ask for food and shelter – a poor unfortunate already at death's door from hunger. But there was neither man nor animal there – though the foul smell remained.

Lying in the dark with the smell of dirt and sickness, the moaning of the dying and the snoring of others, memories of her dead children came and went through her mind. Not in any sequence – so that she saw them as little girls losing their baby roundness, beginning to get a stretch, then as newly-born infants and Statia exclaiming what beauties they were and the luck of them to be born with cauls. Cauls, she said, were always a sign of beauty and a sure protection against meeting their death by water.

She remembered how they had suckled her. Peg more greedily than Nora. Sucking until she could hold no more and her head would loll back and the blue-tinged milk run down her chin. She saw them on the day they went to the lake and disobeying her waded in too far, and cauls or no cauls she was afraid of them drowning and hitching up her skirts went after them and skull-hauled them to safety.

On the way home they had found a dead rabbit and the twins asked if rabbits went to Heaven and she'd said, no, only people went to Heaven, because people had souls. And she'd said that Heaven was the most beautiful place. 'Will we go to Heaven?' they'd asked. 'One day,' she answered, 'but not for a long, long time, please God.' Only it had pleased God to want them very soon. That He might not look so favourably on her remaining children, she prayed, nor on Jamsie either.

Around her she heard the sounds of the dying and thought how they too would have sent up the same prayers for their own and their children's protection. Why should God look more kindly on her prayers? But still she asked Him again. 'Spare us please until we get to America so that we'll be buried in the clay. So that Jamsie and I will lie

47

next to each other and the children beside us. Don't let us die on the ocean and be thrown into the green waves that will move us in their wash until Eternity while the sea creatures devour us.'

Forty people died from the fever and were thrown overboard. Carried from the hold by passengers, for the crew refused to handle them. Into the sea went the bodies clothed only in their rags. No tarpaulin or canvas shroud to bind them neatly – for no law compelled a sea captain to do other than dispose of them. Prayers were said for the repose of their souls, for God to grant them eternal rest and Mary moaned aloud, 'To die without a priest. Oh Katy, girl, how will they face their Maker and their sins not forgiven?'

'Sudden death, sudden mercy,' said Katy.

' 'Twasn't sudden – sick for days they were.'

Oh Mary, Mary, why don't you stop tormenting me, Katy thought. Do you think I'm happy that we haven't a priest – do you think anyone is? Isn't everyone living in dread and fear that they'll die without a priest to absolve their sins. But you wouldn't have your health if you weren't moaning. Every time I refuse Jamsie I'm committing a sin. Every time Eileen went to Larry so was she. We're all sinners – if there was a priest to hand we'd confess and promise to mend our ways. Well, certainly I would. And then I'd have to let Jamsie have his way. I wouldn't want that. Oh God, what am I thinking – that I'm glad we haven't a priest? Oh, I'm sorry, I didn't mean that. God forgive me. I would, after I'd been to Confession I'd have to. I manage to put it out of my mind the sin I'm committing – why did you have to remind me? It's easy for you, Mary, you've no man to contend with. Sometimes I wish you'd never sat by me on the first day, I really do, all you do is worry me.

Her mind was in turmoil. Questioning – questions she should never ask not even of herself. The priest told you what to think – all you needed to know about God, all you had to do to earn God's mercy. But sometimes the questions came into your mind. Of course that was the devil tempting you – and you should discourage the thoughts. Put them out of your mind and say a prayer to Our Lady. Only like now the questions wouldn't go away. When the priest said you should never refuse your husband wasn't he talking about at home, in your own place. Not about in public – cheek by jowl with all the other people on a ship. Surely God wouldn't expect that. The trouble was, you had no way of knowing. All you could do was follow what you thought was the right thing to do – and in case you were wrong say a good Act of Contrition before you fell asleep and ask for God's mercy if you died in the night. God mightn't be half as hard as the priests made out. God might be very kind and understanding.

A scream from Kathleen distracted Katy's further attempts at wrestling with her thoughts. Kathleen was screaming, crying, as if she'd been mortally wounded.

'What ails you, lamb?' Mary was asking as she hurried to her. Kathleen stopped crying for the length of time it took her to say, 'Thomas pucked me in the eye.'

'Did you hit her?' Katy asked, though she knew from his stance that he had.

'No I never.'

'He did so.' Kathleen cried louder and nuzzled into her mother.

Katy caught hold of Thomas and shook him. 'If you don't tell me the truth I'll . . .' Even while she threatened her heart went out to him. Poor Thomas who hadn't a bit of aggression in him. Not like Bridget, Kathleen and Mary Kate, as ready as the next with a pinch or a puck. And the three of them forever tormenting him. He'd been driven beyond himself – but all the same he shouldn't have hit Kathleen in the eye.

'For the last time – what did you do?'

'She hit me first.' His face went red with the shame of being caught out in a lie. 'She hit me hard and Bridget laughed, and then I got mad.'

Katy smacked him. 'Don't be getting mad then, the next time you'll get worse.' She slapped him harder than she felt he deserved, but Mary and her bawling ass were demanding it and she didn't have the courage not to punish him. 'Away you go and let me hear no more tales about you.'

Kathleen smiled triumphantly and left her mother's arms. She and Bridget caught hands and walked off smirking. Katy wanted to murder her and felt a dislike for Kathleen, a little sleveen and spoiled into the bargain. One of these days Mary would live to regret the way she was rearing her.

Thomas amused himself picking pieces out of the rotting hull, picking and then flicking away the splinters of wood. The poor child, Katy thought, all the poor children cooped up like hens at night. It wasn't natural. Especially for boys. The girls managed better to amuse themselves. Copying their mothers and older sisters. Apparently content to sit and talk. Though what, at their age, she often wondered did they find to keep them talking for ages. But talk they did as Kathleen and Bridget were now doing, talking and giggling and playing with each other's hair – Kathleen winding Bridget's into yellow ringlets.

49

Little boys seemed to have no peace inside them – always on the go. She sighed and told her thoughts about little boys to Mary and Eileen who agreed with her. 'Men and boys they're all the same,' said Eileen. 'My father, my brothers, every man I ever knew.'

'I found them hard to rear,' said Mary. 'Into everything from the minute they could crawl, Lord have mercy on them.'

Eileen appeared to be recovering from the first terrible shock of losing Larry. Watching the expressions flit across her face as she talked and laughed Katy was pleased to see that she looked well again, though in her heart Katy knew that her grief was still sore. But Eileen had courage, she didn't beat you over the head with her tragedy. She looked to the future, kept her spirits up by talking about America, the good things of America all of which she knew from hearsay. New York, she said, was twice, maybe four times as big as Dublin. And the style would blind you. It was full of foreigners, a lot of them with not a word of English. And as for money there was hatfuls of it to be earned. 'It's a great place. If you're prepared to work there's nothing to stop anyone getting on. But do you know, there's a queer thing about it.'

'What's that?' asked Katy.

'There's only millions of pigs everywhere, parading up and down Broadway – all over the place, scavenging, eating the slops.'

'Who told you that, Eileen?'

'A friend, Mary.' Her voice wavered and Katy guessed the friend had been Larry. Larry beside her in the bunk after their love-making telling her about New York. 'A friend,' Eileen repeated. 'The pigs are kept by Irish people and turned out every morning to fend for themselves and in doing it they keep the streets clean.'

Katy and Mary marvelled at the strange thing it was to keep pigs in a big city and for cleaning it, too. Katy tried to imagine what a big city would be like. All buildings, she supposed, and never a tree or flower to lighten your heart. She'd miss seeing trees and flowers but it would be a small loss if there was work for Jamsie and food in plenty for the children.

Forty less in the hold made more room for the living. The family that had slept in the section next to Katy's were amongst the dead. Jamsie seized the opportunity to plead his desire for Katy. Once he was sure the children were asleep he climbed into Katy's narrow bunk despite her refusals and protests and tried cajoling her. She was torn between her own desire and her repugnance of making love in public. She liked the feel of him next to her, the warm secure feeling of his nearness, how his nearness drove the worry and fear of another outbreak of fever from her mind.

In his arms she let herself believe that they were lying on the palliasse in the cottage with the sweet clean smell of its straw filling the air. There was a faint glow from the turf fire banked to keep it in through the night. Outside a wind rustled the trees. Comforting, familiar sounds and smells. And she thought of their love-making. Jamsie, sensing the response in her, pressed closer and kissed her. Such a kiss as she hadn't had for a long time and she melted and clung to him and their bodies strained at each other. Then somewhere close by a man let out a terrible snore that brought Katy back to the reality of where she was, and ignoring the ache in her breasts and the throb like a beating heart that was between her legs, she pushed Jamsie from her. She had almost let herself mate like an animal in the hearing of others. Oh dear God, when would they get to America. Please let it be soon. Don't let me be tempted again. But it's been such a long time. Jamsie was pulling at her, his hands doing things to her. 'Stop it,' she hissed, 'stop it!' He'd do it anywhere. Men were queer creatures where their wants were concerned. Jamsie who could blush like a young girl at something said that he thought improper – would take her here in this place if she let him.

He was crushing her to him. She felt how great his need was and buried his head against her breasts to stifle his sounds. Then he slept and she lay wishing he was on his own shelf. It was well for him – his needs were seen to and she was irritable and uncomfortable and his back was squashing her into the wall.

One day Mary said to Katy, 'We've been at sea eight weeks.'

'How do you know that?' asked Katy. 'And why didn't you say when we were six or seven weeks out – and how did you keep track of the days and weeks?'

Mary ignored the first question and answered the second looking very pleased with herself. 'I had a prayer book with two blank pages at the end. I wasn't sure if it was a sin to use them, but I did anyway, sure it couldn't be more than a venial one. What I did was mark the days from the first one we sailed – with a stroke I marked it. When I had seven for a week I tied them with a pencil mark to make a bundle – now there's eight bundles. Tomorrow I'll start the ninth.'

'Well, aren't you the great woman all the same,' said Katy admiringly. 'With the help of God that you won't have many more bundles to make.'

*

During an interval on deck a man shouted excitedly that he had seen seaweed floating past the ship. Surely land couldn't be far off. There was speculation on how soon their first glimpse of America – the halfway mark to Heaven – would come. Then the excitement gave way to fear and despondency and they asked each other, 'Supposing we aren't passed well. Supposing the doctor says we're sickening for fever.'

Mary became frantic with worry, convinced that she and Kathleen would be separated – the sick one sent to the quarantine hospital. 'Promise me Katy,' she pleaded, 'that if it's me with the fever you'll mind Kathleen. I wouldn't die easy thinking of her wandering the streets of America with no one to turn to. Promise me you'll protect her.'

'Tis more likely you than her will get whatever is going, Katy thought, for you have been feeding her like a stall-fed calf, the recipient of more than her share. 'God bless and protect us all from harm and rest easy, if yourself is sick I'll mind Kathleen,' she promised. 'And if the same befalls me or Jamsie I know you'll do likewise. And now,' she urged, 'pull the sad thought away, no good will it do only waste the time and energy we could be putting to a better use. I'd say looking presentable would help us getting into America. So from this day, night and morning I'll wash the children though it's more spit than water I'll be using.'

The children complained about the unaccustomed grooming and screamed when Katy pulled the rack comb through hair that was tangled from lack of attention, salt water and the wind which when they went on deck snarled it into knots. She was thankful they had neither lice nor nits. Since coming on board she'd warned them not to loll against strangers. They had a shyness about them with strangers, thank God. Not like her lovely twins, the Lord have mercy on them. There'd have been no stopping them leaning and lolling against anyone who as much as smiled at them. No more than there was the day the poor woman came to the cottage when the Hunger was at its worst asking for water and a heat of the fire. And she tearing the head off herself, infested with lice through no fault of her own, the poor creature. In no time Peg and Nora were all over her, leaning and lolling against her, their heads close together. Though what lice had to do with 'yalla fever' she'd never know. But it was the strange thing that till that woman came begging, the twins were hale and hearty.

The children went to sleep each night with scrubbed faces and combed hair, in case the ship docked early in the morning before Katy

52

had time to give them a lick. And each night she tidied her own hair and rubbed her face and prayed for God to make the landing soon and to let the doctor pass them, and maybe make the landing not too early in the morning for everyone's hair got tossed while they slept.

Chapter Five

The steerage passengers woke to the sound of a great commotion. Cursing and shouting, crew members as dirty and unkempt as the passengers were moving through the hold ordering everyone up. 'Get the bloody place cleaned up. Get them pissy bundles of straw on deck and over the side. Come on, move them.' Men and women were pushed, pulled, shouted at and cursed. Some protested that their beds were feather, they'd carried them from home, they were clean. 'All of them into the sea. The bleeding quack's coming on board – one look at this shithouse and you'll all finish on Staten Island.'

Katy and Jamsie dragged their straw palliasses from the bunks. The floor became deep in straw spilling from everyone's ticks. A crewman slipped and slithered on it. 'Bloody Irish – live like pigs,' he yelled, kicking at the offending bedding. 'Dirty gets.' Another sailor threw down a pile of rags, pails, brushes and mops.

One of the men who had taken part in the drowning of Larry, a tall, rawboned man with a hatchet-like face, moved to where the crewman stood spewing his foul language.

'Mind your tongue,' said the tall, thin man in a soft, low voice. 'There's women and children listening. Don't call us names or mistake us for fools. We know your concern isn't for us. We know that if the Port Authorities see the den we've been penned in like animals your Captain is in trouble. Go now,' he said, 'and leave us. We'll dispose of the soiled bedding, we'll clean our dirt which until this minute we had neither brush, bucket nor mop to do so. And be warned – we're neither fools nor animals.' His voice never rose nor his eyes leave the sailor's face. 'Fucking Irish,' said the crewman when he was out of the tall man's hearing, but after that he made himself scarce.

The men carried up the bedding for discarding, returning with news that you could see land. The women stopped mopping and swilling, and laughing joyously threw their arms around each other and thanked God that they were almost there. The children catching the happy mood danced, clapped their hands and shouted with glee. The rejoicing continued for a while and then the mops and brooms were wielded with more strength than any of them thought they possessed.

With deck-brushes they scrubbed until their arms ached. They scoured the nooks and crannies where the old, the sick and those with dirty habits had emptied their bowels and bladders. They scrubbed and mopped and swilled and mopped again until the hold was cleaner than they had ever seen it. But to anyone whose sense of smell had not been desensitised by the conditions in which they had spent the last nine weeks, the nauseating stench was as bad as ever.

Katy had as she often said a nose like a needle, a gift in pleasant surroundings. In fields of wild flowers at home; under hedges of honeysuckle, near cut grass or newly-mown hay. Where bread was baking. Nursing her babies and breathing in their warm, sweet milky smell. The scent of Jamsie's body and the smell about the both after making love.

But there was a price to pay for her gift. Bad smells troubled her long before others, if they ever noticed them, as now in the newly-washed hold. While men and women congratulated themselves on the grand job of cleaning they'd done, Katy's stomach turned. And she knew that all the scouring and scrubbing had only removed the top layer of filth and released all the vile odours that had lain buried beneath it.

She fought back the waves of nausea and when she felt a little better said to Mary, 'If we don't get off this ship soon and breathe fresh air I'll collapse.'

'Keep praying then,' Mary said, 'for we might be on board yet for weeks.'

'But why? Isn't land in sight?'

'We've had the fever here. If the doctor thinks it's not finished, it's here we'll have to stay – for months maybe.'

'Oh, sacred heart of Jesus don't let that be so. What'll we do for food? We won't get fed for nothing. Are you sure, Mary? Who told you?'

'The woman who tells me everything.'

'That one, I might have known. I thought you weren't going to heed her talking any more.'

'All the same it's as well to be warned.'

'She could be wrong – she was before and anyway the fever's been gone this long time. When did the last person die? Would your bundles of sticks tell you that, Mary?'

'They would not – 'twas weeks and days only I counted, not what happened during them.'

Agitatedly Katy pressed Mary to try and remember something that would jog their memories as to when the last person had died of the fever. There was nothing. Katy got angry and berated Mary. 'There you were worrying about what would happen to you or Kathleen. Making me make promises – fever was never from your mind and now you can't remember.'

She vented her terror of being cooped up in the ship for an indefinite period. But Mary wasn't to be rattled. 'That was a different thing altogether. Afraid of us being separated I was. Even if we're quarantined we'll be together, please God and the authorities will have to feed us if it's only stirabout. What good would it be, keeping us in quarantine to let us starve to death.'

'I suppose you're right,' Katy said, 'and in any case there's nothing we can do but pray and hope.'

During the night the ship sailed to an area marked off by buoys where it joined other ships awaiting medical inspection. A row broke out amongst those who had wagered on the time of the ship's arrival in America. There were some, those who had guessed short that this was America and demanded their winnings. You could see the shore, they argued. 'No,' shouted the men who had guessed long. 'The bet stands until she's tied up.' A man set hands on Terence McCabe. 'I guessed right – to the minute. Pay up.'

Katy watching the scene could read the man's mind. Like the rest of them he probably had little or nothing to start him when they landed – she could understand his anger and disappointment. The man grappled with Terence and Katy saw how his foot in one of the boots he had acquired lashed out at the gambler's shin. She shivered at his viciousness and felt a foreboding that somehow he threatened her. Why or how she didn't know. Common sense told her that the choice would be hers and Jamsie's as to whether or not they ever had any other contact with Terence, but all the same she was afraid.

By megaphone, the passengers were informed that an inspection by a medical officer was to take place. If fever was found in anyone on board, the ship would be quarantined and the sick transferred to Staten Island. There were many ships waiting to be inspected – it could take some time.

'That announcement is for the benefit of them on the other side – the cabin passengers. They'd tell us nothing,' Jamsie said.

This was the worst moment of the voyage and everyone's nerves were strung tight. After all the hardships they had endured now when they were almost in the promised land – how cruel it would be if they were denied entry. But Katy wouldn't allow herself to believe that. All round her she could hear people speaking aloud their fears. She moved away from them. 'We will land in America,' she kept telling herself. 'There'll be no fever on the ship, please God. It'll be declared clean. We will land in America.'

She avoided Mary, who was wandering here and there forecasting her premonition that never would she set foot on the shores of America. In her heart she knew that fever was about to strike her. But if it was God's will she would accept it. But for all her lamentations Katy noticed she had made preparations to disembark, having tied into a neat bundle her own and Kathleen's possessions. And Katy thought with more tolerance than usual that each one had their own way of dealing with their fears.

'Listen to her,' said Eileen, who had come to sit by Katy. And put into words what Katy had been trying to do in her mind. 'She's imagining the worst that could happen – but not believing a word of it. Easing her mind, that's all she's doing. Mary worries every one else with her troubles real or otherwise. She talks them out of her head, piling them on the unfortunate listener. The likes of Mary sleep easy.'

The ship moved slowly towards the inspection point. Below decks there was speculation as to how the vessels and passengers were faring. It wasn't possible to see much during the brief time they spent on deck – though they learned that the island to which the ships were proceeding was Staten Island and they could see the launch coming and going from the foremost ships.

The crew members with their customary brutality answered questions as to how soon they might expect their turn to come by telling the passengers in foul language the fate that awaited them, laughing and jeering as they did so.

'Scum,' Jamsie said. 'Scum, that's what they are. If ever they were otherwise, sailing these ships and seeing human beings treated worse than animals has killed any bit of decency they might have had.'

'They're not all like that,' Eileen said. 'Oh, they're foul-mouthed and dirty and rough – but underneath it all some are good-hearted.' Jamsie snorted his disbelief. But Katy knew Eileen was remembering Larry with his milk-white skin as soft as a young girl's belly and his poor sore hands. She turned away her head lest Eileen should see the tears in her eyes and ask why she was crying.

★

At last the turn of their ship came and Katy waited with the other passengers to be examined. Around her people were whispering – prayers that they would pass inspections, comments on the American doctor – the neatness of him, the cleanness of him, the speed with which he went through them.

'Open your mouth. Put out your tongue.'

No sir, they replied, their bowels weren't loose. Their head didn't ache. They weren't vomiting . . .

Cursorily he looked at tongues, felt joints and probed bellies. One after another they were passed. Katy saw Mary and Kathleen cleared. Eileen was next in the queue. She laughed and joked during her examination and the doctor responded with quips then waved her through.

Now it was Katy's turn. And now at the last minute she was afraid. Her bowels contracting, giving her cramps, her mouth dry and a heart whose thundering the doctor must notice and suspect that fever caused its racing. First the children were examined. As each one was declared fit she felt calmer. Then Jamsie was being questioned, inspected. She let out a long sigh when the doctor indicated he was well. Her optimism returned. She hadn't got the fever. Not an ache nor pain. Never had she felt so fit. And the doctor confirmed her belief.

Thank you, oh thank you God, she prayed while waiting for the remaining passengers to be cleared. Not a case of fever was found – the ship was clean – they could go up on deck and see America! A cheer went up. Then another. Someone started to sing. Everyone was delirious with joy. Hugging and kissing each other. Calling down blessings on everyone and everything. The ship that had carried them, the Captain, the doctor and America. '*God Bless America.*' Crying and laughing in turns. Shouting their benedictions. 'America!' they said again and again incredulously. 'We're in America. We've arrived. We'll never know the poor day again. If only Mikey had lived to see it,' some lamented. If only poor Mary, Kate, and Padraig, my mother, my father . . . Lord have mercy on them. The litany of names and the floods of tears for those left in Irish graves, for those buried at sea were endless. But the sadness was interspersed with joyous laughter and reminders that all the dead were interceding for them, watching them and knowing well where they were and delighted for them to be there.

Katy too cried for her dead but quickly dried her tears when she saw the bewilderment on Thomas' and Bridget's faces which minutes ago had been transfused with delight as they realised that they had arrived in America. Gathering them to her she hugged and kissed them and told them not to mind her. Her crying was finished. They were in America and everything from now on would be wonderful. Jamsie, Mary Kate and Daniel had their share of hugs and kisses before she calmed down and waited for their arrival in New York.

Up on deck a small portion had been railed off from the cabin class, smaller even than the section allotted previously to the steerage passengers. They were jammed into it and pushed and jostled each other in an effort to get near the rails and catch sight of their promised land. Jamsie elbowed a way through for Katy and the children, ignoring the protests and curses of those he shoved aside.

Mesmerised, Katy watched the land come closer. Now she could see men and women, no – they were ladies and gentlemen, she thought as she caught glimpses of the brightly coloured skirts, the pretty bonnets, the men's good clothes, strolling in what seemed to be a parkland. Now they were visible, now they weren't, as autumn foliage brilliant in its orange, lemon and crimson colours hid the ladies and gentlemen from her view. She heard someone behind her say that the parkland was called Castle Garden – a place where people took their leisure. She thought how beautiful it was and how some day she and Jamsie would stroll there arm in arm.

America was going to be a wonderful place, she could feel it in her bones. They'd have a good life here. She wasn't sorry she had come. Excitement bubbled in her. 'Jamsie!' she kept exclaiming. 'Will you look at that. The colours, the trees. Do you see that one and that one? Oh Jamsie, isn't it grand! And there was me thinking there'd be nothing beautiful to look at. And the sky – it's as blue as a summer's day – and the air – the fresh air. Isn't it wonderful, Jamsie?'

Eileen had also found a place by the rails and was laughing and calling joyously to Katy – drawing her attention to passing sights, as excited and happy as Katy was.

Despite all the noise Katy could hear Mary's complaining voice behind her. Complaining that she couldn't see a thing. That it wasn't fair her Kathleen being deprived of her first sight of America.

'Will I let her in?' Katy asked Jamsie.

'Are you mad? Move an inch and you'll lose your place and it won't be Mary that gets it.'

Now the green parkland was behind and the ship sailing up a river – though it was wider than Katy believed a river could be. But a river it must be, she reasoned, for there were buildings lining one side and ships tied up on the other. So many ships – dozens and dozens of them. Like stabled horses they were, one after the other. Such a sight it was under the blue sky with the sun shining on their tall masts and the seagulls swirling and swooping. Never, thought Katy, never till the day I die will I forget this moment.

The ship was berthed and immediately like a swarm of monkeys came the touts clambering over her sides, veiled threats in their persuasive Irish voices as they sought customers.

'I told you, didn't I, that's them,' said Mary, who with Eileen had come alongside Katy and Jamsie as they waited to disembark.

With Jamsie leading the way they followed the direction most people were taking. Every so often Katy stopped to look round her, or up at the sky, to smile at the children and say over and over, 'We're here, we're in America, in New York.' There were buildings everywhere, huge warehouses from which Katy noticed strange but not unpleasant smells. Then they passed houses and business houses, rows of them and bigger than she imagined houses other than mansions of the gentry could be. Such sights there were. She didn't know where to look. Such crowds – such faces unlike ones she was used to. And so much noise. All the horses and all the vehicles. Everything so new and strange and exciting. And the weather – it wasn't warm like summer for it wasn't summer but felt like it because of the light, the brightness of the blue sky and the crisp dry air. Again and again she stopped to stare, to look about her, to convince herself she was really here and not dreaming. Until Jamsie told her at the rate they were going they'd never find shelter before dark.

Touts and runners who hadn't secured a client were now willing to take on the likes of Katy and Jamsie even though they appeared poor pickings. 'Grand lodgings, sir,' they said. 'Grand rooms and board for next to nothing, ma'am, and every one run by an Irishman or woman.' Jamsie ignored them and the taunts they flung after him.

'You did right,' said Mary. 'Robbers, every one of them.'

'All the same,' said Katy, 'maybe we should engage one, or how else will we find a place?'

Jamsie insisted on going it alone, but as they went further and the light began to go he agreed that the next tout who didn't look a robber altogether he'd engage. However, before he found a suitable one a man stood in front of them barring their way. He said he was a bondsman. He waved a paper in front of Jamsie. This, he said, gave him authority to collect payment from everyone entering the port. From Jamsie he demanded a dollar, from Mary and Eileen fifty cents each.

'For what?' asked Jamsie.

'To guarantee you won't be a liability to the State of New York.'
'We've no dollars,' said Eileen.
'The currency doesn't matter.'
'I haven't seen anyone else handing over money – have you, Katy?'
'I have not,' replied Katy and Mary agreed with her.
'Whether you have or not it's the law,' said the man.

Suddenly Katy felt afraid and aware of how little she or any of them knew about New York, its laws or customs. The man might be fleecing them, on the other hand what he said could be the truth – and God forbid that so soon after landing they should be in trouble with the law. She told Jamsie to pay the money.

'You'll be all right now,' said the bondsman. He rattled off a name and address where he could be contacted if they ran into trouble. With the money pocketed he became genial, asked Jamsie where he was from at home, and said he knew it well. He was from Tipperary himself. Before he left them Katy had the gumption to ask directions to a lodging house.

'There's a decent one in Water Street, 'tis that way,' he said, pointing. 'Turn left when you get to the corner. God bless you now and may you find success in America.'

'What did he say his name was?' asked Katy as they watched him go.

'I didn't understand a word of him except when he threatened us with the law,' said Eileen.

'We weren't meant to,' said Mary. 'That's the way the bondsmen work, didn't I tell you.'

The bondsman had dampened all their spirits. Suddenly they realised how hungry and tired they were, how lost and lonely they felt. The children whimpered and asked for food. The first turning on the left seemed a long way off. Then Eileen let out a screech of laughter. 'Sacred heart of Jesus will you look at that.' Everyone looked and everyone laughed, for down the street came several pigs grunting and rooting in the gutters.

'The best sight I've seen since I left Ireland,' said Jamsie and they all stopped to watch the pigs. They were close enough to smell and see their bristling hair and the curl of their tails and the way they stepped like stout women on small feet.

'Pigs in New York.' Eileen clapped her hands with delight. 'Exactly as Larry said. Pigs, would you believe it. It does my heart good to see them. I nearly feel at home.'

A passer-by, noticing the attractive woman exclaiming with such pleasure stopped and smilingly enquired, 'You approve of the pigs, ma'am?'

'Oh, I do indeed. It's like a breath of home.'

'You'll see plenty of them – they've been foraging all day and are now on their way home. People complain – still they do a fair job of cleaning the city. Good evening.' He raised his hat and inclined his head to include them all in his farewell.

'A real American, a proper gentleman,' Eileen said. 'I hope they're all like that.' Katy thought to herself that he was a nice man and that he was a bit on the thin side, wiry-looking, but his smile was lovely, a crooked sort of smile.

They found the lodging house and got a poor reception after admitting they had no luggage. 'In that case,' said the lodging house keeper, 'it'll be the money down.'

'Why so?' asked Jamsie.

'Couldn't you get up before it was light and clear off without me seeing the colour of your money. Up the top of the stairs there's two rooms, sort them between you.'

'The daylight robber, the fat, baldy oul reprobate. Preying on his own,' Eileen said as they climbed the narrow rickety staircase. 'I only hope to Jesus there isn't a fire in the night – we'd never get out alive.'

The rooms were bare except for several litters of straw and a bucket, each of which were coated in sediment and stank. On each bed there was one dirty rough blanket. 'They'll be lousy and flea-infested,' said Katy.

'To be sure – but it's scratch all night or freeze – please yourself,' said Eileen, trying to make light of the terrible place. 'You and Jamsie and the children sleep in this one and me and Mary'll bunce in together. Here, have this.' She took a hunk of bread from her bag. 'For the children,' she said. 'I was that excited about leaving that kip of a ship I couldn't eat it.'

Chapter Six

Katy woke while it was still dark. There was no swaying motion, no creaking of ship's timbers. There were the other noises with which she was familiar: Jamsie's snoring, a restless child tossing and turning murmuring incomprehensibly. She lay for a while listening. Something had happened. The ship must have docked. Where were all the other passengers, she couldn't hear one of them. She reached out a hand and touched Jamsie. 'Where are we? What's happened?' When he didn't waken immediately her fingers dug harder into his arm. Feeling the hurt he woke and shook off Katy's hold with annoyance on his face as he asked, 'What ails you? Why are you tearing me out of my rest?'

She repeated her questions. 'We're here,' he said. 'We're in America.' His good humour returned, he laughed and put an arm round her. 'Did you forget? We're here – in New York, we arrived last night.' His free hand stroked her face and hair. 'We've four walls of our own at last.' He searched for her mouth and kissed her as his hand reached down in the bed and lifted her shift. 'Oh God, oh Katy, it's been such a long time.' He lay on top of her. 'Katy aghoille!'

She sat up and toppled him off. 'You can wait,' she said, not wanting him, not here, not yet. Her horror and disgust returning as she remembered the first sight of what Jamsie called 'their four walls'.

'Now what's up with you? Aren't we on our own for the first time in months.' He caught hold of her again.

'No,' she said. 'Stop that. Don't do it.'

'Why, in the name of God! It's months since I touched you.'

'I know and I'm sorry, but I can't let you, not yet. First we have to talk.'

'Talk away, so,' he said sulkily, shifting from her and lying on his back. 'I think I'm finished, anyway. Everything has to be used. Maybe you'll be happy now.'

Despite her mood of despair Katy laughed at his attempted blackmail. 'That's very likely and you hardly more than a lad.'

'A lad is it? Amn't I twenty-eight years of age.' He was still sulking and his voice was huffy when he asked, 'What is it you want to talk about that's so important – more important than your husband.'

'About here – this place. We've got to leave. As soon as it's light we'll go out and find somewhere else.'

'If that's what you want,' he said curtly, turning and taking Katy's share of the blanket with him. In the darkness she smiled. He was like a child deprived of something. Then she remembered all the nights of separation on the boat. All the times she had refused him. All the times she had longed to say yes, to lie beside him, to lie in his arms, fall asleep with her head on his shoulder, secure in his love. And she thought about the nights at home. The banked fire keeping darkness at bay. The sweet-smelling straw of the palliasse. The ease of her after Jamsie's loving, stretching like a cat, every bit of her easy, and tears filled her eyes and fell down on her face. 'Oh my love,' she said, 'turn round to me.' Twice she had to say it before he turned and together they banished all the long weary loveless nights.

Afterwards she cried again and when Jamsie became concerned with what he thought was grief she told him it wasn't so. She was crying for joy. They had survived. They were here, the six of them, thanks be to God. She was overjoyed. 'I love you,' she said again and again. 'We'll make a success of America, together we can do anything. I'm that happy.'

'That's what the love of a good man does for you,' Jamsie said, reaching to touch her breast.

She slapped away his hand. 'An hour's sleep works wonders too,' she said, closing her eyes and sleeping.

Later when she woke the children were up. Thomas had dragged a wooden box beneath the window high on the wall and was stretching on tiptoes to try and see out. 'I can't see nothing,' he complained. 'I want to see America.'

'Come down this minute and put on your clothes or you'll get your end. And you Bridget, help Mary Kate get dressed.' She scolded them and told them to mind the splinters and not to step on the insects, big ones, brown-shelled like black beetles at home only bigger.

Jamsie stirred, sat up and announced that he was hungry. 'There's a kitchen below,' he said rising, pulling on his trousers, tucking in the tail of his shirt in which he had slept. 'Hurry up now, I'm starving.'

Bridget standing with legs crossed and face screwed up shouted, 'Quick, quick, I have to go, quick, where is it?' Katy, disorientated in her new surroundings was slow to remember where the bucket was, and by the time she did Bridget had wet herself and cried with shame.

Thomas laughed and pointed to the puddle on the splintered floor making a lake round a cockroach. Danny cried and Mary Kate shouted at all the excitement. And Katy thought she would go mad or break down and cry too. How would she ever manage in this strange place? Where was the water to wash? One of them would get a splinter in their feet and be crippled. Where were they to get the breakings of their fast? And money? She felt weak only considering all that lay in front of her. Go out into a strange place, into such crowds as she had never seen before. Face strangers, speak to them. Maybe they wouldn't understand her. Sometimes crewmen on the boat hadn't. They'd laughed and made fun of her speech. Oh God, how was she to face it all? She wanted to crawl back into the bed and sleep forever.

'What ails you?' asked Jamsie. She thought of telling him but knew he wouldn't understand. In any case the children were clamouring for her attention. So she said that nothing ailed her only that she felt as if she had strong drink taken. 'My head's that light and my legs shaky and honest to God I can still feel the motion of the boat in my stomach.'

'Food, that's what you want, what we all want. Bed and our breakfast – that's what we paid for. Hurry up now with the children and we'll go down.'

Relief that at least one problem was taken care of raised Katy's spirits, and in no time she had found a cold tap on the landing and had everyone dressed. Jamsie took his ease on the bed.

Dead cockroaches crunched under Katy's feet as she came into the kitchen where Mary and Eileen were already seated. Katy marvelled at how well Eileen looked, her hair and eyes and teeth shining, her face full of good humour. Her comments about the lodging house and its keeper making other people sitting at the long table laugh and add their own opinions.

The bread was stale and scraped with dripping, the tea was stewed but even so all tasted better than anything they had eaten on the ship and they ate ravenously. Wiping the lardy grease from her mouth, Eileen suggested that they shouldn't stay another night in the lodging house. Eagerly Katy and Mary agreed. There was a woman sitting at the same table to whom Eileen had talked earlier. She had been in New York for months, moving from place to place, now she and her husband were going inland. Eileen decided she would know the ropes about finding rooms but instead of asking her directly led into it by saying, 'You'll be sorry to leave New York, I suppose?'

'I will not.'

'Oh,' said Eileen. 'I'd have thought it was a great place with all the jobs.'

'Not if you're Irish and Catholic. You don't believe me? Well, wait'll you see the notices everywhere, in shops, offices and the newspapers. *Help wanted – no Irish need apply.* So don't think you're going to plank your arse into a nice easy domestic situation.'

'Women's jobs, you mean?'

'Women mostly, men too if they're not prepared for the pick and shovel. I'm telling you we're the unfortunate people. Little skills we brought with us from Ireland. Little chance we had there of learning them. But in America we thought it would be different. Well, I'm telling you if New York's anything to go by it's not.'

Mary, who had had visions of walking straight into a job looked disconsolate. Katy felt optimistic. Jamsie with a bit of food to build him up was a fine man. He'd be well able for the pick and shovel.

'Tell me now, is there rooms in the neighbourhood we could rent?' Eileen asked, after first sympathising with the woman for her bad experiences.

'Rooms there are if that's what you'd call them. Bad and all as we were at home you wouldn't have put the pig in one. Not far from here there's a place called the Five Points, that's where five streets come together. And the Irish and the tenements are there. Wait'll you see them, you'll think your place at home was a mansion. For if it was only the quarter acre you could piss in privacy, go out the door for a breath of air or close it after you to sit for a heat of the fire. Mind you, the shanties are even worse. There the people have thrown up all sorts of shelters for themselves and their pigs. You're walking through manure, piles of it and it isn't always the pig's either, falling over streels of children running half-naked and their mothers drunk. Take my advice and go for the tenements.'

'How do we get there?' asked Eileen.

'Go out this door, turn to the right and go to the very end, there's a Protestant church there, then ask again for Mulberry Street.'

Eileen thanked the woman and to Mary and Katy said, 'We'd better go.'

Jamsie wanted to know where he would see them later. 'Outside here I suppose, we know nowhere else,' said Katy.

'Right so – but if I get a start you'll have the long wait.'

'I won't mind that a bit,' said Katy.

It was a cold morning, but like the previous day the sun was shining and the women compared the November weather with that in Ireland, the mist and damp there would be at this time of the year. Katy tried to take comfort from the fact, warm herself with it, but the pavements were cold under her feet and her heart ached when she looked at the pinched faces of her children and knew the discomfort there was for them on the hard stones. To herself, she said, 'The first thing I'll buy with Jamsie's wages is covering for their feet.'

But soon Katy's sadness was diverted by all the unfamiliar sights about her. Laying eyes for the first time in her life on black men and women, fire engines with bells ringing drawn by galloping horses. Well-dressed men and women also took her attention, and then again the fears returned. Fears of the unknown, of their reception when they enquired about the rooms. Would they get them? Could they afford them? Would Jamsie get a job today? Where would Mary get one? Would they ever get used to all the strangeness?

'They must have been nice houses once,' Katy said when they got to the Five Points. 'There's more of them black people.'

'Slaves, they are – only they're not now. They escaped, helped by them that's against slavery,' Eileen explained.

'Saint Patrick was a slave,' Mary said.

'That was hundreds of years ago. But them fellas, the blacks they'd still be slaves if they went back.'

'Back where, Eileen?'

'God, Mary, don't you know nothing? Back to the South.'

'The South, where's that?'

'Here, here in America – you know, like Cork is south of Dublin, well the South is south of New York.'

'But who'd own a man or woman black though they be?'

'An American.'

'Glory be to God, I never knew such things existed outside of Ireland where we were slaves to the English.'

'What ails you, we were never slaves,' Eileen said.

'In a manner of speaking we were so, for weren't we working morning, noon and night to pay rent to the English landlord?'

'But he didn't own us, Mary – that's the difference. We could go any time we liked, go anywhere.'

'You could say so, I suppose, if you didn't mind starving and having no shelter – yes, you could go, Eileen.'

'That's all I'm saying – but in America – in the South they own the black fellas the way you would a dog. Anyway, we'd better see about the rooms.'

'Well, talk about the slums of Dublin!' Eileen exclaimed as they entered Mulberry Street, one of five radiating from the Five Points. 'Palaces they are, compared to here.'

Mary and Katy stared at the dilapidated houses, at doors swinging off their hinges, broken windows, some panes stuffed with rags, others boarded over, at the children sitting on the steps, dirty, cold and neglected-looking. And everywhere there was noise, voices of women screaming, men shouting and children crying. Along the pavements were stalls selling bread, fruit, sweets, cooked meats, all sorts of things. Barefooted ragged boys ran round the stalls, the bolder ones passing close, reaching a hand to rob something. 'I'll cut the hand offa you, I'll break your neck if you don't clear off. Get to hell-gates out of it,' the stallholders yelled and brandished knives, choppers or whatever came to hand.

Katy shuddered at the thought of living here, of rearing her children in such a place, amongst such people. Mary declared that never outside the door would Kathleen be allowed to put her foot. Eileen, to whom similar sights were familiar in Dublin said, 'What's worse than the robbers is the knackers – can't you smell it?'

'Knackers, what's that?'

'The place where they boil dead horses, the bones anyway for making glue. In the summer the smell will poison you, can you not smell it?'

Katy said there were so many smells, all of them strange and terrible.

'You'll get to know this one. Wait till the summer comes and it brings the flies and bluebottles in their millions,' Eileen said, then shouted to one of the boys hovering near a stall. 'Commere you, commere, I want you.' He came slowly, staring at her with suspicion. 'Is there rooms to let round here?'

'There's rooms.'

'Where?'

'There, and there,' he pointed to two houses, 'and down in that wooden church they've made rooms in there.'

'Thanks,' Eileen said, and gave him a penny. For an instant he smiled then ran to the nearest food stall.

'There's one consolation anyway,' said Mary. 'So far, except for the black men every voice I've heard is Irish.'

' 'Tis a consolation,' agreed Katy.

'Which one will we go to?' asked Eileen.

'Not the wooden church that would have been Protestant – we'd not have an hour's luck in it,' said Mary.

'The first house then,' Eileen decided.

68

A fat woman coming down the steps said yes, there were rooms idle. If they knocked on the door in the hall they'd get their information. The smell in the hall was appalling, the smell of unemptied privies, damp and cats and vermin and too many people who seldom washed.

'It's this, the shanties or more of the lodging house – will I knock?' asked Eileen.

'Not much of a choice so we'll try it,' said Katy and Mary added, 'For the time being anyway, with the help of God we'll soon be on our feet and out of it.'

Eileen's knock was answered by another stout Irishwoman. There were rooms, two on the top floor and one below them. 'The ones on the top is very small. Gentlemen's houses these were and them the servants' rooms. A grand neighbourhood this used to be, so I hear tell. Then the rich men moved, but held on to the property. One day the tenements will be gone and the ground still here. Sure the rich never lose. About the rooms – have you husbands and more children?'

They told her their circumstances. 'Then you,' she said to Katy, 'would be better with the room below. It's bigger and has a sort of closet. It's a dollar each for the top ones and one and a half for the big one.'

Katy gasped when she heard the price of the rooms. 'I never thought it would be so dear. Could you lower it?'

'I'm only the agent,' the woman said. 'A go-between and God knows how many more there are before you get to the landlord – that's to stop tenants looking for repairs or haggling over the price.'

Mary said she couldn't afford the rent either and Eileen asked the woman to excuse them and beckoned Katy and Mary to one side. 'Listen,' she said, 'the rooms are probably as good and as cheap as any in New York – and if we take them we'll be together.'

'I know,' said Katy, 'but supposing Jamsie doesn't get a job straight away – how'll I manage? As it is I'm almost penniless. We've nothing, not a cup to drink out of, not a bundle of straw to lie on – and if I lay out that kind of money we're finished.' Mary said she was in the same predicament.

'Then let me lend you both the money. Let me finish,' she said when Katy and Mary started to protest that they couldn't borrow money from her. 'I've a few pounds put by. There's only myself to keep – I can spare it until you're on your feet, honest to God. Take the rooms and I'll let you have the money for cups and that – and next week if you, Mary, and Jamsie aren't working I'll give you what you haven't got for the rent. Go on, do it to please me. I'll have no trouble

69

finding work. Go on, say you will. It's for my sake – I'd be lost without the pair of you.'

Embarrassed and grateful and promising immediate payment when work was found they went up to see the rooms. The street, the hall and the stairs had prepared them not to expect too much. Not much was what they found. Walls that had once been distempered were now peeling and stained with grease and God alone knew what else. Windows that neither opened nor shut properly. Through their grime they looked and saw other tenements with washing strung out on poles and rusted fire escapes.

'There's no grate – what'll we cook on?' asked Katy.

'The kerosene stove in the corner – paraffin oil it burns,' Eileen explained.

The room Katy was renting was very dim. Maybe, she thought, the sun had gone down since she was above in the other rooms. It was as dark as the cottage could be but there you'd have the door open or could go outside and see the light. It was a terrible place, it had a bad smell, but she consoled herself it was a shelter and better than the lodging house. And she could improve it. Of course she could. Jamsie would whitewash the walls and she'd scrub every inch of it and get a bit of bright stuff for the window, maybe enough to curtain the closet. So long as Jamsie got a job she'd work wonders in it. Make it into a home. You wouldn't know it when it was finished. If she didn't believe what she was thinking she'd run mad out of it.

'Your children are very good and your daughter, too,' the agent said to Mary and Katy, 'and fine-looking children, God bless and spare them. I'd ask you down for a sup of tea only I'm expecting Himself and he's cranky at the best of times.'

They thanked her and Eileen again became the spokeswoman. Where would they get . . . and she itemised their wants. The woman had all the answers. 'The ticks you'll get around the corner in Mott Street.' She had a young fella below who would get bales of straw from the hayshop. She had advice on where they would get secondhand bedding in reasonable condition and not too dear, either. The same shop sold pots, buckets and mugs; you could get the kerosene and a tun dish to go with it. 'You'll be wanting a brush but for the present I'll lend you mine. Oh, and don't forget candles. We've been promised the gaslight this long time – but sure promises are all we get. Come down now and I'll send for the straw and you can start about your business.'

They bought coffee and rolls at a stall and noticed while they ate and drank how much Irish food there was for sale. All parts of the pig; tails

70

and feet, ribs and backbones, heads and entrails. 'I'll feel that at home with a bit of bacon and cabbage,' said Mary, 'though it's years since I tasted it, not since before the potatoes failed and then not often. For wasn't it on the potato and nothing else but a glass of buttermilk to wash it down that the thousands of us lived. And fine healthy men and women we were, too. A man would think nothing of eating half a stone of potatoes in the one day and a grand feed they were, too. Only when they failed we were left with nothing else. Oh, it was the terrible thing all right to be starving and see the cattle and the grain, the eggs and the butter that we'd made, grown and tended passing our doors, off to the boats and the English people and us at home dying of the Hunger.'

Eileen made a face behind Mary's back, her look conveying that Mary was off again. If she didn't put a stop to it they'd be here all day going back to the time of St Patrick. 'Mary,' she said, 'I don't want to hurry you but there's the ticks and things to get.' Mary finished her coffee and off they went for their shopping.

Irishmen sold them the bedding and all else. Men full of advice and *plaimas*, good salesmen. Having nothing to compare prices with, the women had to be satisfied. The ticks were made from flour sacking with sheafs of wheat and the mill's name stamped on them. Laden down they went back to the rooms. The bundles of straw were laid out in each room.

Katy knelt and undid the bundles then laid her face against the straw, breathing in its sweet smell, fondling silky pieces of it between her hands, letting it evoke memories of home. She was so tired she could have slept, remembering and sleeping, sinking into it, closing her eyes pretending she was far away from this terrible room, from the strange and frightening place New York was, for all that the house and streets were full of Irish people. She forced herself to her feet and began stuffing the tick. For a while she paid no attention to what the children were doing in the closet – then their shouts became more excitable and their laughter hysterical: she had better go and see.

They too had undone their bundle of straw, were dancing in it, flinging it up in the air, throwing it in handfuls at each other – it was scattered and trodden all over the room. It would have to be swept together, sweeping with it whatever might lie on the floor; it was in bits, more chaff-like than straw. 'I'll kill you!' she shouted at them. Her tiredness and sadness, her fears for their existence in this place, suddenly it all came together to overwhelm her and she lashed out first at Bridget, then Thomas and even Mary Kate, slapping and slapping them, slapping Bridget harder and more often because she stared defiantly at her, raised an arm to shield herself and never cried a tear.

71

Exhaustion stopped her and then with horror she saw the marks of her fingers on Bridget's fair skin and Bridget's eyes still regarding her defiantly. She was enraged by the sight of Bridget's face, by the knowledge that she had inflicted the marks. They accused her as did Bridget's eyes. She wanted her to cry, to say or do something that would give her the excuse to take hold of her, beg her forgiveness, cover the raised welts with kisses. But Bridget just stood and Katy lashed out and hit her again. Then she ran from the room and threw herself face down on the half-stuffed palliasse and cried as if her heart would break. To do that to them, she kept thinking, to hurt them, to mark Bridget. Bridget, that was her two eyes.

Bridget, who had never caused her a minute's trouble. To have marked her lovely face. To have hurt Bridget – Bridget, who had nursed her when she had the fever and been a mother to the children. Oh God, please forgive me, something came over me. I don't beat my children. I'll never do such a thing again. Oh God, forgive me and let them forgive me, too.

She was still crying when she felt a hand touching her face. It was Danny sitting beside her, smiling and with his soft baby fingers in her tears. Thank God, she thought, my madness stopped short of beating him. Then she saw the others coming to her. Bridget through tears now falling was saying she was sorry and smiled her forgiveness. Mary Kate sat beside her mother then half lay across her and Thomas said nothing but she knew by how he looked at her that he too forgave her.

'Oh, my little loves,' Katy said. 'I'm that sorry. I don't know what came over me. I'm that sorry. I never meant to hurt you. Come here to me.' They huddled round her. 'Your poor face, poor Bridget, your poor face.' She covered the red welts with tears and kisses, thinking all the while, what sort of a mother am I to harm my own child. They engulfed her with hugs and more kisses and promises to be good. At last she had to tell them to stop now, that the ticks had to be stuffed.

'Let me look at your face,' she said when they had finished. Bridget held it up for inspection. ' 'Tis fading, thanks be to God. I'd drop stone dead if anyone else were to see what I did to you.'

Jamsie when they met him outside the lodging house had obviously had a drink and was in great humour. He had a job for tomorrow. A man he'd got talking to in a saloon, an Irishman, had fixed him up. He'd found plenty of Irishmen who knew the ropes. They'd be all right. New York wasn't a bad place at all, at all.

'What about *No Irish Need Apply?*' asked Eileen.

' 'Tis there to see but not everywhere. And there's ways round it. A sober respectable woman can get a word from a priest that'll walk her into a job. And there's always a shortage of men with strong arms and backs able to swing a pick and willing to work for less than the Americans.'

Terence McCabe was determined to succeed in America – and by his wits rather than with a pick and shovel. He had listened to the stories of touts either robbing passengers of their luggage or bringing them to lodging houses where they were overcharged while the touts got commissions. He knew that bondsmen received fees from ships' captains indemnifying them against further responsibility for the immigrants, that the bondsmen then demanded further fees from passengers and seldom came to their help if they fell on hard times. Bondsmen were hand in glove with minor corrupt government officials and politicians, job contractors – with everyone who was making money in ways that weren't strictly honest.

To find his way into that set-up was Terence's ambition and he reasoned that a tout was his best lead-in. So before the ship docked he secured his money inside his shirt except for loose change and as the touts clambered over the rails looked for one he considered suitable. One about his own size and age, one he could handle if things went wrong. Having found one he asked to be taken to a lodging house, then fixing the runner with his menacing stare warned him that if he tried anything on either him or his brother he'd live to regret it. 'Me, sir? Sure why would I do a thing like that to one of my own? I'll take you to Kelly's. Kelly is a grand man and has the finest lodging house in these parts.' Terence handed over his bag in which there was nothing of value.

To Kelly's, a groggery with lodgings above it the tout brought them. It was at the end of a street called Maiden Lane; Broadway was just around the corner. As they entered the bar the tout explained, 'I stay here myself. It's handy for the docks and if you want a bit of life in the evenings. Broadway's the great place to walk during the evenings, plenty going on and the shops all lit up. I've a little room of my own, because I'm a regular-like. Now you and the brother will have to share one of the big rooms. At least you won't be lonely, eight or nine we do have there of a night.'

Terry nodded and looked round the saloon. There were pictures on the walls of St Patrick, Dan O'Connell, the Young Irelanders and one of Robert Emmet in the dock with his speech beneath it.

'Mr Kelly, this is Terence McCabe and his brother.'

Kelly shook hands. He was a red-faced man with a thick neck and a smile that never reached his eyes. 'It's great to see you, son. Great to have another one of our own arrive. Your man there will take your traps to the room where we keep the luggage safe and sound.' The tout went away with Terry's bag. He knew about this dodge. To keep you in the landlord's clutches until your money was spent on adulterated spirits, your belongings were kept under lock and key. If you ran out of money your luggage was rifled and you thrown out into the street.

'You'll have a drink on the house to bid you welcome,' Kelly said.

'I won't, thanks.' Terence wanted to keep his senses about him. 'But the brother will have a cordial.' While Mikey drank one and then another cordial, Terry was noticing everything, listening to anything within his hearing. Information was being exchanged about building sites, where there were vacancies, where the gangers were bastards, who to approach, who to avoid. Now and then a working man came in and handed something over the bar to Kelly. Money, Terry guessed, payment for a favour Kelly had granted.

Women came in and out to buy groceries, for Kelly seemed to stock everything. He must be making a fortune, Terry thought.

Later in the evening Terry and the tout had a long conversation. Kelly, the tout told him, had been in America no time and was coining it. 'He's a hard man, one you wouldn't want to make an enemy of. What sort of work were you looking for?'

'I haven't rightly thought.'

'You could do worse than take up the running. I'll show you the ropes. I'll fix it with Kelly, you'll get a cut for every passenger you bring. And there's ways of making more.'

'How?' asked Terry.

'Take baggage, for instance. Look for them that have at least one bag, don't bother with women and children, for bundles of rags is all they have. But a good leather bag now, sure even if there wasn't a thing in it the bag's worth something. Get a grip on the bag – a quick sprint and you'll earn more than your cut from Kelly. Anything could be in a leather bag – one time I got a silver teapot. Only don't ditch too many passengers or Kelly'd get suspicious.'

'It sounds grand,' said Terry, 'only there's a drawback.'

'And what's that?'

'The brother. Did you not notice that he's a bit soft in the head, God bless the mark.'

'I did not then,' replied the tout. 'I'm sorry to hear it.'

Terry shrugged. 'It's God's will. At home in the village 'twas no bother – but here?'

'Oh indeed, here it won't be easy.'

'I'll lodge here, but who'd keep an eye on him?'

'For sure and certain Kelly wouldn't. There's the orphanage?'

'No,' Terry said, 'no orphanages, not for my brother. I hear tell they're worse than the poorhouse.'

'You could ask a priest I suppose, the priests know everything. I heard of one that's a soft touch. I've heard him talked about in here. You hear all kinds of things here. It's like one of them societies or clubs. Whatever an Irishman's looking for it's here he comes. I declare to God a man spends more hours here than he does with his wife or family. Everything that happens in the neighbourhood begins here. Hold on now for a minute, Kelly is slack, I'll ask him about you doing the running. But before I forget say not a word about touting to the priest – he's down on us. But sure a man has to make a living.'

When he came back from the bar he told Terence that Kelly had agreed to give him a try. 'You're to start the day after tomorrow.' Then he gave directions as to how Terence was to find the church. 'You could take a short cut,' he added, 'but if you're not in a hurry take my advice and stroll along Broadway – that's where you'll see New York. Only look out for the mad dogs, or any without muzzles. Sometimes they run in packs. Now and again young fellas are hired to kill them.'

'How do they do that?'

'Beat their brains out with shovels. Mad dogs are desperate things – one bite and you'd die foaming at the mouth, not able to swallow, demented at the sight of water though the thirst was choking you.'

The next morning, following the tout's directions, Terence set out with his brother to see the priest. On the way they saw Mary, Katy and Eileen looking for their rooms. 'That's her from the ship,' Mikey said as the women passed without seeing them. 'Her that shifted us.'

'Her and the Dublin hoor,' Terence said and spat. And the hatred he had felt when Katy ran him from the berth returned. Then he remembered how she had looked at him the day he was dealing the cards left-handed. Her eyes accusing him. He was afraid then. From then until the ship docked she had a power over him. She could have told the Dublin one, she could have brought him face to face with the cow who had bitten his finger. Anything could have happened and all through her. But he was safe now. Who'd care in America what had happened on the ship? Who could prove anything? Not even the one

75

he'd taken in the dark. She didn't know him from Adam and in any case he'd kept his ears open on the ship and knew her destination was Boston. Women, he spat again. He hated every one of them. Hated the things they could do to your body, like now, even thinking about them. But most of all he hated the fair-headed one and one day he'd have his own back on her.

They turned into Broadway and Terence forgot about Katy and his vendetta, for the sight of Broadway sent his blood spinning. Crowds, though his only previous experience of them had been at fairs, made him feverish with excitement. People in crowds were easily parted from their money. Giving to beggars, cripples and plausible storytellers, mesmerised by tricksters with cards. Terence was expert in all the ways of extracting their coins and when guile failed, an accidental elbowing followed by profuse apologies blinded them to the hand relieving them of their purse or valuables.

Here in New York the crowd was made up of thousands milling, jostling one another, hardly a hair's breadth between them. People as thick on the ground as flies on a dead horse. There were pickings galore.

'Where are we going?' asked Mikey, interrupting Terence's thoughts.

'To see the priest.'

'Will we go back then?'

'Stop moidering me and keep up,' Terence answered impatiently.

He walked on noticing everything, admiring, envious. The style and the comfort. The confident air of them. You could smell the money. One day, he vowed, he would be like them. One day he would be somebody. He saw the pigs and the dogs and gave them a wide berth. He saw the Irish beggarmen and women dressed in rags and other Irishmen in their imagined finery of blue tailcoats and high hats. But mostly he saw the signs of wealth and with every step his resolve to acquire it strengthened. Not for long would he stay in lodging houses, listening, pretending gratitude to men like the tout and Kelly.

A fire engine came galloping down the street. People stopped and he heard words of admiration for New York's volunteer firemen. Hemmed in amongst the crowd of shouting, gesticulating men and women, Terence slipped a hand as lightly as a snowflake landing inside a man's coat and undid his watch and chain. Holding tightly to Mikey he worked his way out of the crowd and was far down the street before the man noticed he had been robbed.

★

Terence impressed the priest with the story of his devotion to the simple-minded Mikey. So that he didn't hesitate to give him the name and address of a woman who would be a second mother to him. Then he said, 'God bless you – you're a credit to the mother that reared you and the Catholic church. Tell me now, I don't suppose you had a priest on the ship?'

'No, Father,' replied Terence and broke out in a cold sweat, for he knew what was coming.

'You'll be wanting Confession, so?'

There was no excuse a Catholic could make for refusing Confession when for so long they had been deprived of it. Even so, Terence searched his mind for one – anything rather than bend his knee in a confessional. Nothing convincing came to his mind, and in any case if he refused the priest might think twice of the arrangement to have Mikey looked after.

Fear was a stranger to him except when he entered a confessional. He believed in Heaven and Hell. If you died with a mortal sin on your soul you went to Hell. He had nightmares about devils. Yet he never made a true Confession, admitting always only trivial sins, venial ones – missing his morning and night prayers, disobedience to his parents, small thefts. He would no more confess to raping the girl and letting Larry be blamed for it, than he would to missing Mass on a Sunday. He knew that missing Mass was a grievous sin, one that endangered his soul and one day before he died, when he was an old man, when the priest was there with the Holy Oils to anoint him he would make a true Confession. His fear of Hell overcoming his fear of priests in the role of confessor.

As for the other things, he didn't consider them wrong, much less a sin. The wan on the boat was asking for it waddling round with the big fat arse on her. And the oul fella in the cottage would have killed him and Mikey. What he did he did in self-defence – and only a fool would have left the pouch of money. His conscience was clear where Larry was concerned too. He'd never laid a finger on him.

He confessed his trivial sins to the priest, received his penance and absolution and went on his way to arrange Mikey's lodgings.

Chapter Seven

Katy scrubbed and cleaned the rooms until her arms ached. She bought a secondhand table with a rickety leg which, when she forgot to prop something underneath it, wobbled and spilled the tea. She had three chairs; on the third one Bridget and Thomas took turns to sit, otherwise they stood to the table. Danny sat on her lap at mealtimes and Mary Kate on her father's. After Christmas she would buy another chair – after Christmas she would whitewash the walls. Everything had to wait until after Christmas, for by then she would have covering for everyone's feet – that was the most important thing. The boots Jamsie had were falling off him, she and the children were still barefooted – and the freezing weather was coming. Everyone who had spent a winter in New York warned her about the weather that set in in December and could last for months.

The stuff for curtains would have to wait, too. She would have liked them, something bright to relieve the gloominess of the room into which the sun never shone. She knew now that it was because other tall tenements blocked the light. It was a terrible deprivation. She had gummed paper pictures, brightly coloured ones of the Sacred Heart and Our Lady onto cardboard and tacked them to the wall, otherwise the room was unadorned and as the stove used for cooking heated only the space immediately in front of it, comfortless. Yet, she thanked God they had the shelter, that Jamsie hadn't been idle a day since they arrived and that they had their health.

Not everyone in the house did. Day and night you heard them coughing and before Christmas four babies in the house died of croup. And in the street you saw men and women in all stages of consumption. So Katy, when despondency threatened to overwhelm her, when her thoughts went back to Ireland before the Hunger, consoled herself that she was faring better than many in New York. And thanks be to God she had Eileen and Mary for comfort and company.

Mary with a recommendation from the priest got a job cleaning in City Hall and Eileen in a saloon near the docks, where in between washing glasses she sang for the clients.

78

The weather became colder. A north-west wind blew and found its way through the window frames, rattling them, dislodging the paper and rags stuffed in to keep out draughts. Every night when the wind howled, the windows rattled and the icy air came into the room Katy would think that tomorrow she would have Jamsie nail a board across them as many people in the house had. But morning would bring fresh hope that the wind would drop and she wouldn't have to block out what little light came into the room.

It became so cold that they all slept in the same bed and Katy spread over it every bit of spare clothing they had. And when she remarked on how cold the weather was to anyone who'd spent a winter here they laughed and told her to wait – there was worse to come.

On the nights when Jamsie went to the saloon Katy told the children stories about Ireland before the Hunger, and as it came nearer to Christmas one evening she related how the Feast was spent at home.

'At this time of the year there'd be great times up at the Big House. Such excitement there was with all the preparation. Master Charles coming down from Dublin and often bringing young gentlemen for the holidays. And other guests would be expected. Your grandmother, the Lord rest her, was kept busy running in and out to open the gates for the carriages.'

'And what would you be doing?' Bridget asked.

'Working with Nan in the dairy. Churning the butter and skimming the cream. Nan was the dirtiest woman I ever knew. Her face and hands wouldn't see water from one year's end to the next. Under her long nails was enough dirt to grow potatoes. That didn't stop her dipping them into the cream for a taste. How she didn't poison everyone I don't know. But she was the best butter-maker in the county.'

The children laughed at the idea of Nan, then Thomas asked, 'Did you ever have a ride in the carriage?'

'Many and many a time – but only when the family weren't at home. But at Christmas everyone was there, all the family, relations and friends. Ah, Christmas was the grand time there. Do you know something – I can still smell the holly that was brought in to decorate the Hall. It had a lovely green smell.'

Bridget laughed. 'A green smell!'

'Oh, 'twas green alright. With your eyes closed you could tell that. Know something fresh and green from out of doors had been brought into the house. Anyway you should remember, for wasn't our own place filled with the same holly and the green smell every year? You'd come with me to pick it.'

Bridget said she never remembered that. Thomas said he remembered it well. Katy smiled at him. She wasn't sure if he did, but he'd say it to please her. Looking at her children she thought how much she loved them, but Thomas had a special place in her heart. She liked his shy, gentle ways. He wasn't demonstrative, but there were times when in passing he would touch her, a light touch that was quickly gone. She knew it was his way of saying he loved her.

'Tell us more about Christmas,' said Mary Kate.

'Well, the place would be full of other smells, all the lovely things Hannah was cooking, pies and puddings, all sorts of delicious things. And she wouldn't have a minute to talk between the cooking and making stuffing for the geese and larding joints of meat. I feel hungry just thinking about it.'

'Would there be a goose in your house?'

'A fine big fat one every year of my life – a present from the Master.'

'I wonder what a goose tastes like – I think it might be gorgeous,' said Thomas.

'Gorgeous isn't the word. Please God one Christmas we'll have one. And then you'll know. You won't stop licking your fingers for a week. And I'll have a jar of goose grease to rub on your chest if you get a cough. Are you falling asleep, Mary Kate?'

Mary Kate opened her eyes wide and said no, she wasn't a bit sleepy, her lids beginning to droop almost before she finished speaking.

'Anyway it's getting late – but I'll quickly tell you the rest. On St Stephen's Day there was the hunt. That was a sight to see. All the ladies and gentlemen on their beautiful horses, all gathered outside the house. The men wearing red coats and the ladies black riding habits and horses of every colour. There were white ones and chestnut and ones like black satin and bay mares with coats like nutmegs. Such a picture it was. The horses were impatient to be off and the hounds more so. Then the Master would make the move and away they'd go. Slowly at first till they were in the open and then you'd see them galloping and galloping.'

'And did you go galloping too?' asked Thomas.

Katy laughed. 'Indeed I didn't, the servants didn't go galloping. Back to the kitchen we went. You see, there'd be a ball in the evening and we'd lots of preparations to make.

'But for me the best part of Christmas and something I'll never forget to my dying day was Christmas Eve, when with my mother and father we'd go to Midnight Mass. Before we went the Christmas Candle was lit and put in the window to show the Baby Jesus His welcome. When we came out of Mass it would be Christmas and all the neighbours would be wishing you well. Everyone full of joy. Even the crankiest man or woman happy for the time it was. And going home in the dark you'd see in every cottage window candle flames flickering and twinkling like stars.'

'Will we have a candle in the window?' asked Bridget, and yawned.

'Love we won't, more's the pity. The sill is too narrow and the floor so rickety. Someone running up the stairs could set the boards trembling. The candle might topple and the place go up in flames. Maybe next year we'll be somewhere else. I'll miss the candle but God will understand. Now I'll make you a drink and then it'll be time for bed.'

They said, each in turn, 'Ah no, do we have to, tell us more stories.' But Katy insisted it was time for bed. She made the drink from cocoa bean shells. It was a pale colour not like cocoa at all but the taste wasn't unpleasant – and it was cheap and Katy believed nourishing.

When they were asleep Katy had a little cry because she was far from home and wouldn't have a Christmas Candle and little with which to buy the children gifts. Then she dried her eyes and reminded herself that they were lucky to be alive and in America. And that Jesus would find His way into their hearts and home with or without the lighted candle.

She waited until the last minute on Christmas Eve to do her shopping – at the last minute everything was cheaper. For the dinner she got a piece of bacon. The man in the shop wished her a happy Christmas and threw in two pigs' feet with her purchase. She counted her money and decided that with what she'd saved on the meat she could buy a present for each of her family. She chose a yard of scarlet ribbon for Bridget and a blue one for Mary Kate. For Jamsie and Thomas she got stockings and a wooden pull-along lamb for Danny. Christmas was the time for children, she thought, and went back to the ribbon stall and bought one for Kathleen.

Eileen and Mary came on Christmas afternoon. Eileen brought a bottle of port wine. 'You shouldn't have,' said Katy. 'It's a great extravagance.'

'Don't be talking,' said Eileen. 'Didn't I feck it from the saloon. Here, take it and open it, it'll warm the cockles of your heart.' Katy doubted that she had stolen it – and certainly the bags of sweets she gave the children had had to be paid for. Eileen and her generosity. Her reluctance to take back the money borrowed to get them started.

Mary had also bought ribbons and pencils and a pair of thick socks for Danny. The women cried and laughed and remembered Christmases at home and drank the wine and got tipsy and said, all the same America wasn't such a bad place.

At the end of December snow fell and there seemed no stop to it, Katy thought. It was as cold inside the house as out of doors. Ice formed inches up the panes of glass making beautiful patterns, which the children when they rose in the mornings fingered until their fingers grew numb. The tap in the yard which supplied the house with water burst. Katy trudged through snow several feet deep in places to the stand-pipe set up on the street, dodging snowballs as she went, hoping those that hit her weren't the ones inside which boys put stones. Mary had had her head split open by one.

Jamsie was laid off because of the weather, and went out each day looking for any sort of work that would earn enough to pay the rent and feed them. One day he told her he had heard that a man called Ryan who came from a village near them at home was doing well in America.

'Is that so, I don't recall him,' said Katy. 'Is he here in New York?'

Jamsie said he was and Katy asked what had he prospered at and Jamsie said in the building work.

'He might take you on.'

'There's no building work in this weather.'

'I know that, but maybe he'd want other things done, shifting and moving things.'

'I didn't like him when he had nothing. I'd like him less now.' Katy left the subject alone for the time being. But as the days passed, and on some Jamsie didn't earn anything, she knew that somehow more money had to come into the house.

One day when she, Eileen and Mary were talking she mentioned Ryan to Mary, who knew all there was to know about the Irish who were succeeding.

'A farm labourer from Drimoleague who came over two years ago with not a penny to his name and now he's prospering – twenty men working for him. You'd know him to see -- and her, they're in Mass every Sunday, she's a big, fat, red-faced woman.'

'Jamsie knew him at home. I thought that maybe he could ask Ryan for work.'

'And why not,' said Mary.

'Jamsie doesn't like him.'

'What's liking got to do with it?'

'Ryan he says is a bull-driver only short of the whip – but it's pride more than that, I'd say.'

'Men,' said Mary contemptuously, 'and there's me cleaning lavatories and spittoons. Pride indeed, few mouths will it feed. You've to find the rent and he has his pride.'

Watching Katy's face Eileen saw the annoyance on it. Mary, she thought, had never learned that a woman might criticize her man but didn't like another doing it. She changed the conversation by asking Mary to tell about her employers. Mary leapt at the chance. 'Gentlemen,' she said, 'every one of them gentlemen. Never for a minute am I made to feel a servant. Honest to God you'd think I was doing them a favour. It's "Mrs Callinan, might I trouble you to do this". Or, "Mrs Callinan, would you oblige me by doing that".'

Eileen and Katy, who had heard Mary's praise of her employers since the day she started work, listened as if for the first time. They knew it word for word and now waited for the bit with which she always ended. 'And may God bless the priest for getting me the work. Wouldn't we be in a sorry state without the clergy. Lost in this world and the next.'

'There's few gentlemen where I work.'

'They're a different class, Eileen,' Mary said.

'They're not Americans if that's what you mean – but the biggest difference is the drink. I'm telling you, Mary, you'd soon see a change in your gentlemen with drink inside them.'

'That I wouldn't believe,' said Mary. 'No, I would not. I do often think, Eileen, that you'd be as well to look for something else.'

'I love it, wasn't it what I was used to.'

'There is that and then you're snug in the bed hours after I'm out in the morning.'

'I could put in a word for you if you'd like a change,' said Eileen. And Katy smiled at the idea of Mary working in a bar and told Eileen to stop teasing her. Mary said she was well used to Eileen, there was no harm in her. Then Katy said she'd have to find some way of earning.

'How would you – who'd mind the children?' asked Eileen.

'I was thinking of something I could do at home, like taking in washing. I learned at the Big House how to launder fine things – I could do that.'

'There'd be few fine things in this neighbourhood,' Mary said.

'I know that well, but if I had a word with the priest he could let it be known amongst them that are on their feet, but not enough to have a servant.'

'It's worth trying,' said Eileen. 'And to start you off I'll give you my fine things. And another thing – as soon as the weather improves we'll have a change of scenery. We've never been out of the neighbourhood since the day we landed. On the first fine day we'll go and look at the shops on Broadway, how about that?'

'That'll be many months in the future,' said Mary.

'You're the terrible killjoy, Mary. For all we know, the weather could change tomorrow and if it doesn't haven't we something to look forward to,' said Katy.

'How do we put up with her?' asked Eileen after Mary went. 'She sees the black side of everything, knows everybody's business, is that holy she should have been a nun and can't wait to be a real American. I'm telling you, before long you won't be able to understand a word out of her mouth.'

'That's Mary,' said Katy. 'But she has her good points. She wouldn't do you a bad turn.'

'Maybe she ought!' said Eileen.

'Ah, you know well what I mean.'

'I suppose so. All the same, she gets in on my nerves – and as for that young wan of hers . . .'

'Shh,' said Katy and put a finger on her lips. 'Kathleen's 'ithin there in the closet with the children.'

'Jesus! Me and my mouth.'

'I was thinking,' said Katy, one night to Jamsie. 'I'll send the children to school.'

Without looking up from the newspaper Jamsie replied, 'Much good will it do them.'

She bit back the retort, 'True enough if they take after you.' He annoyed her when he didn't raise his eyes while she talked to him. In from work, eat his dinner, read the paper. Not a word to throw to a dog. Not like it used to be at home. There the talk was great between them. She could make excuses for him most nights – he was tired being out from six in the morning, down at the docks looking for work or walking the streets seeking it and not always successful. But what she had to say this evening was important. Deciding to send the children to school was very important. She was working her temper up. In a minute she'd give him his character. But before the minute was up he laid down the paper, smiled at her and said, 'What was it you said about school, aghoille?'

Immediately she forgave him. She loved him. When he smiled at her it was like looking at him for the first time and falling in love with him. 'I was thinking I'd send them to school. I found out where it is and it costs nothing.'

'An improvement on Ireland. Twopence a week my father paid for me to hear the master teach in Peader's kitchen. A waste of my time and my father's money.'

' 'Twasn't much he wasted, for you stayed no time.'

'I did not. I had more sense.'

They were bantering, it was like old times, she felt happy. 'They'll learn how to read and write, like us. I want that for them.'

'Oh, to be sure,' said Jamsie. 'Make scholars of them. Turn them into ladies and gentlemen.'

'Not that, not any of that. Only able to take their place in America. Sure, why else did we come if it wasn't to better ourselves and them?'

'Because we were starving, 'twas the only reason.'

'I know that – but we'd hopes of other things. We did, you know we did.'

'I remember no such thing – nor that we mentioned it, ever. We were as contented as the day was long before the crop failed. We'd everything anyone could want and that's the truth. Weren't you happy the live-long day before the Hunger?'

'Oh indeed I was, the live-long day as happy as a bird.'

'Well then?'

'Well then,' said Katy, 'the Hunger did come and change everything. And maybe we didn't talk about bettering ourselves before we came. But now we're here and I want the children to have an education.'

'Send them so,' said Jamsie, 'but not in this weather.'

'I was thinking I'd send them after Easter.'

'Ladies and gentlemen,' said Jamsie. 'Ladies and gentlemen then you'll be satisfied. Your mother'll never be dead while you're alive – a great one for the quality she was, the Lord rest her.'

'Indeed she was,' Katy agreed, 'but there was no harm in her. She only wanted the best for me.'

'And wasn't it the best you got?'

'The best in the world,' said Katy, and Jamsie smiled at her again before going back to his newspaper.

But that wasn't how her mother had judged Jamsie, Katy remembered. She was heartbroken at the idea of her marrying one of the O'Haras from up on the bog and throwing over the great match that was lined up for her. Her poor mother, she never became reconciled to their marriage. Jamsie she could see would do little more talking tonight. She wouldn't disturb him. There was plenty to occupy her mind. But before

85

she had time to decide what in particular there was a tap on the door and Mary came in.

'Sit down,' said Katy. 'I've something to tell you,' and she told her about sending the children to school.

Mary was horrified by the idea. 'They're all Protestant, the teachers, hymns and prayers, all black Protestant. You'll be putting your innocent little children on the road to Hell. It's as bad as taking the soup.'

'It is not,' said Katy, 'not like taking the soup at all. There's no proselytising in the schools. You're not expected to change your religion.' Mary's mention of 'the soup' brought memories to scald her heart. She remembered well the British Bible Society setting up their kitchens in Kilgoran when the Hunger was at its worst. When the children were like walking skeletons. When soup would have warmed their shrinking stomachs. When she was sorely tempted to take it. But Father Bolger's sermon, the picture he painted of Hell for those who drank the soup, the damnation of the children fed it, had put an end to her temptation.

'Kathleen won't go. She'll wait till we have our own Catholic schools.'

'By that time she may be as old as yourself.'

'Maybe so,' said Mary.

' 'Tis your own business,' replied Katy and decided to say no more about it.

The snow softened, was stained brown and began to melt into grey slush, but on her walks to the shops Katy noticed green shoots pushing up on vacant ground and plants and grass sprouting between paving stones, growing through cracks in walls, and buds on the trees. Spring had come and her heart rose. She felt young again, strong again and without the extra layers of clothing walked with suppleness. She looked oftener in the mirror, a new acquisition and wistfully and hopelessly, she knew, longed for a soft, prettily-coloured blouse or shawl.

An inner core of her also responded to the spring so that she yearned for another baby. And thought of the softness of a new infant, the fragility of its neck. How it would feel in her arms. How looking at it she would feel the glow of love and pride that she and Jamsie had made this child and how while she suckled it, its life was sustained by her alone.

But these thoughts were replaced by ones of relief that for another month at least she wasn't pregnant. That there wasn't another mouth to feed. For it took all her energy, time and resourcefulness to manage her present family. To stretch the few shillings that Jamsie earned, walking from one stall to another finding the food to feed them, worrying that the soles of their boots were wearing thin, constantly having to refuse the pennies they wanted for special treats.

'Turn round,' said Katy, 'and let me look at you.' Bridget and Thomas turned and Katy lifted a thread from the hem of Bridget's skirt and smoothed the back of Thomas' hair that fuzzed when he slept on it. 'You'll do,' she said, 'you're grand. Remember all I told you. Listen to the teacher and be good. Come on now, we mustn't be late on the first morning.'

She wished they had nicer clothes, that Thomas' trousers weren't patched on the seat and Bridget's skirt so obviously one she had cut down from an old one of Eileen's. And now that the moment had come for them to go to school she wished she wasn't letting them go. Never before had they been away from her for any length of time. Never before had she handed them into the keeping of strangers.

She was frightened for them and though she had admitted it to no one, apprehensive of taking and enrolling them, of the meeting with whoever was in charge. An American: so far she had had nothing to do with Americans. Mary said they were nice people but from what she had seen of them they appeared brusque-mannered. Quick in their movements, as if they always knew where they were going and what they would do when they got there. Poor Thomas and Bridget, how would they take to people like that, she wondered? Maybe she was making a mistake sending them. Maybe she should wait until next year. They'd be more used to Americans and their ways. It wasn't as if they had to go to school.

After having warned the children that they mustn't be late she was now deliberately delaying them. Making excuses to put off the moment of leaving.

'I thought we were going to school,' said Bridget.

'You are, now in a minute. I'm looking for Danny's other sock,' lied Katy.

'He has the two of them,' said Thomas.

'So he has,' admitted Katy and knew that now she had to make up her mind one way or the other. And she told herself there was no harm in trying it. If they didn't like it, she wouldn't send them again. The Americans wouldn't eat them, nor her either. If she wanted them to read and write the sooner they started the better. They could try it for today.

'Right then, I'm ready. Bridget – you hold Mary Kate's hand going down the steps.'

The school was in a small, one-storey building two streets away. To one side of it was a vacant space where children, boys and girls, ones as young as five and others that Katy judged to be thirteen or more were running, shouting, playing and some of the bigger ones fighting. Her heart sank as she imagined Thomas and Bridget amongst them.

There were other mothers bringing children to school for the first time. Some of them Katy knew by sight. One Irishwoman spoke to her. 'I only hope to God I'm doing the right thing – they've never been from my side before today.'

'Nor mine,' said Katy.

'All I know is,' said the woman, 'that they'll be at a great disadvantage if everyone else has the schooling and not them.'

'It was the same thought that made me send them,' said Katy as they went into a lobby where behind a table sat a severe-looking woman. While the Irish person was giving her children's particulars Katy looked round. Through an open door she could see into a big room filled with long benches and desks as long, secured to each other by iron bars. Nearer the front of the room there were shorter and lower benches without desks in front of them.

The teacher introduced herself as Miss Cook, then asked Katy for the children's details. While she wrote them down in a big book, Katy was noticing things about her. How short and clean her nails were. How tightly drawn back was her hair into its bun. Katy's nervousness made her give long answers where they weren't required. 'How long have you been in America?' asked Miss Cook.

'Let me see now, it was before Christmas, November it must have been, yes, it was November. I remember thinking how lovely the weather was for that time of the year.'

If only she'd smile at me, thought Katy, but Miss Cook's expression never altered. Katy wanted to tell her that Thomas was shy and sometimes Bridget talked a lot, but there was no encouragement and she stopped herself and smiled at the children whom Miss Cook had told to stand to one side next to the other pupils starting today.

'That'll be all, Mrs O'Hara,' said Miss Cook and Katy was dismissed. Passing the playground she thought of Thomas and Bridget in it fending for themselves. She stopped to look at the children and as she did so Miss Cook came ringing a large handbell. The majority of the children stopped what they were doing and formed into straggly lines. Others ignored the bell's summons, waiting until the teacher came to them. Katy couldn't hear what she said, but the children did and joined the lines. She's a strict woman, she'd take no nonsense, Katy thought and worried again as to how Bridget and Thomas would fare.

She was longing for them to come home. To hear tell of how their day had been. She asked questions. 'Did you like school?'

'It was all right,' Bridget said.

'And the teacher, Miss Cook?'

'She was all right,' said Thomas.

Other questions brought similar answers, so Katy gave up and made their tea. But over the weeks in dribs and drabs she heard that Miss Cook was a fierce woman – she made bold children stand in the corner. Miss Cook was kind; if you weren't well she let you sit by the stove. Miss Cook was a fierce slapper if you didn't do your work. Katy discovered that Miss Cook was the only teacher and there was only one classroom; the infants sat in the front. Bridget and Thomas weren't infants, they sat in the middle and the big boys and girls at the back. And some children couldn't speak any English.

Sometimes she had to bully them to go to school, to be in time, to stay clean and tidy, to make a good impression, not to be classed as dirty, lazy Irish. Once a week she fine-combed their hair for lice and, when they were infested, over the weekend soaked their heads with kerosene to kill the nits.

After a while Thomas complained that he hated school. Big boys bullied him and laughed and imitated how he spoke. And Katy told him to take no notice of the jeering, to think of boys like the Jaegers and the Ginsbergs who hadn't six words of English between them. And to tell the Americans that their own English wasn't easy to understand.

'I was thinking,' said Mary, not long after Katy's children had started school, 'that I made a hasty decision.'

'Oh,' said Katy. 'And what was that?'

'About Kathleen and the schooling. She has me tormented now that Bridget is learning to read. She's a bright child, 'twould be a sin to deprive her of the education.'

'It would indeed,' said Katy. 'You'll send her, so?'

'I'm not happy about it, but I will.'

Katy said nothing but thought – Mary, you wouldn't get your health if you weren't unhappy about something.

Chapter Eight

Now that spring had come Katy felt sure it was the beginning of their luck in America. And to help the luck on its way she went to see the priest.

'Father,' she said, 'Jamsie still hasn't got a constant job. It's hard to make ends meet, so I'm going to take in washing.'

'You're a sensible woman, Katy. God helps them that helps themselves. I'll put the word about.'

' 'Tis fine things I do, if you could mention that.'

'Fine things? Sure, isn't washing washing,' said the priest, a big, jovial countryman.

'I was thinking of ladies' things, chemises and – well, fine things.'

'Washing is what I'll say, girl. When they come you can explain about the fine things.'

'Thanks very much, Father and God bless you,' Katy said and went home to make preparations for her laundrying.

Eileen lent her a tin bath and a clothes horse; she also had a length of narrow strong rope. 'Where it came from I don't know,' she said, handling the rope and to Katy's amazement she began to cry.

'Eileen, what ails you?'

'Nothing, only for a minute I thought of Larry, the way he was always with the ropes – it just came over me.'

'It's early days, there'll be many more when you're overcome.'

'I know,' said Eileen, 'I know. Often when I come back from the bar I throw myself down on the bed and cry myself to sleep. Sometimes a fella takes my fancy and I'll bring him back, but that doesn't always work, either. Anyway don't mind me, I've had my little cry – it's you and the washing we're concerned with. Look – I've an extra big pot and a spare paraffin stove that's easily carried down. What about Mary, has she anything that will be a help?'

'She has a rubbing board and another horse.'

'That's grand, now all you want is the customers.'

'Say a prayer they come.'

Come they did, women from the parish who were getting on their feet but not well enough off yet to afford help in the house. They came first to enquire, then brought chemises and their best petticoats and Sunday aprons, all white, all frilled and flounced and beribboned, all requiring careful washing, starching and complicated ironing.

The following week, Mrs Ryan the wife of the building contractor arrived. Katy didn't like the big woman. She wasn't fat, but tall and broad with a coarse red-skinned face and a manner to go with her appearance. She liked her even less as she saw the woman's eyes dart round the room taking it in while at the same time ignoring the smiling Danny who made friendly overtures to her; and also because Katy knew that Mrs Ryan could well afford to have her washing done at home but was hoping to save money. Her manner was insolent when she said how her husband and sons liked their shirts washed. It was on the tip of Katy's tongue to refuse the work. To say, 'It's fine things, women's underthings and the like I do,' but eight shirts even at the rate Mrs Ryan would bargain for couldn't be refused. At least not for the present.

The lines were strung up round the room and Jamsie forced open the window and fixed another to the fire escape. 'Drying clothes is all it's good for. Look at the lump of it missing from below. God forbidding all harm if the house goes on fire we'll be roasted to death or dash out our brains falling through that contraption.'

When the weather was fine Katy dried line after line outside but on wet days petticoats, the Ryans' shirts, drawers and chemises draped the lines, making it necessary for the family to move about the room only by dodging underneath the drying clothes. Thomas and Bridget complained and often Jamsie used the condition at home as an excuse for his frequent visits to the saloon.

Mary was still full of praise for her American employers. One of them had suggested that domestic work might suit her better. His wife was looking for extra help – would she be interested? She could think it over, perhaps. To Katy she went, to discuss the offer. After Katy heard her out she said, 'So they've changed their minds about *No Irish Need Apply?*'

'It's once they get to know you. Do you think I should take it?'

'And what would stop you?'

'Kathleen. 'Tis the hours you see, from eight in the morning until six at night. She'd be left to fend for herself.'

'Wouldn't I keep an eye on her?'

'God bless you if you would. She'd be no trouble. I'd have her ready for school before I left. If you gave her the bit after school I wouldn't ask it for nothing.'

'Certainly I will.'

'Then in the name of God I'll try it.'

When the weather was fine but not yet too hot as she was warned it would be in July and August, Katy found the Five Points area bearable: the cheerless, washing-draped room, the rickety old house. But these were only temporary stops on her way to a better life in America. Her home laundry would prosper, Jamsie would get a constant job. She was willing it, praying for it.

When the sun shone it was even possible to enjoy her daily foraging for the cheapest and most nourishing food, surrounded by women as poor as herself, mostly Irish and if not always in good humour with sharp tongues and a gift for repartee so that she laughed a lot. The shopkeepers and stallholders knew her by now and *codded*her. She was aware that some of them eyed her appreciatively and often threw on another rasher, a few extra potatoes, or a couple of eggs more than she had ordered.

America, she would tell herself, was a great land. Look at all the advantages. The education for her children. Free education, even though it was Protestant hymns and the Protestant Bible they learned. But for the time being that couldn't be helped. The priests and bishops were working away at it, the people gave what they could afford every Sunday and one day there'd be Catholic schools. Yes, America was the great country. She'd learn about it. Read more. Make a start by reading the newspapers. America was full of them and cheap as well. If only Jamsie felt the same way she'd be the happiest woman in the world. But Jamsie didn't have a good word to say for America. You'd think at least he'd be grateful for the education; the children would grow up with the same advantages as if they'd been born Americans. They could be anything – even teachers, maybe.

One day while she was in the chapel praying, two ideas came into her mind. Kneeling in the cool dim church with the smell of candles and now and then a hint of incense on the air she felt as if God was directing her thoughts. Telling her to suggest to Jamsie that perhaps they should go inland and try farming. She'd have to get used to new neighbours and the children a new school. She'd be leaving Eileen and Mary behind but what did any of that matter if Jamsie was happy. Farming was probably what he had wanted to do all along and hadn't liked to mention it. After all, what else did he know about except working the land. Yes, she would talk to him about it.

The other thought which again she interpreted as God's working was that she should try and get in touch with Peader. Hadn't he said that as soon as he landed he would write to them? Not knowing where they were he would have sent the letter to Carey's. In her mind's eye she saw it lying there amongst the dusty bottles on the back shelf, an old spider maybe spinning a web round it. So to Carey she would write, enclosing her address and asking if there was a letter would he please forward it. And she'd remember to put in the money, for Carey was a skinflint who'd sooner back the fire with a letter than spend the price of a stamp.

If Danny slept for another half hour she'd make a hole in the ironing, then she'd waken him, coax him to eat his porridge and out they'd go to see what there was for the dinner. Using one iron while the other heated she worked out creases and the day's menu. A lovely thick stew made with plenty of vegetables and barley and the bit of meat for Jamsie and for tea she'd make the batter mixture. They all loved that with syrup on it, though Bridget said it wasn't as nice as Mrs Jaeger's. Mrs Jaeger made the batter into waffles, that's what she called them. And the bottoms and tops had crisscross marks because she cooked them on a thing she had bought from Germany. Bridget was forever in and out of the Jaegers' and always on about the lovely things to eat in their house. Right enough, lovely smells came from it – but wasn't the father a baker. She wondered was it right what Mary had heard, that he was taking a lock-up shop and starting his own bakery.

Danny as usual woke before she wanted him to but he was in good humour and ate the stirabout without much playacting. In no time she was back from her shopping, pleased with the big bone from the butcher, had Danny confined behind the upturned chairs in a corner, had a cup of tea, put the stew on to simmer and was back with the ironing. She was singing as she worked an old song her mother used to sing. '*It was early one morning Willy Leonard arose, and it's straight to his comrades the young man did go, saying "Comrade, loyal comrade it's a bright summer's morning and a bathing we will go"*,' when the door opened and Jamsie came in. She knew by the look of him that he hadn't found work today. He smiled half-heartedly and said, 'You're in great humour.'

'And why not – isn't it a lovely day?' He sighed a long sigh and sat down. 'What's that for?' she asked with forced gaity.

93

'I'm just wondering what we'd do if it wasn't for your ironing.'

'Well, don't be – wondering never solved anything. We're lucky, we have our health, food for today and God's good for tomorrow.'

'Ah,' he said, his head bent in his hands. 'I don't think I'll ever get work.'

Katy, looking at him in sorrow for his despondency, noticed the grey in his hair. Her Jamsie that had had hair black as the raven's wing going grey before his time.

'I was thinking,' he said, 'I'll go on the railroad.'

Immediately anger and fear replaced her sympathy and sorrow. With Jamsie not beside her how could she survive in this place? The place which before they came to it had raised their hopes so high – but how different was the reality. Without Jamsie it would have been better to have stayed at home and died. Fury swept away her fear and she shouted at him. 'The railroad? Well, isn't that the grand thought! Fly your kite on the railroad while me and the children stay here and starve. I know you, Jamsie O'Hara, tired already of your responsibility. You were ever the same. Always looking for the easy way out. Well, let me tell you – this time you won't get the chance, not if I have to follow you every foot of the road. You're my husband. Remember that. You're not leaving me defenceless and unprovided for.'

Breathless after her outburst she waited for his response. When it came she didn't know whether to throw the iron at him or burst out crying, for all he did was go into a kink of laughing. And still laughing he got up and came to her. 'You're not right in the head,' he said. 'Provide for you and the children? Leave you defenceless? You that's like a tiger. God help anyone who tried to come one over you. And who but yourself provides the bit we eat. I've hardly earned enough to buy two loaves since we landed. That's why . . .'

'And when you did you spent it on drink,' Katy interrupted.

'Yerra woman,' he said, 'don't cry. I'm not trying to run away from you. But on the railroad I could earn good money and send every penny to you. I wouldn't be twisted inside every time I see you sprinkle and iron Tom Ryan's shirts. I didn't marry you to make you a washerwoman. I want to mind you and the children.' He took her in his arms and kissed her hair. 'Love,' he said, 'you'll have to face up to it – I may have to look for work elsewhere. I hate to see you banging away with that oul iron, the sweat pouring off you and never a complaint.'

' 'Tis more than complain I'll do one of these days,' Katy said. 'A basin of starch I'll empty over the head of Mrs Ryan when next she finds fault with "my husband's fine linen".' She imitated the accent Mrs

Ryan was these days affecting and laughed to make light of her threat so that Jamsie wouldn't know how Mrs Ryan infuriated her and how indeed she would love to douse her with a basin of starch. See a translucent mask set on the coarse grained face, then throw her and 'her husband's fine linen' down the stairs. But fancy was all it was – the price of laundrying the shirts still couldn't be sacrificed.

Jamsie was caressing her and repeating how it galled him to see her slaving over the washing. 'I know,' she whispered, her head against his chest, 'but I'd wash till my fingers were to the bone if the choice was that or you going away. Promise me you'll never do that. Don't ever go without me. I'd be lost. Not much of a tiger I'd be on my own. The strength would run out of me like water out of a tap.'

He held her close and smoothed her yellow hair and wanted her. And remembered how many a time at home he had coaxed her to leave whatever she was doing and go into the bed with him. She'd let on to be scandalised. Protesting about broad daylight and what if a neighbour called or one of the children ran in from where they were playing. In between kisses he'd assure her the children were well-occupied, the baby fast asleep and not a soul likely to pass the door for the next half hour.

But this wasn't Kilgoran. In this rickety tenement you could hear the breath they drew in the next room and confused children, never sure which floor or which door was theirs, often came to the wrong one. And the Irishwomen lost and lonely in America were forever in and out. He kissed Katy and let go of her.

While Katy and Jamsie had talked and fought and almost made love Danny had contentedly dug a hole in the wall with a spoon and was sucking a lump of plaster he had excavated. 'The poor child, he'll be poisoned. Spit it out.' She held her hand in front of him. 'Come on now, spit it out.'

'He likes it,' Jamsie said.

'Hold him,' Katy ordered, then after forcing open the child's mouth with a finger she rooted for the particles of plaster. 'He's like you,' she said, 'there's no filling him. Wait now and I'll dip a crust in the stew.' Danny sat happily on Jamsie's lap sucking the gravy-soaked crust and Katy thought it was as good a time as any to broach the subject of them moving inland.

'I was thinking,' she said, 'that maybe we could go inland and get a farm. It's what we know. You'd be happy and wouldn't it be grand to live in the country again?'

'You're thinking it would be like Ireland – like Kilgoran.'

'Well, wouldn't it? Only better – for one day we'd own a fine farm of land.'

'Aghoille,' said Jamsie, his voice humouring, 'have you any notion of the size of America? But sure, how could you, 'tis only a rough idea I have myself. But it's enormous. Miles and miles of it. Farming here isn't like it was at home. You'll have one and maybe not another for ten or twenty miles. There'd be no gatherings in the evenings, no telling stories or a tune on the fiddle or a bit of a dance. And not a woman for you to pass the time of day with.'

'How do you know all that?'

'Amn't I sick of listening to men who tried it and ran mad out of it.'

'In the bars, I suppose.'

'There and elsewhere.'

'It's not much store I'd put on that sort of advice.'

'Listen to me.' His voice had lost its humouring tone. 'Because a man takes a drink he's not a fool altogether.'

'Of that I'm not so sure, but tell me this – is it on their say-so you don't want to farm?'

'That and my own thoughts.'

'You never mentioned them before.'

'You never asked.'

'Well, I am now. Tell me.'

'All right, I'll tell you. I never want to touch the land again. Never have to depend on it. Few Irishmen do. I don't want to spend my days praying for rain and sun and in the heel of the hunt get too much of one or not enough of the other – then the ground is parched or water-logged and you're in debt for the seed that's destroyed. I want the money in my hand for the work I do.'

'Somebody's farming though.'

'Somebody is – Americans, Germans, Swedes and Irish from the North that came a long time ago. Hard-working religious men with their Bibles to keep them sane. And I'll tell you something else – whatever it is the Irish make their fortunes at it won't be farming.'

If Jamsie wouldn't farm and wouldn't work for Ryan and couldn't get other constant work, she had to try expanding her little laundry. She could offer to do repairs, she had a good hand at the sewing. But without more space where could she keep even an extra bundle? What she needed was a little lock-up shop. Mr Jaeger had found one and his bakery was thriving – any minute she expected them to move out of the house. Where would she find one, and even if she did, how could she afford the extra rent never mind a boiler, mangle, drying racks and the assortment of threads and buttons, needles and ribbons for the repairing? Who could she turn to for help? Who would lend her money to get started?

Peader would. Peader if he had it would lend it with a heart and a half. If only she knew where he was. If only Carey would send word. It was weeks and weeks since she had written to him asking if letters had come for her. He might never answer – never forward letters. But not for a minute would she believe what Jamsie had tried to put into her head when she told him about trying to get in touch with Peader. 'If Peader had wanted to find us he would have long ago.' She had pointed out that Peader didn't even know they were in America and Jamsie had countered with – where else did he think they'd be, except in their grave. Wasn't everything finished in Kilgoran by the time he'd left? Well enough he knew they were in America by this time. And she agreed that was possible – but how could he find them?

Jamsie didn't answer that one. But what he did say put fear into her heart. She wasn't to forget that Peader had married the Master's daughter. And the Kilgorans like all the quality would have friends and relations scattered over the world. In America too, no doubt. Charlotte would have connections and Peader too as her husband. Peader could have lost the run of himself with his connections. Katy wouldn't believe that. Peader and Charlotte wouldn't change. If they were living in New York and for all she knew they might well be – Peader and Charlotte would be the same two beautiful people. She told herself this over and over and over again. But now and then a thought came to her. Miss Charlotte was no longer a child. For so long Katy had thought of her as a little, lonely, neglected child who spent more time with the servants than anyone else that she had overlooked what Jamsie pointed out – she was the Master's daughter. She wasn't the same as them. She might have changed, but please God she hadn't. Jamsie would have to eat his words. Once news came from Peader they'd all get together again and everything would be as it was before.

She prayed every day that soon word would come from Peader. And thought how wonderful it would be if he and Charlotte were living in New York. For all she knew they might be. After Jamsie and the children she loved Peader and Charlotte more than anyone in the world. All of their lives they had known each other. They were like family. There wasn't a name, a place, a happening in their past that you'd mention and immediately it was recalled and understood. Not like in

America with those she knew lately; even to Mary and Eileen you had to explain so much if you were relating something.

The joy it would be to have them living close. To see each other often and help each other learning how best to fare in America. To talk about the old times, to have Peader's steadying influence on Jamsie. If she had that she'd ask for nothing more.

Often she would leave whatever she was doing to sit in a chair and daydream. In the beginning her thoughts centred on Peader and Charlotte together – a married couple, but lately it was Peader alone who came to her mind. Things about him she hadn't given a thought to for years. The colour of his eyes, the red glint to his hair in the sunlight. How it was when she and Peader were courting before she fell in love with Jamsie. And though she had no regrets as to her choice, now and then she wondered how her life would have turned out had she married Peader. With his inheritance they could have survived the Hunger. At this very minute she'd be in Ireland instead of New York.

But then again she'd ask herself – would you? Wasn't the place deserted – everything and everyone dead or gone. It wouldn't have been much of a life just the two of you no matter how comfortable the farm was. And the children – you wouldn't have had them, not Bridget or Thomas or the others. They'd have been Peader's children and different.

One day as she sat musing on such things Thomas came in. Her face had a thoughtful sad expression which Thomas interpreted as signs of his mother being sick. He went and stood beside her. 'Are you sick?' he asked, his eyes full of fear. Knowing why, she put an arm round him and said, 'Thanks be to God I am not, sure I'm never sick.' She saw the relief on his face and was glad. For poor Thomas was going through a bad time.

A week ago she had woken and heard him crying. She went to him and asked, 'What ails you, love?' He didn't answer. Bending low and whispering she said, 'Is it your ear, have you a pain in it? Shh,' she said when the crying didn't stop, 'you'll waken the others. Get up, careful now, don't disturb them.' She put a coat round his shoulders and in the dark guided him to a chair and took him on her lap. 'Tell me love what it is, why are you crying?'

He buried his head against her and in between sobs said, 'I was thinking about dying and you and Daddy being dead.' She rocked him like a baby.

'Ah,' she said, 'sure you'll be an old man before that happens, please God.' And she thought, poor Tom and grieved that so soon was he aware that death didn't only happen to other people and that she couldn't still his fears with lies. She rocked him until he stopped crying and then said, 'I've a good sup of milk, get up now and I'll give you a cup.' She found her way to where the jug of milk stood in a pot of water keeping it cool. 'Drink that,' she said, 'and then go back to bed, like a good boy.'

'Will I really be an old man before . . .'

'As old as the hills,' she said. 'A crochety old man on a stick with a clay pipe scolding me and Dada who'll be sitting in the corner.' He had gone to bed happy.

Now, reassured that nothing ailed her he left her side and mooched about the room. 'If it's food you're after there's a cut of bread, take it, do.'

With the bread in his hand, he said, 'I'm going down to play.'

Thank God, Katy thought, he's young and food occupies his mind more than death. He was growing so quickly – he'd be a big man like his father. Though only in size and maybe a resemblance about the face. He didn't have his nature. She couldn't imagine Jamsie at that age worrying about the death of his mother, father or himself. It was as well to be so.

Peader now, he'd have had a sensitive nature. Poor Peader, she'd treated him badly . . . Letting him believe she loved him when her heart was set on Jamsie. Though it wasn't in the beginning. Then she had never given Jamsie a second thought. She knew him by sight. One of the O'Haras from up on the bog. A family her mother had no look on. And she was content to go along with the plans to marry Peader.

Then everything changed. A spell was cast on her. It was in Mass and Jamsie was sitting on the men's side one row up from her. The same Jamsie who sat in the same place every Sunday. But it was as if she saw him for the first time and at that only the back of him. The curly head of him bent at the Consecration and the pale skin of his neck above his shabby frieze coat. And the magic was working in her so that she had an urge to cross the aisle, bend and place her lips against the white skin below the black curls. And from that moment she knew that Jamsie was the one she loved and would love all her life. But there was her mother to tell and Peader to tell and the village to face with news that the marriage was off. And all the time the wondering and wondering if the magic of the moment had cast a spell on Jamsie.

She sighed and wanted to stay where she was, reliving it all again. But there was a bundle of shirts which she had dampened earlier – they'd be right for the iron. Tom Ryan's was amongst them and Mrs Ryan

99

couldn't be discommoded. In any case, she could iron and think but it turned out she couldn't, for first one child then another demanded her attention and soon her mind was far away from Kilgoran and how she captivated Jamsie and abandoned Peader.

Mary kept Katy and Eileen enthralled with descriptions of her employer's house in Gramercy Park. 'It's the grandest place I've ever seen. Brand new it is, well, not more than six or seven years old and there's this park that the house overlooks. And you wouldn't believe this if I hadn't seen it with my own eyes – the people who live there have a golden key to the park. A golden key – imagine that!'

'What about the work – have you much to do?' asked Katy.

'Little enough. To tell you the truth I wonder what I'm being paid for. They've a house full of servants, or "help" as they call them, and they're black. The cook is as black as a lump of coal. The first day I jumped out of my skin every time I went into the kitchen and saw her. That's where I help – in the kitchen, peeling the vegetables and washing up. Bessie, that's her name, and for all her black face she's a kind creature – look at what she gave me to bring home.' Mary produced a bag full of cold meat, biscuits and cake which she shared with the others. 'That's what they call strawberry shortcake. Have you heard of that before, Katy?'

Katy said she hadn't.

'And the biscuits they call cookies. I've never eaten so much in my life – I'll finish up like the side of a house. They were having a supper party tonight – and the things there were to eat! Eggs that they called scrambled, I never thought there was a way of cooking them except in their shells, and there was a whole ham, and turkey's legs and fish that I'd never seen before and strawberries and all sorts of fruits that I couldn't put a name to. Yellow butter and dishes of cream and then batter cakes that Mrs Jaeger makes. I'm telling you, I never saw so much food in all my days.'

'Isn't it well for them,' said Eileen. 'Tell us more about the house.'

'Well, you want to see the bedrooms. The beds are that high and dark, mahogany I think with four poles, no canopies, only the poles and chests of drawers to match. Of course the beds were made up but I'd say the sheets were the finest linen. I saw the little black girl putting away handkerchiefs that were as big nearly as a pillowcase, gentlemen's handkerchiefs, fine, fine stuff they were made of. And I had a feel of the quilts . . . my fingers sank in them, stuffed with down they were. Eat that bit of food now into you.'

Mary in the days to come regaled them with more descriptions of her employers' house and brought to share the food Bessie gave her. One day she told them how the lady of the house wore gloves to do the garden. She thought that a queer thing, though the queerest thing about it was that with all the servants she bothered her head at all about the garden. And Katy told her that's how it was with women of the quality – they liked gardening. It had been the same in the Big House in Kilgoran.

Mary's first word when she came to Katy's after work was about Kathleen. Was she all right? Had she eaten her bit of food? Had she behaved herself? And always Katy was able to answer yes to Mary's questions, until Bridget and Ulla the baker's daughter made friends and Kathleen became jealous of the friendship.

One afternoon, when Bridget and Kathleen had had their tea, Katy sent them down to play in the street. Soon afterwards Kathleen returned, complaining that Bridget and Ulla wouldn't let her play with them. Knowing how attached she was to Bridget and resentful of Ulla, Katy at first felt sorry for Kathleen and said, 'Never mind, you stay here with me for a while. Sit down and I'll tell you a story, would you like that?'

Kathleen shrugged and looked sullen and wouldn't sit down. Instead, she wandered round the room not avoiding a clothes line where ironed clothes were airing, knocking clothes off, not bothering to pick them up. 'Be careful,' Katy warned her several times, then Kathleen leaving the line alone began tormenting Danny until she made him cry. Raising her voice Katy shouted, 'Behave yourself or I'll have something to tell your mother when she comes home.'

Kathleen started crying and was still crying when Mary came. Mary fussed round her and the more she did the louder Kathleen cried and said she hated staying with the O'Haras, they were all horrible to her. She didn't want to come again. She wished her mother didn't go to work. She hated and hated and hated coming to the O'Haras.

'What'll I do?' asked Mary, with a distraught expression on her face.

'I know what I'd do if she was mine,' said Katy.

'Don't cry pet, wipe your eyes,' Mary coaxed. 'Look at the lovely cake I brought for you. There's a little dote, eat it and stop crying.'

Katy made a pot of tea and when Kathleen had stopped crying Mary said, 'I have something to tell you, Katy. I saw the man today that spoke to Eileen when we first arrived.'

Katy couldn't remember anyone talking to them except the bondsman. 'Ah, you do,' said Mary. 'The American man that talked about

101

the pigs – don't you remember he raised his hat and Eileen said what a gentleman he was?'

'Yes, I do now. He was a thinnish man with a nice smile. Where did you meet him?'

'I didn't really meet him, I saw him – he lives in the house next door. But I have a powerful memory for faces and recognised him. Then I asked Bessie who he was and she said a doctor, a fine man who does a lot of work for the poor.'

'Imagine that,' said Katy.

'I think I'll take her up, she looks tired,' Mary said, nodding at Kathleen. Before she left she gave Katy some of the leftovers she had brought from the house.

By the end of the week Mary had decided to give up her job. Kathleen, she said, wasn't well at all. She was sorry to leave but Kathleen had to come first and she could go back to cleaning in the City Hall. Katy refrained from giving Mary her opinion of Kathleen but with Eileen said just what she thought. 'A little sleveen. Mary has her ruined. If she was mine I'd soon learn her.'

Eileen agreed that a good hiding was what Kathleen needed. 'Do you know what ailed her? She was mad jealous that her mother was sharing the food with the two of us. Haven't you noticed how greedy and mean she is. She'll stand looking up in your face if you ask her to do a message. Not that I wouldn't always give a child a penny for doing one, but that young one demands it without saying a word.'

Chapter Nine

During 1848 the Irish continued to come to America and the majority settled in New York. Like Jamsie they feared depending on the land again and needed the closeness of each other to survive in the new country. In Katy's neighbourhood more makeshift tenements were slung up and people packed in. People who couldn't afford the rooms moved into cellars which were dark, damp and rat-infested. Often more than one family occupied a single one. The living shared beds with the dying, babies were born next to corpses, disease flourished and the death rate was high.

Others squatted on vacant ground and made a shanty town. Boards and planks, anything that would keep out the weather was stacked and nailed into the semblance of houses – they leant against each other and sometimes in a strong wind collapsed. Children, pigs and hens grubbed in the earth, and manure – animal and human, littered the ground. Men and women too drunk or dispirited sat silent or gossiped, apparently oblivious of the children or the filth.

The shanty towns more than the tenements maintained the bad feeling against the Irish. In the shanty tows there were more fights, more drunkenness and more petty crime. Though the fighting seldom involved outsiders. Many of the women who wore men's boots and caps could fight like a man and fight a man.

The women reminded Katy of Jamsie's mother and the shanty towns of the bog where he was reared. The same neglected children, wild children, fearless children. And every time she saw the huddle of houses she was grateful that bad and all as Mulberry Street was, it was better than them.

After Mass, at the shops and stalls, in the streets Katy met the families lately come to live in the tenements.

'How did the potatoes fare this year?' she asked one of the women.

'Better than for the last years,' said the woman. 'This year we might have gone hungry but we wouldn't have starved. Hope was beginning to rise in our breasts when we dug and found sweet new potatoes instead of the stinking filth. But we'd reckoned without the landlords.'

'And what was it the landlords did?'

'Well, as you know, ma'am, we were all in arrears. Wasn't everyone? Where could anyone during the Hunger have found rent. Didn't we have to eat the bit of grain that other years went to pay the landlord. They evicted us.'

'May God forgive them,' said Katy. ' 'Twas His will that sent the blight, but not His will to clear the land. Wasn't that the cruel thing to have survived, to see the crop flourish again and then be dispossessed.'

'That we were, dispossessed and in our thousands – all over Ireland so that the little fields could be thrown together for sheep walks and bullock runs. The curse of God on them and their seed, breed and generation. And don't you ever forget our dispossession, nor let your children, either. Tell them as they grow you didn't come to America from choice. Drum it into them they were made to go.'

Katy made assenting noises as the woman described the evictions. 'They came with crowbars, the polis and the military and tumbled our homes. They came in the rain, the wind and the hail and hunted us out. And nothing softened their hearts. Not the cry of a newborn infant nor the rattle of death, nothing. Not even the fever. For the landlords were clever and the crowbar men in their pay, and the police and military in their pockets. So do you know what the fine gentlemen did? You don't – well, I'll tell you. There was a widow-woman sick and her daughter too with the typhus. "Begor," said the crowbar men, "begor sir 'twouldn't be safe to disturb them two."

"You don't want the money?" asked the gentleman, with the imperious way he had.

"Oh, we do that, but they have the fever." They were grovelling in front of him. " 'Tis not for ourselves we mind, it's the wife and children. If there was a way that was safe now we'd . . ."

"There is a way, you fools," and he dispatched a polisman to bring a winnowing sheet. And as true as I'm standing here this is what he did. Made the men with crowbars cover the bed of the sick and weigh it to the ground with stones. "Now," says he, "you won't have to lay hands on them, tumble the house. But gently, we don't want to kill anyone, do we?" And up on his horse he got and rode away.'

Katy found the telling so harrowing she didn't wish to hear more. But every time she began to inch away the woman detained her by placing a hand on her arm and continuing to talk. 'Hunted we were,' she said, 'from the homes we had known, from the fields and boreens that our feet and the feet of our people had trod. From the place where every blade of grass, bush and hillock was as familiar as the nose on our face.'

'May God comfort you,' said Katy and she thought how selfish she was, wanting to discourage the woman from spilling her heart. The poor unfortunate creature had lived through it. 'We were fortunate, we had a good landlord. It was never known for Lord Kilgoran to evict a tenant, God rest his soul.'

'Nevertheless you're an exile.'

'I am that,' said Katy, 'but it was the Hunger drove us out.'

'Whatever,' said the woman, 'you were driven out. But one day, one day all the wrongs will be righted. There'll be no more evictions. The land that was ours will be ours again. Never again will a family watch the walls of their home being tumbled. That's a terrible sight. A sight no one who witnessed it could forget to their dying day. To see the four walls scattered, the corner by the fire gone, the fire that had lived on the hearth since the first day there was a house, quenched. Not a place to lay your head except under a bush by the wayside, for neighbours were forbidden to give you shelter.'

Katy was crying, wiping her eyes. 'Don't cry, girl,' said the woman. 'Only remember what I'm telling you and tell your children. Never let them forget why they're in America. Tell them about the evictions and tell them about the brave men that tried to hinder the wrongdoers. The men that joined the Societies and went out at night to seek vengeance. Law-abiding, peaceful men who asked no more than to till their land and rear their families. Good-living men turned into murderers and robbers of anyone who persecuted their people. And now in the name of God I'll let you go about your business – I've delayed you long enough.'

Katy couldn't put the woman and all she had told her out of her mind. Her reminiscences had brought back so many memories. Father Bolger, when they were parting at Kinsale, telling Thomas never to forget that they had been forced to leave Ireland. Poor Father Bolger, she wondered if he was alive or dead. And Lord Kilgoran the good landlord, who sold his horses at the height of the famine to buy potatoes for his hungry tenants. But as the woman had said, all landlords weren't like him. Dano Driscoll wasn't and him an Irishman and a Catholic. Dano evicted people from the bog. She hadn't witnessed it but heard all about it. And how as a result the Society came to avenge it, sending Dano's cattle over the cliff, killing the poor oul dog, and into the bargain nearly murdering Dano.

Law-abiding some of the men in the Society might have been before the provocation, but not everyone was so. Jamsie's brother Johnny was one of them. Johnny had no regard for God, never mind the law. For how else could he have let his brother Padraig be blamed for the beating

105

that brought Dano to death's door. Poor Padraig, an inoffensive man only concerned with the welfare of his family. Working morning, noon and night, scraping the pennies together to take them away from the bog. Poor Padraig, 'twas far from the bog he went. All the way to Van Diemen's Land wherever that was, transported for fourteen years. And his wife and family dying from the Hunger and broken hearts. No, about that the poor woman wasn't right; not all that joined the Secret Societies were only in them to avenge wrongdoing. The likes of Johnny O'Hara were in them for the licence to kill, maim and rob. There was nothing to choose between them and the worst of the landlords and agents.

But all the same, it was true that none of them had come to America from choice. Who would have chosen the battle that living in New York meant. The trouble in finding your way about if you went outside the neighbourhood, learning the new money, your heart in your mouth every time you let the children down to play in the streets. In Kilgoran they were free as the birds, but you couldn't cage them, so down in the street they had to be allowed. And sometimes they came back crying after meeting American children who echoed their parents' words and called them dirty Irish, stinking Papists. Yelled after them that their mothers and fathers were drunkards who knew only how to fight and make babies.

It was hard for them. Her children weren't aggressive, weren't able for the bullying and name-calling. 'I hate it,' Bridget would cry after an encounter with the children. 'I hate it when they call me names. I'm not dirty, I'm not!'

'Of course you're not,' Katy would console her.

'I hate living here, I wish we could move somewhere nice.'

'One day we will – but you'll have to learn to ignore the name-callers till we do. 'Tisn't easy. One day it'll stop, one day you'll be an American. We'll all be Americans and one day we'll find another place to live.'

She was expressing her hopes, but hopes she knew they'd remain for a long time. Unless there was a miracle. Unless the money came from somewhere for her to have a shop and expand her laundrying.

The way home took her through Cow Lane. It wasn't far from Mulberry Street and yet seemed a different world. It was so quiet and clean by comparison, with only a few houses and the leather shop. Sometimes she bought laces there. The man was pleasant, not an American but he spoke English and chatted to her while he undid the laces from the big bunch hanging from a hook. She liked him and the

106

shop, with its dim interior and the smell of leather and the boot-making implements spread about, the lasts and awls, sharp knives and hanks of hemp, the strong shining needles.

One day she asked the man if he lived in the rooms above and he told her, no, it was a lock-up shop. 'And soon it will be locked up for good.'

'I'm sorry to hear that,' Katy said.

The man shrugged. 'People don't mend their boots so they don't buy leather. And who in this neighbourhood has footwear made to measure? I made a mistake. I keep hoping,' he spread his hands, 'but hope won't pay the rent.'

'I'm very sorry to hear that,' said Katy and meant it.

At the time she was sorry for his misfortune and then she began to think that if he did leave wouldn't his shop be the very thing she was looking for, if she could get enough money from somewhere.

Now as she passed she looked in – she had no excuse for entering and bringing the talk round to business. And in any case, even if the man was leaving tomorrow she couldn't afford the place. But all the same she never stopped hoping. One day, please God, one day she might have the shop in Cow Lane, a miracle would happen. She would find the money – and then, oh then, wouldn't that be a miracle indeed if whoever lived in the rooms over the shop would leave and she'd move in. Have her laundry on the premises, still be near the school, chapel and Mary and Eileen. She went on home, her head full of dreams and hopes.

Terence continued to find New York to his liking. The woman the priest recommended to look after Mikey was a motherly person who took good care of him. 'Like a son he is to me,' Mrs McGennis would say when he went to visit his brother. 'A son and a second pair of hands, he helps me no end.' And Mikey would grin and look pleased with himself. From money he made touting and robbing passengers Terence rewarded Mrs McGennis liberally and said that one day, when he had his own place, Mikey would come and live with him.

'Please God, though, it's not for a long time, for I'd miss Mikey sorely. With the size that's growing on him he's a great protection.'

So it was with an easy mind that Terence went about his business. He brought enough passengers to satisfy Kelly, robbed enough to keep his savings growing and cultivated anyone who came into the groggery that he judged might be of use to him. And Kelly cultivated him. There was a great future in America, he told Terence, for them that were go ahead. Money and power for the taking and making if you were smart. The Irish were beginning to come into their own. Though it was a hard fight to start with. Terence listened and asked questions, and learned that from as far back as the 1790s, the Irish had supported Thomas Jefferson – for Jefferson had been sympathetic to the French and Irish Revolutionary causes – and following on from that tradition, they still supported the Democratic Party, which Jefferson had helped to found.

Kelly then explained how until 1821 you couldn't vote unless you had property. How before that the thousands of poor Irish had no say in their own affairs. He told of how in 1817, from a meeting in Dooley's Long Room in New York City, several hundred Irish stormed Tammany Hall, wrecked it and attacked the officials who were denying them the nomination of an Irish Leader. They wanted Thomas Emmet for their man in Congress, the brother of Robert Emmet whose picture hung in the groggery. But it wasn't until the suffrage was granted that they got anywhere.

Tammany Hall, Terence discovered, had been founded in 1789 and named after a famous Indian Chief. In the beginning its members were American Protestant working class men and its intentions were brotherly and charitable with a bias against privilege. But with the years, Kelly said all that changed and Tammany became the place that could make or break a politician.

Terence listened and memorised the Tammany history, but it was the present he was interested in – how the Irish were now in with more than a foothold. And it was his intention that one day Tammany might hold the key for his success in America.

Katy had almost given up hope of ever hearing from Peader when one day a package arrived from Ireland. She knew without opening it that inside there was a letter from Peader, and was overcome with delight. She was just about to open the package when Jamsie came in.

'Didn't I tell you, wasn't I right,' she crowed triumphantly. 'It's from Carey – a letter from Peader. So much for you and your advice. I knew Peader and Charlotte wouldn't have lost the run of theirselves.'

'A great suck-in you'll get if it's not from them,' said Jamsie, but his eyes were as hopeful and expectant as Katy's. 'Open it will you, instead of waving it like a flag.'

'It *is* from Peader,' Katy scanned the letter, 'and it's from Virginia – where's that?'

'Yerra woman will you read it!'

'It was written last year – all this time it's lain in Carey's.'

'Will you for the Lord's sake read the letter.'

Dear Katy and Jamsie,

By this time I hope you have arrived in America and didn't suffer too much hardship on the voyage. Write as soon as you receive this as I worry about you and want to help.

As you can see, Charlotte and I are in Virginia. It wasn't our intention to settle here but here is where we are. What happened was a strange coincidence. Not minutes after posting the letter to you from Liverpool, Charlotte and I were walking back to our lodgings. The streets round the docks were teeming. Hundreds of poor starving Irish everywhere, waiting to take passage to America. For as you probably know, the majority sailed from there. We were pushing and shoving our way through the throng or rather I was to make a way for Charlotte when someone called her name. She was so exhausted by the awful crossing we'd had to Liverpool that she didn't hear her name being called.

I did and the heart was put crossways in me. Every minute of the journey since we left Kilgoran I was in dread and fear that somewhere along the way we'd be apprehended, me thrown into gaol for abducting the Master's daughter, Charlotte torn from my side and me never to lay eyes on her again. So you can imagine my fear when this voice – an English one – shouted again: 'Charlotte, Charlotte Kilgoran!' It was a loud voice with a ring of command – it had to be to make itself heard over the babel. I can understand that now. At the time all I thought was – it's the voice of authority. I wanted to run, fight my way through the crowd, push harder, knock people down in my desperation to keep Charlotte safe. At the same time I couldn't resist a glance behind me to see the face of whoever it was about to apprehend us. I saw a young man waving an arm, smiling and again calling Charlotte's name. Had it not been for the smile I'd have rushed us farther from him. But something told me a man smiling in such a fashion meant us no harm. So I let him catch up with us. At first Charlotte didn't recognise him. Then she did. He was a relation of her sister's husband, God rest her. If you remember, Olivia married and went to live in London and Charlotte visited her there.

Anyway, to cut a long story short they fell on each other, laughing and crying as they recalled the London visit. Ages seemed to pass before she introduced me. He congratulated us on our marriage and said how splendid it was that we had eloped. Charlotte confessed that madly in love though she was, the prospect of America frightened her. Of course he asked where we were planning to settle and had we contacts there. We hadn't, as you know, and told him so.

You know me, I'd have been a bit more reticent – but Charlotte did all the talking. And in the course of the conversation it emerged that we were going steerage. Paul, Paul Galloway, that's his name, was aghast. Had we any idea of what travelling steerage was like? It was out of the question – the passage must be changed to cabin class. I needn't tell you I was mortified. All the implications were there. What sort of a husband was I, allowing Charlotte to travel in such a way? I was on the point of thanking and refusing him when Charlotte did the same thing, saying she was well and strong, her circumstances were changed – by her own choice, and get used to them she must.

She was so courageous, so uncomplaining. Not a word had she said about the dreadful trip from Ireland to Liverpool though the seas were mountainous, we were packed aboard like animals and the crossing took thirty-six hours. And here she was, with the prospect of maybe two months facing her in even worse conditions, turning down the offer of the bit of comfort. I couldn't let her. I'd accept Paul's offer, I said, but only as a loan. It was agreed.

Paul was bound for Virginia, where he had inherited a plantation and during the voyage, he suggested we should head there also. Virginia, he told me, had been settled early in the seventeenth century by Englishmen – Charlotte would feel much more at home there than in New York. And as for me, I could be of use to him running his estate. 'At least give it a try,' he pleaded. I could see Charlotte was all for it.

But for me it was a hard decision. Me, managing an estate for someone I'd have spit on in Ireland. But I saw the wistful look in Charlotte's eyes and knew the privations she must suffer if we took our chance in New York, Chicago or Boston. So I said yes, I'd give it a try though all I'd managed before was a thirty-acre farm. Paul dismissed that as of no importance so here I am in Jamestown, Virginia.

Now that you have my address we can write regularly and meet fairly soon I hope, though Virginia is a long way from New York. I wrote to Fr Bolger care of Carey – if I hear from him I'll let you know.

'Well,' said Jamsie, 'what did I tell you? Hasn't she got the bold

Peader by the nose. Sure, come to think of it, he never had much grit in him.'

Katy, who was rereading the letter, put it aside to argue: 'He wasn't a fighter, not a brawler but of grit he had plenty.'

'A scholar and a talker – but not an ounce of grit. Look at how he let me take you from him – I'd have killed a man for trying.'

Katy, who had been that minute admiring Peader's qualities – his consideration for Charlotte, putting aside his pride to borrow from the Englishman, putting aside his principles to let her live where it suited her, now saw him through Jamsie's eyes. And saw Jamsie's through hers blinded by love. His declaration that he would have killed a man for her thrilled her to the marrow. Her handsome black-haired boy who could make her insides melt. What was security and consideration compared to how her heart thrilled at the sight of him. The tenderness that welled in her when she looked at his sleeping face, helpless-looking, like a baby. It was these things which had made her love him in the first place and the lack of them in Peader which had made her throw him over. They were still young, love and passion surged in them. Comfort and security could wait – would do when they were old.

'He said nothing about a priest marrying them,' Jamsie said, going to Katy, looking over her shoulder at the letter she had again picked up. His fingers rested on her neck, caressing it, sliding into her hair, pulling out the pins so it fell about her shoulders. Lovely golden hair, its lustre restored with the better eating in America. She gazed at the letter not seeing a word of it, her whole being in thrall to the sensations Jamsie was arousing. He turned her bent head and kissed her. Raising his mouth he said, 'There's no one here, I'll push the table against the door.'

'Yes,' she whispered, 'do.'

While he barricaded the door she undid buttons and ties, slipped off her shoes. Before lying on the bed she pulled over the curtains. Jamsie laughed. 'Who can see us up here?'

'All the same,' she said, lying down with him, 'it wouldn't seem fitting with the window uncovered.'

Chapter Ten

Katy answered Peader's letter. 'If you could have seen our faces when it arrived. To know that you and Charlotte are here even if Virginia is a long way off. One day, please God, we'll all be together again. All we'll have to talk about. All the questions I have for Charlotte.' She went on to tell about her neighbourhood, how lucky they were to have so many of their own living nearby. It was grand to hear Irish voices, to be able to talk about home. The chapel was only a stone's throw from them – that was a great comfort. She said nothing about their hard times and finished the letter pleading that if ever they had the chance to come to New York how delighted herself and Jamsie would be to see them.

When word came back that Peader was soon coming to New York and would visit them, Katie was beside herself with joy. 'Can you believe it? Him and Miss Charlotte coming to see us.'

'He said nothing about her coming,' Jamsie reminded her.

'Well, of course she'll come,' Katy said dismissively.

'I hope you won't be disappointed,' Jamsie replied and she could have killed him for his lack of enthusiasm. But she felt sure that once he knew the day and date Peader was arriving he would change his tune. When a note did come saying he would be there in two days' time at six o'clock she was ecstatic.

'Your Uncle Peader is coming to see us! You remember him, don't you? You remember him, don't you Bridget and you, Thomas? Of course you do. I can't believe it. He never said a word about Miss Charlotte. He might be wanting to surprise us.'

'He used to fish on the strand,' Thomas said, 'he had a boat.'

'Look at that for a memory.'

'His eyes were a queer colour.'

'What was queer about them, Bridget?'

'They were green like a cat's.'

'Shame on you Bridget – is that all you can remember about your kind Uncle Peader?'

' 'Tis not,' answered Bridget, in a huff for being reprimanded.

'You must be delighted with the news, Jamsie,' Katy said and he told

112

her he was. 'Well, you might show it instead of sitting with a face like a fiddle'

'Aren't you showing enough for the two of us? You haven't stopped talking since the letter came.'

When eventually she calmed down it dawned on her that entertaining Peader might not be that easy. Supposing he meant to stay for the night. 'Where will he lie?'

'On the floor,' said Jamsie callously. Then seeing the shocked expression on Katy's face he said more sympathetically, 'In a hotel, I'm sure.'

'He mightn't have the money.'

'Isn't he coming all the way from Virginia? Isn't he here on business? And doesn't he own a plantation? He's sure to have the price of a bed.'

'But supposing he hasn't – and he only manages a plantation. He doesn't own it.'

Jamsie's sympathy ran out. 'In that case give him the children's shakedown – they can come in with us.'

So relieved was Katy with the solution, his altered tone went unnoticed. 'But do you think Miss Charlotte would object to sleeping on the pallet?'

'I'm going out for an hour,' said Jamsie, and so preoccupied was she with her plans and worries for the visit that he was out the door before she had time or the thought to protest.

More problems presented themselves – sheets for the bed, cups, a cloth for the table. She'd talk to Eileen and Mary about them. Eileen had a pair of sheets never once used. Mary had three cups given to her when she was in service, odd but china and the baker's wife Mrs Jaeger had a tablecloth, hand-embroidered all the way from Germany. All were willingly lent for the big occasion.

Such excitement there was, such planning, such high hopes for the grand reunion. From early on the morning of the day Peader was to arrive, the bed was made up and Danny and Mary Kate threatened with a terrible fate if they even played near it, let alone jumped on it. But the most important thing was what to give Peader to eat. Cost wasn't reckoned, not if they lived on bread and tea for the following week, but the cooking facilities were limited to the top of the kerosene stove. She talked it over with Eileen and Mary. Eileen said not to be killing herself cooking. Half a pound of 'Ausschnitt' with bread and butter and scallions and tomatoes would satisfy Peader.

'Ausschnitt?' Katy was mystified.

'Them cold meats the Germans sell – you get a slice of all sorts.' Katy

113

said no, she didn't trust bought cooked meats – you could be poisoned. Mary asked what more could anyone ask for than a nice head of cabbage and a piece of boiled bacon. 'That would be grand, only I wanted something special.' In the end, Katy decided on a piece of beef with potatoes, onions and carrots. To roast it wasn't possible, so into a pot it went on a bed of vegetables and only a drain of water. Cooked slowly she said you'd be hard put to tell it wasn't roasted.

The table was laid, the children's faces washed for the second time in a day. Even Jamsie agreed to a second splash of cold water. Katy's face shone from excitement and the anticipation of seeing Peader again. Her hair was glossy from vigorous brushing and arranged in a generous knot. Around her shoulders she wore a soft pink, crocheted shawl made and lent by Mary. The ends were folded over and tucked and arranged in such a way to conceal the faded and threadbare front of her skirt.

'If only we could see into the street,' Katy complained, 'then we'd know when he was coming.' Then for the umpteenth time she smoothed Mrs Jaeger's cloth, moved the cups a little to the left, a little to the right and then back to their original position, at the same time warning Thomas and Bridget to raise no contention because there wouldn't be a spare chair.

For the second time she warned Jamsie not to keep Peader in talk about the Young Irelanders nor American politics either – if Miss Charlotte wasn't with him, and secretly now she was hoping she wouldn't be. You couldn't expect Miss Charlotte to sleep on the floor, and Katy wanted to ask him so many questions about her and all the Kilgoran family.

'I heard you the first time and for God's sake sit down – you're like a hen on a hot griddle. Anyone would think it was President Polk himself coming.'

'He wouldn't be half as welcome,' Katy retorted, and gave another pat to the cloth.

There was a knock on the door – her heart jumped – it was him, but it wasn't, only a little boy from up in the house. A pleasant child who played with Thomas. 'Thomas isn't going out,' she said, her voice unusually brusque with disappointment.

'I know,' said the child. 'His uncle from Ireland is visiting, everyone in the street knows. I think his cab is coming down the street. I ran up to tell you.'

'Jamsie, he's here! Go down quick. Quick go on, you know what happens when a cab comes into the street. He'll be surrounded. Go on down.'

She was so nervous and excited at the thought of seeing Peader again. It was natural she supposed, you'd feel like that about anyone you liked and hadn't seen for a long time. But there was more to it than that – Peader wasn't just someone she liked. Peader was the only man besides Jamsie who had held her in his arms, who had kissed her and told her he loved her. That made him very special. She wondered if he thought like that about her sometimes. Was he now excited and nervous at the prospect of seeing her again?

She ran to the mirror to have a last look at herself before he arrived. She smiled at herself and touched her hair. Then she heard the sound of footsteps, they were coming up the stairs. Tears of joy filled her eyes and her heart jumped in her breast. Then they were in the room. Peader's beautiful green eyes were smiling at her, taking her in. He was coming towards her, his arms outstretched. 'Let me look at you,' he said. 'Katy, Katy, it's good to see you.' He held her close, she was very conscious of being in his arms, of feeling his body against hers. And he held her away from him. 'You haven't changed, not a bit.'

'Nor you,' she said. But he had. He was different. She hadn't expected him to be dressed like a gentleman. Or act like one as he did in his first minute over the threshold. She knew him so well. She saw his expression as he took in the room, and knew what he was thinking. 'Is this where you finished up? In this dark hole. In nearly a year couldn't you both have done better?' But acting like a gentleman he never uttered the words. Though she had guessed them.

He had brought presents for the children. Bridget exclaimed delightedly when she saw hers – a model haberdashery with a minute chest of drawers, ribbons and lace spilling from them and tiny hat-stands complete with beautiful decorated bonnets.

Thomas had lead soldiers, their uniforms painted in exquisite detail. For Mary Kate and Danny, Peader produced two horses on wooden wheeled stands. They were covered in real hide, one chestnut with lighter patches and the other as black as ebony. Their reins and saddles were of tooled leather and when Katy touched their manes they were real horse hair.

She was overwhelmed by the obvious expense of the toys. Like Peader's elegant dark blue frock coat, his trousers which on a black background had a matching blue stripe and his gleaming glossy black top hat, they made her uncomfortably aware of the room – its shabbiness, the odd cups and the smell of kerosene overlaying the aroma of the pot roast. She saw herself through his eyes, her faded blouse and skirt, Jamsie's old clothes.

There were presents also for her and Jamsie – a wisp of a shawl in shades of mauve and pink and a china jar with tobacco spelled on it in gold lettering. Lifting the lid, Peader held it towards Jamsie. Katy could smell its fragrance. 'Grown as you might say with my own hands.'

'From the look of them I wouldn't have thought so,' said Jamsie, accepting the jar. By the tone of his voice Katy knew that he too was embarrassed by Peader's appearance and the largesse.

The meal was ready, the children took their helpings and sat on the floor near their new toys. Peader said the pot roast was delicious and he reminded her of meals they had shared in Kilgoran. She was relaxed and happy and thought how she might have misjudged Peader. What did his fine clothes matter? If she was travelling and had the money wouldn't she wear dressy clothes? Peader was the kindest man she had ever known – he wouldn't have looked at the room the way she had imagined. She'd been surprised at how prosperous he appeared, surprised and maybe a bit envious. That was what had ailed her. Peader was still their friend. But all the same she wouldn't speak of her ambition for her laundry – nor ask for a loan.

She plied him with questions: 'How is Charlotte? And what about Miss Catherine – is she still in India, has God blessed her with a child? And Father Bolger and Master Charles, is there any news of them? Tell me everything. I want to hear about everyone.'

Peader smiled at her and for a moment she gazed into his eyes and a voice in her mind said, 'I nearly married you, I could have been your wife.' Then Peader began to answer her questions and the thought was banished. 'Charlotte is very well and sends all her love. No, Catherine hasn't ever had a child, and we haven't, either.' Katy said they had plenty of time, and to herself that she hoped like her sister Charlotte wasn't barren, for those things ran in some families.

'No word from Father Bolger though I wrote to him soon after I got to America – and as for Charles,' he shrugged. 'I don't suppose we'll ever know what became of him.'

When Jamsie entered the conversation it was to complain about America. The false promises that came to nothing. The discrimination against the Irish Catholics, against all poor immigrants but especially the Irish Catholics.

Peader reasoned with him. No country, he said, could accommodate quickly or satisfactorily the vast numbers that were flocking into America. Before 1840 only about six hundred thousand came but in this decade, that figure had more than trebled. 'So don't blame America – blame England and the other European countries where the rights of men are denied. England starved and evicted us – America took us in but she can't overnight. . .'

'Then why didn't she welcome us?'

'Jamsie, America is people. People with fears, fears that their country, cities and little towns will be overrun. Their ancestors like us fled from persecution, they came for freedom to practice their religion. They had a hard time of it. They had to fight for what they've got – first the Indians and then the English. They've made a great country.'

'Where?' asked Jamsie contemptuously.

'They have,' said Peader, ignoring the contempt. 'You must read about it. They valued liberty and freedom and the right for a man to worship God in his own way. They brought with them all that was good in English law.'

'Well,' said Jamsie, 'I've yet to meet one that resembles your description.'

'Now is a bad time for them.'

'Is it codding me you are?'

'I'm serious – it is. No one likes to see their way of life threatened. Why didn't they welcome you, you ask, greet you with open arms? Hospitality, we were brought up to believe, was a prime virtue. You never refused food and shelter – you made the stranger welcome. But no one expected you to receive a tribe. It's the same here. One or two at a time coming in and the difference wouldn't be noticed – now it's millions.'

Katy sided with Jamsie. 'Tell me now Peader,' she said, 'these great Americans sent thousands during the Hunger for the poor starving peasants and yet when we come in their midst they can't tolerate us – explain that to me.'

'Cows in the distance have long horns, Katy. The Irish peasant far away was appealing. You put your hand in your pocket – it makes you feel good. He's a poor starving stranger – then all of a sudden he's here. Everyone fears a stranger.'

Katy thought he sounded pompous – he irritated her. Was Jamsie right, after all? Had marrying Miss Charlotte let him lose the run of himself? She turned on him. ' 'Tis far from Kilgoran you've come, Peader. All reason and excuses. But maybe it's easy for you to be so, for didn't you have a better reception than us.' He reddened and she was glad to see her dart had gone home. Then immediately she regretted scoring off him. He was their friend. He had come all the way to see them. And hadn't he always been reasonable. That had nothing to do with him marrying the Master's daughter. He was a kind, just person.

117

And it was lovely having him here, listening to his voice. It was like long ago at home.

She suggested making more tea, but Jamsie scorned the suggestion. There was something better to drink, he said, and to Katy's amazement took from the press a bottle of whiskey. How hadn't she seen it during the day? Where had he got the money from? On the slate it was, she supposed – her wages would be docked. A pitcher of beer she wouldn't have minded – but whiskey. Never mind the price, the terrible humour Jamsie got into after drinking it.

Until after his second glass he was convivial. Reminiscing about Ireland with Peader, laughing about shared experiences. No, that wasn't how he remembered such and such a thing. Peader was wrong. Peader must be losing his memory. The change in him was beginning. The contradictions became more frequent. Remarks more sarcastic. He was cross-hackling and in an effort to forestall real unpleasantness Katy began to talk about Miss Charlotte. An inoffensive subject, she was sure.

'I had hoped,' she said, 'that she might have come with you. I'd love to see her again. Does she ever come to New York?'

'Not so far. In the beginning she was too upset by her father's death.'

'I didn't think she knew,' said Katy. 'I remember Hannah telling me about it. How she heard the gun go off just as Miss Charlotte was coming down the stairs to elope with you. She suspected something terrible but Hannah, knowing there was nothing to be gained and everything to lose, convinced her otherwise and sent her off to meet you and the cart that was heading for Cork.'

'I don't think she did know, then. She was very upset at the thought of deceiving her father and may have been worried when she heard the shot. But when eventually we heard from Catherine about what had happened to her father, she got the idea into her mind that she had eloped with me despite the fact that her father lay dead or dying, and that in her heart she knew that. She was wracked with guilt.'

'The poor child,' said Katy, 'I'm that sorry. Is there any improvement?'

'Oh, a great one. Now she's too happy and busy in Virginia to consider moving far. She says the life there must be like it was in Ireland before her father lost his money.'

'Like life was for them,' said Jamsie, and unsuspectingly Peader fell into his trap.

'I suppose you could say that. Hospitality is very lavish in the South. England settled it in the seventeenth century.'

'You don't tell me,' said Jamsie, his sarcasm obvious but not to Peader who continued.

'Jamestown was called after King James, and the wealthy still live as the gentry did.'

'Hunting and dancing, balls and eating and drinking while we starved – oh, that's how the gentry lived right enough. 'Twas something you were once bitter about, Peader. Only in Virginia it's negroes instead of peasants, amn't I right?'

Katy could have killed him. He was drunk. He was deliberately setting out to bait Peader. Of course, jealousy ailed him. He had always been jealous of Peader. Of his learning, his way of holding his own without ructions. Above all he was jealous because Peader had once loved her. He was jealous of any man who looked at her. Thinking about this, she saw it as a proof of his love for her. Once upon a time he had fought Peader for her. It made her feel proud and special to be loved so. It made up for everything. Made Peader's description of Miss Charlotte's life not to be envied. It made her happy that she had chosen Jamsie for her husband. Nothing in the world could compensate for their love, nothing in the world compare with it.

But all the same, Jamsie wasn't going to spend the night digging at Peader. It was no way to treat anyone in your home. In a minute she'd send Bridget to bring Eileen and Mary down to meet Peader as she had promised. However, before she had a chance, Jamsie was off again.

'And what business brought you to New York, Peader?'

'The business was more or less an excuse for seeing you and Katy.'

Katy's face flushed with pleasure at Peader's reply. Jamsie noticed and felt a surge of jealousy. Peader done up like a gentleman. Peader coming all this way to see them. To see *her*, if the truth was known. And she like a love-sick girl with her face on fire.

'But there is a bit of business, too. I have to see a man who lives on Staten Island. He imports furniture and silver from England and Europe – Paul is thinking of buying some.'

'Indeed,' said Jamsie, 'furniture and silver. Haven't you come on in leaps and bounds. And I suppose the man on Staten Island is another fine Southern gentleman.'

Peader laughed. 'Far from it – Jacques Demart's origins are as humble as our own. His ancestors came out to Virginia working their passage, promised land when their indentured time was up. In his father's time they succeeded in buying a small plantation. But they were never considered gentry – only a step above the poor whites. And Jacques as he grew up couldn't stomach slavery. So he sold up when his

119

father died, which was a few months after I arrived in Virginia. I was sorry to see him go – we had a lot in common. And now he's an importer.'

Peader tried steering the talk away from Virginia and Katy sent Bridget for Eileen and Mary. 'There are terrible things happening in Ireland, thousands of evictions.' And Katy thought what an eejit Peader was, making the bullets for Jamsie to fire at him.

'I know,' said Jamsie. 'I know all about it. I can read. And if I couldn't, there's hundreds flocking into New York running from the same evictions. First-hand knowledge I have. In Virginia you wouldn't have that. I'm very interested in Virginia. Is it a fact that you have slaves on your plantation?'

'There are black people there, and we've black servants in the house.'

'Slaves,' said Jamsie, his grin malicious. 'There's no servants in America – only slaves and helps.' He laughed and slapped his thigh. 'Slaves and helps, isn't that a good one! Have another drink,' he offered the bottle. Peader refused. Jamsie helped himself to more whiskey. He stood up and walked towards Peader, laughing mockingly, pointing a finger, goading him. 'You,' he said, 'you of all people running slaves. Peader Daly, the great man for the people's freedom – you with a plantation full of unfortunate black men and women owned as if they were dogs. Never, if you hadn't admitted it with your own two lips, would I have believed that of Peader Daly.'

Easygoing as Peader was Katy wouldn't have blamed him had he lashed out at Jamsie. Look at the way he was standing over him, insulting him. He was asking for it. Only much as he deserved it, she didn't want a fight. And it was with tremendous relief that she heard the voices of Mary and Eileen and then they were in the room, and she thanked God for their timely arrival.

Immediately Jamsie turned his attentions to Eileen. Eileen had that effect on men. In minutes they were throwing insults at each other, Eileen at the same time flashing her lovely smile at him so all the harm was taken out of them and everyone was good-humoured.

Peader was courteous but shy with her and obviously more at ease with Mary. She told him how much she had heard of him and Miss Charlotte. She hoped they were well and happy, and was there any sign of a family yet? No? Well, that was a pity, but sure they had plenty of time, she'd do a novena for them. She was sure he must miss Ireland. Maybe, please God one day they'd all be able to go home.

Eileen produced a plate of cake. 'I bought it from Jaeger's. I've had it before and it's gorgeous. Apples in a spongy dough.' Katy wet tea and cut up the Apfelkuchen. Peader said nothing for him, he had to be off, he had an early start in the morning.

'It was grand to see you, please God it won't be so long next time. On the way home I'll be reliving every minute of tonight.' He shook hands with Mary and Eileen. Katy could have sworn his eyes were wet when he took his farewell of her. He kissed the children and told Bridget that soon she'd be a young lady. Bridget giggled and looked embarrassed.

Jamsie had an arm round his shoulders as they left the room. Mary said she had never seen such a handsome man and wasn't Miss Charlotte a lucky woman. Eileen said he was a handsome man, but didn't have enough fire in him for her. 'Would I be right in that, Katy?'

'You might at that,' said Katy.

It wasn't until the next day that Katy found the hundred dollar bill. It was beneath a chalk statue of the Virgin she had on top of the press. 'Peader,' she said aloud, 'may God bless you and the decency of you not to offer it, not to shame us. How sorely I misjudged you. You never altered, you never could. You have the special grace. You wouldn't embarrass us. And with the humour that was on me and Jamsie part of the time last night, our stupid pride might have made us not accept, though we'd have regretted it. I certainly would. You've been my saviour. This will get me a little shop and take us out of the tenements. Wait'll I tell Jamsie. Though it's more than that I'll have to tell him. Him and the slaves! A lot he knows about them. All his information comes out of the saloons. I'll have something to say to him about the way he treated you. Last night wasn't the time to tell him that never mind the Americans, he could do with some lessons in manners and hospitality himself. But wait'll he comes in.'

But by the time he did come home her mind was so full of plans for the laundry, hopes that the bootmaker in Cow Lane would give up the shop and prayers that whoever lived above it might also leave. So happy was she with the bright future she saw in front of her, the different life for Jamsie and her familiy, that she never said a cross word to him.

Chapter Eleven

On his way back from New York, Peader thought about Katy and Jamsie. How lovely it was to see them again, how the children had grown. Bridget was going to be a beauty like her mother. Katy was a marvellous woman. There she was in that terrible place and making the best of it.

Thinking about the room and Mulberry Street, he compared it with Annilaun, the magnificent white house on the James River where he and Charlotte lived. In Paul's house, on Paul's plantation.

'It looks as if we'll have a good trip to Yorktown,' said a man sitting next to Peader in the smoke-room.

'It seems so,' said Peader.

The man was elderly, pleasant-looking, American. At another time Peader would have been glad of the company, encouraged the conversation. Now he didn't feel like talking. The man tried again. 'You're Irish – how long have you been over?'

'Almost two years.'

'Do you like it here?'

'It's a great country.' As he answered the man, he made a pretence of searching through a bag. 'There's a report I have to study – tobacco prices.' The man took the hint and after a while moved to another seat. From his bag Peader took the nearest thing that came to hand – a catalogue of the furniture Jacques Demart imported. He laid it on his lap as a protection against further intrusion, gazing unseeingly at the opened page as he let his thoughts return to Annilaun and the day he had seen it for the first time.

How astounded he had been that this mansion, visible from where the river boat was tying up at the wharf, was the home which Paul had invited him and Charlotte to share. His surprise at the way Paul was greeted by two negroes waiting on the jetty. 'Master', they called him and he called them by name. He had remarked on it. 'I thought this was your first time in Virginia.'

And Paul had laughed. 'I was born here, tell you about it at dinner.'

Then they were being handed out of the boat and into a waiting carriage where again Paul was affectionately hailed by the black driver. And then the drive towards the house. Charlotte's appreciative comments on the rolling lawns going down to the river. Paul's flow of information; the plantation had been in the family since the seventeenth century, there were eight hundred acres of it. The log cabins in the distance were for the slaves, field hands, carpenters, wheelwrights, cooks, those who worked in the house. Those were the drying sheds, smoke houses, packing and sorting places. There nearer Annilaun was the schoolroom for Galloway children, of whom there were now none. The plantation was a completely self-contained unit.

The carriage was nearing the house. Lined up on its steps were a group of black people, laughing and waving, welcoming Paul home. Like the gentry's return to the Big House, Peader thought as he got out. 'Well, there she is – Annilaun. What do you think?' asked Paul.

That I'm a fool and have made a mistake I'll regret, Peader remembered thinking, but seeing the ecstatic expression on Charlotte's face had replied, 'It's magnificient. I had no notion it was so grand.'

'Kilgoran House must have been like this once,' Charlotte said. 'It's so beautiful. And the gardens and the weather. And the servants here to meet us. Oh Paul, it's the most gorgeous place. I can't believe it. I think I'm in Heaven. Oh, Paul, oh, thank you. I know I'm going to love it.'

On that first night in Virginia, Charlotte went to bed early. Peader and Paul sat smoking and drinking and Paul told him the story of how he had come to be born in Annilaun. 'My uncle had the place then and when my mother and father married he invited them out. Papa was a bit of a rake – it was hoped that coming here and with a wife, would straighten him out. It didn't work that way. Apart from the social life he hated the place. He died when I was ten. From fever, my mother said, but my uncle's version was that he drank himself into the grave. Mama was penniless so we stayed on.

'Annilaun was a paradise for a small boy. My uncle had no children and I could do no wrong in his or my aunt's eyes. And the negroes treated me like God. Then when I was a bit older, a visitor from England who also had a fortune fell in love with Mama. I hated him. Not because he was marrying Mama, but because I had to leave here. There was such a rumpus, with my uncle declaiming I was his brother's child, his flesh and blood, and the plantation would be mine. I should be left where I was happy and loved. It was all to no avail. Mama was besotted with her new husband and back to England I was taken, for school and then the army which my stepfather was sure would make a man of me.'

123

'That was unfortunate.' Peader felt obliged to say something and could think of nothing else.

'It was for what seemed an eternity – then fate took a hand in my affairs. Mama and the husband while touring Venice got the cholera and died within hours of each other. No one could have been more surprised than I when I discovered that he had left me all his money. In no time I resigned my commission and was back in Virginia. Do you remember the celebrations, Jake?' Paul asked of the negro who stood by the door when he wasn't pouring drinks or lighting Paul's cigars. Jake laughed aloud and said he remembered well. He and Paul reminisced about the homecoming and then about their childhood. 'Me and Jake were inseparable until I went to school, and even then he'd hang about the schoolroom waiting for me to finish.'

Peader recalled the small building for the Galloway children and his unease about the situation he was now in came again to the surface of his mind. He wanted to get up from the table, thank Paul for his kindness, for the cabin passage and tell him he had changed his mind. He couldn't become involved in managing a plantation run on slave labour. While he was trying to work out the most diplomatic way of saying this, Paul dismissed Jake and began again to talk.

'When the first Galloway came here the place was a swamp – disease-ridden and the Indians less than friendly. The planters were looking for gold and silver, but there wasn't any. Tobacco was popular in Europe and tobacco, they discovered, grew well in Virginia – so that's what they planted.'

'With slave labour, I suppose?' asked Peader.

'In a way, yes, but they weren't negroes. No, they came much later. White indentured fellows worked the land. Seven years they owed for their passage out. At the end of it they'd be freedmen and could grab land, too. Poor blighters, few lived that long. Worked to death probably, with swampy ground and bad food, or not sufficient. Anyway, they died like flies. But they were cheap to replace – only ten pounds for seven years or how long they lasted. Cheaper to buy than a black man.

'Trouble was, they eventually became acclimatised and more and more lived to claim their freedom. Only by the time they did, the price of land was way beyond what they could afford. So Virginia and Maryland had got themselves a wandering band of malcontents. Those were rum times for the planters. Plantations were raided, and firearms needed for Indian attacks were stolen. These freedmen got together under a chap called Bacon and attempted a revolution. They were ruthless, burnt the settlement at Jamestown, robbed and plundered. Then Bacon snuffed it and without him they fell apart. Anyone suspected of being able to replace him was hanged.'

Peader thought how similar were the English methods of planting, whether in America or Ireland – and how summary their justice. He was tired, his head ached, his heart was sore, he had changed allegiances – sacrificed his principles. He pretended interest as Paul went on extolling the virtues of his ancestors. The foresight and faith in the future they had had – the houses they built, the grounds and gardens, the trees they planted knowing they would never live to see them mature – but that someone of their line would. 'That's civilisation.'

Peader kept his thoughts to himself and Paul continued. 'Not easy, eh, not when a band of marauding freedmen might descend on you at any time. But they got round that – stopped bringing in the white indentured fellows and went over to the negroes instead. They cost a bit more – you had to buy them for a lifetime at twenty pounds a head, but it worked.'

'Your uncle and aunt, when did they die?' Peader asked, feeling that he must make some contribution to the conversation.

'Last year. Annilaun and her eight hundred acres – the finest plantation in Virginia is now all mine.'

'Eight hundred acres!' Peader seized on the size of the place to make a last-minute attempt at opting out.

'Paul,' he said, 'I don't think I've ever met anyone as generous as you. I'll never forget what you did for me and Charlotte – the difference you made to our coming to America. But about managing this place for you – well. . .' What in his mind he had planned to say – 'I won't take the job,' came out as a feeble excuse for having only ever managed thirty acres on which little else but potatoes were grown.

Paul waved a hand dismissively. 'There's nothing to it,' he said. 'There's overseers, underseers, Uncle Tom Cobbleigh and all. Everyone knows the job backwards. Rather like the army. I'm the CO and you're my second-in-command. Under you are the blacks, the most loyal, most hardworking army in the world. Growing tobacco is easy compared to cane and cotton. No whips are needed: I look after my troops. They're well-fed – well-fed and happy. They multiply like rabbits – a sure sign of contentment. Occasionally we get a bit top-heavy and some of the young men have to be sold down the river. Unpleasant business – the mothers make a fuss. But it soon blows over. You'll take to it like a duck to water.'

In other circumstances, Peader was thinking as he listened and

125

looked at Paul, I wouldn't have known you. You'd have been 'one of them'. I'd have seen you passing to and from a Big House, as one of the family or guest. I'd have dismissed you as 'one of them' – a runty little man, foxy-looking with your reddish hair and sharp features, a little *siofra* of a man.

In other circumstances I'd not have known of your generosity, gentleness and the good manners of you to everyone, be he crew member, Captain of the boat or Jake. But man – there's an awful want in you, in anyone whose stomach doesn't turn at the thought of owning another man. A crassness that lets you talk of 'the mothers make a fuss', when their sons are sold down the river. Giving it no more thought than the parting of calves from cows.

Paul was now noticeably drunk and airing his views on the secret of how to live. 'Life', he said, 'shouldn't be taken too seriously. Living is for enjoying.'

'So long as you're not harming anyone else,' Peader said.

'Definitely not – never hurt anyone else.'

For the want of something else to say Peader talked about marriage, asking Paul if he was contemplating it.

'Good God, no – a wife's the last thing I want.'

'But with the property wouldn't you be wanting an heir?'

'Some day, maybe – but that's the least of my worries. When I'm gone it's all the same to me who inherits – so long as it's a blood relation and there's plenty of them.'

A strange man, Peader was thinking as he rose to leave. Generous and likeable but not much foundation there. All in all he wasn't someone whose friendship he would have sought. And he promised himself that his job on the plantation would be a very temporary one.

His journey to Yorktown was uneventful. There he boarded the river boat to take him up the James and home to Charlotte. His ponderous, tortuous thoughts were banished as he anticipated their reunion. The disgust he felt each day as he rode about the plantation, his embarrassment at the service he received from the negroes, from Jake in particular, who appeared to have a great affection for him – all these were put aside. He was going back to Charlotte, whom he loved more and more each day.

And then suddenly Katy came into his mind. Katy as she was the night he went to see her. In that first instant when he stepped into the room it was as if they had never parted. As if he was seeing her in her mother's kitchen when he came courting. His beautiful golden-haired girl. So strong had been the feeling that he wanted to go to her, take her in his arms and smother her with kisses. So strong had been the urge that he had had to look away, as if he was looking round the room.

Smother her with kisses indeed, he smiled sardonically. There in the room with her husband and children. Me, do that. Me, that hadn't the passion, the sense or the courage to smother her with kisses when she was single and promised to me . . . Katy was a beautiful woman, a fiery, daunting woman. He could never forget her completely. Though he knew that he had never been the man for her. Katy needed a man like Jamsie – they were made for each other. It had taken years for him to realize that.

Lovely Katy and her lovely family. He wished them well. He would help them. He and his beloved Charlotte would help them. Please God they would prosper in America. Please God this visit wouldn't be the last he would see of them. He closed his eyes and tried to doze, but as he was about to drift into sleep he heard again Jamsie's contemptuous voice. 'You of all people running slaves. Peader Daly, the great man for the people's freedom – you with a plantation of black men and women bought and sold like cattle.' He gave up the attempt to sleep and concentrated on his meeting with Charlotte.

Charlotte had also given up the attempt to have her afternoon siesta and her thoughts, like Peader's, were on their reunion. She hoped the meeting with Jamsie wouldn't have filled his mind again with the injustices of slavery. Why couldn't he see that the negroes on Paul's plantation were happy and carefree. The field hands had cosy log cabins and the ones who worked in the house were treated like the family.

Peader could be very tiresome about the negroes. The number of times she had pointed out how much better off they were than Papa's tenants had been, even though he was a good landlord. His answer to that was always the same – 'at least your father didn't own them.' Which of course was true – but what difference did that make? Surely the negroes didn't go round thinking all the time that Paul owned them.

Poor Peader, he wasn't happy in Virginia. She loved it. The marvellous climate, all there was to do. The social life reminded her of what Kilgoran must have been like before all the money was lost. The parties and balls, picnics and receptions. Exactly how Hannah and the servants described the times in Ireland, except that here the weather was so gorgeous.

She sighed and stretched in the enormous silken bed. Sometimes, when Manty came in the mornings with her breakfast, for an instant

127

after opening her eyes she would think she was dreaming. That any minute the lovely bright room, the furnishings and hangings, the round-faced smiling black girl and the smell of newly-baked rolls and coffee would vanish, and her shabby room in Kilgoran House, damp and dreary, the fire smoking, the once-exquisite curtains faded and threadbare, everything decaying from age, lack of care and money, take its place. Instead of Manty with her gleaming teeth and merry eyes there would be poor old Hannah stiff and breathless from her climb up the stairs, urging her to be a dote, to sit up now and eat her porridge before it went cold. Placing before her on a tarnished, silver tray the grey oatmeal, the pallid, thick cuts of soda bread, the strong bitter tea on which the milk had already formed a skin.

That seldom happened now. She was used to her good-humoured Manty, to her black face and even her different body odour. She wondered why the negroes smelled different, not unpleasant only different. They were very noisy, not at all like Irish servants who never raised their voices in the house. She remembered when she first came hearing what sounded like a furious quarrel in the kitchen. When she went to see what was happening there they were, laughing and shouting, everyone in good humour.

Everything was so different. She was so different. Who would have thought so much change could have happened in two years. She didn't want to keep thinking. She wanted to go to sleep, forget that Peader was coming back. Forget that she must carry on deceiving him. She closed her eyes and tried to think of nothing. But her mind was full of images, full of questions to which she knew there were no answers, for often of an afternoon if Peader was around the place and Paul couldn't come to her, the images prompted the questions to which she had no answers.

What would have happened if they hadn't met Paul at Liverpool? Would she and Peader have settled in New York? Would she have been happy? For how much longer could she go on deceiving Peader? Why hadn't she stopped Paul kissing her that second time? Was she happy? On and on went the questions in her mind and to only one did she know the answer. She *was* happy, happier than she had ever been in her life. And she wasn't sleepy, so she might as well give herself up to her thoughts. Relive again the first time Paul had kissed her . . .

There was a reception and she was introduced to a very old woman. Long, long ago the woman had been a guest in Kilgoran House and now, sixty or seventy years afterwards, she confused Charlotte with an aunt or great-aunt whose name had also been Charlotte. It was very sad, really, listening to this frail old woman. 'Didn't we have such wonderful

128

times, my dear. I remember you were rather keen on Johnny. Whatever became of him? But the weather spoiled everything. Remember how it rained?'

Feeling sorry for her, at first Charlotte had humoured her, inventing answers about what had become of Johnny, remembering the dreadful weather. Then the old woman began contradicting her, quibbling about Johnny, about the rain and when she couldn't think of any more answers becoming quite belligerent. Charlotte was alarmed and signalled to Peader that she wanted rescuing. Peader must have misunderstood, for he did nothing, but fortunately Paul had spotted her plight and came to the rescue.

Charmingly, he disengaged her from the old woman. Once out of earshot they both agreed that there were pleasanter ways of spending the time than pretending to be a ghost. 'Let us walk by the river,' Paul said. They hadn't gone very far before he stopped, turned her to him and kissed her. 'I've been wanting to do that since I first saw you,' he said.

'You fibber,' she said, wiping away the kiss. 'You big fibber, you hardly noticed me when we first met.'

'Ah,' he said, 'you're talking about London. True, I didn't then. You were a child, now you're grown up.' He went to kiss her again.

'No,' she said. 'You mustn't. I am different. I'm married. Take me back, please.'

'Very well,' he said, giving her his arm. 'Never again, I promise. And I'm sorry, but you did give me the impression you wouldn't object to a kiss or two.'

'When! When did I ever do that?'

'Frequently.'

'If I did it wasn't intentional, honestly. I wouldn't even know how to do such a thing. I've never kissed anyone in my life except Peader. He's my husband. I love him.'

'If you say so – but I sometimes wonder.'

'What a dreadful thing to say. What a *stupid* thing to say. You don't know anything about me. London doesn't count and we've hardly been here two weeks.'

'All right, all right, don't get so upset.'

'I am upset. It wasn't a very nice thing to say, either about me not loving Peader or the other thing.'

'You didn't object to the first kiss – why not?'

She was now so mixed up she didn't know what to say. She was more excited than indignant. Paul had that effect on her. Paul had all sorts of effects on her. By a word he could lift her out of bad humour, make her laugh, make her want to touch him. But surely she hadn't ever made any of it obvious? But finding his company so agreeable had nothing to do with her loving Peader

'Charlotte. Look at me, Charlotte. I'm truly sorry for kissing you and for what I said. And of course you love Peader. Now shall we forget all about it and go back to the reception.'

But she couldn't forget any of it, neither his accusation that she had led him on, the kiss, but most of all that he should doubt she loved Peader. It was a monstrous suggestion and for days afterwards she avoided Paul and when they were in each other's company behaved with such correctness, in a manner so different from her usual outgoing self that Peader noticed and asked if anything ailed her.

Kind, sweet Peader, always concerned with her welfare. No, she had said, nothing ailed her. But something did, something she couldn't explain to Peader. Since the day Paul had kissed her and questioned her love for Peader she herself had begun to think.

She looked at the clock. Soon Manty would come to wake her from her afternoon nap, bringing a tray of tea. Reminding her that Peader would be home before long. And again she wondered what effect the visit to New York would have had on him. No doubt he would talk about leaving Annilaun and again she would have to use all her wiles to persuade him to stay. She wanted to spend the rest of her life here.

Oh, yes, Paul had made her think. Sending her thoughts back years to when she first fell in love with Peader. Reinforcing the love she felt for him. They were meant for each other, her and Peader. That's what Hannah and the other servants used to say at home. How often she had heard them. Marriages were made in Heaven. There was a man for every woman – and find you he would, even if you were hiding under the bed. And even though she was scarcely more than a child one part of her mind rejected what they were saying for superstition and foolish nonsense. For if there *was* a man for every woman, who found you wherever you were – why were so many of the servants old maids? But good manners, affection for the women and a half-belief in their pishogues prevented her asking the question.

And often she saw their beliefs come true. People who were dying, miraculously made better with only a lucky charm, a holy medal, water from a blessed well bringing them back from death's door. And had she wanted more proof, didn't Peader come to the secret place, the place where no one else ever came and where she had gone to paint a picture of the holly bush as a surprise present for Papa? For years, at all seasons she had gone there and never had anyone else set foot in it. And then on this day, into it walked Peader, they smiled at each other and fell in love.

What could Paul know of a love like that? Of the kisses they exchanged, of the words Peader spoke to her. His little brown bird, he called her. For hours and hours she recalled their courting. Relived the day her father discovered them together and had forbidden Peader ever to see her again. Ordering her to mount behind him, he had ridden home and imprisoned her in her room. Making Hannah take away all her clothes. And she almost died of a broken heart. Not able to eat, not able to swallow and Hannah fearing she was going into a decline got word to Peader and he wrote to her and the letter was smuggled in. He would take her away, he wrote. But first she must make herself strong. She must eat and then together they would flee and spend the rest of their lives together.

She didn't want to remember the night they had eloped. The sound of the shot as she crept down the stairs. Hannah urging her to go, telling her it was only a farmer shooting a mad dog. The dogs were mad with the Hunger. People said they ate human remains. No, she didn't want to think about that or the night . . .

Hidden beneath a pile of turf she and Peader had gone to Cork. The cart bumped over every rut in the road, and she cried until at last she fell asleep. Crying because she was deceiving her father and crying because she and Peader were at last free to love each other for always.

And Paul tried to make her doubt her love for Peader. Of course, nothing could be as thrilling as the sweet secret meetings. Nothing as intriguing as the letters that went between them with Katy and Jamsie carrying them, the constant fear that they might at any minute be discovered, and Peader banished from Kilgoran. She had been in a ferment all the time. She didn't feel like that now. But she was twenty, a woman and married . . . it was only natural.

Their honeymoon was disappointing. That was no one's fault. The ship was so dreadful and the sea stormy. And she only thought it was a disappointment. Perhaps all honeymoons are like that. How could one know such a thing? If she had a Mama, or sisters to talk to, she might. But Olivia, the one most likely to know was dead and Catherine in India. In any case, she couldn't imagine talking of such things with Catherine.

Manty brought the tea and reminded her again that Peader was arriving tonight. 'I know,' Charlotte said, smiling at her. 'But I'm tired, I'll rest a while longer.'

The ship's cabin was claustrophobic and she was sea-sick. That probably accounted for Peader being so solicitous. If she as much as sighed he wanted to know if he was hurting her. Poor Peader, he was still the same. She wished he was less serious, less reverent towards her. She wasn't his Virgin Mary. Of course she would never say that – he'd think that was blasphemy. She would never say anything to hurt him. He was very easily hurt. She loved him with all her heart. And Paul was a fool for suggesting otherwise.

She drank the tea and thought about the next time she had let Paul kiss her. She had really tried to be circumspect in his company. That wasn't easy. Paul had always been charming, always able to amuse her, make her feel more alive. And gradually she came to realise she was finding him more and more attractive. God knows it wasn't his looks. Paul was ugly. But there was something else. As if silent whispers went between them. Whispers that said, 'Look at me. I'm looking at you. I can see into your mind. I know what you're thinking. I know what you're feeling.' She received the silent whispers and with a blush, a toss of her head, a movement of her body sent back the silent answers. Sometimes the tension between them became unbearable and she made excuses to leave his company.

Then one day a letter came from Catherine telling of their father's death and its circumstances. It was on a day when Peader had ridden to see Jacques Demart who was about to sell his plantation. She was distraught with grief and guilt. Convincing herself that she had known when she heard the shot that her father had killed himself, and that because she cared more for Peader she had let Hannah persuade her otherwise.

Her crying had brought Manty to the bedroom. Manty became alarmed when she could not comfort her and told Paul. He came to the room. He made Manty bring brandy then sent her away. He held Charlotte in his arms and let her cry and listened to her outpourings of guilt. And he rocked her and stroked her hair and when her crying subsided he asked if he could read Catherine's letter. And after doing so, he made her listen while he re-read it to her.

You must never blame yourself for what happened to Papa. Although you weren't aware of it, his mind had been going for a long time. Long before there was anything between you and Peader. You must believe that, otherwise you'll burden yourself with a guilt which will destroy you. Poor Papa's guilt was partly to blame for his tragic death. Guilt at not being able to do more for his tenants. Charles's squandering of the estate didn't help, either. There were lots of things that tipped the balance of his mind. But Charlotte, darling, rest assured his poor mind was demented long before Peader came on the scene.

'Does that make you feel better?' Paul asked, as he put down the letter. It did, of course. Catherine would never say anything that was untrue. And she told him this, and that she was all right now and that he could go. Though she didn't want him to and he must have guessed. It was then that he kissed her for the second time.

And he stayed and he made love to her. And it was the most wonderful thing that had ever happened in her whole life. She forgot about Peader and being married and loving him. Only after a long time, when Paul slept, did she think of all that. She supposed she should have felt dreadful realising what she had done. But she didn't. She could only think how lucky she was. How if it wasn't for Paul she might have gone through her whole life never knowing such ecstasy existed.

Manty came again to take away the tea tray and to tell her Peader was at the jetty. Manty knew all about her and Paul. All the servants probably knew. That was another nice thing about the negroes – they weren't po-faced. Charlotte imagined Hannah's reaction if 'goings on' had happened in Kilgoran. Though come to think of it, they had. She remembered Olivia telling her how guests at house parties swapped rooms round. Then, of course, Hannah was in her place in the kitchen – not the general factotum she had become in her own rearing. But in any case, Hannah and the Irish servants would have disapproved. She smiled, thinking of them in the kitchen gossiping about the goings on upstairs, saying prayers for the souls of the sinners.

No doubt in the kitchen here they also gossiped, but of one thing she was sure – no one would pray for the souls of them that were sinning. They weren't judgmental – at least she didn't think so. Though sometimes she imagined that Jake, a thin scrawny negro devoted to Peader gave her a queer look.

'So how were they all in New York?' she asked, after Peader had hugged and kissed her.

Eagerly he told her the news of Jamsie and Katy. How delighted the children were with their presents. The love Katy sent. How she hoped one day soon they'd see each other again.

While he talked, Charlotte watched him and thought how handsome

133

he was. Much more attractive to look at than Paul, who was a shrimp of a man. She let her mind wander to the delights of lovemaking with Paul, came to herself and realised she hadn't heard half of what Peader had been saying. 'I'm sorry, darling, I slept so heavily this afternoon I feel stupefied. What was it you were saying?'

'That the place Katy and Jamsie have is desperate.'

'But a moment ago you said she had it very comfortable.'

'Oh, she has. Still it's not a fit place to rear children. It's on the Lower East Side where the immigrants settle. You've never seen such squalor. Years ago I lived in Dublin . . .'

'I remember you telling me – wasn't it after Katy had given you up for Jamsie?'

'Yes, well anyway, as I was saying I thought nowhere could be as bad as the Dublin slums – that was until I saw New York. Katy makes the best of it but it's a terrible life. Jamsie wouldn't admit to it but I think he misses the land. Maybe we could do something for them.'

'Such as what?'

'Maybe bring them here.'

'Are you mad? Bring them here! New York may be dreadful but at least they're with their own kind. Who would they have here – blacks and poor whites.'

'Wouldn't they have us?'

The innocence of him, the kindness and the goodness. It was one of the things she loved and admired about him. She didn't want to be brutal. She didn't want to spell it out, that Katy and Jamsie were peasants. They could never live as a happy foursome.

'Darling, it wouldn't work.'

'Why wouldn't it?'

'Well, for one thing Peader, you are always on to me to leave Annilaun. For us to go away from Virginia. You hate it here.'

'I know, but I agreed the last time we talked about moving to put it off for the time being.'

'And you'd want to uproot Jamsie and his family for the time being? You're too impulsive. How on earth would Katy and Jamsie live here?'

'They could work,' said Peader.

'At what? Have Katy washing vegetables for a black cook? We're living in Virginia – here the servants are black.'

'Well, maybe not Katy then – but Jamsie. There'd be something for him.'

'There wouldn't, Peader. There is no work for poor white men.' And she thought – no more than there would be for you, if Paul hadn't come

134

along. 'To bring them here would be the cruellest thing. I hope you didn't raise their hopes.'

'No,' said Peader, 'I didn't do that.'

'We'll help them, send them money now and then. Who knows, I may go to New York and see them. Katy was so good and so kind, I would really like to see her again. And I'm not being heartless. I can see by your face you think I am. That's because you're not a realist. Katy and Jamsie would be lost in Virginia.'

She was right, he knew. He wasn't a realist. On the way home he had imagined Katy and Jamsie as neighbours. Forgetting that most of the time he didn't feel welcome himself. Him with his connections and he didn't feel comfortable with Paul and Charlotte's friends. Wouldn't stay in the place for five minutes if it wasn't for Charlotte, who was terrified at the prospect of settling anywhere else. He had wanted Katy and Jamsie for company, not considering the reality of the situation.

He had to get out of Virginia. One day he would have enough money saved to take his wife somewhere else. He sorely missed having his own land. One day he would buy a farm. He and Charlotte would go far away, have their own home, a family like Katy and Jamsie and never again would he have to tell a black man what to do, however kindly it was done.

That night, Paul was away so only Charlotte and Peader sat down to dinner. 'This is what I like. This is what I want – just you and me in our own home. To eat our meals together, afterwards sit by the fire – just me and you.'

'Oh God,' Charlotte thought, 'he's starting again. How many more lies do I have to tell, how many more acts put on.' The last time the subject came up she had pleaded ill-health, the grief over her father – a move right now would upset her so much. It was a shocking thing to lie so often to your husband. It belittled him and made you aware of how dishonest you had become. Lying, scheming, cheating, anything so that she could remain close to Paul. It wasn't a very nice way to live. But live that way she would.

'Poor darling,' she said, 'you've been so patient and I'm very selfish. I can't plead ill-health any more and I would love to please you. We must have our own home. A lovely sweet little house. Little I mean compared to this. I'll soon get used to the difference in size. After all, most people live in smaller houses, but I will miss servants.'

'You could have one or two to help.'

'Only if you lived cheek by jowl. I couldn't bear that. I couldn't have borne that at home – imagine what it would be like – a black woman in the next room.' Peader didn't answer that and Charlotte continued, 'But don't worry, I'll manage. I'm very capable and learn quickly. In no time I'll be able to cook and clean.' Her voice broke and her eyes filled with tears. 'And when we have a baby,' she sobbed, 'I'll be a wonderful mother.' She broke down and cried convincingly. 'Oh Peader, I'm such a little fool. I'll have to go and lie down.'

She got up from the table. So did Peader and went to her. 'Don't cry, I didn't mean to make you cry.'

She wiped her eyes and smiled tremulously. 'I'm all right, really I am. I'm not unhappy about leaving Annilaun. It's just that I'm so silly.'

Peader held her close. His little bird, how fragile she felt. How small and delicate.

'I was such a flibbertigibbet, wasn't I? All the time I spent in the kitchen with Hannah and never learned how to roast beef or truss a fowl. Not even how to wet a cup of tea. Imagine that, Peader. Can you believe it? I spent all my time day-dreaming or sketching and painting.'

Peader remembered the day he had come upon her in the little wood, her easel set up, painting the holly, the day he fell in love with her.

'Not even a cup of tea,' Charlotte repeated. 'I suppose I thought life would never change. Always there would be Hannah or Katy, always someone to take care of me. But you'll see – I can change – I'll learn how to do everything. Only you'll have to be patient with me. Poor Peader,' she began to cry again, 'what an awful useless wife I am.'

'Hush, astoir, you're no such thing. You're my precious brown bird and I love you.'

'Oh, but I am a foolish, foolish girl. Shouldn't I have realised when I married you that life couldn't be as it was. Shouldn't I have known that we'd live in houses that weren't like at home. That we'd live as ordinary people do and I'd have to work like ordinary women.' She left his arms, walked to the long window and stood gazing out.

Looking at her, at the cloud of soft brown hair falling round her narrow shoulders, the dejected stoop of them, Peader was overwhelmed by a feeling of love and protectiveness and consumed with guilt that he had taken her from her father's house and, had it not been for Paul's generosity, she would now be in a Boston or New York tenement. She, that had been reared a lady and he would have brought her to that. And now to satisfy his ego he wanted, when as yet he didn't have the means to provide her with a fitting home, to take her from here where she was happy and comfortable.

His little bird. His little brown bird that had been reared in the freedom of a great house and he wanted to cage her. He mustn't. He wouldn't. What difference did it make that they stayed in Annilaun for a while longer. They didn't intrude on Paul's life nor he on theirs. He must never do anything to cause her pain. He must never forget all she had sacrificed for him. 'Charlotte,' he said, his voice hoarse with emotion. 'Charlotte, I was hasty. For the time being we'll say no more about moving.'

She turned from the window, her big brown eyes still wet with tears. 'Oh, my love,' she said, coming to him. 'Oh, my love,' she said, again laying her face on his breast, her head beneath his chin so that he didn't see her smile.

It was Christmas before they heard from Peader again. 'Not before time,' Jamsie said when the letter arrived. 'Weeks and weeks ago you wrote thanking him for the money he left.'

Katy made excuses. Peader probably had a lot to do and Miss Charlotte was no doubt kept busy.

'Arranging her flowers and him riding his plantation. Will you never get sense!'

'You know well it's not *his* plantation and after all, Miss Charlotte *is* a lady.'

'A woman she was while courting him and you acting to go-between –but eaten bread is soon forgotten. Tell us what he has to say.'

She opened the letter and saw that it was only a note and that Charlotte hadn't included a line. 'Read it yourself,' she said, handing over the note, after scanning it.

'What's that you have in your hand – more money?' asked Jamsie as he took the note.

'Fifty dollars to buy presents for the children.'

'Fifty dollars! I'm telling you, Peader fell on his feet when he met the man from Virginia. What's the matter with you, why are you looking so down in the mouth?'

'It's an insult – charity, that's what it is. I don't want their money. I'd have thought more of a real letter, a word from her. What do I care about it being the Year of Revolutions, Austria occupying the Italian States, trouble in France. The Young Irelanders seizing their chance. What do I care about any of that. All I wanted . . .'

'God, haven't you the grand memory, word for word what he's written.' Jamsie handed back the letter. 'You're right – he's more flawhool with money than words.'

137

'I wouldn't spend a penny of it, not a penny. I'll send it back, that's what I'll do.'

'Send it back? Have you lost your mind?'

'I will so. I don't want their charity. Five or ten dollars I'd have said nothing about – but fifty – wouldn't touch it. Back it'll go and a letter with it telling them what I think of them.'

'Write the letter if it satisfies you, but hand me the money for I've no objection to it. Money's money, never an insult. I'll soon make short work of it.'

She knew it was Jamsie's way of trying to get her out of bad humour. But it wouldn't work. She was hurt, bitterly hurt to be palmed off with the dollars instead of a nice letter. One that mentioned the children as if he remembered them, not just, 'Buy something for them.' A letter that included her, a word from Charlotte. No matter how busy she was a few lines wouldn't have killed her.

'Of course, if you're serious about the money I can't stop you. But in that case I'd say you should send back the rest.'

'What rest?' asked Katy.

'The hundred dollars he left on his visit – the money you're keeping for the laundry.'

'But that's different.'

'Yerra woman, it is not. It's money from the same man. And when you got that you never stopped blessing him for a week. Send it all back.'

'I suppose you're right.' Hastily Katy added, 'I don't mean about sending it all back.'

Jamsie laughed. 'I didn't think you did. And don't judge him so harshly – generosity it is, not an insult or cold charity. You know Peader better than that. And don't mind me about riding his plantation and her doing the flowers. That's all talk, no more. Peader's the genuine article. Wasn't he the first to write? Didn't he come all the way to see us?'

'He did so,' said Katy. 'God forgive me for the cruel thoughts – I was hurt for a minute, that's all.'

'I know you were. And she could have sent a line and his note could have been longer. But when all's said and done sure they're under no obligation to write at all'

'No obligation at all,' agreed Katy.

'And so you'll keep the money?'

'I will,' she said. 'I'll buy something for the children and we'll have a fine Christmas.'

138

'And after it I'll write to him. Maybe I'll even apologise for the way I took him up on his visit. In some ways he was right.'

'Right about what?' asked Katy.

'About the numbers flocking into the country. About the aggravation they can cause. There's them that haven't been here five minutes and they know it all. What's best for America, what should be done and what shouldn't. And if that rises me that's a newcomer, then I feel sorry for the Americans.'

'He'd be delighted to hear from you. He won't be wanting an apology – for doesn't he know you well enough. A letter will do fine. And please God there's plenty of time for us all to meet again.'

'Tell me this,' said Jamsie. 'What's happening about your plans for this laundry?'

'I'm waiting for the shop on Cow Lane to become vacant.'

'Isn't there plenty of other lock-up shops and shops with rooms to let as well?'

'There is, but I've my heart set on that one. I like it. I think it's lucky.'

'Not for the bootmaker.'

'Don't be discouraging me, you. I've got a feeling that he'll go in the New Year. So don't you say another word.'

After Christmas she went to the shoemaker's shop for laces she didn't need. She wanted to see if there was any sign of him packing up. There wasn't much stock. It was a good sign and she wished she had the courage to ask outright if and when the man was thinking of leaving. But it seemed not only prying but heartless.

The man took down the laces, then reached for another pair. 'I only wanted the one pair,' said Katy.

'Take them for a present. You've been a good customer. The only one this week. Here, take three lots – I'm going. To my cousin in Boston. There, he tells me, people mind their footware.'

'Thanks very much, you're very kind. Let me pay you for the first pair. When are you going?'

'On Friday I close for the last time.

'Do you know if anyone's after it?'

'After what?' asked the man.

'The shop. Is anyone renting it? Only you see,' and then she blurted out all about the laundry and how her heart had always been set on Cow Lane.

'You put the evil eye on me, so?'

139

'Oh no,' Katy protested. 'Oh, I wouldn't do that. When I first came in here you told me business was bad and . . .'

'I am, how do you say, joking you. I will tell you where the landlord lives. Go and see him. But first you see the shop, the shed.'

It was all she wanted; a place for washing and drying, tons of room, everything she could wish for. Part of the shop she'd partition off, and keep the other half for receiving and handing out the finished work.

'Say a prayer now that I get it,' she said to the man, and in her joy and excitement reached and kissed the side of his face.

Chapter Twelve

'Eileen, wait'll you hear! Eileen!' Katy went running up to Eileen's room, calling as she went.

Warned in advance of her arrival Eileen had the door open. 'Come in,' she said. 'I can see by your face it's good news. Sit down and tell me.'

'I wanted you to be the first to know. After all your help, with the rent in the beginning, and then helping me move to the lock-up shop, I wanted you to know first.'

'Then tell me for the love of God.'

'I've got the rooms, the three of them. Oh Eileen, isn't that marvellous? The family there is moving out next week. Three rooms and the shop underneath – I won't know my comfort, can you believe it?'

'You deserve it and all the luck to go with it. Though I won't pretend I'm glad. This place won't be the same without you.'

'I'll only be round the corner – we'll still see each other every day. Be glad for me.'

'For you I am, of course I am – but all the same I'll miss you. What are the rooms like?'

'Dog boxes – a big one partitioned into three. But Thomas and Bridget are growing so I'll need them. I can't believe my luck. It seems too good to be true. First the shop, then Jamsie getting the constant job. He's on that big block of offices, years he said that'll last, and now the rooms.'

'Wait'll Mary hears, she'll be lepping. Wait'll she starts telling me for the umpteenth time about Herr Jalger and his lock-up shop and how he may be moving out of the house. Just wait. I'll let her finish and then tell her your news. Her jaw will drop.'

Katy laughed. 'You make her out to be a terrible woman and she's not.'

'I know she's not, but she is a begrudger. She doesn't mind the Jalgers getting on, they're foreigners, but one of her own, and one that came over with her – for them to get on, that she can't bear. Look at the

141

way she changed her mind about Kathleen and the school once she knew Bridget could read.'

'You're being hard on her, Eileen. She's a defenceless woman without a man.'

'Defenceless me arse! And I wouldn't be surprised if she gets a man before I do.'

'I didn't know you were looking,' said Katy.

Eileen laughed. 'Don't mind me – I'm in bad humour at the thought of you leaving. And venting my spleen on Mary does me good. But I'm serious about her and a man. Leave it to the quiet wans. Them's the sort men want for a wife, especially the second time around. I'm telling you, Mary will finish up with a nice comfortable widower.'

'And what's the matter with you, miss? You haven't said a word since you came in.'

'Nothing,' said Bridget.

'Don't answer me like that.'

'She was in trouble. Miss Cook says she's lazy.' When Bridget reached to hit Mary Kate, Katy stopped her. 'It's true,' Mary Kate taunted. 'She's always in trouble and serves her right!'

'Go from the table this minute.'

'That's not fair – I did nothing.'

'Don't have me to tell you again. Down and mind the shop. Now,' said Katy when the door closed behind Mary Kate, 'what's all this about trouble in school?'

'Nothing,' said Bridget.

In a minute, thought Katy, I'll lash out and hit her. I don't know what's come over her lately, never a civil answer out of her. Never a meal do I sit down to that she isn't the cause of a scene. 'Don't say "nothing" to me again. Mary Kate isn't a taleteller, nor a liar. You must have done something in school and to her as well. I want to know the truth.'

'I hate school and I hate Mary Kate.'

'Since when? You were the best in the class – the best reader, the best at sums. Miss Cook said you'd make a teacher one day.'

'Well, I'm not now and I don't want to be a teacher. I'd hate to be a teacher.'

'Tell me about it. What happened? Something must have happened.' When Bridget didn't answer Katy turned to Thomas. 'What do you know about this? You're all in the same classroom. What trouble was Bridget in?' Thomas looked away from his mother's eyes. 'Don't do that, I'm talking to you! Tell me what happened.'

142

'That's not fair – why do I have to say?'

'Because I asked you,' said Katy.

'I was in trouble for talking back,' said Bridget.

Thomas looked relieved and went back to a catapult he was making.

'I told you never to talk back to the teacher, never to talk back to any grown up.'

Bridget shrugged. 'She said I was lazy. I told her I wasn't. I said it wasn't my fault that Kathleen and Mary Kate knew the answers to everything. And she said it *was* my fault – if I wasn't lazy I'd be the best in the class. So I said I didn't care. I was going to leave school anyway.'

Katy was flabbergasted, not only by what Bridget had told her but by her air of defiance. She didn't know what was the best way of handling this situation. 'Did you apologise?' she asked, while her mind thought of what else to say.

'Why should I? I didn't do anything.'

'But you did, love. You didn't know the answers and then you were cheeky. Were you slapped?'

'I wasn't.'

'You should have been. I'm surprised at Miss Cook, four or five good slaps you deserved. And don't look at me like that or you'll get them yet.'

'I want to leave school.'

'You'll do no such thing. The only place you're leaving is the table. Go down to the shop and send Mary Kate up here to me.'

'I hate the shop too,' Bridget said as she left the room.

'Now,' said Katy, wagging a finger at Mary Kate, 'I want you to sit down there and tell me exactly what happened in school today.'

'Bridget laughs and talks all the time and then she gets mad if me or Kathleen know the answers, and coming home from school she hits me and calls me a dwarf. She can really hurt me, she's much bigger than me. She never hits Kathleen, only me.'

'How long has this been going on?'

'She hits me all the time.'

'I'll check her about that, but how long has she been getting into trouble for not knowing her lessons and cheeking the teacher?'

'For ages and ages. Can I go now, my friend's lending me a book.'

'And why couldn't you have told me that?' Katy asked Thomas when they were alone.

'I didn't want to get Bridget in more trouble.'

When she told him about Bridget Jamsie said, 'You forget she's nearly

143

fourteen. Out of school long ago you should have taken her. She'd be better off helping you in the laundry.'

It was a tempting idea. The laundrying and repairing kept her going from morning till night. Another pair of hands would be a Godsend, only that wasn't what she had wanted for Bridget. 'She's very bright. She'd make a grand teacher.'

Jamsie made a derisive sound. 'A teacher, is it? She'll be married before you know it.'

'She's only a child,' said Katy.

'And were you much older when we married? Don't be wasting your breath talking about teaching.'

'Please God she'll have more sense – she'll get an education first. But you're right – she's not a child any longer. My God, don't the years fly. It's five years since the time Peader came. I wonder how him and her are. Wasn't it a pity we lost touch.'

'What's that you said?' asked Jamsie, who hadn't been paying attention to Katy.

'I said wasn't it a pity we lost touch.'

'That was your fault, you were the letter writer.'

'Ah, it got harder and harder for me to answer letters meant for you. What comment could I make on the transportation of John Mitchell for his part in running the Young Irelanders' paper. The situation in Ireland and how Peader felt about slavery, things like that. Seldom a word about Miss Charlotte, about anything ordinary. A mention that Father Bolger had died, only that, not where or how or when. They were very hard to answer. All I could write about was the neighbour-hood, the laundry, whether you were in or out of work and I wouldn't do that in case he sent more money. You were the one should have done the answering.'

'I was never good with the pen,' said Jamsie. 'Maybe one of these days he'll come up for more silver and furniture. Where was it his friend lived?'

'Even after all this time you can't resist getting in the dart.'

'Sure I'm only codding – where was it your man lived?'

'Staten Island. I often think I'd like to go there. On a fine day you and me and the children – wouldn't that be lovely?'

'Aye,' said Jamsie, 'I'd say it would be nice right enough.'

Bridget wept bitterly when Katy told her she must stay on at school. 'But why, *why*? No one has to, you can leave any time you like. I didn't have to go in the first place,' she cried.

'You didn't. I could have let you all run the streets. I did it for your sake. I wanted you reading and writing.'

'You wanted me to be a teacher, that's all you cared about.'

'And was that a terrible thing to want?'

'I'd die sooner.'

'Please God you won't. And you won't be a teacher – you've seen to that. But you'll go to school and we'll have no more impertinence. It's many a long day since I laid hands on you – don't make me do it again.'

There were no more scenes. Katy hoped the change in Bridget was permanent. And she continued to save a small amount each week in case, by some miracle, Bridget might decide that after all she wanted to be a teacher. And Bridget made up her mind that no matter what happened she was going to work in a hat-shop the minute she left school.

The Jaegers had left Mulberry Street and rented a new shop with rooms over it. Ulla and Bridget were still best friends and better able to communicate now that Ulla could speak English fluently. Her father had made good progress with the language but Mrs Jaeger's English was no better than Katy's attempts at German. Ulla said it was shyness. At home in the house where she practised she could speak English well.

'I admire her courage,' Katy told her. 'I have great admiration for all of them who not only have a new country to contend with but a strange tongue as well. If it was me I'd have run mad out of it.'

'I think Mutti would also like sometimes to run mad out of it. But soon something good is to happen. The brother of my father is coming to America.'

'Well, I'm delighted. Nothing is nicer than to have your own living by you. Many's the time I wish I had a brother or sister to send for. The money that goes from here to Ireland to bring over relations – it must be millions.'

Ulla said it was also thus with the Germans, they sent for their relations. But her uncle had paid his own passage. He was a baker too, but he was going on after a few days in New York to settle in Chicago.

'That's a pity. Still, won't he be nearer there than in Germany?'

Katy was very fond of the Jaegers and particularly Ulla. She was a kind, well-mannered child. Bridget could do well to take a leaf out of her book. Though, thank God she was behaving herself and every day Katy waited for an announcement that she wanted to go to College. Ulla was a bright child, too, but the brightest of them all was Kathleen. It was seldom or ever she now came to call for Bridget. 'Blind she'll go,' Mary was forever complaining, 'for night, noon and morning her nose is stuck in a book.' And Katy thought when Mary complained that she wished she had the same complaint to make. And how you could misjudge people. Kathleen was growing into a nice girl, plain-looking –'as ugly as sin' was how Eileen described her. But she wasn't ugly, only plain. What the Americans called homely.

You had to take off your hat to the Germans. They were the hardest-working, cleanest people Katy had ever seen. Until she saw the Jaegers' rooms she was content with hers. But theirs were an eye-opener. The cleanliness and comfort – nothing like an Irish house. Lovely wool-embroidered cushions, nice mats, pretty curtains and always a clean cloth on the table. They were very particular about the table, it was laid properly even for a cup of tea. A very cosy, inviting home altogether. They were a lovely family and Mr Jaeger's bread couldn't be surpassed. And since he'd acquired the new bakery, for a few cents he'd roast your meat or a fowl at Christmas.

Bridget spent more time in their place than her own and was full of praise for Mrs Jaeger's cooking. Katy was forever telling her to refuse the food, for Mrs Jaeger had enough to do feeding her own family.

Bridget came home one day licking her lips, telling Katy she should have tasted Mrs Jaeger's cabbage.

'Cabbage? I have to force it down you.'

'It wasn't like yours – for one thing it was red, well more like purpley red.'

Katy said nothing. She was tired of comparisons between her cooking and the Jaegers'. In the beginning she had dismissed Bridget's suggestions that she should cook sauerkraut or dumplings shortened with marrow from beef bones. 'Dollops, plocky dollops,' Katy had said dismissively. Now it was purpley red cabbage.

'Will you try it, will you? It's gorgeous. I'd eat loads of it.'

'I'll do no such thing. How all them foreign people aren't poisoned with the stuff they eat, I'll never know.'

'Ah, go on try it.'

'I wouldn't like it, and neither would your father.'

'How can you say that if you've never tasted it?'

'I know, that's all.'

'You'll die in America never having tasted anything but boiled bacon and potatoes. Go on, try it, please.'

'Oh, all right. I suppose there'd be no harm trying it. Ask Mrs Jaeger how you do it, but remember, no more free meals.'

146

The next day Bridget brought home the recipe. 'Seven things, she said. A red cabbage, fat, sugar, apple, vinegar, cloves and a sup of water.'

Katy made a face at the idea of such strange companions for a head of cabbage. But after cooking the dish and tentatively sampling a little she admitted it wasn't bad. Tasting another bit, she said, 'Not bad, not bad at all. I could get to like that.'

Each time she tried a new dish she told Eileen and Mary about it, and if she had some spare let them try it. Eileen was adventurous and copied many of the new recipes. But Mary was a firm believer in boiled bacon, stewed mutton and a nice pot of broth.

In each other's homes where other Irishwomen also came they talked about America, how they were getting used to it at last, though nowhere was like Ireland. In America you were always on the go. Half a day you could spend in Ireland just talking to someone you met on the road. In America if you congregated for five minutes, less, on a path, you'd be pushed out into the middle of the road.

And there was no doubt the Americans were still down on the Irish. Still considered them dirty and drunken and the cause of all the crime, when in reality it wasn't crime at all – a few fights, a broken head amongst their own, a sup too much taken.

Even so, when the question was put to the women one day by Eileen, 'Would you go back home?' in turn after thinking about it each one said no. In America they felt there was opportunity – if not for them, then for their children. They had the education. They could be anything.

Although it was seldom Katy went far from her neighbourhood, she could now with ease find her way further afield. With no more thought than she would once have given to setting out for the chapel in Kilgoran she with Mary and Eileen would walk to Broadway and the Bowery. Or sometimes take the children to South Street and show them where their ship had docked. Though nowadays Bridget and Thomas seldom accompanied her, thinking themselves too big for outings with their mother.

Often, herself, Eileen and Mary reminisced about the first time they had gone far from Mulberry Street. The first time they had walked on Broadway. How the packs of dogs had frightened them and the pigs made them laugh. And they laughed again, remembering the things they had promised themselves when they grew rich in America.

'The eejits we were,' Eileen would say. 'Do you remember Katy, you wanted a big feather bed, a bolster, two soft pillows and a golden chain with an amber stone?'

'To match your eyes,' said Mary.

'I said no such thing. Amber to match my eyes, indeed!'

'You did not. I was only thinking your eyes are that sort of a colour. I was going to eat my way from one end of Broadway to the other. Me,' said Mary, 'that couldn't stomach anything they sell. It was the after-effects of the Hunger then, Eejits, that's what we were.'

'Innocent and ignorant – ah, but it was lovely. We had a great time. We laughed so much. And I was letting on being a Dubliner I knew it all, and inside I was like jelly.'

'Not half as shaky as I was,' said Katy. 'When you come to think of it, it was a terrifying experience. There we were, suddenly, in the middle of all that – the noise, the crowds, surrounded by buildings. At least, Eileen, you'd have been accustomed to some of it. But not me and Mary, out from little villages where in a day you mightn't see more than a dozen people and everyone you'd know.'

'A terrifying experience, that's what it was,' agreed Mary.

On their outings, Eileen always insisted on treating them to coffee or sweets and bought ribbons for the girls' hair. And Mary and Katy scolded her and said she should be putting by her money. Eileen laughed away their protests. 'Walking along here has the same effect on me as a couple of strong drinks. Everything seems possible. The feeling is all round me, do you know what I mean?' Katy and Eileen shook their heads. 'Jasus,' said Eileen, 'you're a real pair of culchies. You *have* to notice it – don't you feel the excitement? It's all round you. You feel strength pouring into you, as if you could live forever. It's fantastic – magic.'

'My feet do get very tired,' said Mary.

Later in the day when Katy and Mary were alone, Mary said, 'God love Eileen, isn't she very romantic and dramatic? 'Tis a pity she missed her chance that time in Dublin. She'd be grand on a stage.'

'Well, she is in a way,' said Katy.

'Ah, no, I didn't mean singing in a saloon, in a real theatre – that's where she should be.'

The audience of drunken men clapped, stamped their feet and shouted, 'More, more!' Nearly suffocated by the heat, smoke and the weight of her petticoat and green shawl, Eileen wished them, *Cockles and Mussels*, *Kathleen Mavourneen* and *The Meeting of the Waters* to Hell and back. But she knew her audience and employer, and more she'd have to give.

While she waited for the foot-stamping and clapping and roaring to subside she noticed a dressy-looking fellow sitting near the platform.

148

She caught his eye – he smiled and winked. He wasn't local, on that she'd take a bet. He'd never been in before – she wouldn't have missed him. Himself and the saloon-keeper had a bottle before them on the table and were knocking it back like water. That he was Irish she didn't doubt. He was good-looking as well. Very interesting, she thought, as the piano played the opening bars for her final number.

'Paddy Kavanagh. Paddy's from Galway – Eileen O'Flaherty – a jackeen.' The saloon-keeper made the introduction.

'You've a grand voice,' said Paddy, shaking hands.

You've a powerful grip, thought Eileen as she thanked him for the compliment.

'And you're a fine woman too,' Paddy said, his eyes on her breasts. 'Sit down, you'll have a drink.'

'Thanks,' she said as she sat and weighed him up. He was handsome in a barbered way. Black wavy hair well-sleeked. A bit on the heavy side. Plenty of gold flashing – a ring, watch-chain, even a tooth. She imagined him without the trimmings, no macassar keeping his waves in place, no jewellery, fine clothes or doctored teeth. She'd still find him attractive. More than any man she had met since Larry. She fancied him all right. All the signals were there, her heart thumping, excited, keyed-up inside.

The saloon-keeper said, 'Well, I'll leave you to it.' Eileen swallowed some of her drink and waited for Paddy to make the first move.

'You're a grand singer,' he said again.

'Not bad,' said Eileen.

'I'm looking for singers.'

'Are you, now? And what do you want singers for?'

'Listen,' said Paddy, moving closer. 'I have this idea. San Francisco's opening up. San Francisco's going to be *the* place. New York'll only be trotting after it. Everyone'll be clamouring for entertainment, theatres, music halls and I want to be in on that. I'll have the biggest and the best. I have it all planned out. I can see it here in my mind.' He tapped his forehead.

He was pleasant to sit close to, he smelled clean, and his breath wasn't foul. Yes, she could really fancy him. 'What's all that got to do with me?' she asked, trying to make her question casual.

'Everything, if you're interested. I'm going to get together a string of the loveliest girls. I could see you being Number One. I want to get away from the green shawl and red petticoat and the songs to make you cry. Leave Ireland alone, there's others in America besides the Irish. I want beautiful girls in gorgeous costumes. I want singers, dancers. There's a fortune in it.'

149

Eileen's head was spinning. She could see all he was describing. In her mind's eye she saw the stage with herself on it, heard the clapping, saw the audience stand to their feet as she had seen them do from her seat in the Gods in Dublin theatres. Standing and clapping and calling 'Encore, encore'. She took another sip of her drink and composing herself asked, 'And when is all this going to take place?'

'I'll tell you no lie. First I have to find the money, get backers.'

I might have known it, thought Eileen. 'Tis only his approach is different from the oul fella in Dublin. I'm an eejit, only I've learned my lesson and he's not getting into my bed on that story. I fancy him all right – but I can't stand deceit.

'It might take a while. I expect I'll be on the road trying to drum up the money for maybe three months or so – but I'll be back.'

'I'll still be here. When you come back I'll let you know.'

'All right, so,' said Paddy. 'Now, have another drink and I'll be off.'

He was either honest, having her on, or playing a hand she hadn't met before, Eileen felt as he stood up, bade her goodnight and left.

She couldn't sleep for ages. Thinking, wouldn't it be great if he was telling the truth . . . if he came back in three months and had it all fixed up. She should have given him her address, asked him to let her know how things were going. Of course he could always find her through the saloon. Tomorrow she must try and find out more about him when she went to work.

'To tell you the truth,' said the saloon-keeper when Eileen enquired about Paddy Kavanagh, 'I know nothing about him except what he told me last night. Why?'

'He spun me a yarn about getting together a crowd of girls for dancing and singing – to take out to San Francisco. He said there's fortunes to be made out there.'

'That'd be no lie. Fortunes there is to be made right enough in San Francisco.'

'If I thought he was genuine I wouldn't mind going.'

'And leave the grand job you have here? Sure, you're the toast of the place.'

'Them fellas,' said Eileen, 'would clap a monkey.'

'Only if it sang Irish songs.'

Eileen laughed. 'If you hear any more about Paddy Kavanagh, let me know.'

'If it's anything bad I surely will.'

'Seriously, try and find out if he's genuine.'

'I'll keep my ears open,' promised the saloon-keeper.

A couple of weeks later he told Eileen that he'd heard from another Galway man that Paddy was single and had had an interest in the theatre since he came to America.

'Are you sure he's single?'

'I've no reason to doubt it. The fella from Galway said it without me making enquiries or mentioning your name. It came out natural like. "Paddy Kavanagh," says he when I put the question. "I know Paddy well, a decent man, fond of a drop, but isn't he single and free to spend his money how he likes".'

She was satisfied he didn't have a wife. And with the help of God the rest was also true. Three months, he'd said. She began counting the days. And she told Katy of her hopes and that Paddy could be the man in her life.

'Every man I've met I compared with Larry and no one measured up. But I took to Paddy straight away. I know I've only seen him the once, but I have a feeling he's the one for me.'

Katy was glad for her and said so, though she thought it was hasty of Eileen having only laid eyes on him the once. Then she remembered how it had been with her and Jamsie – a glimpse and that was all it took.

Sometimes weeks passed without Katy giving a thought to Ireland. Then when it came to her mind and she realised how much time had lapsed since she last felt homesick, she thought – I'm settling, and was glad. Her children and Jamsie were well, her health good, she had many acquaintances, her close friends Eileen and Mary still living in Mulberry Street and her business was prospering.

New American women came to the laundry. At first they seemed distant, not as friendly and talkative as the Irishwomen. But they were polite and great payers. Never any excuses about not having the right money, forgetting their purse or paying on the double next week. And when at last one recognised her in the street she felt now she belonged in America. Another stopped her one day and they chatted. Then the woman asked her did she read much. Katy said she seldom had time to do more than glance at a paper. 'Well ma'am,' said the woman, 'I'd recommend you find time to read *Uncle Tom's Cabin*.' Katy looked blank and the American went on, 'It's a story every Christian man and woman should read. I'm telling everyone about it. You read it. Give it to your children.'

'Where would I get it and what is it about?' asked Katy.

'It's the story of what is going on in the South. The selling of men, the

151

breaking up of families. The buying and selling of human beings as if they were animals. The abomination of slavery – that's what it's about. A good woman wrote it.'

Katy didn't think it was the sort of book she would like but out of politeness asked again where she could get it. And the woman told her it was published monthly in a newspaper. 'I have the back numbers. I'll drop them into the laundry.'

'Do,' said Katy, 'I'd be delighted with them. And thanks very much for telling me.'

'I'll drop them by tomorrow.'

'I'll read them,' Katy promised, thinking there was no harm in the lie. The next night, out of curiosity she glanced at the serial and liked it. When Danny was in bed she settled down to read it.

'What are you reading, Mammy?' Thomas asked. She told him about *Uncle Tom's Cabin.* 'Is it only a story?'

'It's a story – but the things really do happen. The black people are bought and sold.'

'Wouldn't that be a sin?'

'A terrible sin, Tom.'

'You'd be sent away from your mammy and daddy and everyone and never see them again. Wouldn't that be the terrible thing. I'm glad I'm not a slave.'

'Would you like me to read it to you?'

'I would,' said Thomas.

'And me,' said Mary Kate. Bridget showed no interest, but eventually came to look forward as eagerly as the others to the nightly instalments; she was moved to tears and said she'd pray for the poor black people. Mary Kate said she hated all those who owned slaves and Thomas after one reading said, 'Uncle Peader has a plantation, doesn't he?'

'He manages one.'

'There'd be slaves on it?'

'I suppose so,' said Katy.

'I hope he doesn't sell his slaves, not Uncle Peader.'

'I hope not,' said Katy.

The American woman asked Katy when next she came to the laundry how she had liked the book. Katy told her, and of how it had affected the children.

'What about your neighbours?'

'I didn't pass it on, not without first asking you.'

'Do,' said the woman. 'Pass it on by all means.'

'Well, what do you think of it?' Katy enquired of Mary after lending her the story.

'It's very sad right enough,' said Mary, 'but to tell you the truth it doesn't hold me.'

'And why is that?'

'Sure there's enough sadness in the world without reading about it.'

'But don't you think it's a terrible thing that's happening in the South – to those men and women?'

'God comfort them, yes I do – but sure what can me or you do about them? Isn't it taking all our time to fend for ourselves. You're better off not concerning yourself with it.'

When Katy told Eileen of Mary's response to *Uncle Tom's Cabin*, Eileen said, 'Why are you surprised? Sure, Mary thinks of no one but herself and Kathleen. Now, had it been a story of lords and ladies and great romances she'd have been glued to it.'

Remembering Mary's rapt attention when she had told the story of Peader and Charlotte, Katy said, 'You're right. I'll pass on no more of the instalments to her.'

She offered the serial to Jamsie to read. 'I know the facts,' he said, declining her offer. 'Isn't there constant reports in the papers of the agitation between the Abolitionists and the other lot that wants to keep slavery.'

'What about the men?'

'What men?'

'The ones you talk and drink with.'

' 'Tis little interest and less sympathy they have for the negroes.

"Let them stay where they are. Isn't there enough for us scraping for a living. Have the blacks flooding into New York and they'll work for nothing – then what happens to us?" That, Katy, is the general opinion amongst the Irishmen in the pubs, saloons and on the building sites.'

'You're sure Peader wouldn't have anything to do with it?'

'Of course I'm sure, and I wish you wouldn't keep asking the same question,' Charlotte said.

'Do I?' Paul looked surprised.

'Yes, you do – at least twice a week. I've told you before, Peader's too honest to be involved in anything illegal.'

'He doesn't consider slavery legal.'

'He doesn't approve of it. Morally, he thinks it's wrong but that doesn't mean he'd assist your slaves to escape.'

'Well, someone is, and Peader is suspected.'

'That's ridiculous. It could be anyone. Since that woman published her book, people have become hysterical.'

'Not people round here, not plantation owners.'

'Why should Peader be suspected?'

'Have you forgotten his ranting and ravings about the evils of keeping slaves?'

'That was years ago – when we first came. I soon put a stop to that. Told him how embarrassing it was for you and for me – and that it put him in a peculiar light. After all, he was making his living working on the plantation.'

'What did he say to that?'

'Peader is a very reasonable man.'

'Peader is a fool.'

'Why do you say that?'

'He must be, to put up with you.'

'You swine!' Charlotte beat at him with closed fists, pummelling him about the head and shoulders. He roared as if he was being hurt. Then captured her hands and pulled her down on top of him. 'I love you,' he said. 'I love you, especially when you get mad. Give me a kiss.'

'No.' She turned away her face and made him struggle to kiss her, then whispered, 'I love you, too.'

'And Peader,' he said.

'Yes, no. I mean – I love him but not in the way I love you.'

'You still let him make love to you?'

'I have to. Not often – I find more and more excuses – but sometimes I have to.'

'Have to?'

'Yes, have to. God knows you've made it plain enough you don't intend to marry me and I might get pregnant. And don't look so scandalised. I'm just being practical.'

Paul laughed. 'There you go, misreading my expression again. Nothing scandalises me. I was just thinking what a complex person you are. You'll let me make love to you anywhere except in your own bed, you defend Peader up to the hilt when I suggest he may be helping slaves to the North, you tell me you love him – and in the next breath that you'd foist my child on him.'

'I would,' said Charlotte. 'Anyway, it would be hard to tell whose child it was.'

'Touché,' said Paul. 'Do you think he suspects about us?'

'Not for an instant. He's not like you – he's decent and honourable.'

'And if he did?'

'You know, sometimes Paul, I think you are a bit dim. You've known him now for years and yet you know nothing about him. Peader isn't suspicious – to find out about us he'd have to walk in here while we were doing it.'

'I suppose then he'd shoot me.'

'Don't mock.'

'What would he do?'

'Walk away for ever. I should never have married him, never let myself believe I loved him. It was all so romantic and maybe I only know this with hindsight – a means of escape from Kilgoran. Poor Peader – I've ruined his life. He never should have left Ireland or at least he never should have settled here. He's got nothing, absolutely nothing.'

'He's got you,' said Paul and took her in his arms again.

Terence McCabe had graduated from tout to bondsman; he knew many of the minor City Hall officials, was now a personal friend of Kelly the saloon operator and a conscientious member of the Democratic Party, distributing hand-outs to the Irish poor, rounding them up on polling day. In return he received promises. One in particular he intended to see honoured. New York City was littered with manure. Selling it to the farmers on Long Island was a lucrative business – with that contract under his belt Terence knew he would be on his way.

Chapter Thirteen

'Mary, what in the name of God ails you? Here, sit down.' Katy shifted a parcel of laundry and gave the stool to Mary.

'May God forgive me for the careless woman that I am,' said Mary in a mournful voice.

'What's the matter, what's happened?'

'Only my poor unfortunate child starting The Others without a word of warning and getting the fright of her life.'

'Oh Mary,' Katy said with a mixture of relief and exasperation, 'I thought something terrible had happened. Kathleen will be all right and weren't you lucky it's Saturday after dinner and the pair of you at home.'

'I suppose so, but all the same it was very neglectful of me – the poor child. The likes would never have happened at home. An aunt or someone would have foreseen the happening and told her.'

'Yes, you're right – the thought never crossed my mind either and Bridget could start any day, too. You'll tell her for me?'

'I don't think I'd be much of a hand at it. Wouldn't you ask Eileen?'

'It might come better from you with Kathleen having them and you being a mother.'

'All right then,' said Mary. 'I'll do my best. When?'

'Through the week,' said Katy.

At the first opportunity Kathleen told Bridget about menstruation and that she had to go and see her mother after school to be enlightened.

'Why your mother and not my own?' asked Bridget.

'I guess because she'd be embarrassed. Mine nearly died.' They both laughed.

'Come in astoir,' said Mary when Bridget called for her instruction. Bridget handed over a washed and starched pinafore which Katy had used as the pretext for her going to Mary's.

She liked this room. It was always clean and neat and Mary had a collection of cheap pretty ornaments. One day she would have pretty things, lots of them and rooms nicer than anyone else's. She was going to find a job soon and her mother could holler all she liked. She wasn't going to be a monitor and years and years after, a teacher. She wanted a job and money and pretty things.

'You're growing into a fine girl, God bless you,' said Mary. 'I've coffee made, you'll have a cup?'

Bridget said, thanks, she would. And Mary foostered amongst the cups and saucers, trying to broach the subject of menstruation. 'Your mother's a grand woman. I hope you're kind to her. But of course you are. You're a good child. In no time at all now you'll be a woman, you and Kathleen.' Mary stopped talking while she poured the coffee. 'A fine girl, indeed you are. Taller than my Kathleen and look at your lovely hair. God bless it. A child you were when I first saw you on the ship. The years fly . . . as I was saying, you'll soon be a woman.' Bridget concealed her merriment, her head bent over the coffee cup, stirring and stirring. 'Yes, indeed. A woman – Kathleen's the same, grown you might say.'

Bridget drank her coffee straight down and stood up. 'Well, I'd better be going, I've another errand.'

Mary looked flabbergasted. 'No, not yet! Don't go, child – I've something to tell you. Sit down, have another cup.' Bridget refused but sat down. 'Your mammy asked me to say . . .' It was Mary who now paid all the attention to the coffee cup, unable to meet Bridget's eyes. 'Do you see when a girl grows up – well, it's like this. Things happen to her.'

'Do they? What things?' Bridget asked eagerly. 'What sort of things, Aunty Mary?'

Mary raised an embarrassed, flushed face and looked into Bridget's bright, bold eyes and lost her nerve. 'Maybe you'd better do the other message, sure I can tell you again.'

'Very well,' said Bridget, took her leave and hopped down the stairs, laughing as she went.

'And what did Mary have to say?' asked Katy when she arrived home at the shop.

'That I was a fine girl and had lovely hair.'

'Then how were you so long?'

'I had a cup of coffee.'

'And Mary said nothing else?'

'What else was there?'

'Nothing. I was just wondering, that's all.'

The following day Bridget was despatched to Eileen's with another message. Eileen's room was clean but always untidy and smelling of scent and cats. Clothes were piled on chairs, dropped on the floor as if she had just stepped out of them. Sometimes a cat would be sitting on them. One of the cats greeted all visitors by curling itself round their legs and purring, the other if approached made its face into a grotesque grin and spat.

'Come in,' said Eileen when she opened the door. 'I suppose you know already what I'm supposed to tell you?'

'I do,' said Bridget, and they both laughed.

'I thought you might. Kathleen, I suppose?' Bridget nodded. 'Then you'll have Mary's version – enough to put the fear of God in you. All the same, you shouldn't have made it so awkward for her.'

'She gets on my nerves.'

'At your age you shouldn't have nerves. There's another bit of advice you'd better heed: once you start, no messing around with the boys. You'll feel different about boys when you do start and them about you. So be warned – never let a fella touch you further down than your neck. Sometimes it's easy to forget in the heat of the moment – but you remember it. Forget my words and you get a baby. No one wants a baby unless she's married. So slap his hand away if it strays from your neck.'

Now it was Bridget's turn to be embarrassed but she tried not to let it show and promised she'd remember what Eileen had told her.

Dressed in their best, nervous, excited, hopeful and proud they sat on benches in City Hall and repeated after a judge the oath making them American citizens. The Jaegers, the Ginsbergs, Katy and Jamsie, other German and Irish families, Mary and Eileen, all had been five years in America. Afterwards they congratulated each other, then went on their way feeling that from now on they could hold their heads high.

Katy was giving a party to celebrate the occasion. There was an arrangement between the men about the drink and the women had sent loaves, cakes and plates of sandwiches. The Jaegers had given a cake and Katy thought it was a pity they couldn't have come. But their relations had arrived and they were having their own celebration.

Tonight, they were all Americans and for a few hours they'd make merry. Forget the stifling heat of the August night and the thunderstorm threatening. Forget that often they still felt bereft in America, that sometimes in dreams they walked the fields and shores of Ireland happy and secure, for the dreams were robbed of reality; in them were no grasping landlords or their agents, no famine fever, blight-blackened potatoes, no mass graves. Only the happy carefree times came to them in their dreams. Youth, and the sun always shining, the first kiss of boy or girl, the love of caring parents and friends.

But tonight was for celebrations. For the good things of America – money in the hand for work done. Opportunity for you and your children. And opportunity there was. Last week at the official opening of the new Catholic church the proof was there before your eyes. Their pennies and the large donations of those already prosperous had raised the church. There were the successful ones, the Ryans, the Bradys, Jemmy Doyle and Pat Fagan. Up in the front seat, thanked publicly from the altar. In their frock coats, with their tall hats resting on their knees and their wives and daughters decked in silks and satins, frills and flounces, feathers and flowers on their bonnets. And their husbands with big bellies straddled by gold chains and watches, and their side whiskers brushed and trimmed.

Outside the church they were sneered at and ridiculed in discreet voices, behind hands held over mouths. 'There's Mary Ellen, she lived next door at home. Came over on the same ship. 'Tis easy to see she'd be more at ease in her bare feet. The shoes are crippling her. Terrible pair of crubeens she has, as big as any man.'

'And bull-necked Ryan,' said another parishioner. 'Don't tell *me* he made his money honestly. A mansion he has, lace curtains on every window and a black woman in the kitchen.'

'So long as it's in the kitchen he keeps her.' This remark got a laugh. A thin, pious-looking man who had just received the Blessed Sacrament said, 'Every one of them's hand in glove with the crowd in Tammany Hall. The Tammany boys have the dishing out of contracts for public works – from building to selling manure. To get on you have to be in with them.'

Listening to the remarks, Katy had laughed with the others while thinking that one thing was sure and certain – Jamsie was well in with no one. Whatever strides they made would have to be without the assistance of Tammany Hall. Jamsie dismissed them all as a crowd of swindlers who granted one favour in return for another. Once in their clutches you were never out of them. He'd be beholden to no one. That, thought Katy, was all very well while he had the constant work – that he might keep it, she prayed silently.

The men were arriving. The single ones and an old widower came first. 'Katy girl, where's the tumblers?' Jamsie called.

She could hear the talk and laughter as she approached the room. It stopped when she entered. The men greeted her, told her she was

159

looking grand and asked how were the children. 'They'll be here in a minute and you'll see for yourself.' The widower Dan O'Brien, a Clare man, admired her blouse. His wife, he said, had been very fond of that colour green. Katy liked Dan. He was seventy or maybe more but still had a handsome face and bright blue eyes.

Immediately she left, the talking began again. Curious to hear what they were saying, she didn't completely close the door, but stopped and listened. Women, they were talking about. A voice describing one who could fight like a man, no clawing or scrawbing but squaring up with her fist and able to land a punch as well as any man. A powerful woman you'd be as well not to cross – and God help the man married to her!

Then another of the guests talked about the girl he hoped to marry. So far, he couldn't pluck up the courage to ask her. He was encouraged by all not to let the grass grow under his feet. There was a pause in the talking before Dan could be heard telling him he shouldn't lose time. Time was the precious thing. Recalling when he had first met his wife. The loveliest girl you ever saw.

'She had red cheeks and black hair with a curl to it. But through hesitating I nearly lost her – only thank God I didn't. But precious time was wasted. We were walking out for a long time before we got married. Lord have mercy on her, she was a great beauty.'

Poor Dan, Katy thought, poor Dan living alone, his children scattered all over America. 'Tis a pity he never married again. Plenty of widow-women would jump at him, given the chance. But Dan was talking again. 'She was that lovely I couldn't leave her alone in the beginning. Every morning and night for the first year we'd have an intercourse. And a few times a week after that. When she had the first child I used to think how wonderful were the ways of God, for many's the time I found her the tight fit and then she able to bring into the world a fine big boy. Ah, she was the grand girl and grand times we had together. But do you know and it's the truth I'm telling you, after I got to sixty-three he never stood for me again.'

Katy nearly dropped the tray. Dan O'Brien – a decent respectable man to talk like that! The shame of it! He must be losing his senses. She tiptoed from the door.

In the kitchen while rinsing cups she kept going over in her mind the things Dan had said. She shouldn't have listened. The minute he mentioned intercourse she should have walked away. 'And what was so terrible about it?' asked another part of her mind. 'He didn't know you were listening. He was intending no offence. Only describing his lovely wife with red cheeks and black hair that had a curl in it.

160

Remembering how much he loved her. Remembering when they were young.'

'But the other thing?' asked the disapproving side of Katy's mind. 'What about that?'

'Well – what about it? Wasn't it all part of their loving and then growing old. Didn't you hear the sorrow and resignation in his voice and even the bit of amusement at the way Nature caught him out.'

'*He never stood for me again,*' Katy's own voice said aloud and she laughed and washed more cups and laughed again, thinking of all the fine widows who fussed and flocked round Dan. Offering to cook for him, wash his shirts, stitch on his buttons. The spites and jealousies amongst them, the backbiting of each other when Dan singled one out to do his washing or mend his socks. The hopes he raised in them. What a suck-in the one who got him would have had. But Dan was cute. He'd keep his secret and them dancing attendance on him.

She rinsed some cups, thinking and smiling about Dan and the widows then all of a sudden the smile was wiped off her face. Supposing the same thing happened to Jamsie! Supposing he wasn't able to love her any more! Could it happen to a young man? He wasn't so young any more – gone thirty now, like herself. Time went in a minute. If God spared them, one day she and Jamsie would be really old like Dan. she couldn't bear the thought of it – of them changing, everything changing. Her eyes filled with tears and then fell into the basin. She let them fall until she heard Eileen, Mary and the other women arriving. She was wiping her eyes with the damp tea towel when Bridget came in to tell her the others were here. 'Mom, what's the matter? You're crying.'

'I am not,' said Katy. 'I got something in my eye. Tell me now,' she asked, her good spirits restored by the sight of Bridget's lovely eager young face, 'what's thirty-four from sixty-three?'

'Twenty-nine – why?' asked Bridget, looking puzzled.

'Nothing,' Katy said. 'It was a sum I was doing in my head. Twenty-nine – sure that's years and years.'

'Mom' they called her, and she answered to it. She couldn't remember when the change had taken place. One particular day it must have been. Had she been too busy folding laundry, keeping an eye on the dinner, running to the window to see if Jamsie was coming home sober. Was it a day when Bridget was complaining about delivering washing. Maybe she had said, 'Oh Mom, do I have to?' and she'd been so harassed she hadn't noticed the change – the beginning of the new ways.

161

Mostly she was glad. Glad that now apart from an odd word, a certain turn of phrase or a slight difference in pronunciation, it was hard to tell that the children hadn't been born American. It was to their advantage. The less you stood out the better. And she wanted everything better for them.

'Are you going to stay all night in the kitchen? You're supposed to be giving a hooley.' It was Eileen putting an end to Katy's musings.

In the other room the party was well under way. A neighbour had brought a melodeon. There was talking and laughing and congratulations to the new citizens, complaints about American summers and the women undid a blouse button near the neck. There was singing and dancing – only two or three at a time getting up to step it out for there wasn't the space.

Katy laughed and chatted, even got up to dance but wasn't able to give herself wholly to the festivities. There was a sadness about her she couldn't dispel. She saw the women sitting about her dressed in their best, the blouses and skirts worn only for a night like this or to Mass. Clothes hard come by, bought secondhand after great deliberation, their cost weighed against so many other things. Poor women, young women old before their time. Their breasts and bellies sagging from too many babies. Great women who daily worked miracles to feed their families, who carried buckets of water up four flights of stairs, hauling and pulling stones of potatoes, a second or third-hand mattress. Always carrying something, babies in their arms or in their wombs. Confined year in, year out. Nursing sick children, sitting with the dying, keeping watch over the dead. Kind women, ready to come to your assistance with what little they had. Keeping going the traditions of Ireland, singing the songs and telling the stories.

Not saints. Only women. Women who like herself lost their tempers and clattered their children, sometimes undeservedly. Sorry immediately, making amends with an extra slice of bread, a penny they couldn't afford. Women who, when they missed, hoped it was the change in the weather – the heat, the cold, their age, something they'd eaten. Knowing well it was none of those things and accepting when the second course was missed – making a joke about it – praying for God to open another door that another mouth might be filled. On prayers and hopes and dreams they existed.

'Aghoille.' Jamsie was beside her. 'I've seen you look happier at a wake. Are you not well?'

'I'm grand, I was miles away,' she said. He was bending down to her, smiling at her. She saw the love and concern on his face. She loved him.

'Will you dance, so?'

'I will,' she said and lightly and quickly touched his face.

The morning after the party Katy looked out through the window and saw Bridget and Ulla skipping and then, unusually, Kathleen coming to join them. Soon afterwards Ulla left.

'What went wrong out there? Ulla went, why?' she asked when Bridget came in for a minute.

'Cramps in her stomach,' said Bridget.

'It's the heat. I'll be glad when the autumn comes.'

'The fall, you mean. I told you before.'

'So you did.'

'They used to say fall in England at one time.'

'Not in my time they didn't.'

'They did. I learned it in school.'

'All right, they did,' said Katy, not wishing to raise a contention over something that wasn't important.

When Ulla arrived home complaining of an upset stomach her mother good-humouredly scolded her. 'Too late to bed last night, too much excitement, too many tears when your uncle left and too many cakes! I'll give you something for it in a minute.'

While she was making camomile tea, her son Dieter had to run for the privy, then he and Ulla were violently sick.

Not long afterwards, Herr Jaeger came up from the bakery for his coffee, by which time his wife and children were obviously ill.

'Such vomiting, such diarrhoea. So sudden, what can it be?' Frau Jaeger asked her husband.

'Rich things to eat, perhaps?'

'That's what I said – but I never ate the rich things.'

He persuaded her to go to bed. He made a hot jar for her. 'Lie with the others.' He covered and kissed them all tenderly. 'Sleep,' he told them. 'When I've done the next batch I'll come back. Sleep.'

While he sieved and mixed, kneaded and put the bread to prove something was niggling in his mind. Something his brother had said. But then Wolfie had said so many things. They'd drunk a little wine, a lot of wine and Wolfie talked and talked. There was so much to say and so much to ask. Hamburg and how it was. And old friends to ask after. And all the time Wolfie's own questions about America. So much talking, so much laughing. Words flying round the room. But there was something out of the ordinary said. Something about Hamburg. What was it?

163

What was it Wolfie had said about Hamburg that was out of the ordinary? Then his bowels loosened. He ran and as he did he remembered what Wolfie had said. *'There was cholera in Hamburg – a big outbreak. Weren't we lucky to get out.'*

Back in the bakery he soaked a towel in cold water and bathed his burning face. Cholera in Hamburg. So, he said to himself in an effort to control the panic he felt, Hamburg was thousands of miles away and what had Hamburg cholera to do with New York? He was worse than an old woman. Cholera – a pestilence couldn't cross the sea . . .

But terrifying thoughts came into his mind. When he was a boy, there had been a cholera epidemic. He remembered hearing his mother and the neighbours talking about it in hushed fearful whispers. Suddenly it struck. From nowhere it came with shivering, vomiting and diarrhoea, with no stop until every bit of fluid was drained from your body and your hands pinched and withered as if they been in water overnight. Big strong men, sick in the morning, dead the next day. Sometimes in your senses till the end.

He shivered violently, not knowing if it was fever or fright. Only that he was suddenly too ill to bake the bread. But making a strenuous effort he banked down the fires and made the bakery safe in case he couldn't come again for a few hours.

Gisela and the children, he must go to them. With difficulty he climbed the stairs and opened the door. The sights and smells were all there that his mother and her neighbours had described. He had to get help, but knew he couldn't make the stairs again. The window, he would open the window and call a passer-by.

Katy on her way to the bakery was nauseated by the smell of manure which littered the streets. During the night it had been soaked by the heavy rain, now in the hot sun it was steaming and stinking. She put a hand over her mouth and nose and picked her way carefully, trying to avoid stepping in it. If only the weather would change, if only it was autumn, she thought. Then the streets would be cleaned, the tons of horse droppings, tons and tons of it that lay all over the city would be shipped to the farmers on Long Island. During the summer they were busy gathering in the crops, so the manure lay and festered. She hated the New York summers, she slept badly. Last night she had hardly closed her eyes, they were burning this minute in her head. The heat never bothered Jamsie. She was sorry about last night. He liked her to sleep in his arms, or at least let him keep an arm round her. Most times she did, he got offended otherwise. Last night she'd thrown off his arm and he accused her of not loving him. By the time she felt sorry for him he was fast asleep and snoring and that didn't help her night's rest.

No matter how carefully she walked when crossing the street her shoes still got soiled. She'd have to scrape them with the old knife she kept for just that when she got home. Even on the path it was, walked there by other feet, thrown up by passing wheels. 'Bad cess,' she said to herself, 'to him that has the manure contract.' Couldn't it be shovelled and stored somewhere out of people's way until the autumn? Mary, who knew everything, told her it was an Irishman responsible for it – had the contract handed to him by the Tammany Hall crowd. 'A young fella, so I believe,' said Mary. 'I haven't yet found out his name. He might be someone we know.'

Katy began to feel more cheerful. Once round the corner the smell of newly-baked bread would drive away the other one for the time being. Two of Jaegers' crusty rolls and a nice cup of tea and she'd be none the worse for her lost sleep.

But round the corner there was no smell of new bread. The bakery was closed and outside there was a group of women. 'What's the matter?' she asked. 'I've never known the bakery to be shut. What happened?' No one knew. Katy banged on the door. No one answered. 'That's very strange,' she said. She stayed talking and speculating as to why the shop was closed. Then a window on the opposite side of the street was pushed up and a woman shouted something in German and immediately banged down the window. For a few seconds the German women in the group spoke agitatedly then began to move away quickly. Katy caught the arm of one who spoke English well. 'What is it, what did the woman in the window say?'

'Cholera, the Jaegers have the cholera, since yesterday. In the fever hospital they are.'

There was nothing she could do for them but pray and cry when she remembered that only yesterday morning Ulla was skipping outside her door. She could see her hair bound the way the Germans made plaits so they hung to the front of her face bobbing as she skipped. God look down on them, she prayed, and spare them. She was still crying when Mary came.

Mary was as upset as Katy. 'They could all be dead tonight – it takes some that quick. Sacred Heart of Jesus bless and protect them and every one else. In His mercy may He look down . . .' She suddenly stopped praying and crying. 'Was Ulla round here yesterday morning?'

'She was, the poor little child, in the whole of her health, skipping with Bridget.'

'Was that the time when Kathleen came?'

'It was. I was surprised to see her – she seldom comes to play now.'

Mary began to keen. 'And wasn't it the unfortunate thing she came at all. To think I sent her. "Get your nose out of that book for five minutes. It's a lovely day – go and play. Call for Bridget." My poor child, may God protect her. My poor little lamb. The cholera's terrible catching.'

'May He protect everyone. And don't you start meeting trouble halfway – I had enough of that on the ship.'

' 'Tis easy for you to talk so,' said Mary. 'You don't know what it's like to lose a child. The grief it leaves in you and the dread and fear for the living. My poor child, I wish she was home from school. I won't let her stir outside the house for a month. You and Eileen can throw an eye to her. There's a lot of functions at the Hall – I was asked to oblige with the extra cleaning and that.'

The humour that had been on her all day, the news of the Jaegers and her fear for her own children made Katy turn on Mary. 'You,' she said, 'you, Mary Callinan, it's time someone told you the truth about yourself. You're a selfish woman with not a thought in your head for anyone but yourself and that young one of yours. The Jaegers may be at death's door and your only concern is wrapping her up in bed. 'Tis a pity you can't put her back where she came from.'

'My worry is only natural,' Mary began.

'Very, so long as someone else minds her while you oblige your American gentlemen. Let me tell you this – I've enough to do minding my own.'

'Well,' said Mary, her face the colour of a turkey cock. 'I never expected that from you. I wouldn't have asked it for nothing – I'd do the same for you.'

'When?' shouted Katy. 'When do you do anything for anyone? I comforted and consoled you every mile of the voyage. Before I left Mulberry Street I had Kathleen before school in the mornings. I have her now after school. If you hear the gnawing of a rat it's round to Jamsie to set a trap for you and when we lived in the house you had my children as runagates. I could forgive all of that but your only concern when you heard of the cholera was for Kathleen. Well, what about my concern for mine? For Bridget that was wrapped round poor Ulla. But oh no, you're the only one with fears for the living because you buried children.'

'You wouldn't deny me that?'

'No, I would not for only too well do I understand it. Every time I

166

hear of fever, every time one of them has a sore throat or a rash my heart is in my mouth.' Katy began to cry. 'Sit down Mary, I'm that sorry for turning on you. Sure you weren't to know.'

'Don't cry, Katy. I know you never meant half of what you said. Sit down, come on do – and tell me what was it I didn't know.'

Overcome with grief and fear and guilt for the way she had turned on Mary, Katy cried long and bitterly. Mary kindly fussed round her. Telling not to mind what she had said. ' 'Twasn't half of it true? I do make much of Kathleen. I know that. She's all I have, do you see. I'll tell them in work I can't do the extra. 'Twouldn't be fair on you. God help you, you're killed with the work you have. Only don't be crying. I can't bear to see you cry. I do depend on you to keep me going. Will I get you anything?' Awkwardly she put an arm round Katy. 'Gersha, talk to me. Tell me what ails you. Tell me what I don't know. Are you carrying again? Is that what's troubling you?'

'I'm crying for Peg and Nora that I buried at home.'

'And you never told me – that's not natural. Sharing your grief is half the healing. All the things you told me and never that – why?'

'I couldn't. I wouldn't have now, only thinking of poor little Ulla brought it all back. That and fear for the others. Oh Mary, if you could have seen my Peg and Nora. They were twins. You'd have loved them. Everyone loved them. How could I bear it if the same thing happened again?'

For the first time since they'd met on the ship their roles were reversed. Mary gave the words of comfort, reminding Katy of her courage. How many a time she had saved her reason. She was to stop doing what Mary herself always did – meeting trouble halfway. Katy wasn't God – she couldn't see beyond the minute. She had to hold on to that and not try to foresee beyond it.

Gradually Katy regained her composure. Answering questions Mary asked about the twins. Telling her of them, and before she knew it laughing as she recalled the pair of 'divils' they were. The mischief they got into.

Mary made tea and Katy said the cry had done her good. And Mary said she'd take her advice and stop coddling Kathleen. Tomorrow she'd go to school. Everything was in God's hands.

When the children came in from school Katy told them the Jaegers were sick.

'I thought something was up. Ulla never misses school,' Bridget said.

'They're very sick, they have the cholera.'

'Oh Mom, no, not the cholera. People die of that. Ulla won't die, sure she won't,' Bridget pleaded.

'It's all in God's hands. All we can do is pray, love.'

When it was known that Ulla, her mother and brother had died, Bridget was distraught.

'You have to eat,' Katy coaxed, after Bridget had refused several meals. She looked with pity at her tear-streaked face, her yellow hair that hadn't had brush or comb near it all day, and tried again to persuade Bridget that she must eat something.

'I don't want anything.'

'Starving yourself won't bring Ulla back – starving will make you sick.'

'I don't care. I don't care,' cried Bridget and buried her face in the pillow.

Katy turned her round and stroked her hair. 'A cup of tea then, a nice cup of tea and a piece of bread and butter. For me, love, I don't want anything happening to you.'

'No, nothing. I'd rather be dead. Ulla was my best friend. I loved her. Oh Mom why, why did it have to happen? Why did Ulla have to die?'

'It was God's Will,' said Katy.

'Then I hate Him. I'll never go to Mass again. I hate Him.'

'Hush, love.' Katy lifted her from the pillow and held her in her arms. 'Don't say such things. Ulla's in Heaven with her mother and Dieter.'

Bridget screamed. 'I don't want her in Heaven. I want her here. I want to go to school with her. I want to play with her. Oh God, why did You do it.' She sobbed convulsively, Katy held her and said no more. There was nothing else she could say. Only hold her close and wait until she had cried herself out. When she had, Katy laid her down and exhausted, she fell asleep.

She was subdued but controlled when she woke. She drank the tea Katy brought her and let her face be bathed and her hair brushed and tied back. For a while she lay against the pillow and was very quiet, then she asked, 'It wouldn't have hurt her, would it?'

And Katy lied. 'It wouldn't have hurt. The poor child would have got weak and slipped into a deep sleep and never woken up.'

For a while all of the children were subdued and seldom mentioned Ulla until after the funeral. Then gradually her name would come up in conversations and tears fill Bridget's eyes and Thomas became very still and quiet. But as the weeks passed, Ulla was remembered from time to time. Sadly at first, regretfully until the day Mary Kate said, 'I liked the way she laughed.' Remembering Ulla's joyous laughter they all smiled and reminiscences poured out. Thomas said wasn't it funny how she always said winegar for vinegar and wexed and wery. And Katy thought, thanks be to God, the living have to go on and the dead be remembered the way they were. That way you could always have them with you. They were getting over their grief.

On another day when Kathleen, who now had Bridget as her best friend again, came she reminded Bridget how Ulla had shocked Miss Cook by calling a buttonhole a bottomhole.

'Remember how everyone in the class roared and she blushed scarlet.'

'Who – Ulla?'

'No, eejit, Miss Cook.'

They laughed hysterically, even Thomas joined in. And again Katy was glad for the healing process, for their hilarity. Ulla was dead. For a long time they'd remember the funny things she had said. For a long time they'd keep her alive in their memories.

'So far thank God we've escaped,' Katy said one day to Mary.

'You lost a lot of custom, though.'

'People are afraid of having their washing done with other people's clothes. 'Tis a small loss and when the fear passes the customers will be back. I'd sacrifice it all for Mr Jaeger to get better.'

'Wasn't it a miracle he lived?'

'It was,' said Katy. 'But the poor man has a hard road in front of him. 'Tis the lonely house he'll be going back to. I do feel awful thinking of them the day they took sick, the hours they'd have been alone when the complaint was at its worst, the pain they suffered.'

'Sure we weren't to know.'

'I suppose you're right,' said Katy.

'I heard something this morning.'

'What was that?' asked Katy.

'Do you remember that doctor?'

Katy had to be reminded of the doctor from Gramercy Park, the one who had raised his hat to Eileen the day they arrived in America.

'Well, he comes to the tenements and he was telling Mrs Ginsburg that the ship from Hamburg maybe brought in the cholera.'

'Is that a fact?'

'According to him. And if you come to think of it, isn't it mostly Germans that had relations from the same ship that got the complaint.'

'You're right,' said Katy, 'only wasn't there an Irish boy died a few days after the Jaegers?'

'Michael McCabe, there was, but he lived in a lodging house and Germans going inland that had no relations when they came off the boat stayed in it.'

'Had he no one belonging to him and him only a boy and staying in a lodging house?'

'He was a youth more than a boy, but simple in the head so people thought of him as a child. And he has a brother – the one that's got the manure contract. Coining it he is and wasn't he going to buy a house and move the brother in, Lord have mercy on him.'

'Poor Mikey, wasn't it the sad thing he was taken and you about to move him into your place,' said Kelly the saloon-keeper.

'Maybe it was a blessing. Five years he'd been with Mrs McGennis – he'd have found it hard to leave her. Half the time lately I used to think he'd forgotten I was his brother. He'll be happy now, in Heaven with my mother and father,' Terence said.

'He will that, a lovely innocent child. Sure, what sin could he ever have committed? You'll be getting the manure shifted?'

'Everything organised. I've a good gang working for me.'

'For a fella of twenty-three you've done well for yourself. Hard work and a bit up here,' Kelly touched his head, 'that's all you need to get on in America – and the right connections.'

'Indeed,' said Terence and they both laughed.

Hiring the men to shift the manure gave Terence a great sense of power. Deciding who should get work and who not was a grand feeling. Seeing the desperation on their faces, hearing the pleading voices, that satisfied him. 'You,' he'd say, 'and you.' and he felt like a king.

The manure contract was the first of many that would come his way. He'd get building contracts and carrier contracts until he had the Irish labourers in his pocket. The yellow-haired one from the boat, her husband worked at the building. He knew all about her and him. Knew the laundry she had in Cow Lane. The satisfaction it would give him to have them in his power. To have her, as many a wife did, come pleading to him for a job for her husband. Oh, that would be the day and with the help of God come yet it might.

170

Chapter Fourteen

'I was just thinking, Katy and Jamsie are American citizens, too.'

'Yes, of course,' said Charlotte, looking up from a sketch she was working on. 'It's years since you heard from them. I wonder how they are. Why did you lose touch with them?'

'I tried to keep up the correspondence. Jamsie never wrote, Katy answered a few of my letters, then she stopped. I kept thinking that one day I'd go up to see Jacques and call on them.' Peader sighed. 'You know what I'm like, full of good intentions, but as they say at home, I'm inclined to put things on the long finger.' And he thought, the way I've put off insisting that we move from here. But one of these days . . .

'There's nothing to stop you going to New York,' said Charlotte, and wished he would. A week, a few days alone with Paul would be lovely.

'Jacques travels around so much these days. When the time is right for me to leave the plantation he's off in Europe.'

It crossed her mind to say that the plantation could manage very well without him. She stopped herself. Peader knew that only too well: it was something that came up whenever he got on his high horse about them leaving. For a while there had been peace in that quarter – she mustn't provoke him.

'And who's this Maura I hear you talking about?' Katy asked one day when they were making parcels of the finished laundry.

Bridget looked up from the string she was tying. 'You wouldn't know her.'

Katy was taken aback by the expression in her daugher's eyes; several times lately she had noticed it. It had a chilling effect on her. It was like looking into the eyes of a stranger, a stranger who had taken a great dislike to you. My own child, she thought, to look at me like that. Did I ever do that to my mother? God knows she sometimes annoyed and moidered me and put against Jamsie, but I never looked at her that way.

'You wouldn't know her,' Bridget repeated, bending again to the parcel and tying a perfect string bow. And even in the middle of her

171

annoyance Katy couldn't help thinking how good she was with her hands, folding parcels, sewing, tying hair-ribbons, she was very deft.

'I heard you the first time. And know her I might if you gave her a name.'

'Maura Doody.'

'I've seen her in the chapel and her mother and father. Decent respectable people. He's a clerk, I believe. Is Maura in school?'

'She was. She works now for a milliner in the Bowery.' Bridget gave her answer grudgingly.

'That's nice,' said Katy. 'I'll make a point of nodding to Mr and Mrs Doody on Sunday.'

'Don't you go talking to them. Don't you go telling them things.'

'Things, what things?'

'About starving and the smell of stinking potatoes and lice – the things you and Eileen are always on about.'

'Unless Mr and Mrs Doody were very fortunate they'll have come across all them things before they left Ireland.'

'They did not. They're not like us. They're different. So don't you go telling them.'

Katy could contain herself no longer. 'If it wasn't that I'm expecting customers and ones I've only just got back after the cholera, I'd take you by the yellow hair and streel you round the room. I'd make tears come to your eyes. "Them things" as you called them, them things killed my two children, Mary's family and thousands more. Them things were what sent us fleeing for our lives. We talk about them to heal the scars left in our hearts and minds. Please God you'll never know such awful things – but never again in your life belittle me, or them that have. And now take that parcel and deliver it before I forget myself and the customers that are coming.'

What, she asked herself when Bridget was gone, had become of her. What was she doing to make her behave in such a way. Was she doing anything wrong? She made allowances for a lot of things, for the effect Ulla's death could still be having on her daughter. But then Bridget had started showing her teeth before Ulla died. She was like a tinker. The look on her face. The way she talked back to her mother. A tinker. There was bad blood in her – she was an O'Hara. Taking after their side of the family. There was bad blood in some of the O'Haras.

The rows between Katy and Bridget never lasted long. And when there was peace Katy went about happy and contented, for she hated disunity in the family. Rowing with the children upset her. Thinking bad things

172

about them upset her. Likening Bridget to any of the O'Haras except Jamsie or poor Padraig was a terrible thing to do. Please God there'd be no reason for her to do it again.

But the following week Bridget announced that she had left school.

'You can't do that,' said Katy.

'I can. I was fourteen months ago. I've got a job with Maura, in the hat shop, *Madame Renée.*'

Katy took a deep breath. She wasn't going to lose her temper. Bridget was old enough to leave school now, and streeling her by the hair wouldn't alter that. But she could alter her plans. She could work in the laundry.

'I won't,' said Bridget.

'You will,' said Katy.

'I won't. I don't care what you do. You can make me come down every day but I won't work. I love hats and bonnets. I want to work in the shop.'

If I let her defy me over this I'll never get good of her, Katy thought. Then other things came into her mind. What it would be like, day in day out, working with an unwilling helper – the scenes, the tears, the anger, the effect anger had on her. And Bridget was deft. She could do well in a milliners. She would be starting to earn her keep, and that couldn't be ignored. To force her into the laundry wouldn't solve anything.

'I'm not coming into the laundry,' Bridget repeated, with a little less defiance, and Katy's determination wavered. She could use the extra pair of hands, it was true, and Bridget would be there where she could keep an eye on her. Her deft fingers would make short work of the repairs . . . Then she remembered Bridget's open hostility, that expression in her eyes when they quarrelled and she decided.

'Tell me this,' she asked. 'Did you tell Miss Cook you were going to work in the milliners?'

'I didn't tell her anything.'

'Not even that you weren't coming to school again?'

'Nothing. I didn't have to.'

'All right, all right,' said Katy. 'You can go to *Madame Renée* – you can go to your hat-shop. I'll see Miss Cook, it's manners to do so.'

'Oh thanks, Mom!' Bridget threw her arms around Katy and kissed her. 'Can I go and tell Maura?'

'You can,' said Katy. God help her, sure she's only a child. I hope to God I'm doing the right thing, she thought watching Bridget running down the street.

173

So as not to disturb a class Katy went to the school at lunchtime. She hadn't been there since Danny started and that was a long time ago. The small play area now had a low, open-fronted shelter built at one end. It was raining and she could see the children packed into it, so many that she couldn't pick out her own.

The same nervousness overcame her as on the other occasions when she entered the lobby. And she thought that maybe it was presumptuous of her to call. Miss Cook probably wouldn't welcome her lunchtime being interrupted. Miss Cook wouldn't expect a parent to come. The truth was, she was afraid, no not afraid, but uncomfortable about meeting her. Nevertheless she knocked on the door.

'Come in,' a voice called. Miss Cook was as neat and severe-looking as Katy remembered, but now she had a quizzical expression as well. 'Yes, what can I do for you?'

A severe woman for all that the children liked her, Katy thought and walked nearer to the teacher's desk. 'I'm Mrs O'Hara.'

'Mrs O'Hara, of course. I'm sorry I didn't recognise you immediately.' The severe face softened and smiled. 'I've only met you a few times, but I'd have known you, only I'm very short-sighted. Come on in. What can I do for you?'

At ease now Katy returned the smile. 'I've come to apologise for Bridget's manners. She should have told you she was leaving. It was bad manners.'

'Thoughtlessness – few tell me. But it's very good of you to come. I'd like more mothers to come. I only see them at enrolment, – then I'm too busy to be more than civil.'

'You've a lot to do,' Katy said sympathetically.

'It's my life's work. I love it.'

'I wanted to thank you. I won't delay you,' said Katy, not wishing to outstay her welcome, and she made a move to leave.

'You're not delaying me. I'm delighted you came. Your family's a credit to you. Nicely brought up children, always clean and tidy, a pleasure to have in school. I had high hopes for Bridget. She's a clever girl but not much application. Intelligence isn't enough. Has she a job?'

'In a hat-shop, an apprentice I believe.'

'That's good. She'll learn a trade. The real scholar is Mary Kate. Bright, quick and works like a beaver.'

'I never knew that. I knew she was quick, but a scholar, I never thought that. She's a chatterbox, full of energy though it's little of it she spends round the house.'

Miss Cook didn't mention how Thomas was doing in school and Katy didn't ask. She didn't need confirmation that he wasn't a scholar. He could read and write, but he'd not much of a head for figures. Maybe he'd be lucky and get to serve his time to a tradesman. Though she wouldn't pin her hopes on that. She and Miss Cook chatted for a while longer, Miss Cook saying that she hoped for a bigger school now that education was to be made compulsory. Katy joined in with her hopes and before she left, asked about Danny.

'Danny,' Miss Cook said, 'is a puzzle. One week he's the top of the class and the next I wonder if he's the same boy. He's a daydreamer. Don't worry about him, he's only eight, there's plenty of time. And don't forget – you are always welcome to come and see me if you have any problems about them.'

'I think Paddy Kavanagh was a chancer. Three months and not a word from him,' Eileen told Katy a few weeks before Christmas.

'He might be having trouble getting backers,' said Katy, who thought no such thing.

'And lost the use of his arm? A letter wouldn't have killed him.'

'Men aren't much of a hand with the pen. Sure, isn't that how we lost touch with Peader.'

'She never wrote?'

'Never a line, more's the pity.'

'Why so, do you think?'

'When all is said and done I suppose because Miss Charlotte is who she is. In Ireland, at least in Kilgoran, you weren't so aware of the distinction. We were all so young, them things weren't important. Certainly not with Miss Charlotte. Now I'd never have expected to keep up a correspondence with her sister, Miss Catherine. But she was reared when her mother was alive, with all the correctness of the gentry. Very kind, friendly, caring, but the distinction was there. But Miss Charlotte's mother died on the birth of her. Lord Kilgoran never overed that. She was let run wild, reared by Hannah, by all of us because the Master never got a nurse for her. And you forgot who she was. But sure now she's a grown woman – living again with her own kind. What would we have to say to each other?'

'And him – I wonder if he'll ever come to see you again?'

'Maybe,' said Katy. 'I hope so. And I hope for your sake Paddy keeps his word.'

'It'll be just my luck that he won't. Do you know, I've never looked at another fella since the night I met him. I could make a go of it with him. Why is it, Katy, that it's the men who spell trouble we fall for?'

'You're asking the right one.' Hastily she added, 'Not that Jamsie brought me trouble, but I'd have had an easier life with Peader. That's not what we're looking for though, is it? Not me and you.'

'No,' said Eileen, 'but sometimes I think wouldn't it be the grand thing to find a man that had the fire in him and all the rest besides.'

'Miracles you're asking for,' said Katy.

'Aye, I suppose so,' Eileen said and got up to go. 'I nearly forgot, I knew I had something to tell you. Herr Jaeger is opening up again on Monday and he's asked Mary to work a few hours in between her cleaning in City Hall.'

'I knew nothing about that.'

'She'll be round to tell you, to ask your advice. I only heard about it. Did you know she's been in helping him sort out the shop and house. I believe the German women are hopping. Maybe they have a smack for each other.'

'His poor wife's not cold in her grave! Of course they haven't.'

'You're very innocent. Remember what I always said about Mary? It's the quiet wans you want to watch.'

'Shh,' said Katy, 'someone's come into the shop and not rang the bell, it's not a customer.'

'It'll be her, looking for advice. There she is now coming up the stairs.' There was a tap on the door and Mary's voice asking if Katy was in. Eileen winked and mouthed the words, 'I told you so.'

'Come in Mary,' Katy called. Mary did and Eileen changed her mind about leaving. 'I brought these for a cup of tea,' said Mary, offering a bag to Katy. 'They're the biscuits Germans make for Christmas. Mr Jaeger has a mincer like the butchers – the dough goes in and comes out in them shapes, isn't that grand?'

'You're getting to know a lot about German baking. Is it right that you helped clean up the shop and house?' asked Eileen.

Mary went red in the face. 'Who told you that?'

'Someone.'

'Wouldn't they do better to mind their own business. I gave him a hand, the poor man. I just happened to be passing and he was on the door and we got into talk. I felt sorry for him. Well, you would, wouldn't you?'

'Of course,' said Eileen. 'I'm only wondering why the German women didn't offer, they're good neighbours. Of course, maybe you got the offer in first with you being that kind.'

Katy came to Mary's rescue, saying the German women all had

husbands and big families, that would have been the reason for Herr Jaeger accepting her offer of help.

'The very reason,' said Mary, ' 'tis the same reason he's asked me to work a few hours in the shop. I could fit them in between the cleaning and be glad of the money, only I'm not sure.'

'Not sure about what?'

'For one thing when he talks quick and sometimes in German I don't understand him.'

'He wants you to work, not converse with him,' said Eileen.

'But what about the women, how will I know which bread they want?'

'For Jesus's sake Mary, have you no sense or is all this play-acting? They'll point – you're not blind'

'I suppose you're right,' said Mary. 'No tea for me, Katy. I've a lot to do.'

'That wan is setting her cap at him,' said Eileen when Mary went. 'You mark my words.'

Katy laughed and said she didn't believe a word of it.

'Just you wait and see.'

'Mary!' said Katy when she went to the baker's on Monday. 'What have you done to yourself? I wouldn't have known you.'

Mary got flustered and went red. 'It's only an old blouse, I did a bit of renovating.'

'You look lovely.'

'Thanks,' said Mary. 'It's the Germans, they're that clean and tidy, I have to look my best.'

'And you do indeed.'

Every time she went to the shop she was struck by the continuing change in Mary's appearance. It wasn't only renovated blouses. She looked years younger; her skin glowed and her eyes shone and she'd filled out. 'Half of what she's earning is going on her back,' was Eileen's comment on Mary.

'Eileen, you're a terrible woman. You know well Mary will be putting by every penny for Kathleen's education. I think it's working in a pleasant atmosphere. It must be a nice change from washing floors and lavatories. It's the look of her, her hair and skin, and she's nice and plump.'

'You're a terrible eejit. She's fallen for that oul fella. There's nothing like love to put a bloom on your cheeks and a shine in your eyes. She's light about him. There'll be a wedding there, wait'll you see.'

Chapter Fifteen

In the weeks before Christmas Katy always felt depressed. From talking to her neighbours she knew that many of them felt the same way. Christmas in America wasn't like at home. There for as long as anyone could remember Christmas was a holy time. You put the candle in the window on Christmas Eve and went to Mass and the Blessed Child filled your heart and home with love and happiness.

If besides you had a kind landlord there'd be the present of a fowl. In honour of some long ago custom of which they knew not the meaning, their homes would be decorated with holly. It was a time of peace and love with not a worry in your head. No one expected lavishness. Only the gentry could be lavish at Christmas. Wishing to imitate them was like wishing for a star.

But in New York everything was different. At home there might be the one shop that you seldom went to. In New York even the poor shops, the street stalls made you aware of all the things there were for Christmas. You felt a right to a share and were discontented knowing you couldn't afford it. All the toys and clothes and food on display. It saddened your heart to know that not even on this one special day could you indulge your family. And knowing the indulgence was possible for so many you felt the fault was yours. You weren't working hard enough, you weren't thrifty.

In her more placid moments Katy knew this wasn't so. She worked from morning till night, so did Jamsie and seldom now did he squander money on drink. Bridget was earning and yet all that could be provided was necessities. And you wanted to buy lovely things to delight the children, lovely things to eat, something to brighten the room, some of the things that drew your eyes to the shop windows. Katy also knew that once midnight came on Christmas Eve the longings and wanting would be replaced by the true joy of Christmas. The Blessed Child would have entered your heart and home. And the relief it was to know that whether you had the money or not the shops were shut – you couldn't torment yourself with longings of presents to delight the eyes of the children. But she had to get through the days until Christmas Eve.

She slept badly, her mind full of racing thoughts. Bridget liked her work, not that it had improved her disposition at home. She had an air of dissatisfaction about her, turning up her nose at whatever you put in front of her. And an answer for everything.

Jamsie's snoring annoyed Katy, too. Once when she told him he said, 'You want to hear yourself.' She didn't believe him. She had never snored in her life and in any case – how would he know, for wasn't he always asleep before her? When she could bear the snoring no longer she'd say, 'Turn over, you're on your back,' and she'd smile in the dark at how though he was asleep her voice reached him and he obeyed.

On other nights she made plans to find work for Thomas after Christmas. It would be nice to have him serve his time to a trade – only she knew well that the sons of tradesmen were favoured for apprenticeships. He'd have to take what he could get. Danny and Mary Kate would be in school for the time being. Mary Kate could be a teacher, yet. By the time she was, there might be a Catholic school. Wouldn't that be grand.

One night she remembered the official opening of the church and a young man she had seen sitting up in the front amongst them with the money. His face had been familiar but she couldn't place him. He might have been from another parish and just over for the opening. She had meant to ask Mary who he was but forgot. He had passed her while she was still kneeling when the Mass was over and he'd stared at her. It was annoying when you couldn't put a name to a face. She was sure she knew him from somewhere. Her mind went off on another track, thinking that she must remember to remind Dan he was having his dinner with them on Christmas Day. Poor Dan, the New York winters were taking their toll of him. The face of the red-haired young man was back tormenting her memory and while trying to place it she fell asleep.

Terence McCabe had had no difficulty in placing Katy. It pleased him to see her sitting where she was while he had been up in the front. No one had ever got the better of him as she had on the ship – not without being paid back. Her turn would come.

Katy got an abundance of brown, black and white bread and stale cakes brought from Jaegers' by Mary. 'He's a very generous man and very honest,' Mary told her. 'He never palms anyone off with yesterday's baking. He's a gentleman and has all my sympathy. God help him, he's still broken-hearted over the loss of his wife and lovely children.'

Katy watched her while she was singing Herr Jaeger's praises and

179

thought that Eileen might well be right. Mary was falling for the baker. It was the only reason she could think of for the change in her. Jamsie, the least observant of men, one night commented on it. 'Mary's the fine-looking woman. How old is she?'

'Like a lot of women she never divulges her age. But not much if at all older than me, I'd say.'

'There was a time when I wouldn't have thought so.'

'No,' said Katy, but she didn't say why she thought Mary was blooming. Not to Jamsie, nor anyone else, and especially not to Eileen. For Eileen with a drink on her, or in bad humour, or even out of divilment might cod Mary. Mary wouldn't take that kindly – unless Herr Jaeger had shown his feelings. And that she thought unlikely so soon after burying his wife. But in time, maybe. She hoped so. Mary deserved a man. There were German and Irish inter-marriages – not many – but they were taking place. Mary could still have a child. Wouldn't that be grand for the pair of them. He was a nice man, short, a bit on the stout side, but he had nice brown eyes. A good few years older than Mary – but that didn't matter. Listen to me, she said to herself. I have them married, bedded and blessed with a child and for all I know there may be nothing in it.

Unlike other years, Katy's depression lingered through Christmas and after, so that on New Year's Eve she talked about it to Eileen. 'It's been on me this while back. I wouldn't mind if it was only tonight, I've never liked this time of year. We never made much of it at home like the Germans do. But as I was saying, I've been this way since before Christmas. I thought it was the usual thing, wanting more than you could have. But it's persisting. God forgive me for giving way to despair when there's so much to be grateful for. When you think of the poor Jaegers, Lord have mercy on them. Aren't we lucky to be alive. She was a lovely woman. I remember once going to a New Year's Party at her place and such a celebration it was. The delight, the hopes shining out of her eyes as the New Year came in.'

'They're like that,' said Eileen. 'There's a German night in the saloon, for Silvester Abend, that's what they call this evening. But I'm like you. New Year's Eve makes me sad. I do be wondering about all the changes that are coming and it's not on the bright side I'm looking.'

'I'd never have thought that of you. All the years I've known you – I'd have said you didn't harbour sad thoughts.'

'That's my acting,' said Eileen. 'Underneath all that I'm as melancholy as the next Irishman or woman.'

'Melancholy – that's it. That's the way I feel, a great sadness hanging over me, but please God it will pass.'

On New Year's Eve Mary lay in bed fingering the gold cross and chain Mr Jaeger had given her for a Christmas present. Apart from her wedding ring it was the only piece of jewellery she had ever possessed. Since Christmas Eve she had worn it constantly, in the daytime outside her clothes, at night-time inside her nightdress lying against her skin.

Before getting into bed, having first made sure that Kathleen was asleep or not looking in her direction, Mary held the small hand mirror and admired the gold ornament above her breasts. Letting herself imagine while she gazed that Mr Jaeger had placed the chain round her neck, lifting her hair, admiring it as he did so, whispering, 'Such beautiful hair, so soft, so silky,' and then bending to kiss the nape of her neck. Always, before her imaginings went further Kathleen stirred in her sleep or awake demanded Mary's attention. Recalled to reality, Mary knew Mr Jaeger had handed over the cross and chain in a box along with a present for Kathleen – with a smile and a wish for a Happy Christmas. Mr Jaeger had never seen her hair loose. Mr Jaeger had never even accidentally touched her.

Dreaming and hoping and foolish longing was all that it was. But not wrong. She loved Mr Jaeger. He was a kind, good man. Like herself he was lonely and a stranger in America. He was a Catholic. If it was God's will she would like him for a husband and father to Kathleen. For weeks she had been praying to Our Lady for her special intention. And Our Lady was interceding for her. Hadn't she got the golden cross and chain to prove it.

In the dark she lay thinking about other New Year's Eves when Mrs Jaeger was alive. The great celebrations she had made of the feast. And she wondered how Mr Jaeger was spending this one. Lonely and sadly, no doubt, for she had heard him refuse invitations to neighbours' homes, the poor man.

If only she had had the courage to do what she so badly wanted – invite him to her place. Cook something for him. set the table nicely and him, Kathleen and herself sit down like a family. But maybe next year, please God. Caressing the golden cross and thinking to the next year she fell asleep.

She was dreaming. She was in a warm place. She was very happy. She was in the bakery. The bread was rising. Everywhere there were trays and pans of dough rising. Before her eyes it grew and grew, up and up and it rose with a thin skin forming on it. Mr Jaeger was there laughing

181

and talking excitedly as the dough grew to an enormous size and began spilling over and while he laughed his fingers stroked her neck and she felt light-headed from the stroking and the smell of yeast. And then there was a scream and Mary woke up. And it was Kathleen screaming and crying that her ear was paining her.

Mary lit the bedside candle and saw Kathleen rocking from side to side and banging her head against the wall. Mary held her and comforted her and tied a scarf round her head and didn't know what else to do for Kathleen's anguish until she remembered that Eileen had a bottle of almond oil and that a few drops of it warmed up was good for earache.

She looked at the clock – it was half past four in the morning. Eileen would surely be home by now. Anyway, she had to try, for Kathleen couldn't be left to endure the agony. She coaxed her to lie down, pulled the covers from her bed and piled them over her. 'I'll get something to make you better. I'll only be a minute. Say a Hail Mary over and over. Only a minute I'll be and then I'll make you better. There now, my little dote,' she said as she pulled on her skirt and threw a shawl round her shoulders. 'There now, your mammy won't be long,' she crooned, going out onto the pitch black landing where she knew the rats scampered at night and where nothing only the relieving of Kathleen's pain would have taken her.

Feeling her way up the stairs, holding tight to the rickety banisters she climbed to the next floor. 'Thanks be to God,' she said out loud when she saw round the edges of the badly-fitting door the light of Eileen's lamp. She knocked. 'Eileen, it's me. Eileen,' she knocked again.

She heard movement, Eileen's voice cursing. Maybe she'd woken her. She'd be in bad humour dragged from her sleep. But it couldn't be helped – she had to have the oil.

'Who the bloody hell is it? I'm in bed. What d'ye want?'

'It's me, Mary. Kathleen's sick with the earache, out of her mind with the pain – would you lend me the sweet oil.'

'Mary, it's you, hold on now, I'm coming. Come in,' said Eileen opening the door, half-asleep, drunk and half-dressed. 'Happy New Year, come on in.'

'God bless you,' said Mary. 'I wouldn't have disturbed you only the child is very bad. A few drops of the oil. I'll bring it back in the morning.' She went into the room. There was a man asleep on the bed, and after a quick furtive glance she looked away.

'Where the hell did I put that?' Eileen kept asking herself as she kicked clothes and cats from under her feet while searching drawers and press for the oil.

'It could be in the table drawer,' suggested Mary and again she glanced towards the bed and away thinking that there was something familiar about the man. He had his face to the wall so she might be mistaken.

'You might be right,' said Eileen and tugged at the table drawer. It stuck and she tugged so hard the drawer came all the way out, its contents spilling with a clatter on the floor.

'The curse of God on it,' said Eileen, letting fall the drawer and making more noise. Dim though the light was Mary spied amongst knives, forks, spoons, broken beads, twists of string and other odds and ends the bottle of oil. She bent and pounced on it. The man on the bed, disturbed by the noise, sighed and stirred and turned to face the room. Rising from the floor with the bottle clutched in her hand Mary's eyes again drawn to the bed looked on the sleeping countenance of Mr Jaeger.

She ran from the room. Only the thought of her suffering child made her tread carefully, otherwise she wouldn't have cared had she tumbled down the flight and broken her neck. 'Don't cry, Alanna,' she kept saying out loud. 'Mammy's coming. She'll make you better in a minute.' She had to keep talking to prevent herself from screaming.

Kathleen was asleep – the covers thrown off, the scarf slipped from her head around her neck. Mary dropped the bottle on the bed, made the scarf safe and covered her again. Then pulling the shawl over her head she sat in the chair and cried with shame and rage and for the pity of her broken dreams.

As the morning wore on Katy wondered why neither Eileen nor Mary had dropped in to wish her a Happy New Year. Eileen she supposed was sleeping off last night's carousing, but Mary should have called this while back. She was about to send one of the children round to see if everything was all right when Eileen came storming in. 'That oul bitch,' she said, 'she's gone out of her mind. She's after ordering me out and all I did was go in to wish her a Happy New Year and ask how Kathleen was.'

Katy was taken aback by Eileen's vehemence and mystified to what could have made Mary order her out. 'You'd better sit down, have a cup of tea, and tell me all about it.'

'If I knew you had a drink in the house I'd ask for one,' said Eileen taking a chair.

'Have the tea instead, I'll put plenty of sugar in it.'

'That plaikeen of hers had the earache during the night and her mother came up for the oil. There was a man in the room. The oul hypocrite – she knew well it wasn't the first time I'd brought a man back. Though since I took up with Paddy I've asked no one up this long time.'

'Ah, come on now Eileen, Mary has queer ways but she wouldn't turn on you for that. You must have had words. Maybe you were in bad humour when she knocked you up and were short with her – if you had a sup taken you mightn't remember.'

'As God is my judge I wasn't. I gave her the oil and the next thing is she's out the door, running down the stairs without as much as a thank you, kiss me arse or goodnight.'

'Did you give out about that when you went in this morning? If she'd had a bad night with the interruption about Kathleen, then you came giving out as well, that could account for it.'

'I never mentioned anything about last night. Well, you know me – I don't harbour things. In I went and she jumped on me. What she didn't call me.' Eileen looked terrible, her face drawn and pale and Katy guessed it was less to do with the drink than the row with Mary. For underneath all her bluster and blather Eileen was shaken by rows with those she liked.

'You can say what you like, she's an oul hypocrite. It was seeing the man there that caused it all. And I wouldn't mind only he was fast asleep and fully dressed.'

'Very peculiar,' mused Katy, then she asked who the man was.

'Mr Jaeger,' said Eileen.

'Mr Jaeger . . . Mr Jaeger the baker – the one Mary works for?'

'There's only the one – yes, him, what's so extraordinary about him? What are you looking at me like that for?'

'God Almighty Eileen, of all the men why did you pick on him? Wasn't it you that drew my attention to what was going on in the first place!'

'Now don't you start. My head is splitting. Don't you talk in riddles. Drew your attention to what in the first place?'

'Mary and him. She has a strong notion for him. After you mentioned it I watched and put two and two together.'

'Sure I was only codding.'

'All the same you were right, and I think he has notions of her. He gave her a gold cross and chain for Christmas.'

'Oh Jesus, I never knew. Nor about the cross and chain neither.'

184

'She showed only me the present.'

'Why didn't you tell me about her and him?'

'I told no one.'

Eileen looked hurt. 'You could have told me. I tell you everything.' Katy explained her reasons for not confiding in her. 'I might have teased her, but in the long run you've caused more harm than good by your silence. If I'd had an inkling do you think I'd have brought him up?'

'Why did you anyway?'

'I felt sorry for him. He didn't come into the bar until almost twelve. He was well-oiled then, drinking on his own in the house. He kept talking about his wife and the children, Lord have mercy on them. He stayed after everyone was gone and by that time he was footless. I had to link him home and passing my place, I said to come in for a drink.'

'Wouldn't you have thought he'd have remembered that Mary lived there.'

'Listen,' said Eileen, back to her old form. 'By then he wouldn't have known his own name. I'm telling you he was stocious. One mouthful out of his glass and he collapsed on the bed. He was still drunk this morning – I doubt if he'll remember where he spent the night. But how will I get Mary to believe that?'

'You won't – at least not for a long time.'

'Would it do any good if I went round again and said I was sorry.'

'No,' said Katy. 'I don't think it would. Leave it for a while. I'll go after the dinner – if she opens up maybe I'll tell her what you told me.'

'I have to go now,' said Eileen, 'let me know what happens.'

Katy felt so sorry for Mary she could have taken her in her arms and cried for her. The gloss that had lately come on her was gone – her eyes were dull and puffed, her hair straggly, her voice dispirited as she told Katy to sit and then asked, 'I suppose you heard?'

'Eileen told me, she's in an awful way.'

Mary started to cry. 'Didn't I make the fool of myself. A woman of my age that should have more sense. Won't I be the laughing stock of the neighbourhood.' Katy let her cry and said nothing to console her, knowing Mary wanted to keep talking.

'I had notions of him. God knows he isn't a great beauty no more than myself. But a nicer, kinder man you never met. At first that's all it was – his niceness and politeness and the few shillings. Then it changed. I felt different. Like I was a young girl again and courting. Not that he ever said or did anything to lead me on. But I had hopes and when he gave

185

me the cross and chain I thought it might be a sign. I'll never be able to raise my head again.'

'Indeed you will,' said Katy, breaking the silence. 'You did nothing to be ashamed of.'

'Didn't I make little of myself and all the time he was carrying on with her.'

'But he wasn't. That's not how it was. He was lonely, sad because it was New Year's Eve. He stayed in the house drinking on his own and when he couldn't bear it any longer went to the saloon near midnight. There's nothing between him and Eileen. God help her, she's head over heels in love with that chancer Paddy Kavanagh that she only met the once. Living in hopes of a word from him.'

'And she took my man to console herself and spite me,' Mary said bitterly.

'No, that's not true. For one thing, Eileen knew nothing about your notions for him. No one suspected anything about you. I had my suspicions, but I never breathed a word, as true as God.'

'You wouldn't tell me lies?'

'I would not.'

'Oh Katy, what am I going to do? Apart from how I feel about him I love the work. It's a lovely change from cleaning the City Hall – I look forward to it. If, I was thinking, but that was before last night, if I could have had more hours I'd have left the Hall. I don't think I could ever go near the bakery again. How could I face him?'

'I told you, Eileen said he was so drunk he wouldn't have recognised anyone.'

'She would, wouldn't she?'

'You saw him – is that the truth?'

'Every word a concoction of hers. The last thing I want is to throw up the bit of work. But how could I ever face him again. And what do you think it would be like for him?'

For the time being Katy decided it was no use trying to heal Mary's hurt or convince her of Eileen's innocent part in what had happened. But she must make her keep the job. Then maybe time would take care of the rest. After more questioning, Mary admitted the possibility that the baker was too drunk to recognise her, even to know where he was. Having done this she agreed reluctantly that she would go back to work, but couldn't immediately. She'd need a day or two to get over the terrible experience.

'All right, so,' said Katy. 'I'll go and tell him you're sick and see what he says.'

'I'll do it then, but only if you swear again that no one knew about my foolish thoughts, and that wan in particular.'

'No one, and Eileen didn't have the slightest suspicion. Wouldn't I have been the first she'd have come to with the news.' And Katy thought that before going to the bakery she must find Eileen and warn her that she was supposed to know nothing.

I'm becoming the accomplished liar, Katy said to herself after seeing Herr Jaeger, and he's either a great actor or was as drunk as Eileen said, for he was genuinely concerned about Mary's health. She must stay home until she was better. The job would be waiting for her, he assured Katy and as she turned to go he called her back and made two parcels of fancy bread and cakes, one for her and one for Mary.

He was a kind, good man and Katy hoped all would go well for him and Mary. With all that had taken place she had been too preoccupied to dwell on herself. Now that the problems were seemingly solved a black, fearful feeling descended on her. An anxious state, a foreboding that something terrible was going to happen in the future.

Mary was overjoyed with the news Katy brought and wanted to detain her, to quiz her again about the baker's reaction. Did he look sheepish? Did Katy think he remembered? Even when Katy had reassured her Mary wanted to keep talking. Wanted her to have tea and eat the cakes. Katy refused. Mary asked, did anything ail her and Katy said nothing, only work she had to have ready by teatime. When the mood was on her she wanted to be on her own, walk for a while, let the cold wind blow through her brain and blow away the lost, sad and fearful feelings.

Jamsie too was in a black mood as he walked away from the job where the bad weather had made it impossible for the labourers to work. Maybe he'd be laid off a week, maybe more. He hated American winters, the freezing winds, ploughing through snow that came up over your boots, or when it thawed plodding through the icy slush. His feet were permanently cold and damp, his toes parched white, the skin crinkled when he undressed. Life in America was terrible. And he thought of Ireland. The easy living there was before the Hunger. Winter, spring or summer the weather was neither harshly hot or cold, the rain was warm, the winds seldom piercing, the sun never unbearable and snow he had seen there only once in his life.

On the rare days when the wind was from the north-east you could stay in by the fire. Potatoes needed little care or cultivation. A man could spend his days living, living as his father had before him. Never getting into a lather of sweat. There was time for everything and everyone. At your leisure you could enjoy the bit of food. Have time for your wife and children. Time to talk, to listen, to look. To poach a salmon, snare a bird. In Ireland before the Hunger he had been as content as the next man. Ambition was a word he didn't know. Ambition was for the gombeen man. Breaking his neck and racking his brains and the hearts of them he robbed to make his pennies. A figure to be despised.

In Ireland, no one measured your progress – only your decency, your kindness, your willingness to help another. On those things you were judged. But in America it wasn't like that. Here people had a dream. One day they would be successful. Everyone had the same chance of succeeding. Work hard enough and you could be anything. It wasn't true. Never had he worked so hard in his life. And what had he achieved? Nothing. What little progress they had made was Katy's doing. Katy's and the help from Peader.

He hated America because it infected you with the disease everyone else suffered. And the disease was money. Without it you were done for. Money was a curse. In Ireland you lived happily from one year's end to the other without handling much. In America without it you were nothing. And when you had it it was swallowed wholesale. The little house had the big mouth. Pots and coppers, coal for the fire. Though he'd admit the coal was better than the kerosene in Mulberry Street. But it had to be paid for and it was filthy stuff. At home you had your own turf, lashings of it, cut on a good day, dried and stacked by the gable wall. Sweet sods of dark brown turf that threw out twice the heat of the oul coal and didn't choke you with its smoke. And not a penny to pay for it.

In America you had covering for the floor. At home the earth was trodden beneath your feet, packed hard from years of feet trampling – what better floor could you ask for? Food and warmth and shelter with little or no expense, and you were as comfortable as ever you were in America and more contented.

The trouble in America was that every man wanted what the next one had. In Ireland there was only the gentry – only a fool tried to imitate them. There were the few comfortable farmers. Wise, thrifty men and their women the same. What money they had was put by. Not squandered for rugs and ornaments, fancy curtains and clothes. And the rest were labouring men who when they laid hands on a shilling put it to good use slaking their thirst.

188

In America you were led to believe that Jack was as good as his master. And no matter how hard you resisted the belief sometimes it got to you. That's what caused the discontentment. For in your saner moments you knew it was a lie. You worked until you felt like dropping. Katy worked, now Bridget was working, Thomas would be next. All of them slaving, chasing the dream and in twenty, thirty years time – where would they be? If not dead, not a penny the better off for all the slaving. And all for what? So that by buying the coppers and kettles, and boots and coal and floor-covering they had made other men rich. He wished to God he had never set foot in America. He wished he was back in Kilgoran with nothing on his mind except persuading Carey to give him his porter on score.

A glass of porter, that would be the fine thing. Lately he'd had little of it. Well, he'd soon change that. The first saloon he came to he'd wash the taste of America out of his mouth.

While he was doing it he got into talk with a man from Kerry who was going to work on the railroad. The money, the man told him, was good. 'Later on,' he said, 'I'll send for the wife and children. Or I might get the fare together for a passage home.'

'You're not settled, so?'

'Settled?' said the Kerryman. 'I am not. I hate cities.'

'I do too,' said Jamsie, 'but I wouldn't want to farm either. Like yourself I'd say I'm not settled.'

'Go on the railroad – you're in the country without depending on the land for a living.'

'I've a wife and children.'

'Tell her you'll send for her. Tell her maybe you'll buy a farm of land.'

'She knows I wouldn't do that. I had enough of the land.'

'Tell her you've changed your mind. No doubt she's a good woman. She'll wait for you. But get out of the city. Sure a man is caged in them. A city could break your heart. Do you know there's days when I never lift my eyes from the ground. Digging, one foot after the other, breaking the rocks and digging again, and the ganger shouting "Dig, dig, dig" '

'I'd say there wouldn't be much difference on the railroad.'

'Oh, but there would. You'd be moving from place to place. There'd be fields around you and mountains behind you, you'd not be caged. And if you didn't like the railroad, sure wouldn't you be nearer to where there's gold?'

'Aye,' said Jamsie, 'you might be right.'

189

The idea of the railroad became rooted in his mind. He imagined being away from the city, the fields round him, the mountains behind him. Daily he came more and more to resent 'the ganger'. One day, he promised himself, he would take no more of it. No more gangers would stand over him. If there was one thing he hated it was being stood over. One day he'd go to the railroad and earn lapfuls of money to send home to Katy. Then she wouldn't have to take in washing any more. And he'd send for her, or maybe have money enough for a passage home where he'd work the small fields that needed little attention. And he'd work on his own with no one to tell him when or how.

In the meantime he would be escaping from the city. He'd be a caged bird no longer. And as the man had said, if he didn't like the railroad wouldn't he be nearer to where the gold was. He'd make Katy a fortune.

Katy's feelings of depression came and went. One day in Confession she mentioned them to the priest. 'Father, I have this terrible unease about me. It's as if something terrible is going to happen.'

'Child,' said the priest, 'put your trust in God. We are all in His hands. Now make a good Act of Contrition and for your penance say a decade of the Rosary.'

The floor was hard beneath her knees and the repetitious praying kept her mind off herself for the length of time it took to say the ten Hail Marys, Glory Be to the Fathers and Our Fathers.

'You're working yourself into the grave,' was Eileen's answer when Katy mentioned her anxious feelings. 'I could count the number of times on two hands I've seen you sit and do nothing since you moved to Cow Lane.'

'Amn't I sitting down now,' said Katy.

'Like a hen on a hot griddle, up every minute to see if the boiler's working, the whites blueing, the stew simmering.'

'It's the way women with a family get, always working against the clock.'

'Only in America. At home you wouldn't be trying to run a laundry and rear children.' Then Eileen changed the conversation to talk about Mary and the baker. 'I saw them the other day like a pair of turtle doves gazing into each other's eyes. The next thing you know there'll be a wedding.' Eileen laughed. 'I couldn't,' she said, 'imagine Mary doing it, could you?'

'Now Eileen,' said Katy in mock severity.

'Still she must have, she's got the plaikeen to prove it. God forgive me, I shouldn't mock them. But I can't help it. If I know someone as pious as Mary, or an ill-suited pair where the woman's as big as a house and him a skinny little fellow I do see them in my mind's eye and all the contortions.'

'Eileen, you'll never see Heaven unless God takes into consideration the number of times you've made me laugh when I started out wanting to cry.'

Then Eileen talked seriously and advised Katy to take life easier. 'I know you want to get on, everyone in America does. Look at me waiting to hear from Paddy, hoping to make my fame and fortune in San Francisco. Six months and not a word. Take my advice and don't be killing yourself.'

Katy said she would, pretending all that ailed her was ambition and overwork. But knew that whatever ailed her went deeper than that. It had nothing to do with loss or gain of things. Her fears were for those she loved. One of them was threatened. Something terrible was going to happen.

Paddy Kavanagh after leaving Eileen that night in the saloon went back to Philadelphia, where there was another attractive woman with a good singing voice. To her as well as Eileen he had outlined his scheme for San Francisco. To her he told the story of visiting New York and having the promise of backers. 'Since you went away I have talked to my father,' she now informed him.

'Oh yes,' said Paddy. He wasn't keen on becoming involved with fathers. 'You never mentioned your father.'

'You were here no time, I never got round to it,' said the girl whose name was Norah. 'Anyway, my father thinks San Francisco is a good idea.'

'Indeed,' said Paddy. 'Don't mind me asking, but what would your father know about it?'

'He knows everything. When he first came from Ireland he travelled all over the country.'

'I see,' said Paddy. 'What does he do for a living?'

'He's a builder, he made a lot of money from building.'

'Then how are you singing here? I wouldn't have thought he'd want his daughter singing in a saloon or in San Francisco for that matter.'

'He doesn't – but you don't know me. I'm a singer – that's what I want and that's what I do. He might back your show. But first he'd have to meet you.'

Paddy dabbed at his sweating forehead with a handkerchief and said, 'Isn't it very warm in here.' Backers he wanted, dancing girls and singing girls he wanted, but fathers as backers – that was another thing altogether. His intentions of getting a troupe to San Francisco was genuine enough, but in his own way, in his own time. Half the thrill was in collecting the girls, having them dotted round the country, going from one to another. Being careful at the first meeting to arouse no suspicions in their minds. On the second visit they usually fell into his hands like ripe apples. By the time he got to San Francisco he'd have a harem. And what better way of buying loyalty than with love. He was the soul of discretion and would bank on it that with five or six girls he could keep them all happy, convince each in turn that she was the girl he would marry. In blissful ignorance they'd live happily. And one day maybe he would marry one of them. He had taken a great shine to Eileen in New York. She was the one he'd have to be careful about, for Eileen was no fool.

'Why does your father want to meet me?'

'Well, he would if he was thinking of putting money your way.'

'I don't know,' said Paddy. 'I know a few fellas that made a bit with gold and want to invest it. Fellas about my own age. With businessmen like your father he might want too much say.'

'Maybe,' said the girl. 'Tell me, while you're waiting to get this troupe on the road what do you do for a living?'

Paddy was taken aback by her directness, but truthfully could say, 'I have independent means.' He had five hundred dollars left from the sale of his father's pub in Galway. With the help of God before it ran out he'd be set up for San Francisco so long as he tracked down his miner friends and so long as they hadn't squandered their money.

'You've nothing to lose by meeting my father.'

'I suppose not. Right then, I will.'

He went to supper later in the week. The house was all decked out with the newest and most lavish of furniture. Mr and Mrs Molloy were welcoming and thanks be to God, Paddy thought, apart from the furniture the money hadn't gone to their heads. The food was simple and there was plenty of it; the girl who brought it in was Irish and treated like one of the family. The father told him of his hard beginnings in America and how he had got on. And the mother said they had buried two children while they tried farming in the west. 'Norah, God bless and spare her, is our only daughter, our only child.'

Norah talked and laughed and Paddy could see that she had both parents round her finger. When they had finished eating, Mr Molloy asked Paddy to come into the parlour. 'We'll have a glass of whiskey and you can tell me about your plans for San Francisco.' Once they were seated and the bottle and glasses set out Mr Molloy began to talk about Norah. 'We've spoiled the child. And she's grown up headstrong. It nearly killed her mother when she went to sing in the saloon. You can imagine the talk there was. The looks in Mass, the priest coming to talk to her. But she wouldn't budge an inch. The wife wanted her voice trained, wanted to send her to Italy. But I'll say this for Norah – like myself she's a realist. She knows the sort of voice she had and it's not for training in Italy.'

So, thought Paddy, you'd be glad of me to take her off to San Francisco where she could indulge her passion for singing and your wife would be spared the nods and winks of the neighbours. It wasn't such a bad idea if the father coughed up the money. He mightn't keep such a sharp eye on the finances. He seemed to have plenty and wasn't his main concern keeping the two women in his life happy.

Paddy outlined his scheme. Mr Molloy asked pertinent questions and now and then jotted down figures on a piece of paper. 'It might very well work. There's plenty of openings for that sort of thing. And as you say there's others besides the Irish in America wanting different songs and music. Yes, I'd say it could work.'

Everything was going grand, Paddy was thinking. He might be out of there tonight with it all fixed up.

'Have another one,' offered Mr Molloy.

'Thanks,' said Paddy then raising his glass added, 'Slainté.'

The older man returned the toast, lit his pipe, puffed for a while and said, 'Of course, it's not something I could decide in a minute. I'll have to talk it over with my wife, the bank and my solicitor – that's how it is in business – but it doesn't have to take too long. You're not in a terrible hurry.'

'Not terrible.'

'That's good. Anyway, the weather's bad – you wouldn't be wanting the journey west till it improved.'

No,' said Paddy, 'that mightn't be wise.'

'Then I'll see you again. You'll come and eat with us. And I'd be very obliged if you'd see Norah home from the saloon of an evening.'

After eating their food and drinking their whiskey he could hardly refuse. 'Certainly,' he said. 'And don't mind me asking, but would you have any idea how long it might be before you make your decision?'

'Not long, a few weeks I'd say at the most.'

They shook hands on that and promising to come to supper on Sunday, Paddy went back to his cheap hotel.

Norah, he soon discovered, was one of those apples that didn't fall into his hands. A kiss, two or three – that was all he got. All his charm and protestations of love went for nothing. 'I thought,' he said one night, 'that you were a headstrong girl, doing what you wanted.'

'I am,' said Norah, slapping away his hands that were straying near her breasts. 'I'm doing what I want,' and she kissed him chastely and went into the house.

'I'll have you yet,' Paddy said to himself as he left.

He was getting fatter with all the food he ate at the Molloys'. They had him now going to Mass with them, a thing he had avoided since leaving Galway. From time to time Mr Molloy gave him small pieces of encouragement. A friend in San Francisco had been in touch – he knew the very site for a theatre. He was following it up – another few weeks should see the enquiries complete.

At the end of three months Mrs Molloy said one night, 'Do you know, Paddy, isn't it the sin you paying money in that hotel and four empty bedrooms here. Would you not think of moving in for the while until the business is finished.' She was a nice kind woman, the house was warm and comfortable, the hotel was a kip, so Paddy thought he had all to gain and nothing to lose and moved in.

Lapped in luxury, fed titbits of good news about the San Francisco venture, six months had flown before he knew it. Then one evening in April Mr Molloy said, 'Come into the parlour, Paddy. There's something I have to say.'

As he left the table Paddy noticed the pleased and excited looks passing between Norah and her mother. 'This is it,' he thought following Mr Molloy out, 'this is the night the money's put on the table.'

'Sit down, Paddy, have a drink.' Mr Molloy poured himself one and made himself comfortable in his chair. 'Well now,' he said, 'I think we've gone into everything and I've had the best advice and the venture seems a sound one. Only a matter of a few papers and you're all set.'

Paddy was bursting with joy. 'Mr Molloy, I don't know how to thank . . .'

'Ah, now hold on a minute Paddy, there is one other thing.'

Jesus, thought Paddy, what's he come up with now? 'Yes, sir?' he said and waited.

194

'What are your intentions towards Norah?'

'Towards Norah? I don't understand.'

'Don't be bashful. Haven't you been courting my daughter for the last four or five months? I was thinking we'd announce the engagement, a short one and have the two of you married before you set off for California.'

For the first time in his life Paddy was at a loss for words. Marry Norah, marry anyone . . . not if he never got to San Francisco, not if he never got to Heaven. The crafty oul bastard – that's what it was all about. Norah after singing in the saloon wouldn't have the local successful Irishmen beating a path to her door. Mr and Mrs Molloy were killing two birds with one stone. Get Norah a husband and out of Philadelphia at the same time. The trap had been cleverly laid and into it he had fallen. He wondered if Norah was a party to it. Probably. As a means of getting away.

'Well,' said Mr Molloy. 'You've been mulling over what I said for a while.'

'Norah's a beautiful girl and I have a great regard for her. But to tell you the truth I hadn't thought of marriage . . . that's not the truth, I had but sure I didn't think I'd stand a chance. You're a big man in this place, I didn't think it was a fella like me you'd have in mind for a son-in-law.'

'You've become like a son to us and Norah is light about you. Like a good man go off to your bed now and think on what I've said. I think I'll know what your answer will be. Norah's an only child, don't forget that.'

Paddy stood up and went to the older man, offering his hand. 'You've done me a great honour, so great I'm overcome by it. I'll take your advice and go to bed and first thing in the morning I'll be down with my answer.'

'Good man,' said Mr Molloy, slapping Paddy on the back. 'Good night and God bless you, son.'

'Son, me arse,' said Paddy to himself, and went on tiptoe past the room where Norah and her mother might be sitting. In his room he waited and waited until there wasn't a sound in the house, looked round the door and saw the lights were out. Then he packed his belongings, crept down the stairs, fearfully opened the front door, waiting every minute for Mr Molloy's hand to descend on him, to hear Norah or Mrs Molloy scream but everywhere was silent. He slipped out the door and ran and ran. When it was daylight he set about getting back to New York.

195

Eileen screamed when she went into the hall and a hand caught hold of her. When Paddy identified himself, she yelled, 'What did you want to do that for? You gave me a terrible fright.'

'I wanted to surprise you,' said Paddy.

'You could have surprised me without waiting in the pitch black hall. Feel my heart – it's leppin'.'

Paddy put his hand on her breast. ' "My heart," I said,' remonstrated Eileen, but all the same she let his hand remain. She was thrilled he had come. As excited as a young girl in love for the first time. And it wasn't as dark in the hall as she had said. She could see his face, his lovely smiling handsome face. 'Come up,' she said, 'but don't make any noise.'

Inside the room they embraced and he gave her a long kiss. 'I missed you,' he said.

'I missed you, too. Three months you said, it's been six.'

'I know and I'm sorry I was delayed. You spend days, weeks trying to locate someone. You make an appointment. Then he doesn't turn up or does and isn't interested. You have to start all over again. I'm that worn out.'

'I bet that wasn't all that delayed you.'

'God, Eileen, you're a desperate woman. A disbeliever. Business, that's what kept me.'

'How did the business go – are we off to San Francisco?'

'We are that – but there's a hitch. Two men I thought I had in the palm of my hand dropped out. So you could say I'm back where I started. You'll have to be patient and above all, trust me. One of these days we'll have a show like no one has ever seen before. If you'll only trust me. Say you do.'

She was in his arms again, hungry for his love. Wanting to hear him tell her she was beautiful. That there was no one else. Wanting him to love her, wanting to love him. Wanting to be desired by only one man, her own man. Wanting to trust and believe in him.

'You came back to me, so it must mean something,' she said. 'You will be starving – we'll have a bit to eat and then we'll go to bed.'

'Darling,' said Paddy, 'I couldn't eat a thing but I'm jaded. I could sleep on a bed of nails. Will we go to the bed?'

'Where are you heading for now?' asked Eileen the next morning.

'Nowhere for the present. There's one or two contacts to see in New York, why?'

'I was thinking you could stay here for a while.'

'Would you like that?'

'I would love that,' she said.

Paddy stayed for a month, then left to see a man in Buffalo. To Katy, Eileen said on the day he went, 'I love him. In the long run I think he'll let me down. But I'll face that when the time comes.'

'Don't mind me asking,' said Katy, 'but how does he live?'

'I never enquire too closely. I know he has something from an inheritance. Anyway he's never short of money – whether he comes by it honestly or not I couldn't say.'

Katy thought, poor Eileen you are unfortunate with your men and said aloud, 'My acquaintance with Paddy hasn't endeared him to me. He's not a man to be trusted. That I may be wrong and you may find happiness and go to San Francisco, though for my sake I hope you're still here for many a day.'

Chapter Sixteen

Eileen was still in Mulberry Street the next year. Paddy came and went and kept up her hopes with promises and fed her longing for declamations of love by telling her she was the grandest woman he had ever met. The words and his love-making kept her content.

She noticed the frequency with which his rings and watches changed and suspected that he received stolen articles in one city and sold them in another, for how else was he managing for money? His inheritance must surely be long spent on the trips he made, looking for backers and finding the right girls to take San Francisco by storm.

Sometimes the thought came to her that Paddy was nothing but a chancer. That his plans for a troupe of singing and dancing girls was no more than talk. That he was a liar and a thief, a womaniser. That in ten or twenty years she'd still be in her tenement room, too old to sing in the saloon. And where, she wondered, would Paddy be then. But she never let such thoughts linger. Replacing them by brighter, happier ones. Herself and Paddy in California. Herself delighting an audience. Herself and Paddy married.

Katy's black moods came and went, though as she told herself time and time again she had no reason for feeling depressed. Hadn't she and her family their health. Wasn't Jamsie still working at the building, only idle in the bad weather and didn't they love each other as much as ever. Sometimes she wondered why God hadn't blessed her with another child. Few women of her age living with their husbands escaped this long. And she'd smile, remembering Statia and her advice on how to avoid having another child. 'Afterwards always get up and pass water.' Statia, the Lord have mercy on her with a remedy for everything. Statia, who wasn't put off giving advice no matter how often it failed. Whether you got pregnant or died Statia had the ready answer. 'It was God's Will.'

Bridget had nothing but praise for Madame Renée and the shop. 'Such hats and bonnets,' she told Katy when she was in good humour. 'I'm learning how to block the felt ones, though we don't get much call for them. But Madame Renée says it's all part of the training. What I love is the decorating of the straws and silks. I'm good at that. Madame Renée says I have the knack.'

Mary Kate was proving to be the student Miss Cook had said she was. Ask her to do a message and you'd have to ask umpteen times, for she was always with a book or pencil and paper. Katy would look at her two daughters and think how no one would take them for sisters. Bridget was tall with yellow hair like her own and the same big, brown eyes. With a good figure already and a grace to every move she made. And poor Mary Kate. God wasn't fair in the handing out of figures and faces.

She was low-sized, though there was nothing of a dwarf about her. And Bridget had stopped calling her one a long time ago. But unless she suddenly got a stretch a low-sized woman she'd be. Low-sized and bunty. Her hair was nice and thick but neither one colour nor the other, brownish-fair with greyish, blueish eyes. But she had the sweetest mouth and the loveliest smile Katy had ever seen.

'She's the nicest child I've ever taught,' Miss Cook told Katy when she went to see her again. 'Mary Kate will be a teacher, she has everything it takes. She'll grow into a fine, uncomplicated woman with her feet firmly on the ground. But first she'll be a teacher. For girls must be educated and their talents not go to waste but more important, Mary Kate will be independent – able to earn her own living.'

'I'm all for the education of girls as well as boys. But I never thought of it like that before. You're right, every woman should be independent. And I'll see to it, God willing, that Mary Kate has her chance.'

'Good woman,' said Miss Cook.

Thomas was out of school. Katy made enquiries about him serving his time but no one, not even the priest could help her. Apprenticeships went to the sons or relations of tradesmen. Disappointed though she was, he'd have to go labouring with Jamsie. Jamsie refused to ask for him.

'What's the matter with you, why won't you speak for him?'

'He wouldn't be right for labouring.'

'Look at the size of him – he's as big as you.'

'There's more to it than size. That fella'd be swinging a pick, suddenly see a worm in its way and stop to pick it up.'

Katy laughed, for what Jamsie said was true. Tom couldn't bear to kill a fly. He'd go out of his way to avoid stepping on a cockroach. 'He'd soon learn with you to keep an eye on him – he has to have work.'

199

'I thought,' said Jamsie, 'you didn't want him with a pick and shovel. Wasn't that why you sent him to school?'

'He can read and write – maybe he'll get something else when he's older. But in the meantime I don't want him hanging about the street. You'll speak for him?'

'I will not. It's hard enough having someone standing over me. I don't want them over him then coming to me to complain.'

'God bless us,' said Katy, ' 'tis you are the unnatural father. You'd see your own son idle.'

'Let him find work for himself – there's more than one building site.'

Katy said no more about jobs. Lately Jamsie had been very cantankerous. You never knew when you had him. Sometimes he seemed miles away. Thomas would find something, anything for the time being. When Jamsie was more himself she'd broach the subject again.

Jamsie, as Katy had noticed, often seemed miles away. Since the conversation with the Kerryman he was coming closer and closer to a decision about leaving New York. In another couple of months it would be winter again and he vowed it would be the last one he'd spend in the city.

Jacques Demart had come on a short visit to Virginia. He stayed in one of the less grand houses but one day came to see Peader at Annilaun. 'It's good to see you, Jacques,' Peader said, warmly shaking his hand. Charlotte presided over the afternoon tea and kept Jacques engaged talking about furniture. Paul was looking for a writing table. Jacques promised to keep an eye out for a suitable one.

When it was time to leave Peader walked with him to the jetty. Before boarding Jacques asked, 'What do you do with yourself all day? How do you stay sane? I don't understand you.'

'I don't understand myself, Jacques. And you know exactly what I do – nothing that's worthwhile.'

'Then why do you stay? I'd help you get started in New York. You've friends there, you're an educated man, there's a big Irish community, you'd be more at home there. Here you're nothing, no more than I was. You're only tolerated because of who Charlotte is.'

'Leave it, Jacques. What you say is true but Charlotte's my wife. I love her. She loves Virginia. I think she'd die if I forced her to leave. I never should have taken her from her own kind. Now she's found them again I can't make her go. I can't break her heart. Can you understand that?'

'No,' said Jacques, 'I cannot. If she was mine I'd have had her away from here years ago.'

'How could you understand – you haven't a wife.'

'No, thank God. You married the wrong woman. Katy, the woman you've told me so much about, the one in New York with the children, she'd have been the woman for you. I'm sorry Peader, I've overstepped the mark. If one day you see sense, come to me. Whether or not I'm there the house is yours. Well, I'll be off. I'm glad I saw the old place, and the old ways before, thank God, they disappear forever.'

'Goodbye, Jacques,' said Peader and envied him his return to New York.

One day in the spring of the following year when the sun was shining, the washing dried quickly, the women in the street were singing as they strung out lines of washing and Katy felt it was good to be alive, Jamsie came home from work early. Her heart sank. Something was wrong. He'd been sacked. Quickly she reminded herself that wasn't the end of the world. New York was booming, with new buildings going up everywhere, factories opening. More ships coming and going.

'I'm going away,' he announced before sitting down, without smiling at her. 'I'm going on the railroad.'

'You can't,' she said, 'you've a job.'

'Not any more.'

'What happened? Why were you sacked.'

'I wasn't sacked – I walked out. No jumped-up Dublin Jackeen not five minutes in the job, not six months in America, is going to stand over me giving me orders.'

'Sit down love, there's soup in the pot, have a cup.' His face was pale with suppressed anger. She felt sorry for him. Lately he had tried so hard, seldom drinking, minding his work. She humoured him. Not asking any more questions – hoping the going away was only a threat. She ladled out the soup and put it in front of him. 'Drink that,' she said, 'your poor stomach must be empty.'

He pushed it away. 'A cantankerous Cork bastard – that's what he called me. First he told me to dig the footing one way, and then said no, the other. Then I told him what he could do with his footing. "I've watched you," he said. "You're a trouble-maker. A cantankerous Cork bastard." So I hit him and when he stood up I hit him again.'

'You did right,' said Katy. 'I'm proud of you. The cheek of him. He got what he deserved. Take a little of the soup. Did you bring home the pick and shovel?'

'A fella on the job is minding them for me.'

He was right to have defended himself. She'd have thought less of him for letting another man insult him. She'd coax him to have a lie down and when he got up make him something to eat. Talking about the railroad was bravado. He'd got all that out of him long ago, please God. Tomorrow he'd get another start. She was sure of it only she would have felt happier had he brought his tools home. She suggested that he threw himself on the bed for an hour. 'No,' he said, 'I'm going out.'

'Where?' she asked.

'Just out,' and he went and she was afraid, for never before had he acted like this. This, she thought, is what has been coming. This is what has been hanging over me for months. Life was too good and now it's time to pay the price – he is going – he is going to leave me. She left what she had been doing – not caring that the washing boiled over or the dinner dried to a stick and sat on a chair staring into space. She had known all along that life was too good to last as it had for so long.

A woman came to collect her laundry. Katy had to rouse herself to find it, the woman was pleasant and wanted to make conversation but Katy pleaded a headache and returned to sit in despair. The children came home from school. 'Where's our tea?' they asked. 'I'm sick,' she said, 'you'll have to make it.' Never having had to fend for themselves they were disconcerted and then alarmed that she who was up before them in the mornings, and never in bed before they went should be sick. She was never sick. When she didn't stir or give them instructions what to do they asked would they call a neighbour. 'No,' she said, 'I'll be all right.'

When it got dark they asked where Dad was – why wasn't he home from work? She didn't answer them. Only when Danny came and laid his head on her lap and cried and said he was tired did she rouse herself. 'Are you better?' asked the older children. 'A bit,' she said. 'I have a terrible headache, but it's better than it was.' And she fried cold potatoes for them and an egg and said it would have to do. And would Bridget be a good girl and put Danny to bed and then go herself with Thomas and Mary Kate in a little while. For she knew that Jamsie was going to come home very drunk and she didn't know what might happen and she didn't want the children to witness a scene.

Nothing did happen, for Jamsie had drunk so much he passed out as soon as he sat down. He had a crumpled paper clutched in his hand, and as his hand relaxed the paper fell to the floor and Katy picked it up. It was a printed advertisement in big black letters. She smoothed it out and took it near the lamp to read.

Wanted: 3,000 labourers on the 12th Division of the Illinois Central Railroad.
Wages $1.25 a day.
Fare from New York $9.75.
By railroad and steamboat to work in Illinois.
Constant work for two years or more.
Good board at $2 a week.
This is a rare chance for persons to go west being sure of permanent employment in a healthy climate where land can be bought and for fertility is not surpassed anywhere in the Union.
Men with families preferred.
For further information call at the Central Railroad Office
173 Broadway, corner of Courtland St New York.
H. Phelps agent. R. B. Mason. Chief Engineer. July 1853.

Eighteen fifty-three, she sighed with relief – the pamphlet was a year out of date. Only something he had picked up. Tomorrow everything would be all right – he'd go out and find another job and sure if he was unsuccessful straight away they could manage for a while. She thanked God that he had been too drunk to quarrel with. Everything was going to be all right. Her and her premonitions. Eileen was right, all they were was being run down. She undid and took off Jamsie's boots, loosened the neck of his shirt, kissed the top of his head and after covering him with an old coat went to bed having put away the railroad advertisement.

But the next morning after the children had gone to school, Jamsie asked had she seen a paper anywhere. She was tempted to say no, but didn't and brought it to him.

'This,' he said, unfolding it, 'was what I was telling you about. It's where I'm going.'

'Sure that's last year's – how can you go there?'

'They still want men, I've been to the office.'

'You're not serious, Jamsie.' she sat down, for her legs were shaking and she feared they wouldn't support her. Then she remembered how the bill had said, *Men with families preferred.* She didn't want to go to Illinois, she didn't want to leave New York and go out into the wilds where maybe they'd all be killed by Indians, but at least she would be with Jamsie.

'I suggested us moving a long time ago and you wouldn't hear tell of it. It's a pity that it's now you want to go. Bridget likes her work. And there's the laundry, it's doing well and the children are settled here – would you not think it over?'

'I have,' he said, 'over and over, long before the bust-up with the ganger. I've thought it all over – the children, Bridget, and you happy here with the neighbours and that's why I'm going on my own.'

'You're leaving me – deserting us. Walking out on your wife and children like so many of them have done. Off to the railroad and not a penny nor a word ever coming from them again. Their wives and families destitute.'

'Katy,' he said and his voice was coaxing, 'what sort of a man do you think I am? Surely to God you're not comparing me with them that ran off.'

Anger had replaced her weakness, but she curbed it and argued. 'I read the bill, they want men with families. I'll go with you. I don't care what we have to face, so long as we are together. Don't leave me on my own. Sure you wouldn't do that. We've never been parted a night since we married.'

He argued forcefully. Of course the company wanted family men. Family men were more settled, less likely to leave the job, more likely to work harder if there were bonuses. The company were no fools. But what did they care about the women and children living in a wilderness. No, first he was going on his own. He'd send her money and when he was sure the place out there was all right for her and the children he'd send for them.

'But I won't mind, honest to God I won't care where we live, what hardships I have to face so long as you're there,' she pleaded.

'No,' he said, his mouth set firm. 'I'm going first on my own.'

'But why? What made you decide all of a sudden to do this? Why, tell me, why?' Her voice rose. 'Everything was lovely. We were getting on our feet. We were happy – I thought you were happy. Why, why? Tell me,' she screamed when he wouldn't answer her.

'I'm doing it for you. For you and the children. Why else would I be going off to God knows where to dig tunnels. Can't you see that? Do you think I like the prospects of what's in front of me – do you?'

'Oh, no, you're not. It's not for me and the children. Tomorrow you could go out and get a job in New York. If there was nothing else you could get in the police. There's no bar against the Irish nowadays in the police. There's more building in New York than ever there was. It's not for me and the children – it's your freedom you're looking for. Strange places and strange faces, that's what you're after. No wife to ask where you've been or have her hand stretched waiting for your money. Free to spend it on yourself with men like yourself. Being a family man doesn't suit you. Like your father before you, like everyone of the O'Haras you're no good.'

'Leave my family out of it.'

'Your family!' she said scornfully. 'A fine family they were indeed – never a day in their life sober. Living up on the bog like the pigs they kept.'

His face was white with anger. Say something to me. Make me stop pouring out this hate. I don't want to be saying such things. Raking over the bones of your mother and father who never harmed me. But she couldn't stop herself. She was distraught at the thought of him leaving her. Not in control of herself. Thinking how she hated him. How she loved him, how if he left her she would die. She hated him. The callousness of him. Leaving her, not caring that she'd be without him. Not caring that he'd be without her. Leaving her in a strange place. Not hearing his footsteps, his whistle on the landing of an evening. Not having him to lie with. Without him she would surely die. She could kill him. If she stayed in the room a minute longer she would, or goad him into killing her.

She ran from the room into the street and all the way to the tenement house, to talk to Eileen or Mary. To hear them tell her none of it was true. To hear them say, 'Jamsie wouldn't do a thing like that. Tomorrow everything will be all right. It's the drink talking. Tomorrow it will all blow over.' Only when she reached the house did she remember that Mary would be at the bakery and Eileen in work and there wasn't anyone else to open her heart to.

Then she walked not knowing where she went, not caring. Oblivious of the people passing, of the rain which began to fall. She crossed streets, unconscious of her narrow escapes from the horse-drawn vehicles, not hearing the curses or seeing the threatening fists of the drivers. Tears and rain ran down her face. In her head pounded Jamsie's voice. 'I'm going on my own. On my own. On my own.' The rain drenched her. Like another skin her clothes clung to her. And her only thought was, he's leaving me. In a while he'll be gone from me and then I'll die.

Her skirt was sodden and water squelched through the soles of her shoes, but on she walked unaware of discomfort.

Eventually she came to South Street where the ships were, where she had first set foot in America and she remembered the day. And all the fears that had possessed her during the voyage and on the day they landed. But never, not even in the blackest moments of her life had she known such fear and despair as now. Not even when Peg and Nora died, for Jamsie was beside her. And for always she had believed he would be beside her.

Far away, over there, over the ocean was Ireland. If only all this was a dream, a bad dream from which soon she would waken. If only when she woke the tall ships and the grey sky were gone and above her were the cottage rafters and the smell of turf smoke. She closed her eyes and saw again her little home.

The wind rose and her hair that had come undone flew back in it. The cloth of her skirt moulded her thighs and the blouse her breasts. Like the figurehead of a ship, apparently lifeless she stood until a hand gripped her arm and a voice spoke to her in a language she didn't understand. She opened her eyes and looked into the face of a smiling man who squeezed her arm harder, laughed and gabbled and began pulling her.

Terrified, she wrenched herself free and ran back the way she had come. Aware now of the cold, of being drenched, of the darkness falling, of the danger she had been in. I could have been killed and worse, a knife plunged into my heart and my body thrown into the sea, she kept thinking. And it would have been all Jamsie's fault. He'd have been sorry then and it too late.

She looked behind her, but there was no sign of the foreign man and she stopped running. It was a long time since she had left the house, hours and hours. Jamsie would be worrying about her. Thinking as often she did if he was late that something terrible had happened to him, that he had been run over, was dying, even dead. This minute he could be thinking the same thing. Saying her name, telling her he meant none of it. Going on the railroad was all talk. What man in his senses would leave the woman he loved. Talk, that's all it was. Tears would be running down his face as he talked and called her name and said how sorry he was, and wished he had the time back.

She began to hurry. His face would light up when she came in. His face would light up at the sight of her. And he'd say again the things he had said when he thought she was dead.

Mulberry Street was just round the corner, and Cow Lane two minutes away. She turned into it, she was nearly home when on the other side of the road passing a lighted window she saw Mary and Herr Jaeger. They were arm in arm. The sight of them jolted her mind and Jamsie's reassuring words fled from it. Jamsie didn't think of sudden death every time someone was late. Jamsie would have spent the hours sleeping or reading the paper or in the saloon. And if he had noticed how long she was away would have thought she was gossiping or in the chapel. Jamsie worried about nothing.

She ducked into a doorway as Mary and the baker crossed the street. They were laughing and talking. They were happy. She wouldn't burden them with her troubles. They passed and their laughter drifted back making her feel sad and lonely. And she thought how strange were the turns life took. Mary had a man and soon she would be without one.

Jamsie was out. A man, Bridget told her, had come to call for him. She had heard them talking. The man had brought money, saying it was what was owing for the tools. So he had sold them, Katy thought – he wasn't going to look for another job. He was really going away.

'Will we go with Dada – when he goes on the railroad?' Thomas asked when she told the children.

'Not at first,' Katy said, 'but soon afterwards. Would you like that?' Thomas said he would. There'd be great things to do and all them Indians.

'God forbidding all harm,' Katy said and told the children it was time they were in bed and as usual they protested and asked for more time and she gave them a little.

'You were a long time gone,' Jamsie said when he came back with little sign of drink on him.

'You sold the few tools,' she said.

'I did – I'll get more where I'm going.'

'Why are you going, why, Jamsie?'

'Ah, for God's sake don't start all that again.' He unlaced his boots and stretched his feet nearer the stove.

She thought, he's acting as if it's any night of the week and him just getting ready for bed. Sitting there wriggling his toes, not a bother on him and her heart breaking.

'You can't go,' she said. 'You can't leave me. We've not been parted for a night since we married.'

'We were,' he said. 'Years ago when I went to Cork to look for work.'

In her sorrow she had forgotten that. When they were starving during the famine he had gone away in desperation to find a job. It wasn't long after the twins had died. But then it truly was for their sakes he had gone. Unwillingly he had left. And heartbroken as she was by their separation it was a different thing to what was now going to happen. Then he was leaving her in the cottage, in her own place. He had only left her when there was no alternative. Now he didn't have to go – there was work. He didn't have to go – he chose to go.

He yawned and stretched again and said he was going to bed and asked if she was. 'No,' she said, 'I've a few things yet to do.'

She sat and thought of all the lonely nights in front of her. No one to talk to after the children were in bed. No one to talk over the day's happenings, to hope with for tomorrow. Or when the mood took her to remember Kilgoran, laugh and cry about the old times. What would she do without him.

During the night her sleep was disturbed by Jamsie's arm going round her and her heart leapt with joy. He was sorry. He had changed his mind. She lay close to him waiting for him to speak. She waited. 'Jamsie,' she whispered. He didn't answer. He was asleep – reaching for her in his sleep. It meant nothing.

She wouldn't let him go. Her life revolved round him. The sound of his footstep on the stair made her heart leap with joy. When she planned the meals they were planned with him in mind. With all the washing she had to do his received special attention. His chair was placed nearest to the stove. She loved him. She wouldn't let him go. She'd fight to keep him. Pray. Go herself and ask Mrs Ryan for a job. She went, though her pride was killing her. A servant, a young red-faced Irish girl in a maid's uniform opened the door.

'Yes, ma'am?' asked the girl.

'I was wondering,' said Katy, 'if Mrs Ryan is in?'

'She is,' said the girl.

'Would you tell her then that Katy O'Hara would be obliged if she could spare me a few minutes.'

'I will indeed, ma'am,' replied the girl and smiled at Katy.

Already Katy was regretting having come, telling herself she could have achieved the same ends by asking the priest and less likely to be turned down. But now it was too late. She could hear Mrs Ryan's voice scolding the servant. 'Will you never learn. Haven't I told you before not to say I'm in before finding out if I want to see the caller.' And then she was walking down the hall, as fat and coarse-looking as ever. 'Oh,' she said ungraciously, 'it's you. Well, now that you're here you might as well come in. Into the parlour.' Katy followed her into the room which looked like one of the furniture stores on Broadway. Everything in it was brand new. Grass green damask chaise longues – two of them, corner cupboards and whatnots, small tables and chiffoniers covering every inch of wall. Glass shades of wax fruit and stuffed birds – a piano and in the middle of the mantelpiece a figure of the Sacred Heart. 'What was it you wanted?' asked Mrs Ryan.

She was so rude and ignorant, a cabog of a woman, nothing was to be gained by the niceties of manners and not even for Jamsie, Katy now decided, could she fawn before this woman. 'I'm asking for a job for my husband.'

'Lord bless me,' laughed Mrs Ryan. 'You're asking for a job for your husband. Has he lost the use of his tongue?'

'No,' said Katy, 'he hasn't. He doesn't know I'm here. He's planning on going on the railroad. I thought if I told him there was a job with your husband he might change his mind.'

'I see,' said Mrs Ryan, her fingers stroking a satin cushion. Thick fingers well-ringed, Katy noticed, rings with blue stones and another with ruby ones and an emerald one as well. 'My husband's prospering, as you know. I'm sure there's jobs. But things have changed since the beginning. Men are only taken on nowadays through the office. Tell your husband to call in.' She stood up. Katy did, too. 'You're still taking in washing, I suppose?' Mrs Ryan asked as she led Katy out.

'I am.'

'I must remember to send you down a few things now and then.'

'Thank you,' said Katy barely able to contain herself.

'Not at all,' replied Mrs Ryan.

Katy O'Hara, you're a fool of a woman. You got what you deserved. Making little of yourself to her. Didn't you know what to expect. And didn't you know full well that had she handed you a job on a plate Jamsie wouldn't have taken it. But he might, she said to herself after finishing her castigation. If I could have told him it was sure and certain, he might. Now of course she wouldn't mention it. He'd kill her for giving Mrs Ryan the chance to humiliate her. But there was the police. She had mentioned that to him before, she would again. He was the right height and build, there was no more discrimination. After the Americans the Irish were in the greatest numbers, more than the Germans.

She fought and prayed and coaxed and pleaded. And Jamsie said no and no, and no again. His mind was made up. He was going on the railroad and he was going next week. There were towns springing up round them. Good small towns, where they could have a house. Wasn't she always wanting a house? Fresh air, fields. As soon as he could he would send for her. What ailed her? Why was she so unreasonable? Other men did the same thing and their wives waited and then joined them.

209

'Other men,' she said, 'take their wives with them.'

'In no time I'll be sending for you.'

She knew he wouldn't. The knowledge that she was to lose something had hung over her for so long. She had been expecting a tragedy. 'What is tragic about going away to earn money for a better life?' Jamsie asked her when she told him of her premonition coming true. She couldn't answer him. He had become a stranger. Jamsie had never given a thought to improving their life. The Jamsie she had married wasn't like that. This was a stranger. A madness had taken hold of him. Please God it would pass. She'd cry no more nor fight him. She'd be patient and silent and hope for the madness to pass.

A miracle could still happen. God would answer her prayers at the last minute. Jamsie would come and say 'Aghoille, I can't do it. I can't leave you.' And she'd hold him and say how glad she was. And make a vow that never again, whether he worked or he didn't, whether he drank or he didn't, never again would she say a cross word to him.

He went. The children kissed him and Bridget cried and said she'd write to him every week and he promised he would do the same. He told Thomas to be a good boy and mind his mammy and that soon they would all be together again. 'You'll do that, mind your mammy, won't you Thomas,' he said. And Thomas holding back his tears nodded his head.

Then he came to say goodbye to Katy. She was weary and defeated. She couldn't look him in the face. She wanted his arms round her. His strength to lean on. His love enfolding her. 'I'm going now,' he said and she drew back. If he touched her she would scream, throw herself at his feet, wrap her arms round his legs and scream and scream. For the sake of the children she stood still as he kissed her and all she said was, 'God bless you and take you safely.'

'I'll write and send the money regularly, honest to God.'

'Yes,' she said so quietly. 'I know you will.'

'Goodbye so.'

'Goodbye,' she said and he went and still for the children's sake she didn't cry.

She carried a heart like a lead weight inside her breast. Every minute of every day she was conscious of his loss. And when night-time came and the children slept she gave reign to her grief and fears. Some men deserted their wives when they went on the railroad. Tale nor tidings of them were ever heard again. The number of women there were in the parish living on charity. Some outspoken women said their men weren't a great loss; they managed on the charity, scrubbed floors, took in washing and waited for the children to grow up and earn for them. Their sons from an early age sold papers, picked rags, begged and raised money for their deserted mothers in any way possible.

There were other women genuinely widowed, so many were the fatalities on the railroad. Hardly a week went by without a word coming that a man had been blown to pieces, buried beneath a rock fall, poisoned by a snake, killed in a fight. She prayed for God to protect Jamsie from all harm.

Eileen was her greatest consolation, coming to see her often late at night when they would sit talking. Eileen made her look at the advantages of moving out of New York. It was, she said, a kip of a place to bring up children. She herself couldn't wait to leave it. Out where Jamsie had gone they'd have a great life. She'd heard tell it was a grand place. Out on the prairies you only had to look at the land for something to grow. This time next year herself and Jamsie would have their own house, land, a farm, everything. He wouldn't stay on the railroad forever.

Chapter Seventeen

Jamsie went with the intention of working for Katy's benefit. Every spare penny he would send to her. Not a drink would cross his lips, not a hand of cards would he pick up. He was sad that they had parted bad friends. God, she was a fierce woman – fighting him every step of the way since he first mentioned going on the railroad. Not a day had passed without a scene of some sort. Anyone would think he was deserting her. That he took pleasure in the prospect of going. Women were contrary creatures. All these thoughts went through his mind as he walked to the railway station.

At the agent's office where he had to report for instructions and a small advance on his wages, there were other men heading for the railway. The majority were Irish. Some Jamsie had met on building sites, others he knew from saloons. Soon they were greeting each other, nervous and excited, talking, laughing, making jokes, speculating about the job. Some congratulating each other that there were no women travelling with them. Women had a way of making you watch your tongue. And when a man had a drink the tongue often ran away with you. Jamsie was as excited, nervous and garrulous as the others so that thoughts of Katy and their parting no longer occupied his mind.

On the station platform the train was admired and marvelled at. The engine inspired a sense of awe. Many of the men had never seen a train before. The majority had never been aboard one, had never travelled in any vehicle, had in Ireland seldom moved outside their parish. And never would have, if hunger hadn't driven them to take ship to America. Now they were embarking on another momentous journey.

In their shabby moleskin trousers, patched and broken boots, old coats and an assortment of caps and hats, with their possessions bundled into large kerchiefs they stared in fascination at the engine. Asked questions of the firemen. How fast could 'the ingine' go? Did it need a powerful lot of wood? How far was their destination? When would they get there?

On the wooden benches they grouped, those already acquainted sitting together. Some had brought food which they started to eat before the train moved. They ate and drank then filled their pipes and talked, convinced they were doing the right thing going on the railroad.

One talking to Jamsie said, 'Five years I've been in New York. Once I went on the ferry to Staten Island. The brother was in the quarantine hospital, Lord have mercy on him but little else I saw of America.'

'You saw more than me, so,' said Jamsie.

'We're doing the right thing travelling. We'll see America if not the world.'

'We will indeed, and them red skins, so I believe.'

'Fearful savages, from all accounts,' said Jamsie's acquaintance.

Fed by wood, the engine pulled the train through narrow mountain passes. Above it the Appalachians soared. Older men talked of having worked on this part of the line, of this one and that, workmates killed by rock falls and they told the young men where they were going the land was flat; there was nothing to laying rails there.

The flat dry lands went out from each side of the track to meet the horizon. Here and there, a long way apart were log cabins. Close to them Jamsie saw figures, men and women, children, a cow, a dog, chickens. His eyes ached from staring at the monotonous scenery. He closed them and thought about the lonely people, their separateness from neighbours, the desolate place they lived in.

Sometimes, the train came to what were the beginnings of a town. It slowed as it went through. People waved, boys ran after it as it passed the groups of clapboard houses, the saloon, the church higher than anything else.

The journey to where the railroad was, finished by steamboat. There was a tented camp and alcohol was forbidden, the ganger threatening that if men were discovered drinking whiskey they would be sacked and their wages already earned, forfeited. But as they moved on, working from dawn until the sun set, their picks hacking at the baked earth, earth in which the roots of plants and grass had bound the soil in a grip of iron, the lodgings and their keepers were more tolerant of drink. And the company store gave credit.

Sweat mixed with their dirt, hands and fingers burnt in the sun, the skin broke and festered and healed of its own accord. Dehydrated, the men swallowed cold tea brought in bottles, water, small beer – anything to replace the fluid that poured from their bodies. Gangers, Irishmen, oversaw them. Tough, ruthless men motivated by the bonus for mileage. From dawn to dusk the men worked clearing the way, bringing up the iron rails and laying them. It was hard monotonous work, the sameness of the flat scenery which stretched as far as the eye could see, not even relieved by the sight of a tree, adding to the boredom. Only now and then when clouds crossed the sky and their shadows were thrown on the flat prairie land was the scene temporarily altered.

Men with families lived in rough shanties hastily erected and as hastily dismantled when they moved on. Bad and all as the tenements were in New York, Jamsie thought Katy was better off in Cow Lane than here. The occasional guilt he felt at having left her behind was assuaged every time he saw the shanties.

In the evenings the unaccompanied men bought drink on score from the company store. When the alcohol relaxed and mellowed them they talked of home, New York, Boston, wherever their families were. When they became maudlin they remembered their real home, Ireland and sang sad laments for the leaving of it. Recalled their happy times, the leisure and the pleasure of the living in Ireland. The decent men and women, the gatherings in the cottages. The wakes and the weddings. The softness of the climate. The fools they were ever to have left it. The curse of God on the English and the landlords who had made them go. At the end of the week came the reckoning – half of their wages was owed to the store for drink, tobacco, food and sundries and the money sent home was short by many dollars.

Jamsie, abstemious for the present, renewed his vow that never would Katy suffer the loss of a penny. For the first two weeks he wrote and sent money and felt very noble . . .

He wasn't much of a hand with the pen, Jamsie reminded Katy in his first letter. Yet in a few lines he let her know how much he missed and loved her. How at night he lay in bed thinking of her and wishing she was beside him. Imagining him laboriously writing, the pencil gripped too tightly, his face screwed up with the effort, spelling aloud the long words before putting them on paper, she laughed and cried, kissed his letter, held it to her breast, reread it several times and forgave him for going away. Telling herself she had been too hard on him, had misjudged his reasons for going. It was for her sake and the children's he had gone. So that they could have a better life. She'd work harder than ever in the laundry and save all she could from the money he sent. And please God soon they would be together again.

After reading the letter once more she put it safely in the press and went about her work which since Jamsie left had become a trial, but now in her high spirits it seemed effortless. It was finished in no time,

214

leaving her with energy, restless and eager for the children to come from school and hear the good news.

The younger ones were delighted that a letter had come from Dada. Bridget showed little emotion. And when Katy asked her why, she shrugged and wouldn't answer. Katy thought how humoursome she was. Crying her eyes out after Jamsie left and many a time since she had heard her sobbing when she should have been sleeping. Now not interested in the letter, not like Mary Kate and Thomas asking her to read it again.

After they had eaten Bridget asked if she could go to Maura's and Katy let her. When she was gone Mary Kate said, 'She doesn't want to go.'

'Who doesn't want to go where?' asked Katy, who was composing a letter to Jamsie in her head and had forgotten about Bridget's lack of interest.

'Bridget doesn't want to go to Illinois.'

'What put such a thing in your head?'

'She did. She told me. She cries every night in bed – she wants to stay with Madame Renée.'

'People,' said Katy, 'wear hats everywhere.'

'Mom!' Mary Kate looked at her mother as if she was simple. 'Don't you know nothing – out there everyone wears poke bonnets.'

'I know no such thing, and don't you be impertinent, Miss,' said Katy. But her tone of voice took the severity out of the reprimand. She was too happy to be cross and goodnaturedly chivvied the children to help her clear the table so she could answer Jamsie's letter. And when she was done they all had to add a few lines.

She wrote him a long letter. She told him how delighted she was to get his. How much she loved and missed him. How sorry she was for fighting with him before he went away. She thanked him for the money and hoped he wasn't leaving himself short. She reminded him not to wear damp clothes and if there was a chapel in the vicinity not to miss Mass.

Then she wrote about how the laundry was prospering. Maybe when she joined him they could start one out there. She wanted to say how lonely the nights were without him. That sometimes she dreamt about him, lovely dreams that ended too soon. But couldn't think of how to express such things in a letter and even if she could, wouldn't, for they were too private. So instead she wrote about the neighbours.

Eileen would soon be off to San Francisco. And by ship at that! Going all the way from New York on one of them clippers that were racing

215

each other. Paddy Kavanagh had been down last week and made all the arrangements. Or so he had told Eileen. For her sake she hoped it was true. He was always making promises – so far that's all they'd been.

Then she said that he'd never guess who was courting. Mary and Herr Jaeger! Sometimes they went to Mass together. There'd be a wedding there before long. Poor Dan O'Brien was very bad with his heart. He wouldn't last long by the look of him. But then there was a good age on Dan and something had to come for everyone's end.

Kathleen wasn't at all pleased about the baker's attentions to her mother, so Mary had confided. A puss on her every time he called. It was to be hoped Mary wouldn't let her interfere too much. A few slaps was what she wanted in her rearing. But now that she'd turned out such a scholar and wanted to be a teacher, there was no holding her nor Mary.

Bridget came home before the letter was finished and added a few lines. Katy was very nice to her and felt sorry that she would have to leave her friends when the time came for them to join Jamsie. But she wasn't going to talk to her about it. Bridget was only a child and children had to do what their parents said.

Later on she made them cocoa and they talked about Illinois. Katy wondered how far away it was.

'Hundreds of miles, maybe even a thousand,' Mary Kate said.

'And what sort of place will it be?'

'Wild, with mountains and forests full of Red Indians that come out every night and kill the white people,' Thomas said.

Bridget said he knew nothing. Illinois wasn't like that at all and not the worst place for Indians. Thomas said she was a liar and how would she know, anyway. Mary Kate said that tomorrow she would ask her teacher all about Illinois.

'Would it be anywhere near Virginia?' asked Katy, who had suddenly thought about Peader and Charlotte.

The older children laughed and Bridget said, 'Mom, you don't know anything about America. Virginia is in the south.'

'I don't,' Katy admitted. 'No more would you if you were my age and not five minutes in the place and no master teaching me every day. But I do know one thing – you're all getting too big for your boots. In my day you wouldn't back answer your mother.'

Another time she might have said more, might have slapped Bridget or Mary Kate for their cheek. But not tonight. Tonight they could do no wrong. They were hers and Jamsie's beautiful children. God bless and spare them. She was full of love for them and happy to be surrounded by them.

Mary Kate came home from school the following day and gave her mother a headache repeating the information about Illinois which she had got from her teacher.

'Miss Cook says you're not to worry about the Indians. They used to live there. Black Hawk's tribe, the Sauk and Fox Indians, but Abraham Lincoln beat them in a battle and they had to move to the other side of the Mississippi. Terrible savages they were. But we won.'

'The poor unfortunates,' said Katy. 'They sound like the Irish and what Cromwell did to them. They had to move to the other side of a river as well. Into Connaught.'

Mary Kate looked uncomprehendingly at Katy and then continued to tell her exactly how far Illinois was from New York. 'And there's a great big city, Chicago, and Miss Cook says there's bound to be lots of hat-shops there.' And on and on she went about Chicago and Illinois until Katy told her that would do and to say nothing to Bridget about Chicago or hat-shops. When the time came to move she would do all the telling.

'With the help of God it'll be no time. Dada won't delay sending for us. A month or six weeks, I'd say.'

Eileen was full of plans for her move to San Francisco, Katy, she said, could have every stick of furniture, cups, pots and plates.

'God bless you for your kindess, but furniture now I wouldn't be able to take, not with the move.'

'I forgot all about that. Sell it then, and get a few dollars for it.'

'If you're sure,' said Katy.

'Of course I'm sure. And during the week I'll be sorting out my clothes. There'll be plenty I won't be taking – you could alter some of them for Bridget or yourself and sell the rest for rags.'

'I'll be sorry to lose you. I've known you so long I forget there was a time when we were strangers.'

'I know,' said Eileen. 'We've been through a lot together. I don't know what I'd have done without you when Larry died.'

'Poor Larry, Lord rest him,' said Katy and only in time stopped herself saying hadn't he the terrible end.

'Most of the time I put it out of my mind. But now and again when I can't sleep I go over it and I cry for the injustice and to think that somewhere, maybe here in New York the real culprit is walking around.'

It was years since Katy had thought about Terence McCabe, but now

217

his face came back to her. The brutal face with its blackened broken teeth. And she remembered the girl he had raped and wondered what had become of her. He, as Eileen had said, could be living here in New York. With the help of God she would never cross his path.

Terence was still living in New York and doing very well. The blackened broken teeth had been attended to, his wild red hair was slick with oil and he could afford to pay for shoes and suits. As the number of immigrants had increased so had the bondsmen and touts. Kelly, unable to handle the extra work load had split his pitch with Terence. One night when they were drinking the only unadulterated rum in the shop, Kelly said, 'I heard a whisper there's a move to have the immigrants come in at Castle Gardens.'

'Why and when?' asked Terence.

'Would you believe it, they say there's complaints! The immigrants say they're robbed by the touts. Did you ever in your life rob an unfortunate passenger or lead them astray?'

'On my mother's grave, never,' said Terence with a serious face.

'No more than myself. Anyway, if they regulate entry our profits will be down. So keep putting your money into property and look about you for a wife. A wife gives a man standing in the community.'

'I'm in no hurry for a wife,' said Terry.

'Thanks be to God we have our foot well in the door. We're here to stay. There's a big future in America for young men. You could be anything – the Governor of New York, the President. Take my advice and find a wife.'

During the week when Katy received her third letter from Jamsie, Dan O'Brien died. Old though he was and his death not unexpected, Katy was very sorry when she heard the news. On her way to his Mass she remembered the night of the party to celebrate becoming American citizens. How happy everyone was that night. Poor Dan was talking about his lovely wife with the red cheeks and black hair that had a curl in it. She hoped that tonight he was with her in Heaven.

The chapel was crowded, for Dan had been a popular man in this parish and the one in which he had lived before, so that people had come from both. After the Mass when groups were gathered outside talking, Mary, who was standing beside Katy nudged her and said, 'Do you see who that is? Look – over there standing next to Kelly.'

'I don't know either of them. Who are they?'

'Kelly's one of the big bugs in Tammany and the other one's not far behind. You remember him from the ship – he hadn't a shoe on his foot and look at him now.'

At that moment Kelly and his companion left the priest and turned round. 'I never saw either of them before,' Katy said to Mary.

'Yes, you did. I remember well you telling me about the young fella that tried to take your place on the ship.'

She wouldn't have recognised him. She'd have passed him in the street and not known him. But now beneath the careful barbering, good clothes and dentistry she saw him for who he was. He walked by her and their eyes met. She felt cold, and shivers ran down her back as if someone was walking on her grave.

Two to five miles of track were laid each day. The rails were brought up by a horse and cart, dumped half a mile from where it was to lie and then manhandled by a gang who at a word of command dropped it into place. Thirty seconds per gang per rail. After a month of working like that Jamsie broke his pledge and had his first drink. One, he reasoned, didn't matter. He could afford one, he was entitled to one. Then he had another. It quenched his thirst as nothing else had. As the drink flowed into him his pains and aches went, his grievances against gangers, railroad bosses and America disappeared. There was a game of cards starting and he accepted a hand. On a winning streak the first night, he came on the second with money to spare and still enough for Katy. Again luck was with him, the next night he lost all his winnings. But his luck was bound to change. It didn't, and at the end of the week there was nothing to send home. He couldn't send a letter without money. What would he say? He couldn't tell her he'd been drinking and was in debt. Next week his luck would change. He'd send her money on the double and let on he'd been sick, nothing serious he'd say so she wouldn't worry.

Katy's letters kept arriving. What ailed him, she asked. She was out of her mind with worry. The children cried for him, were convinced something terrible had happened to him. They knew children in school whose fathers had been killed on the railroad. Maybe he was dead, that's why the letters had stopped, the children said, but she knew he was alive. He could never die, no matter how many miles he was distant, without her knowing. But he could be sick or injured. If he had the power of himself at all, or some kind person to oblige – just one line would put all their minds at rest.

Never a word about him not sending money. Not one complaint that she was going short. He got so that he dreaded the letters arriving. Not tearing them open as the other men did. Putting them in his pocket and sometimes not opening them until the next day. And the more into debt he got, the longer were the intervals between him receiving the mail and opening it. Until the time came when he no longer did but pushed them into the bag where he kept his few spare clothes, pushing them well down out of his sight.

Weeks and months passed and still no letter came for Katy. She became irritable with the children, and not even Thomas getting work in a warehouse and bringing home three dollars a week helped her rise above her despair.

The savings she had once intended for Bridget's education were being used up and she was incapable of thinking how she would manage once they were gone. Eileen and Mary were sympathetic but each of them had their own troubles. The trip to California had once more been postponed and Mary had given in to Kathleen's whims so that when Herr Jaeger proposed, she asked him if he'd wait until her daughter went to college.

Everyone Katy knew enquired about Jamsie. She lied, said he was well, soon they would be joining him. But as time passed and knowing people weren't fools, she began avoiding them. She printed two notices which she put in the window and on the door of the shop. *If there's no one in, leave the laundry on the counter and please collect after four o'clock.'*

After four o'clock one of the children had to man the shop. Some customers objected to not being able to drop in any time to pick up their washing and many took it elsewhere. Better that, Katy thought than having to face them, answer questions and tell lies that weren't believed. But at the back of her mind she knew that the more customers she lost, the quicker the savings would be eaten up – and then she wouldn't be able to afford the rent.

One night, Katy and Eileen were commiserating with each other. Eileen said, 'I don't know what to do about Paddy. In one way I know he's no good for me, that half of what he tells me is lies. And if I'd the sense I was born with I'd throw him over.'

'Do,' Katy wanted to say. 'Get rid of him before he throws you over for someone else. He's codding you up to the two eyes.' But she knew that wasn't what Eileen wanted to hear. So she made excuses for the postponed trip. 'It probably was the truth that the backers he had hoped for let him down at the last minute. After all, if he wanted to run out on you all he has to do is not write or come to see you again.'

'I suppose so,' Eileen said. 'Only sometimes I'm aware of time slipping by, especially first thing in the morning when I see my face in the glass.'

'Go off out of that! You're as lovely as ever you were. You don't look a day over twenty-five.'

'A lot of good it's done me so far. I don't know,' Eileen sighed, 'and there's Mary who God knows isn't a raving beauty and that man panting for her and now having to pant for another few years. You and I weren't as lucky in the men we got.' Katy started to cry. 'Oh God, Katy, I'm an awful mouth. I didn't mean it like that. All I meant was that Paddy and Jamsie wouldn't be fobbed off by excuses. Don't cry, love, I didn't mean anything. Jamsie was the loveliest man, the greatest husband. And there has to be a good reason for you not hearing. Listen Katy,' she said and came to sit next to her and put an arm round her. 'I've been wanting to say this to you for a long time. Jamsie had his faults, he liked a drink, but you and the children came first in his life. I think something happened to him. There's no other reason under the sun why he wouldn't write. I think Jamsie's dead, and I think in your heart you know it.'

Katy cried more bitterly. 'Cry for him, and in a while you'll come to accept it. I'd be the last one to want to say such a thing but it breaks my heart to see you making yourself believe he's still alive. What you're doing now is natural. Crying the way you are is the beginning of the cure for grief.'

'Eileen, Eileen, oh Eileen, don't you understand? I don't think Jamsie's dead. He's not. If he was I'd know. If he was I'd cry and pray for him and accept it as God's will. I'm going mad and my tears are the tears of a madwoman. I'm going mad because Jamsie has deserted me. I don't know why but I'm as certain of that as I am that he isn't dead.'

'Oh Katy, I wish I'd never brought the subject up. I thought I'd be helping you. Now I don't know what to say.' And for a few minutes Eileen remained silent before saying, 'Well, surely to God you could find out one way or the other. That agent, the one where he went in the beginning – they'd know if he was alive or dead. Ask the priest to find out. I know what you say may be the truth. Some people, some women, believe they know if a person close to them dies even if they're miles away. But you could be wrong and spend the rest of your life living in hope.'

'No, no, don't say it, don't ever say it again! Jamsie isn't dead.'

'All right, all right, I won't. But Katy, love, how are you going to manage? How will you be able to stay on here?'

'I won't.' Katy wiped her eyes. 'I'll have to get out. The thought of

221

that is killing me as well. I love it here. We were so happy. I was making a go of the laundry.'

'If you could get a room back in Mulberry Street it wouldn't be so bad and maybe the landlord here would let you keep the little shop – it's separated from the rooms.

'I wonder if he would?'

'There's no harm in asking and then if Paddy Kavanagh keeps his word you could have my place. The minute I'm sure I'll let you know.'

'You'll be gone as well.' Katy started to cry again.

'Come on now,' said Eileen, 'I'm not gone yet. I know in my heart I'm a fool to bother with him. What makes us do it, Katy?'

'You love him – love makes us do the queer things.'

Katy kept writing letters to Jamsie, which without opening he pushed to the bottom of his bag. Drink blotted everything from his mind. He was drunk when he fell into bed and its effects lasted well into the following day so that only for brief moments did the thought of having deserted Katy trouble him. And during those moments he swore that tomorrow he would turn over a new leaf. Stop the drink, leave the railroad, go back to New York. Not let Katy know until he had a job. But when tomorrow came there was another one the day after, and on that he pinned his hopes for salvation.

It wasn't to San Francisco, but Paddy was taking Eileen away. He had an engagement booked in Buffalo – five girls and Eileen, singing and dancing.

'Where's Buffalo?' Katy asked when Eileen came to tell her news, and forced herself to smile though her heart was heavy at the prospect of Eileen moving.

'New York,' Eileen replied.

'Oh, thank God – I thought you'd be going far away.'

'It is far, Katy – more than two hundred miles. It's in what they call New York State, you know like Cork city is in the County of Cork. But I'll write to you, honest to God, and now you'll be able to give up the rooms over the laundry – that'll save you a few shillings. I know it's a come-down moving back here, but the room isn't too bad and I'll leave you my bits of furniture. Come on now and don't cry – I couldn't bear that.'

Katy forced herself to smile and Eileen said, 'We'll go down this minute and tell her that's the agent you want the room.'

★

222

Katy moved back to the tenement. Herr Jaeger, still courting Mary and still objected to by Kathleen, helped her move her things in and what she didn't want of Eileen's, out. Life, Katy felt, was now harder than at any time since she had come to America. To live at all she had to keep the laundry going, and that meant a journey to and from Cow Lane each day often carrying big bundles of washing that people, knowing she had moved back to Mulberry Street, dropped there for convenience.

Bridget became even more humoursome and complained bitterly about how they now lived. Her friend, she said, had a proper house. Maura's brothers didn't sleep in the room with her. Maura's house had a parlour. How could she ever bring anyone to this place! Two beds in it, it was a disgrace. And that sofa of Eileen's that Thomas slept on should be thrown out. Katy prayed for God to grant her patience and understanding. Bridget was unhappy, the room was terrible, Bridget was very difficult, maybe she couldn't help it, but one of these days Katy knew her patience was going to snap and that she and Bridget were going to have a reckoning.

Eileen wrote, sent five dollars and said Buffalo was a kip of a place. But Paddy had another city in mind. Gradually he was moving them west and on to San Francisco. She hoped it wouldn't take as long as the move to Buffalo had or there'd be hairs on her chin. She told Katy to mind herself – not to wear herself out with children, you got no thanks in the end.

Her letters continued to come at first from Buffalo and then from places Katy had never heard of and all of which Eileen described as kips. But for all that she said herself and Paddy were getting on well. Often there were dollars in the letters.

One day, Mary came in to ask Katy had she heard about the house in Cow Lane. Katy said, no, what was there about it that was strange? And Mary told her that she had heard in the bakery that it had been sold and that fellow from the ship, the one that Katy had had words with had bought it.

'I hope to God,' said Katy, 'he doesn't put the rent up.'

'He'll do more than that – he wants the shop.'

'Oh no, what'll I do? Without the little shop the laundry'll be finished.'

'Maybe you could go and see him – tell him your circumstances. It's not as if he wanted it for himself. He's buying up lots of property – try it.'

'How would I get hold of him?'

'I'll find out for you,' Mary told her.

But before she did Terence paid a visit to the laundry. 'Mrs O'Hara,' he said. 'I have bought this place and I want you out by the end of the week.' Whoever had rented the laundry, he would still have wanted possession – that it was Katy gave him satisfaction.

Katy looked at him, seeing beneath and beyond his expensive tasteless get-up to the splaw-footed ugly menacing boy on the boat. She saw him again as she had on the day Larry was thrown overboard, singing in the crowd and again, dealing the cards left-handed because his finger was bandaged. All her thoughts registered on her face. Terence McCabe felt as he had at their first confrontation, humiliated by this woman, by the disdain in her eyes, the mocking smile about her mouth and he hated her and promised himself a sweeter revenge than taking back the lock-up shop.

'By the end of the week,' he said and walked out.

Part Two

1856

Chapter One

He has been gone for two years. She remembered the day, the date, the time of day when he went. Two years – and after the first letters no word of him since. Her heart felt like a heavy weight. It dragged her down so that she walked more slowly. She felt its sullen beat affecting her mind so that she was confused, forgot things, answered the children absentmindedly.

She washed herself and no more. Her hair was pinned carelessly and she never glanced in the mirror. What did her appearance matter? Who was there to care how she looked? She made the meals and cleaned the room and did the washing, not particular whether she took in fine or coarse garments. Forcing herself to be civil when she had to face customers, for without the extra money she couldn't manage. And without Mary's help in letting her dry clothes in her room while she was at work and Kathleen in school, she would have had to abandon the laundrying.

She missed Eileen sorely. She missed their gossiping, Eileen's ability to make her laugh. Sometimes she was too tired to eat, sometimes she forgot and sometimes there wasn't enough for her to have a share. Days passed without her saying more than one or two words to the children or they to her. Bridget went and came from work, hurriedly ate her food and went to see the girl who lived in a house with a room of her own. Mary Kate spent every spare minute reading and Thomas and Danny when the weather was fine escaped into the street. They seldom mentioned their father and weren't particularly interested when sometimes Katy, desperately wanting to talk about him, wondering where he was, what he was doing, brought up his name.

Once upon a time she wouldn't have let Thomas and Danny out into the street. But eventually their pleadings had worn her down. And as Jamsie had argued with her in the beginning – they lived here, they went to school here – they had to play here. Then she had objected to the roughness and toughness of the other children. The fights they had, the gangs they formed. Their reputation for stealing, roaming the neighbourhood and beyond.

But now she had given in. Thomas was gone fourteen, as big as a man. Thomas was earning, he couldn't be kept tied to the room. Sometimes he brought home fruit and vegetables. He'd found or been given them, he said when Katy asked where they'd come from. She had her suspicions but not enough energy to follow them up. Often he brought pieces of meat and offal from the shambles where butchers threw away meat not likely to keep in the heat. At first Katy made him get rid of them but as money became scarcer if the meat wasn't visibly decomposed she cooked it.

Everything became too much of an effort. What little energy she had must be reserved for the laundry, without which they would become destitute. Once she had been particular about what time the children came up from the street of an evening. Now she seldom noticed if they came in late. And so on one summer's night when the heat was stifling she sat lost in thought. Wondering, where at this very moment was Jamsie. Was he thinking about her. Was he sorry for not writing. Wanting to, but not knowing how to start after such a long time. Why had he deserted her? Hadn't he loved her as she loved him? Weren't they happy? When her thoughts became unbearable she cried and comforted herself by spinning fantasies. This was the night he'd come back. He'd creep up the stairs to surprise her. Knock on the door letting on he was a stranger – and then . . .

From away down in the street she could hear the children's voices, laughter and the chants of games they were playing. Sometimes there were angry shouts and the laughter faded and a child could be heard crying. Coming out of her fantasy world she assumed hers were amongst the laughing, playing, quarrelling children and went back to thoughts of Jamsie's arrival.

Then she became aware that the voices were louder and she could hear footsteps on the stairs: her heart leapt with joy. He was coming! Only people had seen him, greeted him, were coming up with him, welcoming him home. There was a knock on the door. He was playing the trick on her – she ran to open it. As she did so, other doors opened on the landing. Her head was spinning and her eyes blurring. There were so many people everywhere. 'Mrs O'Hara,' someone was saying and Mary was running down the stairs.

'Mrs O'Hara,' said the policeman. Someone was crying. 'Mrs O'Hara, ma'am,' the policeman said again. Katy stared stupidly at him. Mary Kate had come out behind Katy and was pulling at her arm screaming. 'What happened, why is Thomas roaring crying?'

'It's your boy, Danny,' and then Katy screamed.

'Danny, where is he? What's happened to Danny? Where is he? Where's Danny?'

'It's God mercy he's not drowned. Going down for the third time. But we got him. He'll be all right.'

Katy fainted then. When she came round Mary was slapping her face. 'Killing yourself – that's what you're doing, not minding yourself, keeping everyone at a distance.'

'Danny – where is he?' Katy sat up.

'In the hospital being pumped.'

'I'll kill him,' Katy said, getting up. 'When I get my hands on him I'll kill him. And you too,' she added, catching sight of Thomas. 'Didn't I tell you never to play near the river? Didn't I? Didn't I? Didn't I always tell you that? How many times did I say it?'

'We weren't in the water,' Thomas said. 'Oh Mom, I thought he was dead. Oh Mom,' he came to her crying and she held him close. 'The other kids were swimming – they kept yelling at me to come in. I wouldn't then they said we were scared and Danny jumped in.'

'In his clothes,' said Mary, and Katy laughed hysterically.

She fainted again the next morning as she got out of bed. Mary, who since she was betrothed to Mr Jaeger didn't work in City Hall, was at home when Bridget ran up to say her mother was sick. By the time she arrived Katy had made two attempts to get up but each time was overcome by dizziness and had to lie down.

Mary told her to stay where she was. Thomas could take a note to Mrs Ginsberg who now lived along the street. 'I don't like the look of you and I'm getting the doctor.'

'For the Lord's sake, Mary, there's nothing wrong with me but a bit of a weakness. I want no doctor. I've never had a doctor in my life.'

'Well, you're having one now.'

'Mary, I haven't what would pay for the dinner never mind a doctor! No more nonsense – but I'd be glad of a cup of tea.'

'It's nearly ready and don't you worry about a fee.'

'Mary, I'm taking no money from you.'

'You won't have to – you and your pride. Mrs Ginsburg will ask that nice Dr Purcell to come round. I happen to know he goes to her of a Wednesday. Lucky for you the day that's in it. Her Issy has consumption, the poor child, and Dr Purcell throws an eye to him.'

Katy broke out in a cold sweat – how could she have a doctor come? She hadn't a stitch of a nightdress and the bed was like a heap of rags.

'I'll bring you down a nightdress,' Mary said when Katy confided her worries to her. 'And the bed is spotless. Drink the tea and I'll be back in a minute.'

David Purcell examined the small sick boy. He was very gentle with him and when he had finished the examination he smiled at the child and said, 'You're doing fine Issy, just fine.'

'How is he?' Mrs Ginsburg asked in a hushed voice as they moved away from the bed. Her beautiful sad dark eyes were swimming in tears. The child was dying. She knew it, mothers always knew, but never lost hope, there were miracles. He wouldn't deny her hope. 'He's not very well, Mrs Ginsburg. You do a wonderful job of nursing him, you're a remarkable woman,' he said picking up his hat, preparing to leave. 'Now don't forget – if he should have a relapse, send for me. Day or night – I'll come as soon as I can.' If he couldn't cure the boy he'd see that his dying was as painless as possible. He bade Mrs Ginsburg goodbye.

'Ah,' she said. 'I forget, for you come this – ' and she gave him Mary's note.

Wonderful, remarkable woman, he thought as he walked to Katy's house. Such courage and spirit, such selflessness. His admiration for the tenement women went back many years. Back to his days as a student when often he was called to the immigrant districts to assist at a delivery the local handywoman couldn't cope with. Initially appalled that human beings in America should live in such conditions, nauseated by the smells as he entered the tenement halls and often frightened by drunken incoherent men who viewed him with suspicion and hostility, it didn't take him long to become accustomed to habitats and manners so different from his own New England upbringing, and beneath the squalor he recognised the qualities of these poor people, the women in particular.

Their valiant efforts to keep the rooms clean, to bring a touch of beauty into them, a single flower, often a brightly coloured weed, a sprig of blossom, a few green leaves in a jam jar or bottle. Some Holy pictures in the Irish homes, in the German ones a wool-embroidered cushion. The courage of them, their forebearance, their acceptance of the infant born dead and the joy and wonder on their faces when a live child was born, whether it was their first or twelfth. Such women! They inspired him and made him resolve that when he qualified some of his time and knowledge he would give to the tenement people.

While Mary was fetching the nightdress Katy fell asleep and woke to see

230

a strange face bending over her and Mary at the foot of the bed holding up the nightdress and making mouths that she was sorry for the delay. David smiled at Katy. She thought it was a nice smile, a boyish sort of smile as if he were shy. His teeth were lovely and as he leant forward a strand of his fair hair fell onto his forehead.

She began to sit up. 'No,' he said, 'stay there.' She liked the sound of his American voice.

He asked her if she was in pain and she said no. While he took her pulse Mary was talking. 'She collapsed, doctor, in a dead faint. I've told her she's killing herself with the work and doesn't eat enough.'

He ignored Mary's comments and gently questioned Katy. What had happened? Where had she fainted? What was she doing?

She answered his questions and then he told her to sit up and examined her heart and listened to her lungs. 'Fine,' he said, 'your chest is clear.' She was embarrassed by the old chemise she wore, it wasn't decent and she clutched at its neck. She had watched his face while he was examining her. She had seen him before but couldn't remember where or when. He had a narrow, thin face and his eyes were brown and his skin was sunburnt.

'Open your mouth, Mrs O'Hara,' he said. 'Fine, now let me have a look at your eyes.' He pulled down her bottom eyelids and made a little sound. 'Hmnn.' Then he lifted her hair and looked at each ear lobe in turn.

He was very young-looking, Katy thought, and wondered how old he was.

'Are you pregnant, Mrs O'Hara?'

'I am not,' Katy said indignantly.

'She's not, doctor,' Mary added. 'You see, the way it is her husband's been away this long time.'

'I'm sorry,' he said. Katy went scarlet and now she couldn't look him in the face. 'You lie back and rest. You're run down, nothing serious. I'll give you a tonic. Have you someone who'll collect it from the dispensary?' Katy nodded. 'It won't taste nice but take it all the same.' He replaced his stethoscope and Mary handed him his hat. 'Don't overdo things for the next few days and I'll call again a week today.'

Katy thanked him and Mary blessed him profusely and now that the professional part of his visit was over he chatted to her as she saw him out.

'A gentleman if ever there was one,' she said when she came back. 'Eileen was right when she said that. You know he buried his wife and little girl with the cholera.'

231

'So that's who he is. We saw him the day we landed. Doesn't he live in Gramercy Park?'

'That's the very place.'

'Where they have a gold key for opening the Park.'

'Pure gold. What washing have you for today? I'll lather it out.'

What that woman needs, David thought as he went from the tenement, is a new life. A different environment. Space, fresh air, good food, leisure. It was what all the tenement dwellers needed and had as much chance of getting as finding gold at the end of the rainbow.

The women in particular needed it, for their men at least had a certain amount of leisure, an escape in drink and they were given the lion's portion of food, while the majority of women were undernourished, overworked, constantly pregnant or nursing. Women grew old before their time, had prolapses which went untreated, varicose veins which ulcerated and ruptured – and almost all of them were for long periods of their child-bearing years anaemic. That, without a more thorough examination, was his diagnosis of Mrs O'Hara. So far she had escaped the ravages wrought on many of the women. She was beautiful. Different, a great dignity about her. The course of iron and an improved diet which he would suggest on his next visit should help – then he'd see.

During the following week he thought oftener about Katy than he did of his other patients. And his thoughts were nothing to do with her anaemia, its cause or treatment. It was the colour of her hair, the softness of it and her lovely mouth which occupied his mind.

The tonic tasted horrible but after taking it for a few days she felt a new woman. Full of energy and her appetite restored. Feeling so well, she had the energy to take stock of her life. Because of her carelessness Danny had nearly drowned. Two mornings she had slept it out and Thomas being late was sacked from the warehouse, Bridget and Mary Kate didn't lift a hand to help in the home. And all because she had neglected her duties as a mother. From now on she'd make big changes.

First, she'd have a word with the priest about work for Thomas and no matter what it was he'd take it and she'd get him up in the mornings. The girls would do the dishes and help with the simpler repairs. Then she could work harder at the laundrying, get back the customers she had lost by moving from Cow Lane. The laundry was her only means of support so she had to make it succeed. And because she felt so much better physically she grieved less over Jamsie's absence. Telling herself that he couldn't stay away forever and that it was wrong of her to have

232

stopped writing: she would start again. Supposing, as she sometimes thought, he had been injured, a bang on his head that had sent his wits astray so that he didn't know who he was or where – how would he or anyone find the truth about him if no letters came?

One by one, she tackled the problems. The priest found Thomas a job in a slaughterhouse. Bridget and Mary Kate, after moaning, picked up and put away their clothes and stitched cloth buttons on to the newly-washed underwear. She scrubbed and blued and bleached, pressed and ironed and did the repairs.

'It's as if new life was poured into me,' she told Mary.

'You look it, too,' Mary said. 'Though your teeth are queer, all black in the front. What ails them?'

'Divil the know I know. I'll ask the doctor when he comes.'

Katy was full of curiosity. What was the latest with Mary's marriage plans, or were they still postponed until Kathleen went to college?

'They are,' Mary said. 'Herr Jaeger is very understanding – he knows it wouldn't be fair on the child.'

For a minute Katy felt a pang of jealousy – the baker loved Mary so much he was prepared to wait and Jamsie had run away from her. But quickly she banished the thought – feeling sorry for herself did not a bit of good. They talked about Eileen, Katy lamenting that it was a long time since she'd heard from her and hoped all was well with her.

'It's as well she has no children and can earn a living, for I'd not put much faith in Paddy Kavanagh and his promises.'

Katy had to admit that Mary was right – that was her feeling about Paddy, too.

'I'm glad to see you looking so well.'

'Thank you, doctor – I'm grand, except for my teeth.'

'Let me see.'

Katy opened her mouth. 'Ah, yes,' said David, 'your front teeth are black.'

'Will they fall out?' Katy asked anxiously.

'No,' he said, 'they won't fall out,' and he smiled at her.

'Thanks be to God, what ails them?'

'The iron medicine causes discoloration. Try holding a cube of bread between your teeth when you take it. Difficult but worth a try. In any case, once you stop taking the tonic the staining goes.'

He spun out the visit, asking her questions that weren't relevant to her condition. He was enjoying her company, enjoying the sight of her. He hadn't seen her standing before – she was tall and had a lovely figure.

233

At last decorum made him bring his visit to an end. He would, he said, drop in again some time. In the meantime she should keep on with the tonic which could be renewed from the dispensary.

When he left, Katy looked at herself in the mirror – something she hadn't done for a long, long time. She studied her face, smiled at herself, smoothed her hair and was glad that the black teeth weren't permanent.

She worked twice as hard without becoming tired or irritable. She was tolerant but firm when the girls lapsed into their old untidy habits. She wrote another letter to Jamsie and another to Eileen's last address. Thomas hated the slaughterhouse. She reasoned with him: he didn't have to stay there forever – he must keep his eyes and ears open and something else would turn up.

She could cope, she was coping. She'd bring up the children well, see they minded their duties, that Mary Kate got ahead in school, that with God's help they were healthy. She could cope, she was coping. Never again would she let herself go so far down that her children were neglected. They were all she had until Jamsie came back.

Occasionally the face of David Purcell came before her mind. She remembered his smile and the way his fine hair fell onto his forehead. She wondered if he would call again. She felt so much better that she didn't finish the second bottle of medicine and in a little while the staining of her teeth disappeared.

For several weeks everything went well, then Bridget began again to make unfavourable comparisons between her home and that of her friend. She hated to come in from work and find washing all over the place. The smell of starch, soda and chlorine gave her a headache. It wasn't fair – why did they have to live like this? No one else did.

Katy placated her. 'Soon,' she said, 'if things improve maybe we can get another room, or maybe I'll find another lock-up shop. You'll have to be patient, that's all.' Bridget flounced about and Katy said an aspiration not to lose her temper. The next day, Thomas gave up the job the priest had got him in the slaughterhouse.

'Thomas,' she said, sitting down and cupping her chin in her hand. 'Thomas, that was a terrible thing to do. I depended on the money. I need it to feed you – why couldn't you have waited till you found something else before walking out?'

He wouldn't answer her – his mouth was set in a stubborn line that reminded her of Jamsie. Another O'Hara, she thought with bitterness and had an urge to hit him across his sullen mouth. But Thomas was the size of a man, you couldn't slap him like a child. For the first time since her recovery she felt her confidence leave her. She couldn't keep going – it was too much for anyone, she couldn't keep going. For the first time for a long while she wanted to cry. She got up and paced in what space there was, willing herself not to cry, not to lose her temper.

Then Thomas said, 'Mom, I'm awful sorry. I know it's hard on you. I know how you work. I should be making it easier for you – I promised Dada I'd mind you. But honest to God I couldn't stay there. Neither could you or anyone when you see how they kill the animals. I couldn't do it. I'll find another job. First thing tomorrow I'll find another one.'

Poor, gentle Thomas who couldn't kill a fly, step on an ant. 'Ah,' she said, 'never mind. You'll get something else.'

She forgave him, but even so her sense of well-being was gone so that when Bridget came home from work and again found fault with the place Katy's restraint went. 'You,' she shouted at Bridget, 'morning, noon and night you're finding fault, making comparisons with your fine friend's house. Well, you listen to me – your fine friend has a fine house and a mother who doesn't take in washing – and do you know why? No? Well, I'll tell you! Because she has a father who didn't desert them like yours did.'

Bridget glared at her and Katy hit her hard across the face. They stared at each other – the marks of Katy's fingers were coming up in a red weal across Bridget's cheek. The sight of it, the thought that she had inflicted it made Katy angrier. 'Go from my sight,' she shouted, 'go on, get yourself up to Kathleen, now, before I hit you again.'

'It's a lie, you're only saying it, Dad wouldn't do that. Dad never deserted us.'

'Go,' Katy said. 'Just go.' Bridget ran from the room crying.

'It isn't true, is it Mom, Dada didn't run out on us?' Mary Kate was crying and so was Danny. 'He was sick, wasn't he and maybe,' she hesitated before saying any more, then in a rush of words said, 'maybe he's dead.'

'No,' Katy said, 'he didn't desert us. I didn't know what I was saying. That one has me tormented. He didn't desert us. Something ails him but he's not dead. He'll come back, one day he'll come back – you'll see.'

Her sense of well-being waned. She became pale again, her body ached and the slightest exertion made her breathless. She was irritable and often too tired to eat at mealtimes, postponing eating until later, then found she could stomach little but tea and bread.

Some nights she fell into an exhausted sleep from which she woke still tired, dragging herself out of bed, forcing herself to work. Other nights she lay and listened to her frantic heart, hearing its echo through the pillow. Faster and faster it pounded. Any minute it would stop beating. Then what would happen to her children? What lay before them but the orphanage. Please God, don't let me die, she prayed. Spare me until they are reared or until Jamsie comes home. Praying she relaxed, her heart became comfortable and she slept.

One morning there was a knock on the door. Katy left what she was doing and, wondering who it could be, she opened the door. David Purcell was there. 'I was in the neighbourhood,' he said, raising his hat, 'and I thought I'd call. I hope it's not inconvenient.'

It was, very, for clothes were scattered in piles over the floor waiting to be washed, and she was untidy. It was very inconvenient and yet she was glad to see him. 'Come in,' she invited.

'Well,' he said, 'and how have you been keeping?' His eyes were scrutinising her.

'I'm grand, grand,' Katy replied.

'Your appetite all right?'

'It is,' she said.

'Mrs O'Hara, I don't wish to pry. I know your husband is away . . . I was wondering how you manage – for money, I mean?'

'I work and my daughter works. I manage, thank you.'

'Are you still taking the medicine?'

'I finished the second bottle,' she lied. He didn't believe her. She looked more ill than the first time he had seen her. And she had evaded his question about her husband – he obviously wasn't sending her money. She was proud. He would have to be very tactful. She would resent interference.

'You're bloodless,' he said, using the term the women themselves used. 'It'll make you tired.' He listed the other symptoms of anaemia – all of which Katy had. 'It also leaves you open to anything that's going – it undermines your constitution. You need red meat, liver. Do you eat red meat and liver.

'Sometimes,' Katy said. 'Sometimes I do.'

'You have a lot to do, a big family and your work. You must eat and you must take more of the medicine.'

'Hard work never killed anyone,' Katy said.

'You'd be surprised how many it does kill. You'll be sensible now, the medicine and the red meat and rest, yes?' He smiled at her. 'You do that and I'll call again. Two weeks, and I'll want to see a big improvement. I won't delay you any longer.'

She was easier with him on his next visit – admitted to not getting the tonic, to existing mostly on bread and tea. He was more candid with her. Telling her of the high incidence of consumption in the tenements through overcrowding, insufficient fresh air and rest, and malnutrition. All of which left you prey to the disease – and so did being bloodless.

On further visits he elicited the fact that Jamsie wasn't in contact nor had been for more than two years. And Katy's belief that he wasn't dead.

'How can you be so sure?'

'I'd know,' Katy replied, with such convinction he didn't argue.

'Then he's a fool and you're to be greatly admired for the way you manage.' He hadn't meant to be so forthright, and apologised. He must say no more for fear he said too much. Said what he thought of a man who left his wife and children to fend for themselves. He cleared his throat, looked away then back again, hoping he had regained his professionalism. 'It's admirable, Mrs O'Hara to strive as you have – but not to kill yourself in the process. You'll have to give up the laundry or have help.'

'Help!' Katy laughed. 'I couldn't afford help – you know enough about my circumstances, you should now that.'

She had spirit, too. He deserved the reminder that not only had he pried but had put the information to no use. He had better leave, as this visit was by the minute becoming less and less professional. He was enraged at her circumstances, enraged by her physical condition. She was a beautiful woman, a good woman, she deserved a better life. He had to find a way of helping her. A plan was beginning to form in his mind. He wanted a housekeeper. For a long time he had been meaning to engage one. When his wife died, the one who had been with them since their marriage left. The two black servants remained and for the time being he found their service adequate. But he did need someone to run his house.

'Would you consider other work, less strenuous than the laundrying and paying probably more?' he asked.

'Where and at what?' asked Katy. 'Housework, washing, cooking, sewing, that's all I know how to do.' She shrugged. 'It's all strenuous – at least with laundrying I'm more or less my own mistress.'

'But supposing this other job didn't require you to do all those things – would you consider it then?'

'For the likes of me those jobs don't exist.'

'I might know of one – think about it and when I call again we'll discuss it.'

The next time he came he enquired about her health, the state of which was evident from her pallor. Then he spoke about the job, telling her he wanted a housekeeper. 'Would you be interested?' he asked.

'I would,' she replied, for she recognised that housekeepers didn't have to kill themselves with hard work. Well she remembered Lord Kilgoran's housekeeper, at whose beck and call the servants were. Not that she expected in a doctor's house to find the same conditions as in the Big House – but certainly the work would be easier than laundrying. And she had no doubts about being capable of running a house. 'I would,' she repeated, 'only housekeepers have to live in and I couldn't do that.'

'Of course not – you have a family. I wouldn't expect it. You could come in the mornings, not too early. I'd make arrangements for a cab to fetch you and bring you home in the evenings.'

'I could walk. From here to Gramercy Park is no distance. I could do the job too, I was well-trained. Once my mother hoped I'd be a housekeeper – long ago when I worked in the Big House. If you didn't make a good match that was a great ambition. Oh, I could do the job with no bother. China and glass and linen, silver and food, I know all about it.' She was so eager for this job that she continued to talk on, repeating herself, boosting her abilities. 'I was used to it all, guests and parties, the stillroom, everything. I could . . .'

'Mrs O'Hara. I wouldn't want you to think I have such a grand establishment. Or guests or parties – I can't remember when I last had anyone to dinner. It's only a small house, with just two other servants.'

'Oh, Dr Purcell, you must think I'm an awful fool of a woman prating on. I know well it isn't a mansion you have. Though it's a beautiful house – I've seen them on the Park. It's that I'm so nervous and excited and delighted at the prospect.'

After accepting the job, Katy then found many reasons not in its favour. Supposing the black women resented her? And why wouldn't they. They'd had the run of the house since Dr Purcell's wife died. Now she'd be poking her nose in – asking questions, changing things. Relying on their help in the beginning. She had been too hasty in taking the job. Carried away by the prospect of an easier life.

There was Danny to consider. Could she trust him to come straight from school and stay in until Mary Kate came home? And Thomas, who'd give him a bit to eat when he came in after his fruitless job-searching? And in any case, supposing she did take the job – what would she wear? Memories of the sedately-dressed housekeeper in Kilgoran presented themselves. Black she wore. Never a crease, a stain or a fold of the dress out of place. Black shoes in which she glided about the place, her hair severely scraped back. Maybe Dr Purcell wouldn't expect her to dress exactly the same, but neither would he want her arriving in a worn skirt, patched blouse and her turnover.

No, she couldn't take it. She'd write a note, leave it at the dispensary apologising. She couldn't take the job. There were too many things against it. She must have taken leave of her senses when she agreed. Telling him all she knew about housekeeping, boasting about china and silver, linen and guests. And what did she really know about any of them? How to wash the china, polish silver, lay a table. That wasn't housekeeping. The black women could do any of that as well. Housekeeping was running the place. Being responsible for ordering everything, keeping accounts, keeping the servants in order. Mad she was to have said yes. Fitter for her to stay home and mind her family. She'd get her strength back and the washing would be no bother. She'd go with Thomas right up to a building site and wait while he asked for a start. Half the time she didn't believe he tried hard enough. If he was earning they wouldn't be too badly off.

For hours she found more and more excuses for not becoming David's housekeeper. If solutions to any of the problems came into her mind she banished them, until she was finally convinced. She really couldn't take the job. Yes, she would write a note and apologise – she'd send Danny with it to the dispensary. She'd send him the minute he came in from school. It wouldn't be fair to deceive the doctor, keep him waiting when he could be looking for someone else.

When the note was written and Danny impatiently waiting for instructions as to where he was to take it, Katy wavered. Was she doing the right thing throwing away the chance of a living that would improve all of their lives? According to the doctor, her health would also improve. So would Mary Kate's chances of becoming a teacher. If she wasn't earning, out of school Mary Kate would have to come. And as far as the black women were concerned, so long as she didn't immediately make sweeping changes, didn't find undue fault with their ways, found her feet slowly – they might tolerate her.

Mrs Ginsburg, the poor woman who had buried her little son, she'd let Danny stay in her place until Mary Kate came home from school. Most of her problems could be solved. The book-keeping and ordering wouldn't be on such a scale as Kilgoran, for hadn't Dr Purcell said he didn't keep a grand establishment, didn't have parties or guests to dine. It wouldn't take her long to learn what was needed. But there was still the question of what to wear. She had nothing suitable, nor money to buy anything. Then she remembered the clothes Eileen had given her and to which she had paid little attention at the time. They were in a sack under the bed. She dragged it out and tipped the clothes on the floor. The smell of Eileen's scent wafted about the room. Bright, garish-coloured dresses, there was nothing suitable there, Katy thought and smiled – Eileen wasn't the sort to go in for housekeeper's clothes. But at the bottom of the pile she found a grey dress. She picked it up, shook it out, and examined it. It had long sleeves and a white collar, the stuff was soft, it wouldn't cling nor stand out too much. It was very suitable for a housekeeper's dress.

Where, she wondered, as she put the other clothes back in the sack, had Eileen got it – and why? Then she remembered. The saloon had put on a sketch in which Eileen had played an American country girl – the grey dress, a straw basket, a shawl and a bonnet was her costume. 'Like a bloody nun or someone out of an orphanage I look,' Eileen had said when she tried the outfit on. 'It's not my style. All the same, it doesn't stop me getting a man. A beauty who gets me pregnant, deserts me and then my father throws me out in the cold, cold snow. You want to see the eejits of men – letting on not to cry. All the same it's an awful-looking thing. You know me and what I like to wear.'

Frills and flounces, low necks and the brightest of colours. Katy wondered if Eileen had got to San Francisco and bought the crinoline her heart was set on. She missed her so much, her gaiety, how she made her laugh. She hoped things were going well for her friend, that Paddy was being good to her and that some time she would see or hear from her again.

How Eileen would have laughed at her in the housekeeper's get-up. But she'd encourage her to take the job. Katy could hear her voice. 'You're mad if you don't. A lovely house to spend the day in – good money and your keep and plenty to bring home.' And Katy wouldn't put it past her to have said, 'And there's more to housekeeping than that – many's the man who married his housekeeper.' For Eileen, though she had never after the first time of mentioning it, spoken of it again, was convinced that Jamsie was dead. Katy tore up the note turning down the job and sent Danny instead to buy blacking. With a good rub of it her shoes could be improved.

Chapter Two

It was a pleasure to wake in the morning and know that her day was to be spent in the house in Gramercy Park. For a few minutes before rising she lay thinking about all there was still to be done there, planning how she would approach it and still remain on the good terms she had with Rachael and Sarah, the two black women who helped. Rachael was old and took little interest in what went on outside the kitchen, but sometimes Sarah's expression altered from a wide smile to a broody questioning when Katy wanted cupboards turned out, rugs beaten, all the things that must be done, that hadn't been done since Dr Purcell's wife had died.

It was such a beautiful house. It was the only other house except for the Ryans' she had ever been in in America. And even though it was dusty, dirty and very neglected, Dr Purcell's place was so much nicer. There was nothing in it that looked as if it had come straight from a store on Broadway. There were books and soft chairs, old silver, miniatures of people in old-fashioned clothes, paintings of ships. There was quality about everything. It reminded her, though on a much smaller scale, of Kilgoran House.

To be in such surroundings had a beneficial effect on Katy's health. So had the good food and the security of money in her purse once a week. Sufficient money to nourish her children, encourage Mary Kate with her studies and not be too downcast at Thomas' failure to keep a job. Her improved circumstances also made her brood less about Jamsie. She still loved him and longed for his return but now it wasn't foremost in her mind.

She rarely saw David Purcell. In the mornings, ever. Occasionally in the afternoon he would come in and have tea – which lately she had taken over making and serving. Eventually, she intended preparing all the meals. For although Rachael's cooking was good, Katy considered that for the doctor it wasn't good enough. Though he never complained – no more than he complimented. The silver, furniture, mirrors and rugs to which with Sarah's help she had restored bloom and lustre went unnoticed. She would have loved a word of praise. Surely, she often thought, he must see the difference. Then at other times she would console herself that he was too busy, that men rarely noticed things about a house, that had he been the noticing kind he would have had a housekeeper long ago.

The library she had left last for putting in order, and there she wouldn't have Sarah to help. There were books in piles everywhere. Books taken from shelves and not replaced. She was full of purpose and contentment as she set about her task. With a soft brush, she attacked the dust coating the books and it made her sneeze many times. Some books obviously belonged together but this she could only judge by size and colour, for the titles of the majority meant nothing to her. One set – the Waverley novels, she remembered having seen in Kilgoran House. Carefully she removed those already on shelves, dusted and replaced them, wondering as she did so had the doctor read all the books? All the things that people knew, who read books. Mary Kate, if she stayed on at school, would read a lot of books. She glanced at titles, of medical books and ones about botany and insects. Some she opened and looked at the drawings. Carefully and methodically she worked until there was only one more set of shelves to arrange. Going through it, she saw a title she recognised, a book she had read even though it was only in a paper. She was thrilled. She knew what this story was about. She sat in a chair near the shelves and opened *Uncle Tom's Cabin* and began to read. Unaware of time passing, unaware that about now was when David often came in for his tea.

He came as he did whenever it was possible. He came not because he was thirsty but because he wanted to see Katy, sometimes deluding himself that his interest in her was of a medical nature. Her health was vastly improved. He liked confirmation of that and the satisfaction of knowing his treatment had provided the cure. When he was being honest with himself, he admitted that none of these reasons were true. He was in love with Katy. He wanted her in his house for always. He wanted to find proof that her husband was dead and ask her to marry him. He had already made some enquiries. Putting them to people connected with the railroad, saying they were for a patient of his. The replies had been discouraging. There were few records of the thousands of labourers employed. They came and went – finding one would be like searching a beach for a particular grain of sand. The best course was for the patient to try the last place where it was known the husband had been. Sometimes a workmate would have information.

He didn't know the last place where Katy's husband had worked. He knew very little about him, not even his first name. But most important,

242

he had no idea how Katy would react to him making enquiries. To rush into anything might result in him losing what little contact he had with her. He needed time, time to build up a relationship of trust between them. In her presence he became tongue-tied, gauche, so that in an effort to disguise his unease his speech was abrupt, impersonal – the manner of a bad employer to his servant. Kate, his sweet Kate, never did he want her as a servant.

He was delighted to see her in the library, so engrossed in the book that she didn't hear him come in. He said the first thing that came into his head. 'You like books?'

Startled, Katy turned. She felt guilty, as if she had been found prying into something that wasn't her business. 'Oh,' she said, putting down the book and standing up. 'I was supposed to be dusting them, I'm sorry. 'Tis little I've read though I always meant to. I was surprised when I saw this one,' she indicated *Uncle Tom's Cabin*, 'for a woman lent it to me. I read it and to the children as well.'

'Sit down,' he said. 'And did you like it?'

'I did, I knew nothing about the slaves before. Yes, it was a grand book.'

'Indeed,' said David, 'and a hornets' nest it stirred up. Many more people in the North knew nothing either about slaves – now they do and have great sympathy for them. Take it home, if you like. Borrow any of the books – I'd like to share them with you. There's one there your boys might like to read. This,' he said, taking a copy of *Moby Dick* from the shelf. 'It's about a great white whale. About whalers from my part of the country.' He couldn't stop himself talking. He wanted to detain her. 'My grandfather was the captain of a whaler – that's what I wanted to be. Lots of small boys want to go to sea.'

Katy didn't know what to say though she searched her mind frantically. He came to her rescue by handing her the Harriet Stowe book and telling her to keep it as long as she liked and to take *Moby Dick* as well.

She had a reason to speak, thanked him and then remembered his tea. 'I forgot all about it – I'll make it now this minute, if you'll excuse me, and thank you again for the books. I'll take good care of them.' She left him.

He cursed himself for not having the gumption, the courage to say, 'Have tea with me.' He could think of nothing nicer at the moment than sitting with her, she pouring tea and them talking, getting to know each other.

★

243

Katy reread *Uncle Tom's Cabin* and began *Moby Dick* so that the next time Dr Purcell spoke to her about books she would have something to contribute. He occupied her thoughts a lot. She liked and admired him very much. She had never known a man like him. She compared him with Peader, the only man she had known well other than Jamsie. She compared them physically – one was as tall and fair and handsome as the other, but Dr Purcell had brown eyes and Peader green. It was years since she had seen Peader so it wasn't really fair to make a judgment but she did, and guessing that they were about the same age she thought that Dr Purcell was wearing better. Peader, she remembered, had had a softness of the flesh about him, he'd get heavy. No, he definitely wouldn't wear as well as the doctor. At the first hint of her mind wanting to further the comparison between Dr Purcell and Peader, she busied her mind with other thoughts.

She got to know him better. Once, he invited her to have tea with him and it became an afternoon ritual. He talked about books and his childhood, asked her if she read a newspaper and when she said no, told her to read his *Tribune*. And she did and would sometimes speak to him about an article she had read and didn't understand and he would explain it to her. Now she compared him in other ways to Peader. Peader was well-read and years ago used to explain things to her. Now she realised that his explaining had been different. He, maybe not intentionally, made her aware of the little she knew. David, for in her secret thoughts she had started to call him David, never made her feel like that. She felt bright and alert listening to him, questions coming to her mind that she wanted to ask and he answered them.

She learned so much during their tea sessions. That once upon a time New York had been a trading colony of the Dutch, and was known as New Amsterdam. A Dutchman, Peter Minuit, bought Manhattan for the equivalent of twenty-four dollars. Then the English took New Amsterdam and called it New York but again the Dutch won it back and renamed it New Orange.

While David talked she listened and watched his face. His smile, slightly crooked, as she had noticed on his first visit. His lean boyish face with its smooth skin except round his eyes where when he smiled there were lines. Sometimes she wondered what it would be like to lay her cheek against his.

She had noticed the use of her name and after their tea when he had gone back to the hospital she let her mind dwell on it. Did it mean he had a special regard for her? But then remembering that he also called Sarah and Rachael by their first names she thought not and took herself

244

to task for mooning like a young, lovesick girl. Dr Purcell was a very kind, gentle, polite man. Having tea with him, him calling her Katy meant no more than that. And thank God for it. She was a respectable married woman with a husband who admittedly didn't possess her thoughts every minute of the day any more but whom until the day death closed her eyes she would love and wait for.

Now she cooked the meals for David. Rachael, becoming more infirm, seemed relieved to hand over. She spent most of her time in the kitchen huddled close to the stove – even on a warm day she complained about the cold. Sometimes her mind rambled and she talked about her childhood on a cotton plantation in South Carolina. Her very good master, all the pork and corn they had, all the singing and their own plots to keep pigs and grow corn. On these occasions she'd sing snatches of songs and keep an eye on Katy if the meal she was preparing was of Southern origin. On the days when her bones ached she was melancholy and her memories of the plantation were bad ones. The brother or lover, Katy was never certain which, who had been flogged, many times, before the master sold him down the river. Then Rachael would cry and Katy think the poor men, the poor men everywhere being flogged and sold down the river or transported – wasn't it the same thing. And all the tears shed by the women, mothers and wives and sweethearts.

Once, talking to David about Rachael's tales he told her how she and Sarah had come to him, on what was called the Underground Railway –an organisation in the South and North of people who were against slavery. Slaves willing to risk it left the plantations at night, creeping over fields to meet up with a sympathiser who would send them on the next stretch of their journey to the North. Some slaves made the journey without help from the organisation, sleeping by night and stealing enough food to keep them going. One enterprising fellow disguised his light-skinned wife as his master and made it that way. David supposed that Rachael and Sarah were moved to make the break after the lover or brother was sold down the river.

Katy told him of Peader and Charlotte living in Virginia. And how she could never understand him staying on a plantation worked by slaves. 'For Miss Charlotte it could well be different. She was used to servants, though her father had been a good kind master. Even so in the last few years, since I've been in America I can see that good and all as he was, his owning us, as he did in a way, our cottages and whether we had work or not, was wrong. So I could understand her, Miss Charlotte, not

245

seeing anything wrong in slavery so long as they were well treated. But him – Peader – there was no one more for freedom than Peader.'

'In that case,' said David, 'the South won't be the most comfortable place for him now.'

'Why is that?' asked Katy.

'Things are coming to a head – sides must be taken. In the long run I think it'll mean war.'

'I hope to God then Peader has the sense to clear out long before that and bring Miss Charlotte with him.'

'Why do you call him Peader and his wife Miss Charlotte?'

'Well, she was the Master's daughter, Lord Kilgoran. I always called her Miss Charlotte, even when she was a little girl. Everyone who wasn't family did.'

'You don't have to any more.' David smiled his lovely smile. 'You're in America now. We don't have lords, nor their daughters called Miss. You don't,' he said and his voice became quieter, 'have to call me Doctor. My name is David, I'd like you to call me David.' Katy blushed. 'Try it – go on. Say David.'

'David.' She said the name.

'No more Doctor, then?'

'No more Doctor then,' she hesitated and then added, 'David.'

She made an excuse soon after saying his name, gathered up the tea things and left the room. David thought, at least now we are on first-name terms. It had taken a long time but it was an achievement. They were getting to know each other. He hoped she no longer considered herself a servant. She talked to him about many things, her life in Ireland, the children, Eileen and the progress of Mary and Herr Jaeger. But she never mentioned her husband. He still didn't know his name.

The library in which he and Katy had their tea was a sunny room, but without her presence the light seemed to have left it and a chill crept in. It was, he knew, only his imagination. The chill was in his heart and the gloom in his mind at the prospect of never having Katy for a wife. He wanted her as the mistress of his home, wanted to ride out with her in his carriage, wanted her to be a friend of his friends, a daughter-in-law of his parents. He wanted her in his bed. And he wanted her husband dead.

Jamsie was alive and kicking, working on the railroads, hating them and the gangers as he had when working as a labourer in New York. Sometimes he cursed himself for ever having listened and been influenced by the Kerryman. But again he was listening to men talking and an influence being exerted. Like the Kerryman they talked of gold. Of men who had made fortunes digging for it. Men with no more than a pick, pan, an Indian basket and a shovel finding a fortune in one digging. Millionaires ten times over. He became obsessed by the thought.

One day, during the hours when he was sober and thoughts of gold were mixed with guilty ones of Katy, and a longing was on him to hold her in his arms and tell her how sorry he was, how he loved and missed her, how never in his life would he look at another woman . . . something in his brain went snap. He would leave the railroad. He would seek a fortune for Katy. He'd come back to her and lay it at her feet. At the time he made the decision he was running with four men who between them held a length of track – they ran until they reached the spot where it was to be dropped. When it was, Jamsie walked away. He had one dollar and seventy-five cents in his pocket. He had no idea where he was going, only that he was setting out to make a fortune for Katy which he would bring home and place in her lap.

She called him David, had tea with him most afternoons and left his supper ready before she went home. There she cooked another meal for her children, calm and unruffled. Able to give her attention to Danny's news and reports of Mary Kate's progress in school and plan with her for the years ahead when she would go to College and become a teacher. To Thomas who seldom had work she slipped fifty cents – not enough for him to get drunk on, but at least he had something in his pocket. And every night she marvelled again at how beautiful Bridget was. Not that she ever told her so. Bridget was vain enough. Forever in front of the mirror arranging her hair or trying on hats, failures from the shop that she remade.

Like herself, Katy knew her family benefited from her working. Though they were still crammed in the one room, without the washing at least there was a little space to move. And please God one day she would find somewhere better to live. Often her thoughts of improving their living conditions revolved round Jamsie reappearing and finding a job – with the two of them working they would be very comfortable. Her only worry was that David might bring in a wife who didn't approve of her. And she knew that she would find a mistress difficult, for as it was she had begun to think of the house as her own.

Sometimes she let herself imagine that it was, and from there her thoughts would go to who she was living in the house with. Who she

247

would want to live in the house with. And in her mind she said the name. And for a few moments indulged herself by pretending, seeing her days as they would be lived as his wife – a life so different from her own. They would have friends come to supper, they'd go for visits to his relations, she'd see the place where he'd lived as a boy and dreamed about being the captain of a whaler. She'd hear his voice explaining things to her, talking to her about little things, making her laugh.

Beyond that she wouldn't think. It would be a sin. Impure thoughts, a cause of Confession. But the other thoughts were harmless, like a fairy story. A girl dreaming of becoming a princess. Even so sometimes she took herself to task for dreaming of princes – she was a grown woman, married these years. With no place in her mind for such nonsense.

One evening when she came home from work Bridget was arranging roses in a big jug, one of the ornaments Eileen had given. The roses were red and Katy quickly counted twelve. The room was full of their scent. 'Who gave you them?' she asked.

'I don't know,' said Bridget.

'You don't know?' What do you mean – you don't know. Where did you get them?'

'Someone left them in the shop.'

'Then you should have let them stay there – they'll be looking for them in the morning.'

'They were left for me. A boy brought them, there was a card.'

'Now, what's all this? Roses and a card – that doesn't happen. People don't have money to throw away on flowers and then not let on they sent them. Come on Miss, you're not telling me the truth.'

'Honest to God – look, there's the card.'

Katy took the card and read, *from an admirer*. 'Well,' she said, sitting down, 'that beats Banagher.'

'Who's Banagher?' asked Mary Kate.

'I don't know – 'twas a saying of my mother's. You'll have to find out about them. Ask in the flower shop and leave word you want no more flowers. You're to take presents from no one without me knowing who they are.'

Bridget made an exasperated sound.

'You'll do what you're told – do you hear me!'

'Oh, all right.'

After supper Katy went up to Mary's and told her about the flowers. Mary's eyes lit up. 'She has an admirer, isn't that grand?'

'What ails you, Mary! An admirer – she's only a child.'

248

'She's eighteen years of age nearly. I was well married by then.'

And so was I, thought Katy. But still to her Bridget was only a child. 'I'm not surprised – she's a beauty, God bless her. It's many an admirer she'll have.'

'Lord, doesn't the time fly. Little Bridget with an admirer – and Kathleen away to College next month.'

'Aye,' said Katy, and suddenly she felt old and dispirited. Her Bridget eighteen and Jamsie gone all these years – half a lifetime and more flown.

'I've been waiting to tell you, it's all settled between me and Günter. We'll be putting in the Banns and please God getting married on St Stephen's Day.'

'That you may both be very happy,' Katy said. 'You deserve it,' and she thought how that was the first time Mary had ever called Herr Jaeger by his Christian name.

For the first time in months Katy couldn't sleep. She kept thinking of Bridget, nearly the age she was when she married Jamsie. Only yesterday she was her first baby. Now there was a man admiring her – sending flowers and not declaring himself. He could be anyone – a bad-hearted person, maybe. America wasn't like the village where you knew everyone. It was a dangerous place for a young girl. At home you'd know all about him – here he could be anyone. Her child with a man – it didn't seem possible. It didn't seem right. Bridget with an admirer and Mary with a husband. It wasn't fair. She wasn't old, not yet she wasn't old.

The next morning she reminded Bridget to leave word at the flower shop that no more were to be sent to her. 'And another thing, Miss,' she said. 'If you've any more admirers I want to know about them. You'll bring them here for me to see, remember that.'

Bridget, ready for work, laughed. 'Bring them here?' She looked with scorn round the room. 'Are you mad? I wouldn't bring a dog here.' She was gone through the door before Katy could say anything.

She talked to David about Bridget's secret admirer. Showing her indignation, her worry, her determination to put a stop to any more presents.

'Perhaps it's someone who is shy – a young boy smitten with Bridget who can't pluck up courage.'

'A young boy with money for twelve roses? More likely an oul fella old enough to be her father.'

'I suppose you have a point – few young men would have such money.' He wished he could send her flowers, shower her with gifts, take her to the theatre or out for a drive. He couldn't, for he wouldn't compromise her. But one day he would give her everything.

'I shouldn't,' she said, 'be bothering you with my worries. Home for a rest you come in the afternoon, not to hear my prate.'

'Katy,' he said, 'you rest me just by being here.' He could see by her face that she was disconcerted. Hurriedly he said the first thing that came into his mind, wanting to restore the ordinariness of the situation. 'Your friends in Virginia – do you ever hear from them?'

'No,' Katy said, remaining occupied with the tea things, not wanting to meet his eyes, waiting for the blush to leave her face. 'No, not this long time.'

He liked her. 'Katy, you rest me just by being here,' that's what he had said. Didn't that mean he liked her – liked her for herself, not because she was a good housekeeper, not because his house was spick and span or his supper tasty. He liked her for herself. The thought pleased her enormously so that throughout the afternoon she kept recalling what he had said – so often that it eventually became confused in her mind and by evening she was no longer sure of his exact words. Had he said, 'Katy, you rest me just by being here,' or 'Katy, I'm rested just by being here.' Meaning at home, away from the hospital he was rested.

That night she dreamt about Jamsie. A dream in which they were physically close, then the dream changed and it was David in whose arms she lay. David who was kissing her, fondling her breasts, lifting the hem of her nightdress. She woke with a thudding heart and her insides contracting and she moaned with pleasure.

In the cold light of day the dream appeared sinful. She had had such dreams since Jamsie went away. Almost always they finished too soon. Even so she felt impure, unchaste though she never confessed them, reasoning that she didn't control her dreams, that it wasn't sinful to miss your husband, to think about him and long for him before you slept.

But to dream such a dream about David! To have such pleasure in it. That had to be a mortal sin. All day yesterday she had dwelt on him. Pondering the meaning of what he had said. She had put him out of her mind before going to bed and thought instead of Bridget being grown up and of Mary and Günter getting married. But she remembered that before she fell asleep her last thought was pondering again on what exactly David had said. It was a mortal sin committed deliberately.

250

She took herself to task, telling herself she was a married woman, Jamsie's wife and she loved him. He would come back soon. He must come back soon. She prayed for his safety, for his return. She needed him.

On her way to work she reminded herself that she was just a housekeeper: she must remember that and behave like one. There would be no more Daviding – if she had to give him a name, it would be Dr Purcell. He might think the sudden change odd so whenever possible she would avoid using any title. And there'd be no more staying in the library for tea. She could always find an excuse – something she had to do – but definitely no more time in the library, otherwise she'd start making a fool of herself again.

David noticed that Katy stopped using his name and invented reasons for not having tea with him. It saddened him that the little intimacies were over. He had been too freemaking, too eager to make headway with their relationship. Katy was a respectable woman, convinced that her husband would return. He must bear in mind that never by look or gesture had Katy shown signs that might be interpreted as other than those of a friendly, kind woman. His love for her was no guarantee that even if she were free the love would be returned.

Chapter Three

After a while Katy forgot her resolve and 'David' slipped out now and again. Eventually tea in the library was also resumed. Supposedly engrossed in pouring tea she covertly glanced at his face, admiring its narrow leanness, his beautiful teeth and his fine fair hair. As covertly and admiringly he watched her but took great care never again to say anything that might cause offence.

They talked about the weather, each saying how glorious it was, how the fall was their favourite season. She borrowed and returned books and they talked about them. He had lent her Walt Whitman's *Leaves of Grass*. She said it was nice, but found some poetry hard to understand. Once she apologised for Danny taking so long to read *Moby Dick*.

'Is he enjoying it?' David wanted to know. And Katy said he was. He loved anything to do with the sea – he was mad about the sea.

'I remember,' David said. 'He jumped in in his clothes and nearly drowned – I met you soon after.'

'You did,' Katy said and he thought her reply was more than a casual answer. Was he imagining it or did he detect a hint in her tone, an expression in her eyes that showed she was glad they had met. But the next minute she was talking about Thanksgiving in a matter-of-fact manner. He had imagined it. Imagination was all he had, imagination and his fantasies of Katy as his beloved wife.

Sometimes he talked to her about politics. Asking her was she a follower of the New Republican Party.

'I read about them but I'm not sure I always understand what I read. It's late I've come to reading newspapers or trying to understand politics. At home what you knew about them was learned by word of mouth. The men read the papers and pamphlets and the women were told about the news. In any case the problem in Ireland was simpler – there was Them and Us – the English and us.'

David explained how the New Republican Party were anti-slavery and Katy said yes, she had read that. That was a good thing.

'And Abraham Lincoln – you'll have come across his name.' Katy nodded. 'He's a man of great integrity – one day he may be the

President.' David smiled at her and she looked away, for his smile had an effect on her that she liked but mustn't allow herself to indulge in. In David's company it was beginning to become difficult to remember that her heart was pledged to Jamsie. Once she wondered how she would react if David touched her, caught hold of her hand, put an arm round her. Not that he was ever likely to, for he was a gentleman who treated her with respect. And she a foolish, lonely woman starved of love, starved of affection as the children grew older and became indifferent to her. Even Danny shrugged off her embraces. She longed for the closeness of another human being – the touch of someone, someone to hold. For Jamsie – for David. But such thoughts of David must be put from her mind lest one day she wrongly interpreted a friendly gesture and frightened the life out of him with a passionate response.

'That's two turkeys we've had this year, one for Thanksgiving and this one for Christmas,' said Mary Kate, helping Katy make stuffing. 'Isn't Dr Purcell very generous with his presents.'

'He is that,' said Katy. 'Now, be a good girl and take it round to Jaeger's and ask what time it'll be ready.'

They sat down to dinner at two o'clock. 'I hope,' said Katy, 'that your father has a nice bit of food for today.' Her eyes filled with tears.

Thomas reached and touched her arm and squeezed it. 'He'll be fine, Mom.'

'Please God,' said Katy. 'It's just that I was thinking we could never afford a turkey when he was here. He'd have licked his lips over it.' They had a Christmas pudding made as puddings were in Ireland, a rich heavy one that had been boiled in a cloth and hung for weeks. It was lovely hot or cold and could be sliced like rich fruit cake. By the end of the meal Katy was happy and contented with her family round her, well-fed and in good humour, and looked forward to the afternoon when they'd stay together, talking, maybe having a song. Then Bridget stood from the table and announced she was going out.

'Not on Christmas afternoon, Bridget,' Katy protested. 'It's a time for families to be together.'

'We have, for hours.'

'I'd like you to stay.'

'Well, I'm not,' said Bridget. 'And another thing,' she pointed at Mary Kate, 'don't you touch my things while I'm out.'

'I wouldn't want to touch anything belonging to you,' Mary Kate retorted.

'Then don't. Anyway, they're not meant for dwarfs.'

253

'Bridget!' Katy's voice was loud and angry. 'Take that back at once. Tell Mary Kate you're sorry. I won't have you calling her names. Tell her you're sorry, do you hear me!'

Bridget stood mute. Katy got up, intending to get hold of her and slap her face till she brought tears to her eyes. The wicked girl, to torment Mary Kate, to spoil the Christmas.

'Don't, Mom. Don't get yourself in a temper. Let her go. Don't upset yourself,' Thomas said and made his mother sit down. 'You know what she's like. Half the time she doesn't mean what she says.' To Bridget he shouted, 'Go if you're going, let's have a bit of peace.'

When she had been gone a few minutes, Mary Kate said, 'I bet she's going to see the man who sends the flowers.'

'Flowers, what flowers? What are you talking about?' asked Katy.

'All sorts of flowers. Her admirer sends them – they still come to the shop.'

'Now Mary Kate, I know you don't tell lies, so you're only saying this because you're angry with Bridget. When she comes home I'll put a stop to any more name-calling.'

'It isn't lies. She does have flowers. I'm always keeping her secrets – well, after today I'm not any more.'

'Shame on you, Mary Kate.' Better to think she was a liar than Bridget receiving flowers and being deceitful about it. 'Commere to me this minute and no more prevaricating. What made you say such a thing?'

Mary Kate shrugged. 'You'd better ask her when she comes in.'

'You know it isn't true. You know I put a stop to all that business about the flowers.'

'There's more than one flower shop in New York. Maybe he sends them from different ones.'

Though she didn't want to, Katy believed Mary Kate. The turkey dinner stuck in her gullet, it felt like a lump of lead. The lovely atmosphere of Christmas went, to be replaced by fear and anger. She was angry that all this time Bridget had deceived her and terrified that at this very minute she was somewhere with a strange man. She vented her feelings on Mary Kate, grabbing hold of her, shaking her roughly and demanding to know all she knew about it.

'Mom! Let go, you're hurting me. Bridget told me and made me promise not to tell you. I'm sorry I did. She'll kill me when she finds out. I hate her. She spoils everything. She has spoiled Christmas.'

Without relaxing her hold, Katy asked, 'And did she tell you she was seeing him today? And was she with him on Thanksgiving – she went out then as well.'

254

'No, she's only gone to Maura's house. She doesn't know who he is, honestly. But she gets off everything. I was thinking of all the dishes to wash and then when she called me a dwarf, I got mad at her.'

Katy let go her arm. 'I'm sorry, love. You did right to tell me. And don't mind her name-calling. You're a lovely, good child. You sit there now and read your book and never mind about the dishes – I'll do them.'

While she did she talked to herself. 'For two pins I'd go round to that girl's place. Mary Kate only knows what Bridget told her. It may be lies. Hasn't she been lying all the time. Only I can't go to the Doodys' on Christmas Day and cause unpleasantness. But the day after tomorrow I'll go to the hat-shop. I'll see she gets no more flowers. I'll take her out of the place, so I will. That's what comes of having no father. Wait till she comes in.'

Mary Kate was trying to read her book, a present from David, but Katy's long monologue was interfering with her concentration. But having put the cat among the pigeons she thought better of asking her to stop talking, letting out long-drawn exasperated sighs instead, hoping they might penetrate Katy's mind. If they did Katy ignored them and carried on talking.

It was Kathleen coming to ask Katy to go and see her mother's wedding dress that eventually shut her up. Mary Kate heaved a sigh of relief and settled down to her reading when the door closed.

It was a lovely dress, a soft woollen one, beigey-brown in colour. A German woman had made and embroidered the collar and cuffs. Katy admired it and said it suited Mary and that well might she wear it. All the time she was talking and listening to Mary's plans for tomorrow her mind was with Bridget. She wouldn't have a minute's ease until she was in and Katy knew the truth of where she'd been. And another thought occurred to her – there was Kathleen, the same age as Bridget, at home with her mother. Grown up into a sensible girl even, apart from the fuss she had created about her mother getting married – a nice, polite girl. She that had been the cranky, demanding, greedy child was now a model daughter – while her own . . . It went to show you never knew what you were rearing.

Bridget thought her mother was making a fuss about nothing. 'They're only flowers. No, I don't know who he is. And, yes, I told the first shop not to send any more. So he went to another shop. What am I supposed to do – go round every shop in New York saying no flowers for me, my mother won't allow it?'

255

'You know who he is, you're lying.'

'I don't and I don't care. It's a scream, that's all. The girls think it's the funniest thing and very romantic. I didn't tell you because I knew this is what would happen.'

'And tonight, where were you tonight?'

'With Maura – where did you think I was?'

'Listen, love.' Katy altered her tone. 'I don't want to be fighting with you on Christmas Night. You wouldn't lie to me. Tell me again you don't know this man – you aren't seeing him. Tell me that and I'll say no more about it."

'How many times do I have to tell you? I don't. He's probably mad. He must be, spending all that money on someone he's never seen.'

'He must have seen you.' Katy was worked up again. 'He must have. How else would he know your name or where to send the flowers? I'm going down to the shop. I'll see the woman you work for, this Madame Renée. I'm putting a stop to it.'

'Mom, if you do that, I'll never go there again. I'll never work again. I'll run away. I mean it. If you go to the shop and make a fool of me in front of everyone I'm leaving home.'

She would, too. It wasn't an idle threat. She couldn't lose Bridget as well. She'd have to leave well enough alone and hope the man got tired of sending flowers. And pray that if he didn't, sending flowers was as far as it would go.

Mary had a quiet wedding. Katy was her bridesmaid and a friend of Günter's the best man. The four of them walked to the church, the men in front and Mary nervously clutching Katy's arm a few paces behind. As the bride and groom stood in front of the altar Katy remembered her own wedding, the beautiful dress one of Miss Olivia's, which her mother had altered for her. Her poor mother, her father, Miss Olivia – all dead and gone. And Jamsie – where was Jamsie? Why had he deserted her? She loved him and had never doubted his love for her. Tears filled her eyes. But she told herself she mustn't cry. This was Mary's day, she mustn't let her sadness spoil it.

After the service Günter shyly kissed his bride and Mary blushed like a young girl. Back in their apartment, German neighbours had a wedding breakfast laid out. Katy had a glass of wine and then another. The wine cheered and warmed her and for a few hours she put aside her own heartache and rejoiced for Mary and Günter's sake.

A German neighbour said it was the custom at home after a wedding to put a baby carriage up on the roof to bring the couple many sons and daughters. 'No,' said Mary. 'No, nothing like that,' as a flush of embarrassment tinged her cheeks.

And in any case, Katy pointed out – who'd have a baby carriage there and if anyone had, wouldn't the weight of it and the man on the roof putting it there maybe bring the roof down on top of them! The idea was abandoned and the wedding breakfast proceeded.

He knew now that his name was Jamsie. Katy had let it slip and also the place to which she sometimes sent letters. It happened one day early in the New Year. They were watching the birds squabbling for the food Sarah put out for them during the cold weather, and Katy had asked, 'Does it snow in Illinois?' He told her it did, that the winters in the mid-west were very severe. 'Poor Jamsie, if the weather's like this in Racine how will he manage to look after himself, dry his clothes and air them?'

'He'll know how to look after himself, they'll have stoves.' He kept looking out through the window pretending great interest in a robin, willing himself not to say what he really felt about Jamsie and whether or not his clothes were aired.

'I hope you're right, I hope they do have stoves. The winters in America are desperate. Not like at home, for only once in my life did I ever see snow there.' He encouraged her to reminisce about Ireland. He would have encouraged her to talk about anything other than her concern for Jamsie's welfare.

During the following week he passed on the names to his friend with the railway connections. 'It's better than nothing,' the friend said, 'but not a lot – there would be dozens of James O'Haras. It's not an uncommon name, but I'll pass it on.' While he waited for word David wondered if the news was what he hoped, would he break it to Katy? How would he explain his coming by it? Grief did strange things to people. He'd seen bereaved people turn on the innocent messenger who brought news of a tragedy and blame them for it, and many harboured resentment long after reason should have shown them otherwise. Katy, full of superstitions, might believe he had brought bad luck on Jamsie. Bad luck by making the enquiries. If she did, then what chance would he have when he told her he loved her? For days he tormented himself until he hit upon a solution. He would go and see Katy's priest, tell him of his feelings for her, his intention of marrying her and ask if he would break the news. Catholic priests had contacts with others all over the country. It would be feasible that word could have come to him. However, before very long David's hopes were dashed, for his friend from the railway contacted him. Time-sheets for the section of the line on which a James O'Hara had been employed were turned up and showed a man of that name working until June 1856 – but nothing thereafter. He consoled himself that even if it was Katy's husband it proved nothing, but all the same he was downhearted.

On the June day in 1856, when Jamsie dropped the rail and walked away his head was full of dreams, full of a hundred stories of men who had found gold in California. With a hand in his pocket holding his dollar seventy-five he walked briskly, his dreams buoying him up, and now and then he whistled. The further he walked from the railroad the more continuous became his whistling and now and then he looked back over his shoulder, fearfully, in case he was being followed. Then in between backward glances he reasoned that there was no one to follow him. Men left the railroad all the time. He was a free agent – he could go where he liked. Yet as the afternoon wore on he still looked back until he realised his fear was more than a fear of men. The silence, the solitude, the vast empty space stretching for miles in front of him was unnerving. By the time darkness fell he would have welcomed a human being, even a pursuer.

His mouth and throat were parched, he craved water. Too tired and weak to walk any further he lay down on the ground and thought of his foolishness. To have walked off with no plan in his head, no provisions, no water and nearly a week's wages owing. He could have waited. But waiting wasn't his way. When he wanted to do something he had to do it now. Like the way he'd left other jobs – the way he'd walked out on Katy. Never thinking ahead. Taking hold of the minute. Only before was never like this. Then there were places and faces, the sound of a voice, the chance of earning money.

His head ached, his eyes burned and seemed too big for their sockets. His lips were cracked. He ran his tongue over them: like his eyes it seemed to have grown bigger. He fell asleep, the light was pale when he woke up. His eyes hurt less but his mind was going – of that he was sure. Hunger and thirst had sent him mad, for why else would he be seeing creatures all round him, leaping and jumping, running in circles. He closed his eyes to block out the crazy vision, but when next he opened them he saw that the creatures were rabbits, cavorting. When he stirred and attempted to sit up, they scurried away.

Thank God he wasn't mad, only demented with hunger and thirst. He lay back on the ground; the sky was lighter now, the greyness tinged on the horizon with red. Soon the sun would be up again to crucify him.

If only he could find water, if only he could snare a rabbit – with the food would come strength enough to search for water. What was the use moidering his brain thinking – he had nothing to make a snare and if he had and caught a rabbit, no way of cooking it. Unless there was a miracle he was finished. The thinking further exhausted him and he fell asleep again.

When he woke the next time he thought that either he was dead or a miracle had come to pass. For in front of him on his hunkers was a man and the man spoke to him and the man was an Irishman. 'You're all right, hold on now,' said the man. 'What you want is water.' He got up and Jamsie's eyes watched him go to a horse nearby and take from its saddle a canvas water bag. And then the tin mug was having water poured into it and the man knelt beside him and raised his head and water slid over his swollen tongue and down his parched throat.

'What in the name of God are you doing out here with nothing?' asked the man, when Jamsie's thirst was slaked. He told him about the railroad, California and the gold.

'And you were thinking of going to California as you are? How much money have you got?'

Jamsie told him. The man laughed. ' 'Tis not far you'd get on that – if I were you I'd head back to the railroad.'

The man, Jamsie saw, was about fifty. Much of his face was hidden by a beard and a big old black felt hat – the little that showed was tanned and tough like leather.

'I won't go back. There is gold in California and I might find it.'

'Indeed you might. You've as much chance as the next one – luck is all you want. It's the lucky ones that find it, not the mining engineers. I've seen fellas like yourself, fellas out of school, men that never handled a pick in their life strike it rich.'

'You've been there?'

'Twice. This is my third trip.'

'And did you find the gold?'

'By the bucketful.' The man laughed ruefully, pushed back his hat and scratched his head. 'Finding it is easy – hanging on to it is another thing.'

'Go way,' croaked Jamsie, 'and how is that now?'

'Drink, women, madness. There you are, penniless, working knee-deep in freezing rivers, filling up the pan with dirt, then into the water, giving it a great shake to get rid of the sand and dirt – a hundred times, a thousand times and then one day you spot it – gold gleaming up at you and suddenly you're rich. No more fat bacon and sourdough bread – the

259

world is yours. You go to town and are fleeced. There's the touchers –
men whose health left them after the dysentery and all the other things
you are open to in them conditions, there they are with their hands held
out, poor bastards – so you give to one and how do you refuse the next?
You can afford a new shirt and the man in the store charges you sixteen
dollars. A fifty-cent box of Seidlitz powders and another twenty-four
dollars goes over the counter.' He shrugged. 'Others are out for money.
Little hotels and eating-houses have grown like mushrooms and you
pay through the nose for everything. The girls come in, girls you've
never seen the like of before, painted and powdered, only short of
showing their arse and that they show as well when the price is
right . . . If I'd had any sense I'd have opened a store or a whorehouse.
Have another drink of water.'

After he'd drunk the water the man handed Jamsie what looked like a
strip of tobacco. Jamsie turned it over in his hand wondering what he
was supposed to do with it.

'Chaw it,' said the man. 'It's meat, dried bullock, not much taste but
it'll keep you alive.'

After chewing for long enough to soften and swallow a few mouthfuls
of the meat Jamsie asked, 'What happened then? How long did you
stay?'

'The best part of a year, digging it out and spending it until I got a bit
of sense, left the girls alone and accumulated enough dust and nuggets
to sell for five thousand dollars. Then I packed it in and headed back
home. I'd a wife in Baltimore. She was gone when I got there.'

'She died?' asked Jamsie.

'The hoor she didn't – she ran away with a fella from the same village
at home in Ireland. I never heard tale nor tidings of them since.'

'You'd have thought she'd have waited.'

'That's women for you,' said the man. He continued talking, telling
Jamsie how after discovering his wife's desertion he went on a bender
and while still drunk met a man who talked him into becoming a
business partner in a firm selling patent medicine – pills for women
which cured everything from backache to cancer. How he had parted
with a lot of money and never saw it or the man again.

Two years afterwards, he headed back for California. This time he
looked after the gold he found, determined to settle in the west and buy
a farm. But luck wasn't with him. On the way to Missouri he was held
up and robbed. He lost the appetite for gold then and had worked at
various things since – but he hated being beholden to another man, so
here he was again on the trail.

'My name's Mike Doyle, what's yours?' he said when the telling of his story was finished.

'Jamsie O'Hara.'

'Well now, Jamsie – what am I going to do with you? You're off to California and have as much chance of getting there as I have of going to Heaven, God forbidding all harm.'

'I'd heard tell,' said Jamsie, 'that people walked all the way there. That sometimes you'd get a lift in a wagon, could help out and get a bit of food as well.'

'You've had great advisers. Walk, is it? Let me tell you, it would take a tougher man than you and as for a lift on a wagon you can forget that – they're laden down already. A lift on a wagon you'd only get if all the men dropped dead – then a lone woman might consider you. A horse, that's what you want, a horse and then we'll make for Independence and the Oregon Trail. For the time being you can ride with me.'

Bridget continued to receive flowers from her secret admirer. Once a month they arrived at the hat-shop and had become a great talking point. The other apprentice and the proprietor Madame Renée were visibly more excited and intrigued than Bridget. 'Who could it be?' they asked each other. 'He must be very rich. He must have a great shine for Bridget.' One day he was bound to come and declare himself. Bridget said little but her imagination ran riot. He was very rich – and tall, with fair hair. An American. He'd come in a carriage and before he asked, 'Is there a Miss O'Hara here?' she would recognise him. He would take her riding in the carriage, tell her he loved her and wanted to marry her.

Madame Renée would fuss round him, offer him a chair the way she did with special customers and say yes, of course Miss O'Hara could take the afternoon off. He'd escort her to the carriage, hold her elbow and be very polite. He would tell her that one day when he was passing the shop she had been dressing the window and he had fallen in love with her at first sight. And she would ask him why he had waited so long to declare his love. 'You were so young, my dear. I knew it would be hopeless to ask for your hand too soon.'

Each time Bridget reached this part of her imaginary meeting with the secret admirer she felt sick with fear. Ask for her hand. Ask her mother. Come to the house, see where she lived. Meet her mother who would fly into a rage once she knew that the flowers had been coming behind her back. But the worst thing was the place – how could she let him see where she lived. She'd die. Then one day she had an idea – she would pretend she was an orphan. Her mother and father had died of

261

the cholera. There was no one to ask for her hand. She could marry any time she liked. It was a grand plan until she realised she would have to live somewhere – even orphans had to sleep somewhere. Her friend might let her stay in her house for the time before the wedding. But then where would she be married? The minute she spoke to the priest in her parish he'd ask if her mother knew about it. And before the night was out she would.

The only thing to do, she finally decided, was to leave home. Move to another district, another parish and then she could play the orphan to perfection. But she didn't earn enough money to keep herself and pay the rent. If they married quickly she might be able to manage for a week or two. She began to save, cutting back on her little treats of candy, cutting back on the dimes she gave to Mary Kate and Danny. Once she thought of asking her mother to take less of her money. Invent a story of a lovely dress she had her heart set on. And probably her mother would agree – only she'd want to know all about the dress. Where had Bridget seen it, how much was it? Ask for the name of the shop so she could go and look it over. If only her father hadn't gone to the railroad. If only he'd write, so that she could send him a letter telling him about the man who sent her flowers. He'd understand and help her. Her mother spoiled everything. She hated her mother.

She picked spring flowers, daffodils and tulips and arranged them in David's house. Later in the season she brought in plumes of lilac and the fragile columbines that grew in a shady place by the path. She remembered them growing wild in Kilgoran. All the wild flowers there were at home and in May – the hawthorn, all the hedges full of its white blossom and heavy scent – and everyone's belief that to bring the blossom across the door brought bad luck with it.

She wore gloves in the garden and smiled at the idea each time she put them on. Like the gentry with her gardening gloves, out with her gloves and basket to bring in the flowers. Her hands felt awkward wearing them but she did it to please David. 'You have pretty hands,' he had said one day in the garden when she was cutting flowers and she'd thought – it's as well you didn't notice them when I was doing the laundry. She was pleased with the compliment, but then he had said, 'You can't be too careful in gardens. A prod of a stem or thorn and you could get a badly-infected wound.' It was the doctor in him minding her health – and she wasn't to go imagining any other meaning. It was a great temptation and there were so many things he said and did that she could take in the wrong way. She had to keep reminding herself they

262

were only part of him being such a gentle, kind, considerate man and not be filling her head with nonsensical and sinful thoughts. How would a man like him, a gentleman who tomorrow could go out and choose a wife from his own kind, have notions of her . . .

And in any case, she had a husband that she loved and was waiting for. And would wait for until the day she died. She felt guilty when sometimes days passed without her thinking of Jamsie, when it was hard immediately to recall his face. When she was miserable and unhappy, before she came to work for David, his face was always before her. When she had spent all day in her own place she could see him everywhere. But now her days were well spent, and she earned sufficient money to provide more than an existence. The children were less demanding and her health was good. No longer was she exhausted in the evenings, but had the energy to do what was necessary – to listen and talk to her family, to sew dresses for Mary Kate and Bridget, to visit Mary in her rooms above the bakery. To listen with interest about Kathleen's progress in College and talk about her hopes for Mary Kate and wonder when Bridget and Kathleen would meet nice young men.

Mary thought there was plenty of time. People shouldn't rush into marriage. Years ago in Ireland they had all married too young. Nowadays you should be prepared – a few shillings put by. Some evenings they would wonder what had become of Eileen and often Mary would bring up the talk of Peader and Miss Charlotte. Very seldom was Jamsie mentioned. Katy knew that Mary purposefully avoided bringing up the subject and was grateful to her. Herr Jaeger would sit in the room reading and smoking his pipe, only occasionally taking part in the conversation. But when he addressed Mary his voice and manner were full of affection. And watching the glances exchanged between them Katy would feel a pang of envy.

Returning from Mary's after such an evening her mind would be full of Jamsie. Where was he now? Did he realise that next year they would be twenty years married, that Bridget and Thomas were grown up? And she would continue thinking about him as she got ready for bed, and pray for him and ask God to send him home soon.

Chapter Four

It was early summer and Virginia was beautiful. Wild roses twice the size of those in Ireland grew in the hedges, scarlet and crimson, pink and paler pink, their scent sweet and delicate. Magnolias, azaleas – white, yellow and pink, Virginia creeper climbing the tallest trees. Clouds of butterflies were everywhere, some as big as small birds, bigger than the lovely humming birds, butterflies coloured like a rainbow. Peaches in the hedgerows and strawberries by your feet. Such an abundance of everything, so much to delight the eye.

And yet, thought Peader as he rode from one place to another performing his charade of overseeing the slaves, he would run from it this minute if only Charlotte would go with him. For nearly ten years he had lived in another man's house, worked at a job made for him by Paul's generosity, supervising the slaves who knew more than he ever would about growing tobacco. They needed no telling how to mix sand with the thousands of seeds, thirty or more to grow an acre, no supervision in planting out the seedlings, nor telling when it was time to snap flower and sucker off – the minute the bottom leaf, the one to ripen first, was ready they were there to harvest it.

It was a useless job, leaving him with too much time on his hands. Too much time to think and read and brood on his own shortcomings. To realise that another man would long ago have insisted Charlotte left Annilaun and set up home with him elsewhere. He couldn't offer her a replica of her previous life, but she'd known that when she married him and left her father's mansion. Much as he loved her, he had come to feel that she was unreasonable and selfish.

But the trouble was, he *did* love her. He idolised her and up until now had never forced the issue, accepting her pleas of delicacy, the unpleasantness of living in a smaller house, the change in her status – for how could she possibly entertain in such a place – who would visit them? Nothing would have pleased him more than not seeing her friends, for hers they were, not his. Oh, they were pleasant to him, received him with hospitality but he wasn't one of them and they had subtle – no, subtle was the wrong word, they were too arrogant to attempt subtlety – ways of making him aware of it.

The last time he had discussed this with Charlotte she had assured him it was all in his mind. He was imagining the snubs and insults. 'The trouble is, you can't forget you're Catholic and Irish. You see slights where none are intended.'

'That's not true,' he had contradicted.

'But it is. I know. I've watched you. If anyone criticizes the Irish or the Catholics for demanding financial help with their schools you go red in the face like a turkey cock. What you never understand is that it's a compliment they do so in front of you. They think of you as one of them. Can't you see that?'

'No, I can't and won't – it's ill-mannered and arrogant.'

'Nonsense, absolute nonsense! You can't expect everyone every minute to guard their tongue because you're in the room.'

'Well, what about when they suspected me of helping the slaves escape?'

'That was understandable at the time. We were new here and you did have a habit of airing your views on slavery. Honestly, you worry too much, Peader, everyone adores you. You silly thing – come over here to another one of your adorers.'

And he went as he always did and in her arms his worries and discontents went and again he conceded to her wishes.

He was, he knew, a man of little grit – a talker and a dreamer rather than a doer. But now things were different. Trouble was coming to the South. The slavery issue was reaching fever pitch. There would be violence – it had already begun with John Brown last year. Some said he was a fanatic but the anti-slavery men hailed him as a hero. Peader thought there was nothing heroic about Brown and four of his five sons brutally murdering five men. The city of Lawrence may have been sacked, the printing press of the Free-Staters destroyed, a blow struck for the pro-slavers but nothing justified John Brown taking the law into his own hands. Once violence was unleashed it spread quickly. There would be more, there would be war. Paul as a Southern gentleman must take sides and the side he'd take was obvious. He and Charlotte must leave Virginia long before that happened. He would go now and talk to her again, and this time not take no for an answer.

Charlotte was lying on a sofa, her soft brown hair falling loose round her shoulders the way Peader loved it. She greeted him affectionately and listened while he told her of his fears of war and the terrible predicament he would be in if they stayed and the danger he feared for her. She appeared to give weight to all he said and agreed how appalling it would be if war came, how terrified she would be for her own and his safety. 'You're quite right,' she said, 'we can't possibly stay here.'

His heart leapt with joy. He had misjudged her, she wasn't selfish or unreasonable.

'How soon do you think we should make a move?' she asked.

'As soon as possible. We'll talk about it tonight, decide on the best place. A place where you would be happy. I've enough money saved to make you a good home – it'll have to be in the North, of course.'

'Of course,' she agreed. 'But it couldn't be for at least a year.'

'A year? Oh, no. It has to be now. In a year we could be in the middle of a war. And even if I'm wrong about the timing, it would be as well for us to be settled long before anything did happen. It must be very soon.'

'Darling, I'm afraid that's not possible. I know a year sounds an eternity, but there's a reason, a very special reason. I wasn't going to tell you for a while, but now you have to know. The doctor thinks I'm going to have a baby.'

A baby! Their child. He was so overcome with joy he stood motionless and speechless staring at Charlotte until she said, 'Well, aren't you pleased?' Then he went to her and took her in his arms, and he cried and kissed her and told her how delighted he was, how much he loved her. That she must take care of herself – and that of course they couldn't think of moving before a year.

She eased herself from his arms. 'Darling,' she said, 'it won't be certain for a little while – that's how it is with having babies.'

His face fell with disappointment . She touched it and said, 'Don't be downhearted. I'm almost positive, only I know how long you've waited to hear this news and I don't want you building your hopes too high, but I'm sure it will be all right. In the meantime, I'm not to have any worry and must rest a lot, doctor's orders. That's why I've been so – well, you know – all the times I've refused you. It broke my heart. I should really have told you the reason.'

'Oh love, don't, it doesn't matter. Nothing matters except that you are well and that please God there will be a baby. You lie down again, I've got to get back to the fields. Sleep and mind yourself.'

'You are sweet and I love you,' she kissed him on the lips. 'Now off you go and I'll have my nap. I nearly forgot, there is something else. You mustn't touch me until the doctor says it's safe to do so – this is the dangerous time of carrying a child.'

'I'll do no more than kiss you goodnight for the whole time if it's necessary.'

'Good,' she said, and waved him off.

'Paul,' said Charlotte, 'I'm such a liar.'

'I know, my love,' said Paul and bent to kiss her. 'Who have you been telling lies to now?'

'To Peader. I've just told him I'm having a baby.'

'You're not, are you?'

'Of course I'm not.'

'Then why?'

'He's restless. He thinks there's going to be a war, and he wanted us to leave immediately. I had to say something.'

'Maybe he's right about a war – things are coming to a head. But what about this baby when the time comes for you to deliver?'

'I haven't thought that far.'

'Do let me know when it's official. I'd like to be the first to congratulate Peader.'

'Sometimes I hate you,' said Charlotte, rising from her sofa. 'Here I am distracted with guilt for raising false hopes in Peader and all you can do is make silly jokes.' She walked towards the door. Paul barred her way.

'So he still bothers your conscience if not your heart – still has an influence on you. The pity is, he's all talk. If you had been my wife I'd have dragged you by the hair out of another man's house. You'd have liked that, wouldn't you?'

'Let me pass. Let me pass, please.'

'And what'll you do if I don't?'

'You,' she said, 'I hate you, I hate you.'

'He'll be gone until dusk – will I come up after your nap?' He held her arms. 'Will I? I won't let you go until you answer.' He saw the beginning of a smile and her effort to suppress it. 'Will I?' he repeated, slackening his hold.

'If you like,' she said, breaking free. 'In half an hour.'

Peader went round in a daze of happiness. Please God this time next year he would have a child. He hoped for a son. He would like to think of the Daly name going on into the future. When the baby was old enough and Charlotte recovered from the birth, they would move. Where they went he would leave to Charlotte to decide. Sometimes he imagined her choosing Ireland and he let his mind dwell on that. He had enough money to buy a decent house there and rent a good farm of land. Their child, their children for with the help of God they would have more than one, would grow up in their own place. In a country where the Dalys had for hundreds of years been a respected family. It was a name to be proud of – the name of the poets and lawmakers until the seventeenth century.

He had kept abreast with events in Ireland, had pinned his hopes on the Tenant Right League and their aims of fair rent, fixity of tenure, and freedom of the tenant to sell his interest in his holding, all to be won by parliamentary means. Its failure had saddened him, but now something else was afoot. Another organisation would spring up – the struggle wasn't over.

He dreamed of being part of it and if in his lifetime it didn't succeed he would have children who would pursue the dream. Sadly, he would then think of Charlotte and how unlikely she was to choose a return to Ireland. Ireland held only bitter memories for her. Kilgoran House, her beautiful home lost, her sister and brother thousands of miles distant, one in India, the other in Australia. And worst of all, she had placed herself outside her own class by marrying him. Ireland wouldn't be her choice and he couldn't blame her. But there were places in America, places where the curse of slavery didn't exist. They could buy a farm there. They could live a good life there and his children would know of their heritage, he would see to that.

Charlotte told Manty about the baby she was supposed to be having and how in two months she would miscarry. Manty clapped a hand over her mouth and her already big eyes grew bigger. Then Manty giggled and Charlotte laughed and then instructed Manty how she was to behave when the time came and on no account, no matter how much Peader insisted, was the doctor to be called. It was the women's business and the women would take care of it. Manty continued to giggle and nod her head and giggle louder until it got on Charlotte's nerves and she sent her from the room.

Peader prayed for the doctor to confirm Charlotte's pregnancy. He knew it irritated her if he enquired too often about her health so he asked seldom. He consoled himself that had the doctor told her she was not carrying a baby she would have said so – no news was good news. Then one day when he came in from the field he met a tearful Manty who told him the mistress was sick. Charlotte was in bed, her face tear-streaked. 'Oh Peader,' she sobbed when he came to her. 'I'm sorry, I'm so sorry – I've lost our baby. I've lost our precious baby. Please forgive me. I know how much you wanted a baby.'

He comforted her. 'It's all right,' he said. 'It's all right. Nothing matters except you. My poor love don't cry, it's all right. God will bless us with other children. Hush now, don't cry.' He sat with her until she fell asleep, then quietly left the room. On the landing Manty was hovering. 'Did the doctor come?' he asked and Manty told him no. 'Why wasn't he sent for?' he demanded. And Manty told him there was nothing for the doctor to do. It was women's business.

Not satisfied, he found Paul who pretended surprise and sorrow when he heard what had happened. 'A baby? Charlotte lost a baby? I thought she was just indisposed. I'm terribly sorry.'

Peader expressed his worry that Charlotte hadn't been seen by a doctor and Paul assured him it was unnecessary – the women took care of all that sort of thing, only if there were complications was the doctor called. But of course, if it would put his mind at ease the doctor could be called. 'No,' Peader said, 'there don't seem to be any complications.' He left Paul and went out and walked for a long time and he cried for Charlotte's loss and for the baby who was gone.

One morning, Eileen stood before the mirror and didn't like what she saw. The lines at the corners of her eyes had deepened, she saw or imagined she saw the beginnings of more lines, one at each corner of her mouth and there was no mistaking the grey hair that here and there was sprinkling the black. 'My Jesus,' she said aloud, 'I look terrible. I look old. But is it any wonder? How could you keep your looks leading the life you do. Dragged from pillar to post, three nights here and three nights there and this fecking climate – the baking heat is no sooner over and you have weather that would freeze the balls off a brass monkey. And it's all his fault. All the fault of that hoor's melt, Paddy Kavanagh, who has as much intention of marrying me as he has of taking me to San Francisco.' A snore from the bed where Paddy was sleeping off his excesses of the night before infuriated Eileen further and muttering that she'd fix him, once and for all she'd give it to him, she went over to the bed.

Paddy lay flat on his back, his knees up making a tent of the bedclothes, his big dirty feet sticking out of the sheets, his mouth open and the fumes of last night's drink poisoning the air. Eileen looked at him with disgust. 'Mad, stone mad I must have been ever to let myself get entangled with him.' She shook him roughly. 'Waken up, I want to talk to you.' Paddy half-opened his eyes, closed them again and rolled over taking the bedclothes with him. 'Get up,' shouted Eileen. 'Get up this minute or I'll douse you with the jug of cold water.' He stirred and pushed at the covers, moving them away from him so that between his rumpled shirt and the waist of his drawers his big fat white belly showed. 'Look at you – you're a disgrace – you've a paunch on you the size of a camel's hump. Get up when I tell you.'

Slowly Paddy sat up holding his head, complaining about the thumping in it and asking, 'What do you want, wakening me at this hour of the morning?'

'To ask you a few questions, like for instance – whatever happened to San Francisco?'

'Ah, for the Lord's sake don't start that again. You know well we're heading there.'

'Oh, indeed I do – in circles.'

'I had a few setbacks, that's all.'

'Setbacks me arse!' retorted Eileen. 'I'm fed up with you and this bloody country. I've been up the Mississippi and down the Mississippi, across the Missouri, along the Erie Canal. Had every bone in my body nearly smashed to smithereens travelling by covered wagon to Boulder and Denver, Bullock's Creek and Bollock's Creek, anywhere you could get me to show a leg without the Pilgrim Fathers running us out of it. I'm sick of it – of you and dirty drunken miners making a grab for me diddies and you doing deals with barmen, encouraging me to encourage the lousers to buy drinks, whiskey for them and coloured water for me and you making money hand over fist and little of it me or the other girls see.'

'Ah now, Eileen, don't be like that. And don't keep shouting – me head is very bad.'

'Shag you and your head. What about San Francisco? Whatever happened to that, eh?'

Paddy got out of bed, pulled up his drawers and tucked in his shirt. 'I told you, I had a few setbacks, but honest to God this time we're on our way. Isn't that what I've been doing with the money, putting it by for the journey.'

'I've been hearing that since we left New York. There's hairs on that story.'

'Sure you know I wouldn't let you down. Commere to me, you know how I feel about you. You know the great plans I have for you. I'm telling you, there won't be one to touch you when we get there.'

He was beside her now. He put an arm about her and squeezed her. She shrugged it off. 'And don't think you can get round me like that – you've done that once too often.'

He had hold of her again and this time she let his arm remain. 'You've a fine arse,' he said, and his hand caressed a buttock. 'I'd never let you down.' He kissed her neck and his hand moved from her buttocks and

270

started doing things to her. 'Look at me,' he turned her to face him. 'You know how I feel about you. The minute we get to San Francisco we'll get married. Give us a kiss.' Without stopping the kissing he began manoeuvring her towards the bed. She let him. One of her hands was in his hair pressing his head, keeping the contact with her mouth while the other was undoing her clothes. Together they collapsed onto the bed.

He fell asleep as soon as they had finished making love. The bastard, Eileen thought. Every time I fall for it, every single bloody time. He knows my weakness and plays on it. Well, she'd give him one more chance. One more chance to take her to San Francisco – and if it didn't come off then she'd show him what she was made of.

She lay listening to his snores and thinking about the fools women were and she thought about Katy. Poor Katy, another fool. Poor women, they were all fools if they had feelings for a man. Only the cute oul things like Mary made a go of it. They set a price on themselves, knew their own value. Passion would never rule Mary. No by dad, and more luck to her.

She wondered about them all. Had Jamsie ever come back? Had Mary let the German marry her? One of these days she must write to Katy.

It was against David's principles to have an affair with a married woman. He was a Christian and fornication was a sin. But he was also a man who loved and desperately wanted Katy. He wanted her for a wife but that wasn't possible, and might never be possible – for there was no way of proving whether Jamsie was dead or alive. He was tortured seeing her every day, standing close to her, breathing her smell, seeing her beautiful face, her lovely shape and never being able to even lay a finger on her.

If he couldn't have her as his wife he would have her as his mistress. But not in a hole and corner way. He loved and respected her too much for such furtiveness. He would defy convention and have her come to live in his home. Her children should come, too. Thomas and Bridget being grown up might not want to. If so, he would make other arrangements for them. But the younger children would come with their mother. He'd have a family and his adored Katy. Never again would she have to worry, look for work or be deprived of the comforts she deserved.

It seemed so simple when all he thought of was the positive side. But Katy had never shown in any way that she considered him other than

271

her employer. He would have to woo and win her, convince her of his love. Convince her that if she were free it was marriage he would be proposing. Make her realise that whether Jamsie was dead or alive it was highly unlikely that he would ever return. Tell her that she was still a young, beautiful woman who shouldn't spend the rest of her life unloved. He had to start his wooing now. No more time must be wasted. It was nearly Christmas again, another year almost gone. Tomorrow he would invite her to stay one evening for supper and have the children come, too.

'Katy,' he said the next day, 'I was wondering if one night you and the children would have supper here. Not much of a treat I know, as you'll be cooking it. But it would give me great pleasure if you said yes.'

Katy didn't know how to be coy and so accepted the invitation with delight. 'That would be lovely! Thank you, thank you very much. But mightn't it be a lot of trouble for you?'

'For me, why? All I'll have to do is eat and try to entertain you.'

'I'm not sure that Bridget and Thomas would come. Bridget is forever with her friend or there's church socials and that – and Thomas – well, he'd be a bit shy, but Mary Kate and Danny will jump at the chance of coming to the house again.'

'They like it?'

'Don't they love it. One afternoon not long ago when they came to meet me here they were enchanted. Mary Kate would have stayed in the library all day if I'd let her.'

'I never knew they'd come. I'm glad they did, they're welcome any time.'

'They were passing, so they said. I told them they must never do such a thing again, they mustn't make so free. When would you like us to come – and will I do anything special?'

'Of course, it's a special occasion, a sort of Thanksgiving and Christmas rolled into one. Let me see – what about a big fat goose and blueberry pie and mashed potatoes – all sorts of things – whatever else the children like. And we'll have it next Wednesday night, how about that?'

Katy said Wednesday would be grand and thanked him again and said wait until she told the children, they'd be beside themselves with joy.

My sweetest love, he thought, watching her animated face – not half as delighted as I am.

She put no interpretation on the invitation other than that it was a very generous thing for David to do. To spoil his peaceful evening after

272

working so hard in the hospital and seeing his poor patients. She didn't think she had ever known anyone so unselfish.

She would wear her new dress, the one she had made for Christmas. She had copied it from a fashion magazine that Bridget brought home from the milliners. The skirt was flounced from the waist to hem and the bodice had two wide reveres, enclosing a white silk pleated inset. Katy had adapted it to her liking, with two flounces on the skirt and a plain bodice to which she had added a narrow white collar. She trimmed the cuffs with the same white and was pleased with the result. Her fair hair and colouring went well with the nutmeg shade of the dress, she thought.

When the goose was stuffed and the pies ready for baking she instructed Sarah when to put the food in the oven and went home to collect the children and change into her new dress. She was very excited. Never before had she gone to a social event, never anywhere except to work and the chapel. Danny told her she was pretty and she kissed and hugged him. Mary Kate said she looked real nice but Bridget, busy getting ready to go out herself, said nothing. Katy warned the children to behave themselves, not to talk too much, not to eat too much. She warned them before they left the house, in the cab and again when they arrived.

Sarah met them at the door and said there had been a message from the hospital. The doctor would be delayed, but not for long. Katy's heart sank. Supposing he was very late, the evening would be ruined. The goose smelled delicious. Danny asked when they'd have their supper and Katy warned him again to behave himself. She was all on edge in case David had to stay away for a long time and the supper be spoiled.

But he came at the right moment, just as everything was ready, only waiting to be served. She had set the table as usual with David's wine glass, and put ones for water for herself and the children. He carved the goose and sent platefuls to Mary Kate and Danny. She could have hugged him for the way he received the children, straight away putting them at their ease.

Sarah poured his wine. 'Katy,' he said, 'you'll have some?'

'A little,' she said.

She didn't like the first sip but the next tasted better. Halfway through the glass she felt light-headed in a pleasant way, happier than she had for a long time. She forgot to scold the children when they said yes, they'd love some more of everything.

When it was time to go, David called a cab and as they were leaving

273

said he hoped they'd come to supper again. On the drive home Danny said wouldn't it be grand to live in a house like that and eat goose every night. Katy giggled and said it would be grand, though the doctor didn't eat goose every night. And Mary Kate said she wouldn't care if they only ate bread and butter, for bread and butter would taste like goose if you were living in that house.

David thought the evening had been a great success. Katy looked gorgeous. He had wanted to compliment her but was afraid of alarming her by being too attentive or effusive. For the same reason he had left her sitting by Mary Kate though he would have liked her by his side. He believed that the children had taken to him. It was important they should like him. Next year, 1858, he hoped would have them and Katy living with him. Katy had done so much for them: together they could do so much more.

A horse – where were they to lay hands on a horse, Mike Doyle asked aloud. 'They're the precious asset – people won't part with them easily or cheaply. Are you sure a dollar seventy-five is all you've got?'

'As true as I'm sitting behind, not a farthing more,' said Jamsie.

Mike had some money, enough to buy another horse or see him comfortably to California. He'd be a fool to part with it. On the other hand, he'd taken a liking to Jamsie and two men could work better at the digging than one. Maybe he'd stake him out.

'Hold on now,' warned an inner voice. 'You know nothing about him. If he's honest, can he work, how will he stand up to the journey . . . As it is, he's made a hole in your supplies. And look at the size of him. Before you go much further he'll have crippled the horse.'

'I know all that,' said Mike to the voice in his head. 'But what'll I do with him, geesh him off, ride away – he'd be dead in the morning. And anyway, I've taken a liking to him. But I'll do nothing rash. The horse can take the strain for another couple of days. I'll give it a day or two to think it over.'

For the next two days he thought about nothing else. 'Ah, to hell with it,' he said in the long run. 'I'll buy a horse. Maybe Jamsie will bring me luck.'

If you wanted a job, to get into the police, have bricks or anything else delivered quickly, have your tender viewed favourably, Terence McCabe was the man to see. Mary heard all the gossip in the bakery. When her knowledge of German let him down, Herr Jaeger did the interpreting and in turn she passed on the news to Katy.

★

274

'Wallowing in money he is, influence everywhere and owns streets of houses.'

'You can be sure he's come by none of it honestly.'

'Isn't that a fact. No favour does he do without having his palm greased or getting another in return.'

'I wouldn't give him a drink of water if he was dying.'

'You've a terrible bitterness towards him, Katy. Wasn't your disagreement with him on the ship a long while ago – you shouldn't harbour it still.'

Katy thought of the girl who had been raped, God alone knew what had ever become of her, and Larry reeling in the rope and the half-scream of him and Eileen's broken heart and shattered hopes – and the feeling of malice, of evil that was about Terence McCabe, as plain to her as the glow round a candle flame. Even now thinking about him she felt the feeling. 'You're right and I shouldn't,' she replied to Mary's question, 'But I do. I hate him. I'd starve and let every one of my children do the same, walk the streets idle for the rest of their lives rather than be beholden to him.'

'All the same haven't you great principles. My own now wouldn't be that strong – if Terence McCabe or anyone else for that matter could put a word in for Kathleen when she wants a teacher's job, how they came by their wealth or influence wouldn't stand in my way of asking.'

'That would be your business, Mary – we all have our own way of looking at things,' said Katy.

Chapter Five

Katy and the children went to supper many more times. The invitations were a highlight and she looked forward to them. Then one evening after she had prepared David's meal as usual and was about to go home he arrived early and asked her would she eat with him. Thinking it was another invitation to supper she asked, 'When?'

'Now,' he said, 'please.'

'I couldn't,' she said, 'the children will be waiting.'

'Not even for an hour?'

He looked so disappointed. It was lonely, she supposed, eating every night on your own. He asked so little of her. Gave her free reign in the house. If the children were sick she was free to come and go as she pleased. He never asked her to work late or come in on Sundays. She didn't have the right to refuse him.

'Well, not supper then, but do stay for an hour, half an hour,' he suggested. 'We'll have a glass of wine. I'll drive you home, have you back in no time. How about that?' He was smiling his crooked smile, his face eager, boyish-looking.

For days he had been steeling himself for the moment when he would tell her he loved her. Going over and over in his mind what he would say. How he would convince her, persuade her to overcome the objections she would raise to coming to live with him. 'Please,' he said now. 'Please, Katy.' All his carefully-rehearsed words fled and he blurted out, 'Katy, I love you. I want to marry you.'

She wondered if he had drink taken. She'd noticed his flushed face and how he didn't seem himself. Nervous and excited-like. She had never seen him drink more than a couple of glasses of wine. But what else would make him say such things. He'd regret it tomorrow. Be ashamed for having made a fool of himself, and making a fool of her. Sober he would never do that, he was too kind, too good a man.

'Are you all right? Will I make you some coffee?'

'Katy,' he said, ignoring her questions. 'Katy,' he said again and took her hands in his. 'I love you. I want to marry you but I know you can't do that.' She left her hands in his, conscious of his touch, of how pleasant it was, trembling a little.

276

'David, don't say any more, don't talk any more. I'll have to go home now, the children will be wondering where I am.'

'I have to talk and you have to listen.' He drew her to him. 'All the time I've wanted to say these things. If you only knew. I've loved you from the first moment I saw you. I know you can't marry me. But I want to take care of you, cherish you. If it was possible, if you were free I'd marry you tomorrow. But you're not. Come and live here with me, you and the children. I love them as if they were mine because they're yours. Please, Katy.' He put his arms round her and kissed her. She had forgotten what it was like to be kissed. The sweetness of it, the pleasure of it. She let his lips remain on hers until she felt the urge to kiss him back. She stopped herself and moved from him. She didn't know what to say. She felt like crying. He wasn't drunk. He meant it. He loved her. She had to go from here quickly. She made excuses about the children waiting, she must go and no, he mustn't drive her home. A cab would be grand.

While she waited for the cab he asked her to remember what he had said. To remember that if she was free he would marry her. 'I know you'll be thinking about sin and your priest and the neighbours, but don't. The sin is the waste of your life. I'll take you away from here, anywhere you like. Anywhere in the world, so long as I can be with you. You're young and beautiful and I love you so much.'

She kept her face turned from him so he wouldn't see that she was crying and prayed for the cab to come soon.

No one had missed her. She went about what had to be done in a stupor. David loved and wanted to marry her. And because she couldn't, he wanted her to come and live with him. She went to bed and cried silent bitter tears. He had spoiled everything. She could never go to Gramercy Park again. She could never be near him again. If he kissed her again – if he kissed her like tonight . . . 'Oh, God, oh God,' she said angrily. 'Why did You let it happen? Why did You show me another man to love, another way to live? Wasn't it the cruel thing. I had one man and he went away. And You sent me another I couldn't have. And such a man. Oh God, it's not fair. I love Jamsie. He'll come back, I know that and I'll wait all my life for him. But it wasn't fair.'

She fell asleep thinking of David kissing her, but she dreamed of Jamsie in a disjointed sequence. She was married to him though at the same time they were only courting. They were living in Ireland but all the people were strangers – Americans and Protestants who pointed at Jamsie and called him 'dirty Irish' and blamed him for taking their jobs, for working for less money.

In the dream Katy was crying because the American children tormented Bridget and Thomas, made fun of their brogue and said that when their mother went to Confession she slept with the priest. All the Irishwomen slept with the priest. Everyone knew that. Maria Monk wrote a book about it. And she should know, she was a nun.

Then Jamsie said he was leaving to go to America. She screamed and clung to him. But he went. Her screams woke Danny and Thomas. They were frightened and asked what ailed her, was she sick? Was there a ghost? No, she told them, she'd only had a nightmare. Thomas offered to make her tea. She didn't want any. He sat on the bed holding her hand. She let on to fall asleep so he could go back to his couch. Poor, kind, thoughtful Thomas.

In the morning, when the children had left for school and work she cried again for all she had lost and then with great difficulty wrote a letter to David. She thanked him for loving her. For asking her to share his home. She knew he meant no disrespect. She reminded him of her belief that Jamsie was alive, that she was his wife and was waiting for him.

He mustn't come to see her. He must never come to see her again. She couldn't bear it. She hoped he would understand what she meant by the last two lines and take consolation from them.

When the letter was finished she went into the street and found a child and gave him a dime. 'Run all the way to this house in Gramercy Park, ask for Sarah and give her this letter.' She wanted David to have the letter when he came home in the afternoon. Thinking of him arriving, going into the library, expecting her to be there she nearly changed her mind. 'Go on now like a good boy,' she said, swallowing the lump in her throat and handed him the note. David had to have the letter as soon as he returned and missed her, otherwise he would come looking for her. He mustn't do that. She must never lay eyes on him again. But for the rest of her life she knew she would remember him. See his thin boyish face and his smile. She'd remember him and pray for him and be glad that once in her life she had met such a man.

Why, the children asked, didn't she go to work any more? She lied and said David had a new housekeeper. 'Does that mean we'll never go to supper again?' Danny asked and Katy said it did. Danny said that was mean of David and Mary Kate said she'd miss the house and the library. Bridget said that now that her mother wasn't earning she would look for a job that paid more. She would soon be out of her time and maybe one day have a hat-shop of her own. Thomas promised to get a permanent job. If they all pulled together everything would be all right.

Spring came and filled Katy with great sadness. She thought often of David. She missed him. She missed the house and the garden. The time they had spent together.

The lines which Katy hoped might console David, didn't. He read them at their face value. He must never come to see her again. She couldn't bear that. He had insulted her. Asked her, a decent good-living woman, to be his mistress. He could see it from her point of view. The scandal it would have caused. The trouble with her older children. The loss of her Irish friends, even the life she was familiar with in the tenements.

What a fool he was. A selfish arrogant fool. Thinking that because he loved her she should love him. Thinking he could snare her with the offer of comfort. A soft bed and good food in exchange for all that she lived by. Her love for Jamsie, her belief that he was still alive, her religion. But Katy wasn't an item in a shop, Katy couldn't be bought. His arrogant thoughtlessness had lost her. Lost him her presence from his home and deprived her of a living. And now what would become of her? She'd have to go back to laundrying. He remembered the first time he had seen her. How ill she had been. Why hadn't he just treated her? Not interefered in her life. Above all, why had he let his selfish desire blind him to what sort of a woman she was. Recognised her love for Jamsie and her fervent belief that he would come back. Because he was a self-centred man dressing his selfishness in the guise of love.

He sat for hours lost in thought. Sarah brought his tea and he left it untouched. She came again to draw the curtains, to ask if he wanted anything. He told her no and to leave the curtains. He sat in the dark remembering Katy, the times they had spent in this room. His elation the day she had let Jamsie's name slip out and his hope then that soon he would have proof of his death. Never considering the grief such news would cause Katy. The heartbreak for her children. He had wished another man dead so that he could have his wife. His only concern had been for himself.

Now he had to think of her, genuinely think about her welfare. He devised plans for going to see her. Explanations, apologies, reassurances of his admiration for her faithfulness to her husband. But convince her that she must come back to work. And promise that never again would he say a word to offend her. She didn't have to see him again. He would be away from the house before she arrived and not return until she had left. For her own sake, for the sake of the children she must come back.

But if she refused and thinking about the letter he believed she would – how then could he help her? She wouldn't accept money. Putting himself in her place he imagined how she would think of such gifts. He considered again seeing her priest, explaining what had happened. Arranging to send money through the priest. But what priest, what man unless a saint wouldn't suspect his motives. He could do nothing for her except hope that Jamsie was alive, that one day he would return to love and take care of her.

He read the letter once more. It was the only thing of Katy's he had. He would keep it always.

Katy also lied to Mary about her reasons for leaving Gramercy Park. Blaming Sarah, saying she didn't get on with her.

'Them blacks, they've lost the run of themselves with all the talk and stuff in the papers – anti-slavery this and anti-slavery that,' Mary complained.

Katy didn't argue the point nor remind Mary how when she first came to America she had been horrified at the idea of slavery.

'I'm telling you,' Mary continued, 'they'll overrun the country. They'll work for nothing. Think what that'll do for the likes of us.'

Katy listened with her mind on other things. Mary Kate with her head in the clouds or in a book, with her hopes of being a teacher . . . she would have to leave school. Thomas the size of a man with a man's appetite giving up nothing or seldom. Only Bridget bringing in anything. Poor Bridget carrying the burden of them all. Once she had wished that Bridget would meet a nice young man, but now she prayed it would be the long day coming.

She let it be known that she was taking in washing again and gradually the sheets, pillowcases, shirts and chemises came in. Bridget's reaction was to be expected. 'I hope this is only a summer thing.'

'We'll see,' said Katy listlessly.

'You'll see – well, I like that.'

'Lump it then,' snapped Katy.

'I'll do more than that – I'll move out.'

'And may all my bad luck go with you.'

She was sorry for saying it and didn't mean it. But Bridget was the hard child to get on with. Bridget had a way of looking at her so that sometimes she felt Bridget didn't like her. If she said one thing, Bridget said the opposite. She disagreed to be disagreeable. Maybe she missed her father, but didn't it ever cross her mind how much Katy missed

280

him, too? She wasn't a child any more. All the times she longed to talk to her – but at the first hint of intimacy Bridget withdrew.

Her mother's reception of her threat to leave pleased Bridget enormously. For after a long lapse between bouquets another, the biggest and most beautiful, had arrived last week. And this time there was a message on the card: *See you soon.* She had been in a ferment of excitement ever since. Every day she thought this might be the day, and when it wasn't, pinned her hopes on the next one. And she was glad she had waited, had made short work of the boys at the church socials. She wasn't going to spend her life like her mother. She was going to marry a rich American. He'd come in his carriage and take her away. And so much the better if she wasn't living at home. Her mother, not the priest nor anyone else would stand in her way.

It took a long time for Charlotte to recover from her miscarriage. Out of concern for her and because it was so long since they had made love Peader would ask periodically, 'Are you any better?'

'Not enough,' was Charlotte's usual reply.

Sometimes she said it with a sweet smile and asked him to be patient a little longer. Then he would feel ashamed of his grossness and embarrassedly lie and say it was only of her he was thinking. She'd laugh and tease him, tell him he was silly. Of course it wasn't only of her he was thinking. She hoped not. Other times she answered his enquiry curtly. Accusing him of having no consideration. Thinking only of himself. Didn't he realise what she had suffered, what she was still suffering?

When finally she did let him make love to her, he swore he never would again. She had suffered him and made it obvious. Complaining that he hurt her, that he was too heavy. Had he shaved, she asked. While he kissed her, she kept her eyes open staring at the ceiling. Then she told him to for God's sake hurry up. He lost his erection and she pushed him off.

Angry and ashamed he went from the room. But as always he found excuses for her behaviour. He had been inconsiderate. She was delicate, she had been ill. She must, like him, be grieving for the child. He was clumsy and awkward, and she so little. But all the same it wasn't natural for her to be sick for such a long time. But maybe it was – how would he know? He knew nothing about women and miscarriages. She lay about a lot, though she was well enough for parties and her appetite wasn't affected. It could be something wrong

281

with her insides. He had always thought she should have had a doctor when she lost the baby.

The next morning he suggested this to her. 'Why?' she asked, putting down the letter she was reading.

'Well, you know, last night.' He always found it difficult to talk about their love-making. He paused and began again. 'Last night, it shouldn't . . .'

'Oh, for God's sake Peader, don't be so Catholic. It's not a sin, we're married, you're allowed to do it, to mention it. What was wrong with last night?'

'You were in pain.'

'Was I?' She returned to reading her letter for a few moments then left it to speak again. 'It's from Catherine, listen to this. "Last week I heard from Charles – the first time in years. And believe it or not he's doing very well for himself in Australia. Turned over a new leaf at last. He's ranching, has thousands of acres and millions of sheep. I'm glad for him but can't help wishing he'd learned sense sooner. How different everything would have been for Papa and for Kilgoran." '

Charlotte then went on reading the letter to herself. Once or twice she read out bits to Peader. 'Catherine's asking about Katy and Jamsie. Do we have an address for them?'

'From long ago,' said Peader. 'When I went to New York.'

Charlotte wasn't listening, absorbed again in the letter. Then suddenly she exclaimed, 'Oh, Jesus! How awful. Poor Catherine!' and she read once more the letter to Peader. ' "Jamsie's brother – Johnny O'Hara – was here in the regiment. I say *was* because last week he was executed. He was calling himself by another name but I recognised him and I'm sure he did me, though neither of us acknowledged the other. Edward said lots of men gave a false name in the army. Usually they had something to hide at home. Sometimes a deserted wife, more often trouble with the law. It didn't stop them making good soldiers. Johnny, he told me, was a good soldier and up for promotion. Then the next he heard of him he was charged with killing an Indian in the bazaar – found guilty and executed.

' "Wasn't there some suspicion that he had killed or nearly killed someone at home? It's so long ago and my memory's not what it was, I think the heat addles one's brain. But I've a vague recollection that his brother, the one who was like his double was wrongly accused and transported to Van Dieman's Land. Do you remember anything about it? If so, write and tell me. I suppose if you ever have contact with the O'Haras you should let Jamsie know – that's why I was asking earlier in the letter if you had their address." '

282

'Johnny O'Hara – fancy that!' said Charlotte, laying down Catherine's letter. 'I don't remember his brother being transported. But wasn't there something about O'Hara's wife and Charles? I seem to remember talk in the kitchen, what was it?'

Everyone knew about Johnny O'Hara's wife and Master Charles. Everyone in the village knew about everyone else. Peader's thoughts went back to Kilgoran. To the time before Charlotte when he was to marry Katy. When their future seemed settled. They'd marry and live in his father's house, their children would be born there and grow up as he had, part of a community, knowing who they were. How happy and contented he was then. What a worthwhile life he led. Working the land and taking part in the struggle for Catholic Emancipation. And Charlotte was a child in the Big House, a little girl he saw occasionally passing through the village in her father's carriage or with one of her sisters in a dogcart.

Who could have foreseen then the turns life would take. His flight to Dublin to mend his broken heart. His return when it had healed. The day her father came upon them in the wood. Her willingness to run with him, leaving everything she had known and loved behind.

'Peader.' Charlotte's voice recalled him from his reverie. 'Peader, I asked you a question. What happened between Johnny O'Hara's wife and Charles?'

'It was nothing, love. Talk, that's all it was,' said Peader and remembered the talk – the dead baby, the running of Johnny's wife from the village. 'Talk, you know what it was like at home.'

Charlotte sighed. 'I do,' she said. 'I think about Kilgoran often, and wish we were there. Wouldn't that be grand. Imagine if we could go back. Imagine if we could have the House again. Oh darling, do you think we could?'

He fell as she knew he would into the trap. 'Maybe not Kilgoran House. But we could go back, I've enough put by to get us a grand little place.'

'Then let's do that. Let's make plans.'

'Do you mean that? Do you really, Charlotte?'

'Of course I do. I only want for you to be happy. We'd have been gone by now if I hadn't lost the baby.' She began to cry. 'But we'll have more. When I'm truly well we'll have lots of children.'

Please God, Peader prayed silently, make her well soon. Let us leave this place. Let us get away before the war comes. In Ireland, even somewhere else if she changes her mind, we'll be happy again. Like we used to be. And please let me not always be misjudging her. Let me be

283

the patient, loving husband she deserves. She made such sacrifices for me, let me remember that.

'How much longer can I go on stalling him, Paul?' Charlotte asked after relating what she had promised Peader.

'Indefinitely, I should think – the man is a fool where you are concerned.'

'But I don't want to go on indefinitely. Supposing he went away, supposing he died, would you marry me?'

'I wouldn't marry anyone.'

'Oh, I know you said that ages ago, in the beginning. But it's different now. We've been together so long, I love you.'

'No, you don't. Like me you love yourself and no one else.'

He would become, she thought, when he was old a little wizened man. Already the signs were there – he was drying out – like a withered stick he would become. It was true, she didn't love him, but she liked him a lot. And in bed could believe that she was in love with him. She wanted to marry him, to secure her position. Despite his protestations that he never intended marrying, he could at any time. Then where would she be?

'You know that's not true. I do love you, I've never loved anyone else. And you should have an heir.'

'By whom?' he asked, and she knew her tactics had been wrong. In ten years and with two men she hadn't produced. She had better change the subject.

'Tell me,' she said, 'what's happening about the slaves and the Free-Staters – I never understand anything I read.'

'A lot and it's gathering momentum.'

'Then why don't we free the negroes, or pay them, anything rather than go to war,' said Charlotte.

'Then who'd plant my tobacco, harvest it? The Southern economy is geared to slavery. And as you well know they're not all badly treated. And in any case you can't just free them, send them packing. Where would they go? How would they live?'

'That's not your main consideration.'

'No,' said Paul, 'it's not, but the planters do give it serious thought. Unlike the Northern abolitionists we're not sentimental fools. Slaves are valuable property. We understand them also as people. We feed and clothe them. Look after them when they're old. We care about them and they about us, unlike the Northern businessman and his employees.

'Whatever dissatisfaction there is among the negroes has been drummed up by Lloyd and his anti-slavery movement. He was bad enough but that Harriet Beecher Stowe and *Uncle Tom's Cabin* gave an appalling picture of the South. Had people in droves putting pressure on their Congressmen to end slavery. People who'd run a mile if they saw a black face, never mind live at close quarters with them.'

Charlotte had already lost interest but Paul was now in full flight so she arranged her expression to pretend interest.

'There's more to it though than bleeding hearts for the slaves. It's a struggle for power between the North and South. We want free trade for our raw materials. To get it we need votes. But if more and more new States go for free labour we'll be outvoted on any motion.'

Charlotte was now confused as well as bored. But the possibility of war troubled her greatly. If Paul went to war and was killed, what would become of her? If Peader died she would be broken-hearted – but if Paul died, her future died with him. Paul sat on the bed, she moved her feet into his lap. 'Darling,' she said, 'don't let's talk any more about it, it makes me so sad.' She smiled seductively at him, but Paul wasn't in the mood for seduction and made an excuse to leave her.

Manty gave birth to a baby. It was a boy, with his mother's beautiful big dark eyes. His skin was pale, almost white, and his hair a definite ginger. Charlotte's heart froze when she saw the child who was unmistakeably Paul's. He was proof that her charms were no longer enough to keep Paul faithful. Supposing the next time he sought a mistress he found a white one. Supposing despite his intention not to marry, not to care about an heir – this white woman captured him. It wasn't only the war she must fear. And she must in future be more considerate of Peader.

Chapter Six

'In politics a wife's the grand thing to have. If you're serious about entering them, get yourself a wife,' Kelly had counselled Terence on several occasions. Eventually he took the advice and cast an eye among the young Catholic women. He fancied none of them until the night of Dan's funeral when for the first time he noticed Bridget, thought she was beautiful and realised she was Katy's daughter. She was the one he would have for a wife.

'She's a lovely girl, O'Hara's daughter and they're a decent family,' Kelly had said approvingly when Terence acquainted him with his choice. 'Mind you, she's young for marrying yet.'

'I'll wait,' said Terence.

'Put your claim in then.'

'How will I do that?' asked Terence, who though determined to have Bridget because she was gorgeous to look at and her mother's daughter, was terrified at the thought of approaching her. America had given him wealth and a certain ease with strangers but girls had a terrible effect on him. In their company he was awkward, tongue-tied, generally ill at ease. He believed they scorned or pitied him or laughed at him behind his back. If Kelly hadn't convinced him that a wife was an asset he would never have considered taking one.

'I know the very thing. You're in America so be the wealthy American and send her flowers.'

'Flowers?'

'Yes, flowers, bouquets, from one of them expensive shops. Send a card with them – no name, only a message. Let me think now what to say. *From an admirer*, that's what you'll say, *from an admirer*. And keep sending them until you're ready to start courting.'

'Flowers,' Terence said again. 'Sure aren't flowers only for funerals?'

'Begod then they are not, not in America if you can afford them. They'll do the trick. The girl will be up in the air, wondering who you are, thinking you're one of them wealthy Americans. The guessing there'll be. Who is he? What's he like? And everyone telling her you must be mad about her.' Kelly rubbed his hands together. 'I can see the whole thing, the excitement there'll be.'

'Where will I send them?'

'To wherever she works. Yes, that'll be the best place. I heard tell it's in a hat-shop. The others working there will be hopping with the thrill of it – flowers from a stranger – making the young wan feel ten foot high. She'll only be waiting for the day you declare yourself. And it's smart work she'll make of any lad with a notion of her. Won't the mother see to that. "What do you want throwing yourself away on him and a rich American waiting for you?" That's the advice she'll be giving her daughter. And when you come out and reveal yourself, it's with open arms she'll receive her prospective son-in-law.'

'That she won't. Whatever about the girl it's no grand reception I'll get from the mother.'

'That's a queer thing to be so positive about it. Tell me now what makes you think so?'

Terence told him about his row with Katy on the ship, but didn't mention the rape or Larry's death.

'Ah,' said Kelly dismissively, 'wasn't that years ago. Wouldn't Mrs O'Hara have long forgotten a little thing like that. A row on a boat is one thing – a great match a different thing altogether.'

'You may be right,' lied Terence. 'What do you know about her and him?'

'By all accounts a decent couple. He went away years ago and hasn't been heard of since. She's a hard-working woman, used to take in washing, but sure you know that. Wasn't it her had the lock-up shop in Cow Lane.'

'Aye 'twas. Any scandal about her since the husband went?'

'Not a breath. She's housekeeping for a doctor up in Gramercy Park.'

'And no talk?'

'No talk, not a word,' said Kelly.

A pity, thought Terence, knowing that Katy would oppose his marrying Bridget. Marry her he would, but a lever on her mother would have made things easier and given him a great satisfaction.

'From now on keep your eyes and ears open. I want to know everything about that woman.'

'Tall orders,' said Kelly half-jocularly, for he was annoyed at Terence's tone. He had come a long way from the night he'd arrived looking for work. He had as many connections as he had himself and might in the future have more. 'Tall orders,' he repeated, this time with a pat on the back for Terry, 'and if that's what you want that's what you'll get. I'll tell you what the O'Hara woman has for breakfast. Only don't forget, one day I'll be wanting all the favours returned when you get where you're going.'

Both men laughed and had a drink on the request and promise.

He sent the flowers, with the card and message. When the first florist told him she had been instructed not to send Miss O'Hara any more flowers he took his custom elsewhere and there were no more complaints. Many times he passed the milliners and sometimes he caught sight of Bridget. She was what he wanted all right. She was old enough now for courting. Very soon he would make himself known to her. So far Kelly had found nothing to discredit Katy, but he might yet.

The Oregon Trail stretched for two thousand miles, a great highway along which rolled covered wagons, men attempting to walk it pushing handcarts which had come into vogue, and the men like Jamsie and Mike Doyle riding. Forty-five miles a day could be made, if everything was in your favour, Mike had told Jamsie after the purchase of the second horse. Mike was a great talker and whiled away the hours describing other journeys made by other men along this and the Sante Fe Trail. 'Only hearsay,' he would add before relating incidents. 'At the end of the Twenties there were some terrible massacres on the Santa Fe – white men and redskins. The Indians attacking the whites and they taking fierce reprisals. Indian scalps had a price on them, a hundred dollars for a man, half that for a squaw and half again for a papoose.'

'I thought it was only the Red Indians that scalped,' Jamsie said.

'It wasn't. According to many a trapper and hunter I knew the white man was handy at the business, too.'

'They were brave men and women who set out in the early days – how in the name of God did they find their way?'

'Furtrappers and hunters became guides. There were hunters and trappers from the earliest times, from up Canada way. Working for the Hudson Bay Company in the beginning, they knew every inch of the country. Knew the Indian tongue, had squaws for their women. Beavers they used to catch, set traps in the river, steel cages and the beaver drowned. Queer creatures, sometimes they'd chaw off their toes or a leg once they were caught. A cured plew, that's a beaver's pelt, used to fetch four to six dollars the pound. The Americans had their own company in Twenty-Two. A fella by the name of William Henry Ashley with a mate, Andrew Henry started it – the Rocky Mountain Company. It lasted till about Thirty-Five, when there wasn't the demand for beaver any more.

'They were hard men, the trappers – hard-living and hard-drinking. I remember once years ago being at a trading post where them and the dealers met to do business. And as they had skinned the beaver so did the middlemen skin them. First there was the drink which put a hole in the trapper's pockets. A thousand dollars' worth of catch he might have brought in, he was lucky to get out with his shirt. Twenty and thirty shillings for a pint cup of coffee, a plug of tobacco ten to fifteen shillings. Drink twenty to fifty shillings, everything over the odds. Their money melted like snow in the sun, on food supplies, gambling – then the fights would start. And more gambling, cards, poker, seven-up, euchre – until they hadn't a penny, but credit was there – they pledged against their next season's catch. Poor fools, with one catch they could have settled on the land. But I guess they weren't that sort of men. Them that didn't die, or get killed took up the guiding when the beaver trade was worn out.'

Jamsie listened and believed he'd never walk straight again – and there were still more than fifteen hundred miles to go. He swore to himself as every jog of the horse sent fiery pain through his bones that if he found only enough gold for his fare back to New York he'd take it and run. Sometimes he imagined Katy's reaction when he arrived and painted a rosy picture to keep up his spirits. At other times he remembered what Mike's wife had done. What would he do if Katy had run away with another man? However, these bouts of pessimism didn't last long. Katy loved him. Katy was a good wife who wouldn't look at another man. If God spared her she'd be waiting.

There were times when Katy's certainty that Jamsie would return deserted her. He had been gone such a long time. A lost, lonely feeling would envelop her. Jamsie had deserted her. She would grow old and never know love again. Desire would plague her and she'd remember the past. How it was to be held in Jamsie's arms, how he had kissed her, made love to her. How the days, whatever trouble or burdens they brought, were made bearable because he spent the nights beside her. The pleasure there was in pleasing him. To look nice for him. To have him touch her arms, to love their roundness, the soft smoothness of them, her breasts. His hands caressing her body, his hands lingering in places, his fingers stroking, holding, squeezing. Making her know and love her body because he loved it.

And now before her stretched the remainder of her life, growing old, her skin shrivelling, her body's shape altering, her skin growing crêpey and yellowing. In the bodies and faces of the widows and deserted wives she saw herself in the future. And at these times she curled on her side in the bed she had bought for herself and Jamsie and cried herself to sleep.

Then for weeks or months she would be too tired, too occupied with the day's worries to think about her loveless plight. The loneliness was buried and like the deserted wives and widows she functioned, talking, walking, working, even laughing. Going to Mass, taking part in neighbourhood gatherings, wakes and funerals, occasionally a social evening in the church hall, attending a house wedding, thinking no further ahead than tomorrow.

Once, when walking in the street she thought she saw David coming out of a tenement house. She ducked into an open doorway, peering round the door's edge. It wasn't him. She hadn't wanted it to be him, hadn't wanted to see him and yet she was sad and noticed how her heart was beating, how much despite what her head told her she would have liked a glimpse of him. David, who had told her he loved her and would have married her. David, who would never have deserted her. David, who had once kissed her. David, whom she deliberately kept out of her mind.

He wasn't American, nor tall and fair, and he didn't come in a carriage. All the same Bridget fell in love with him. And Terence, standing in the hat-shop being fussed over my Madame Renée and assured, though he hadn't asked for it, that of course Miss O'Hara could have the afternoon off, was reminded of flowers he had seen in the shop where he went to order Bridget's bouquets. He never looked at women's faces unless it was unavoidable. He couldn't have said if a woman was beautiful or described why she was. But now, looking at Bridget he suddenly thought of flowers, long-stemmed creamy yellow flowers with a sweet smell and brown speckles at their centre.

The sweat poured down his back and silently he cursed Kelly for the situation he had talked him into. 'Go to the shop itself,' Kelly had said.

'Couldn't I meet her somewhere else? Stop her outside the shop?'

'What?' Kelly had roared. 'Is it to ruin the whole thing you want! Stop her outside the shop, indeed. She'd think you were a man molesting her and run a mile. Go in like a man and introduce yourself.'

His hands tightly crushed the brim of his hat. 'I'm Terence McCabe,' he said. 'I hope you don't mind me calling.' Madame Renée said, not at all, he was very welcome, wouldn't he sit down, wouldn't he . . .? He waved a hand as if shooing a fly and fixed Madame Renée with a stare. 'Go away,' said his expression. 'Get out. Leave us alone.'

And the cocky little woman, well able for disgruntled customers, local hooligans or unscrupulous salesmen flinched before his gaze and suddenly remembered something urgent in the workshop that required her and the other assistant's attention.

Watching the incident, Bridget thought again that he was neither American, fair nor tall but he had a quality about him that excited her, that fascinated her. 'I've been wanting to meet you for a long time,' he said when the workroom door closed.

Why didn't you then, she wondered, but didn't ask, saying instead, 'It was you that sent all the flowers. They were gorgeous, thank you very much.' She couldn't believe it was happening at last. That her fairy prince had come to take her away. That it didn't matter she was still living at home. He was Irish and a Catholic. Though he was rich, once he must have been poor. Not like a well-off American, he would have seen rooms like hers. And her mother wouldn't object to him.

'Did you bring them home?'

'What?' she asked, looking puzzled.

'The flowers, did you bring them home?'

Bridget laughed and he thought how like her mother she was and about the creamy lilies he had wanted to buy. To fill his room with them – to look at them, touch them, smell them when he was alone. But hadn't done so, because of what the woman who cleaned for him would have thought and said all over the neighbourhood. 'Imagine that – Terence McCabe with his room full of flowers, hothouse flowers – isn't that the queer thing?'

'The first ones I did, but my mother went mad so after that I never let on.' He was glad she told the truth. So her mother had gone mad. She would go mad again when he declared his hand. He hated her mother.

'She thought they might have been from anyone. Someone dangerous, an old horrible man, maybe waiting one night to pounce on me and lead me astray. Mothers,' she laughed dismissively. 'But she'll be all right now that she'll know who you are.'

'I'd like to see you, to walk you out.'

'Yes,' said Bridget. It was what she had expected. It was why he had come. 'Yes,' she said again, 'that will be fine.'

'I would have come sooner but you were too young.'

'I'm still young, but I know what you mean.' He was hard to get a smile out of.

'Will we keep it a secret for a little while from your mother?'

'If you like.' She was disappointed. Why should they keep it a secret? 'But my mother won't mind, not now.'

'All the same we'll keep it a secret. I have a good friend, his wife is a nice woman – we can meet in his place. Will we do that?'

It wasn't how she'd imagined her courting would begin. But instinct told her that though he appeared to leave the decision to her that wasn't so. It was a command, and he took it for granted that she would comply with it. So she agreed to meet him at the Kellys' on the following Sunday afternoon.

On Sunday afternoons Bridget made excuse after excuse for not being home for tea. She was going to her friends. Maura's father was taking them on the ferry to Staten Island. Madame Renée had asked her to come in for the afternoon. Having no reason to suspect otherwise Katy accepted the reasons, though sometimes she wished Bridget would keep her company for an hour. Sunday, once Mass was over was the lonely day. But, she reminded herself, it was little of her mother's company she had wanted at Bridget's age. When she married and settled down, and had children it would be a different story. She'd be glad to pass many an hour then, glad for someone to take the baby. Girls became more understanding of their mothers when they had their own children. Often on Sunday afternoons while she sat sewing or mending, she would wonder who Bridget might marry. Someone from the parish, for she met no other men. A decent Catholic boy. With the help of God he'd be working so they wouldn't have such a hard struggle. Occasionally the thought crossed her mind that the lads were a long time showing interest in her.

There was Kathleen, that no one could call a beauty, 'homely' as the Americans said, with plenty of fellas after her. If you were to believe Mary Kate who was Bridget's confidante – once they'd made up their quarrel over her telling about the flowers – Bridget didn't have anyone after her because she was stuck-up. Plenty of fellas fancied her but she would have none of them. Ah well, Katy would think, when she found the right one there'd be no hesitation. Not having found him yet wasn't bothering her – she was as happy as the day was long. No more complaints about the washing, no more niggling and wanting to fight with her nails. She was a good girl, a beautiful girl – the child of her love for Jamsie. Conceived in those times so long ago, so far away, such happy times before sorrow or care had touched her life. And she wished for Bridget and for all her children that if only for a little while they each should know such times.

On Sunday afternoons Mrs Kelly showed Bridget into the parlour where Terence was always waiting. On the first visit he had brought her sweets and flowers. She ate the sweets nearly making herself sick, then reminded him that as he wanted their courting to be kept secret from her mother not to bring flowers again.

He seldom talked about anything but his political ambitions and how much money he intended to make and, without having proposed, talked about where they would live when they were married. 'You'll have the best money can buy. Whatever you want you'll have.' She liked his masterfulness, but wished that sometimes he'd look her straight in the eyes instead of half-turning his head away. She wished he would say something about love, or tell her she was beautiful. And as week followed week and he made no attempt to kiss her she wondered if he was changing his mind and didn't intend marrying her. Then no sooner would she have thought this when he would again be outlining their future.

Halfway through each visit Mrs Kelly would knock on the door then bring in tea. While she served it she talked, making references to when the two of them were married. What a wedding they would have. What a lucky girl Bridget was. Bridget longed to get Mrs Kelly on her own and ask her a few questions, like – 'When is this great wedding going to take place? And when can I tell my mother? And why does he never lay a finger on me, hold my hand, kiss me.' But the opportunity never arose. Terence took her to the door, telling her each time that he would have sent her home in a cab only they were still keeping the secret, weren't they.

She stuck it out for another while then one Sunday interrupted him as he talked about their future. 'Terence,' she said, 'would you not sit beside me?'

'Why?' he asked, genuinely surprised at her request.

'Well, that's what courting couples do. They sit together and hold hands and kiss.'

'I never courted anyone before.'

'I didn't either – but that's what people do.'

'Listen,' he said, coming to where she sat but not sitting with her. 'I'm going to marry you. You're going to be my wife. When that happens we'll do all we're supposed to do.'

She felt afraid of him. She thought for a minute he was going to hit her. But it was a thrilling kind of fear, like when you stood somewhere too high and looking down you had a strange tingling all over and a queer feeling in the pit of your stomach.

'I'll be glad when we get married then,' she said. 'Will it be soon?'

'As soon as it can.'

She was so proud of him. He was such an important man. Such a rich man. People looked up to him, you could see that by the way the Kellys treated him.

He could marry her tomorrow. Without as much as a word from her mother he could marry her tomorrow. But he wanted the word with her mother. He wanted to see her face when she forbade him to marry Bridget. When she fumed and flustered and at last begged him not to. And when that failed, threatened him. Threatened to expose him to Bridget. He would beat her every inch of the way. His plans were carefully made and laid. Love, what did he know or care about love? Bridget was a beautiful possession that he wanted and would have. She wanted what he could give her. Her eyes shone when he talked about where they would live, what he would give her. Like himself she had had nothing all her life. He knew the overpowering want that sowed in you. Like him, she had been no one in America – he would make her someone. He would dress her like a lily, put jewels in her hair, ride with her in a carriage, display her for all to see.

But first her mother had to grovel. He would find something about her, something of which she was ashamed. Something to shut her mouth when she talked about the ship. She would come to their wedding. A big happy family wedding and a party afterwards for all the neighbours – all the people who in the years ahead would vote for him. For McCabe the Irish, Catholic, family man.

Manty's child was a constant reminder to Charlotte of her precarious position in Annilaun. The little boy was almost a year old, and almost white. He had the tightly-curled hair of a negro but its colour was red. There was no doubt who had fathered him.

She reasoned with herself – many white men, many plantation owners fathered children on black women. But they didn't acknowledge the children as theirs nor marry their mothers. Paul wasn't likely to, either. But reason deserted her when she thought that in the eleven years since she had come to live in Virginia, no other child had been born on the plantation that resembled Paul. Paul had been faithful to her – and now he wasn't. And if he had slept with Manty mightn't he be sleeping with others, too? With the daughters of other planters, with one of the many, young, attractive widows. Supposing he made one of them pregnant. What then of his, 'I never want to marry. I don't care about an heir.' She had always considered that bravado. It wasn't natural. All men wanted their name to go on, wanted a child to inherit what was theirs.

If only she had conceived a child. Sleeping as she did oftener with Paul than with Peader she could have convinced him that the child was more likely to be his. Her future would have been secure. Then she would have sent Peader about his business.

Now she was between the devil and the deep blue sea. If war came and Paul was killed she'd have no claim on the estate. If he married, his wife would soon send her packing, certainly out of Annilaun. Then she'd be stuck with Peader for the rest of her life. And Peader was slowly driving her mad with his constant talk of the approaching calamity about to overtake the South. Pleading with her to leave before it was too late. How many more excuses could she think up, for stalling him further. One day even Peader would get fed up and go North. And where would that leave her? Praying that Paul wouldn't marry, praying that if the war did come he would survive. Almost praying that if anyone was to die it should be Peader. Worrying about not being so young any more – twenty-eight was no longer a girl. What would become of her if she made the wrong choice?

If she went with Peader, at least she'd be sure of a roof and food in her stomach. If she gambled on Paul, she had one chance in three – if luck was against her, she would finish up homeless and penniless. Peader was the safest bet. But inside a month of living with him away from Annilaun she would be insane. Everything about him irritated her. He was like a great affectionate dog, an obedient fawning dog, but a dog with a voice and opinions which he enjoyed airing. He was good and kind, he would have made a nice brother or pet, you could have made allowances for him. But as her husband he was intolerable and when, as seldom as she possibly could without arousing his suspicions, she let him make love to her – she felt like screaming.

What was she to do? What could she do? Sacrifice her life with Paul for the security of a future with Peader? For weeks she thought of nothing else. Her predicament haunted her day and night. She couldn't eat and didn't sleep so that she grew to look wretched and had a genuine excuse for refusing Peader's amorous advances.

Then one morning she had another letter from Catherine, in which she sent more news of Charles together with his address. Suddenly the solution to her problem was clear. She would put her money on Paul. Peader could go. If Paul married or was killed she would go to Charles in Australia. Charles was wealthy and in Australia she would have no trouble finding a husband. Bigamy was the least of her worries – Australia was a long way off.

From this moment on, she would take life as it came – but first make it quite clear to Peader that she had no intention of ever going North with him. If a war was coming and his high principles prevented him staying in the South, she had no objection to him leaving.

Not long after she had reached this decision, Peader came to her and said how swiftly they were drifting towards war. She humoured him, pleading her ignorance, knowing how he would enjoy explaining the reasons. She'd let him, for the last time she would listen and pretend interest and then, when he thought she was finally convinced they must leave, she would give him her answer. He was a pompous idiot who deserved what was coming. But first she would play him along.

'Tell me,' she asked, 'is slavery the reason why we'll have a war?'

'Anything as evil as slavery is bound to result in war.'

'But is it the only reason?'

'It's the base of all the other reasons. Slavery is an abomination and the South is corrupt. It's still feudal. Here men own other men, brand them like cattle, sell them, while those with wealth live as the English did in Ireland – they're the same breed. But this is America. From Ireland and all over Europe men came here to find freedom, to escape from the remnants of feudalism. Slavery is a blemish on the face of America.'

He was a handsome man, Charlotte was thinking. His hair was beautiful, its fairness bleached by the sun, and physically he was much more attractive than Paul.

Peader had been about to explain the events which had made war inevitable; the Missouri Compromise which forbade slavery north of latitude 36° 30'N, the replacing of it by the Kansas/Nebraska Bill, the Supreme Court's decision in the Dred Scott Case. In the face of such arguments she'd have to agree that the time had come for them to go North, but he saw the glazed look film her eyes. He knew she found him tedious. On many occasions she had told him so; he couldn't continue with what he had intended saying.

She was bored, but it wasn't his arguments that were responsible for her expression. His mention of Ireland had sent her thoughts far away. Back to Kilgoran. To when she had believed he was the most handsome of men, that she would love him forever and that she was the luckiest, happiest girl alive. She felt suddenly sad and sorry for him, and was deciding that he should have a reprieve for a little while. Today she wouldn't tell him that war or no war, she was staying at Annilaun and that he must make his own way North.

★

'Will we ever strike it?'

'We have,' said Mike.

'In pennyworths,' replied Jamsie.

'The same pennyworths have kept us going.'

'I suppose you're right – but it's not much we have to show for a five months' journey and placer mining for nearly two years.'

'Think of the experience – the compensations.'

'What compensations?' said Jamsie, looking round the wooden shack at their meagre possessions, the two tin mugs and few utensils hanging from nails, the wooden stretcher beds, their mining equipment – the sieves, cradles, hammers and shovels in a pile on the floor. 'Compensations how are you – by this time I thought I'd have been living in the best hotel in New York.'

'I was thinking about the travelling, the sights you saw. Across America you came. You've seen more than many a man will in a lifetime. You've been in Kansas and Colorado, Utah and Nevada and now you're in California.'

'You're having me on,' Jamsie said, seeing the suppressed smile in Mike's eyes.

'I'm trying to give you heart. I told you it was all about luck – we haven't been lucky yet, that's all.'

'I'm afraid.'

'Afraid of what?'

'That Katy won't be there when I get back. Once I started out for California I had this picture in my mind. I was going to find all this gold and go back to her and lay it in her lap.'

'Jamsie, isn't it you that's the great romantic, sure. God help your senses. If I hadn't come across you you'd be bleached bones – a long way you'd have got with a dollar seventy-five.'

'Do you think she'll be waiting.'

'You're a lucky man, I gambled on that when I made up my mind to stake you out. I don't know what luck is, but I know that some men have it. You're one of them, and so I'd say yes, Katy will be waiting and we'll strike it rich.'

'Honest to God, is that what you really believe?'

'Honest to God, Jamsie.'

Jamsie sighed with satisfaction. 'I'll shower her with everything. Everything she ever wanted. It'll be great. Katy's the grand woman, wait'll you meet her. I might even take her back to Ireland. There'd be no limits to what I could do. And the stories I'll have to tell the children.

297

Wait'll I describe the buffaloes. Jesus! Wasn't that a sight. Millions of them – holding everyone up for days. How far was it you said they could roam?'

'Texas to Canada,' said Mike.

'Is that a fact. Powerful creatures, queer-looking with all that black matted fur and the great humpy necks of them. Right enough we had some experiences. Some I wouldn't care to live through again. Like the snake – the heart went crossways in me when I saw it rear up and it making a noise like the buzzing of bees that were holed up in some contraption. From nowhere it came.'

'We disturbed it. We set up vibrations.'

'I thought my end had come. An evil-looking thing if ever I saw one. 'Twas as well you had the rifle handy. I had a good look at it the next morning. Very brave I was, moving it with my boot now that its head was gone. You're a great shot. There was a length on it, maybe four or five foot. Browny grey it was, and zig-zaggy diamond patterns on it.'

'You took a good look.'

'I'd never seen one before.'

'You were lucky so. America never had a visit from St Patrick.'

'More's the pity,' said Jamsie. 'I'll never forget that snake. Nor all the burials, neither. Seldom a week passing without someone on the Trail dying. The little wooden crosses the families dug in to mark the spot.'

Mike took off his hat and boots and lay down on the bunk. 'It wasn't all rattlesnakes and burials, though.'

'It was not. I remember the other things, too. Them mountains rearing up to Heaven with snow on them and we roasting in the sun. And the forests where the giant trees grew that had a queer name.'

'The sequoias.'

'That's them. What a sight that was. And the view of Carson Valley, the way the land went in waves toward the mountains and the trees growing up their sides. Oh, 'twas beautiful. And the gorgeous red flowers of the wild peach. Weren't they sights to remember, Mike? Grand things to tell about.'

Mike didn't answer, nor when Jamsie asked the question again. Mike was asleep.

'Talking to myself,' said Jamsie and went to bed where he lay imagining arriving home laden with gold and Katy's reception of him.

On Sunday afternoons in Kelly's parlour Bridget and Terence continued their courting. She had over the months enticed him to sit beside her on the sofa and for short periods he let her hold his hand.

Each week he brought her gifts – bracelets and chains, filigree brooches, bottles of scent, lace handkerchiefs and rings. She gloated over each present, put on the bangles, made Terence fasten chains and pearls round her neck and felt the trembling of his fingers. Her heart raced and her face grew hot and she knew this was love. She dabbed scent on her wrists and her temples, held up her hands to admire the rings and bracelets and fingered her necklaces. When it was time to leave she removed the jewellery and lovingly placed each piece in the velvet padded box, another of Terence's gifts. Then Mrs Kelly was entrusted with it until the next visit.

Katy noticed the smell of scent, said it was lovely and asked Bridget where she had got it. From her friend, or Madame Renée, Bridget told her. The scent became so much a part of Sunday afternoons that Katy grew used to it and after the first time no longer enquired though sometimes, when she was sorting Bridget's clothes for washing, she would hold a dress or blouse close to her face and inhale the perfume that still lingered. And think how beautiful a smell it was and that never in her life had she owned a bottle of scent. Then she'd plunge the garment into the bowl of suds and laugh at her fanciful notions, and say to herself, 'Bottles of scent, indeed! As if that was all you're short of.'

Yet all the same the perfume evoked memories and feelings. Thoughts of Jamsie when she and him were courting, walking through the narrow lanes at home in the summertime where the hedges were twined with wild woodbine and the air heavy with its lovely fragrance. Now and then they'd stop walking to embrace and kiss and his mouth tasted of the honeysuckle. And in her memory there was the moon coming up or the sun setting so that the light was beautiful. Jamsie was beautiful, her life was beautiful. She loved and was loved, no one she cared for had died or deserted her. Tears fell from her eyes into the soapy water and she wiped at them with hands covered in suds which stung her eyes, and the smarting put an end to her lovely memories.

Kathleen was a teacher now and had a job in a neighbourhood school. Katy thought Mary would burst with pride. At every opportunity Kathleen's name was introduced into the conversation. Katy stifled her pangs of envy. She understood Mary's pride and had Bridget been the one to make her mark she would have been as proud. It was a great achievement – what all parents wished and wanted for their children. And Kathleen despite her spoiling and pouting as a child had grown into a pleasant young woman. Katy liked her, she was kind and helpful.

Always ready to help Mary Kate with school work she found difficult. Poor Mary Kate, who still wasn't aware that her days in school were numbered.

A factory or a shop was her future and sorry for her though Katy was, her wages were desperately needed. Thomas when he earned was generous, but there was no depending on him. What would become of him, Katy wondered and worried. Always full of good intentions. Full of promises. When she left David's house, all the promises Thomas had made then were quickly forgotten and Bridget's ambition to have her own hat-shop was another castle in the air. Though she mustn't criticize Bridget, for without her money she couldn't manage, and she had lately been a model of good behaviour. Well, at least she didn't complain about the washing any more or make unfavourable comparisons with her friend's house. She seldom went outside the door except on Sunday afternoons. Sometimes she seemed too good to be true. Her only fault was her vanity. She'd spend hours arranging and rearranging her hair, gazing at her face in the mirror. Not one of Katy's predictions that one day she'd look in the glass and find oul Nick looking back had any effect.

She was so beautiful, Katy never tired of looking at her. The neighbours said, 'God bless her, she's the image of you.' Katy would say, 'There's a resemblance,' but knew that's all there was. Bridget had better features, a classiness about her she had never had, and resemble her was all she did.

Wouldn't Jamsie be the proud father. A child she was when he'd left. If he could see Bridget now. See the young men when she came into Mass craning their necks. She could have any one of them. Sometimes Katy wondered if she had a vocation and hoped she hadn't. A sin it would be for someone so beautiful, so made to be loved to spend her life locked away in a convent. In any case, if it was a convent she had on her mind what was all the preening with her hair and face for?

Mary told her that David was leaving Gramercy Park. They were in the rooms above the baker's shop where Mary had asked her to come because she had something to tell her.

'Dr Purcell's going back to where he came from, so you wouldn't have had the job much longer anyway. I heard it in the shop. Isn't that a pity, he was a grand man. Though mind you, he stopped coming to this neighbourhood about the time you finished. A young fella took over, not half as good as him, so I believe.'

'He'll be missed,' said Katy. She missed him, but seldom allowed thoughts of him to linger. He could have been her undoing. And had she agreed to move in with him, she his. Not that at the time she had considered his position. Only much later on. His neighbours, friends and private patients would have been scandalised – his job in the hospital could have been threatened. How he must have loved her to have risked so much.

'I think he came from New England. I seem to remember him saying that,' said Katy aloud. 'I hope he'll be happy. Was that what you wanted to tell me?'

Mary blushed and became very concerned with the arrangement of the cups and saucers. 'It wasn't,' she said. 'There's something else,' and without looking Katy in the face told her she was expecting a baby.

'Oh Mary, I'm delighted. God bless you and bring you safely over it. When is the child expected?'

'About Christmas, please God.'

'And Günter – I'm sure he's beside himself with pride and joy.'

'Like a fool, not wanting me to lift a finger. If he had his way I'd be laid up till the confinement.'

In the middle of her rejoicing with Mary, Katy remembered the conversation she'd had with Eileen years ago when it was known Mary was to marry Herr Jaeger. Eileen's joking reference to whether or not Mary would or could do it. She could see Eileen's face and hear her remarks. They'd made her laugh. And she thought how Mary had the last laugh, certainly on her. She hoped Eileen had fared better.

The prospect of another winter in Chicago terrified Eileen. The snow, the wind and piercing cold would kill her. Already she had a frozen place in her heart, for Paddy no longer paid her constant attention. He had used her. Fooled her up to the two eyes. The number of times she had had it out with him. Bargaining for a few more dollars. Tackling him about San Francisco. Telling him he was 'a bloody chancer'. And always it finished the same way. With him sidling up to her, kissing and loving.

But he'd fooled her once too often. She could have settled for him, would have settled for him. San Francisco and fame was only a dream. She wasn't a great singer, a great performer. She'd always known that. In a marriage she'd have settled for touring with him. But Paddy didn't want marriage – not to her, anyway. The young one in the troupe had his eye and more now. Eighteen years old, young enough to be his daughter and hers.

She couldn't take that. She didn't have to. Love or whatever you liked to call it had kept her chained to him. Well, not any more. No more scenes, no more pleadings. She'd lay her plans, then up and go.

Chapter Seven

It was cruel not to tell Mary Kate that next year she must leave school, but Katy kept hoping, hoping that Jamsie would come home, that Thomas would find work. Night and morning she prayed for her special intentions, pleading with God to answer one of them, not specifying which one, adding always at the end of her supplications, 'If it be pleasing to Thy holy will.'

Then one day Thomas came in and announced he had got a start on the docks. Katy was delighted and offered up an Act of Thanksgiving. She was always saying prayers of thanksgiving for Thomas' jobs and sometimes wondered if they arrived in Heaven before he was idle again. But this time, please God, he might take a liking to the docks. The difference it would make to have two regular wages. If Thomas did stay with the work she might with careful managing keep Mary Kate in school. She deserved the chance, poor child.

Weeks passed and Thomas was still working and Katy thought that at last maybe her luck was changing. God was doing it. Hadn't He answered one of her prayers and mightn't He answer the other? Maybe her long wait was nearly over.

Mary was beginning to show and so rarely went out except after dark when sometimes she'd come to visit Katy. It being unlucky to talk about the unborn child Mary's condition was seldom referred to. But as her belly grew bigger and sometimes Katy saw her place a hand on it and knew the child had leapt within her she was overwhelmed by feelings of her own loss. Her loneliness and lovelessness. The awful aching loneliness for Jamsie, her need to love and be loved. If Jamsie didn't come soon there was nothing in front of her but old age. Love kept the sap in you, without it you grew like a withered stick.

One night after Mary had been to visit, Katy lay in bed unable to sleep and thought about Jamsie. Wondering where he was: was he well, was he happy. Was he maybe at this hour lying awake thinking of her. When would he come home . . . she missed him so desperately.

Let him come soon, please God. Sick or well I'll welcome him. If he never works again I'll work for the two of us. If he's sick I'll mind him. Like a child I'll mind him. But he'll be well and strong. He's still young. There's years before us. He'll be young and strong. I'll lie in his arms and he'll stroke my hair and kiss me.

She was drifting towards sleep, thinking about the kissing and hoping to dream of Jamsie when she heard the singing and was wide awake again. Drunken men, Irishmen in the street singing. Staggering home, singing the way Jamsie had many a time. And I'd have a puss on me, she thought, about the drink and the money spent on it, money wasted. Money squandered that deprived her and the children of so much.

An affliction: men who drank had an affliction, that's what the clergy said and the priests were lenient on the men afflicted. Though it was little leniency they showed to women who had the same affliction. 'A disgrace to their womanhood' – many a time she had heard a priest say that. And as often heard them say, 'Drink is many a good man's failing.' 'Twas to be expected, for weren't they men and many of them with a liking for the drink, too.

Thanks be to God I am lucky, I have no liking for the drink, she thought. And thanks be to God again for though it wasn't fair that the priests had less sympathy for the women who drank, there was no doubt that a woman in its clutches was a terrible sight. A poor creature, herself destroyed and what was worse her family. Neglected and hungry, unwashed and unloved and carrying the shame of their mother's plight. Many a blind eye was turned on the drunken man, but not on the poor woman.

The singing in the street grew fainter. She settled herself for sleep once more. The singing stopped, now she could hear voices calling to one another. The men parting, saying their goodnights, going their separate ways. For a little while there was silence. And then a lone voice, a voice that came nearer – a lovely clear tenor voice. She listened. She knew the song. She had last heard it in Peader's house the night his father was waked.

Her mind went back to that night. There was a clear cold sky full of brightly shining stars. People coming into the wake remarked on the hard frost and hoped the gravediggers wouldn't have trouble breaking the ground. The keeners came, thin gaunt women dressed in black like starved birds, and set up the keen. A piercing wail, an anguished wail of desolation that made you feel cold all over and think of death and the waiting grave. And you were glad of the bright fire with its living flames and the nearness of your neighbours, the warmth and sound of breathing while you waited for the keen to end.

When it did, the wake began in earnest. Drinking and dancing, hot tea, tobacco, sights and sounds and smells of life banishing the thoughts of death.

The sound of the street singer grew fainter but the song went round and round in Katy's head, together with other thoughts and images of the night long ago when Peader's father was waked. She remembered how, when she heard he was dead, she had gone with Statia to help with the laying out. And how, while taking linen and candlesticks from the press, she had fantasised that this was her home. These were her possessions for she had never married Jamsie, she was Peader's wife. At night they lay in the big bed, she in his arms and he kissed her, but beyond that she didn't let her imagination stray for once before in Peader's house she had given reign to fantasy. And so lost in it had she become that her thoughts showed on her face each time she gazed at Peader. Jamsie noticed, dragged her outside and inflamed with drink and jealousy, threw her to the ground. She struggled and fought, inflaming his passion further and he took her where they lay. Such loving it was. Under the sky and the stars looking down on them, such loving it was.

Oh Jamsie, Jamsie, where are you now? Oh, that you were beside me and my arms around you. She thought and thought about him and relived the lovemaking under the starry sky and longed to dream a lovely dream about him. One that would leave his presence about her when she woke, keep him close to her so that she could imagine all she had to do was reach out and touch him.

But when she slept she dreamed of Peader. Peader was in her bed. His breath smelled sweet. And she thought how pleasant it was to sleep with a man whose breath wasn't tainted with porter. She raised herself on an elbow and looked at his sleeping face. And wondered why once she had preferred a dark man. Who he was, she couldn't remember. Once she had loved him and he had taught her how to love. Poor Peader, he didn't know how to love. But now she'd teach him. All she had learned from the dark one she would teach Peader. She traced the outline of his lips. In his sleep his mouth smiled. She lay on him and kissed him. He opened his eyes and looked into hers. 'Katy,' he whispered. 'I love you, I've always loved you.'

His presence had been so real, their lovemaking so fulfilling she expected him to be beside her when she woke. Daylight was coming in through the thin curtains. She shivered in the bed that had insufficient covering and bitter thoughts of Jamsie came to her mind. Jamsie was responsible for her plight. Jamsie had deserted her. Left her lonely and

305

unloved, a prey to dreams of other men. Dreams of Peader, a man happily married to Miss Charlotte.

What a fool she was, believing Jamsie loved her. Believing he would come back. Keeping herself going on dreams and hopes. Foolish hopes. For reason told her she was a deserted wife. Her and her children thrown to one side. Like the men she had heard singing in the street last night, Jamsie loved only two things – himself and drink. Jamsie always had to have his own way.

If it wasn't for him, today she would be Peader's wife. They mightn't be rich but he would never have reneged on her. He'd have stayed by her side, cherished her and their family. Peader wouldn't have left her to grow old and lonely and unloved.

From today she would put Jamsie from her mind. See him for his true self: a handsome, selfish man who had left her and her children to starve in America. No more would she daydream about his return and living happily every after. She would in future get through her life a day at a time. Keeping her mind on what she was doing. She'd grow old, everyone grew old, but it would bring its compensations. Her body would cease to plague her with its wants and longings. But as she went through the day performing her tasks that required no thought, the vacuum she had created by banishing Jamsie filled itself with images of Peader. Scenes of their youth when always it seemed to be summer, with remembered snatches of last night's dream. Peader's kisses and caresses.

Sometimes Jamsie tried sneaking into her mind, but she blocked him out convincing herself it was better to do so. For with the humour that was on her only his faults came to mind. His drinking, his desertion. She couldn't remember one good thing, one caring act of his. Whereas all her memories of Peader were good. And so she thought about him, brought him alive.

Up the side of the mountain were pitched the tents, and leaning into it the makeshift shanties of the placer miners. From morning till night they hacked at the rock and shovelled it into their cradles, then carried it to the river and rocked it in the water, washing out the loose dirt and gravel, their eyes probing the remainder for the gleam of gold.

Some days Jamsie and Mike found five dollars' worth, ten dollars' worth, some days nothing. Pennyworths, as Jamsie said. But they kept hoping, for always above, beyond or behind them someone was striking it rich. And one day, Mike was convinced their turn would come.

On the nights when they had enough to buy a beer they sat in the store that sold everything and bought dust, and listened to the stories of those who'd struck it rich; of the miner who'd been pushed down a well and his claim jumped, of the gold nuggets and packets of dust robbed at gun and knifepoint as their joyful owners were making for the assayist.

Jamsie's thirst for adventure had long since been quenched. The sun and the cold, the snakes, diarrhoea, chills, coughs and bone weariness made the prospect of New York seem like Heaven. He wanted nothing more than to go home to sleep easy, without the fear of his head being knocked in for the sake of a rocker, pick and shovel. But he'd come this far, suffered this much and wasn't going back empty-handed. He was lucky. Mike kept telling him that – he'd strike it yet.

Eileen counted what money she had saved and went through Paddy's pockets on the nights he came to her drunk. He had robbed her all these years, now she robbed him.

She outlined her plan to four of the original girls who had set out hoping for great things in San Francisco.

'Do you know how long Paddy's been fooling us?' she asked.

'Too long,' one of the girls replied.

'So why don't we get out of it? Why don't we go off on our own?'

'But how would we live?' asked another.

'No worse than we are now. We're women and there's men out there. If we pool what we've got we'll go into business on our own, right?'

'You mean dancing and that?'

'Yes,' said Eileen. 'We'll get a couple of rooms first – then a house. We could make a fortune. We could – all by ourselves. Think of that! No more travelling. Money to spend. Money to save. No more worries about our old age. Think about it. But not a word to Paddy.'

They thought about it. It appealed to them. Nice dresses, paint and powder, scent and soft beds. And money piling up. And so they left without saying a word to Paddy.

In the summer of 1860 Peader came home one day when he should have been in the fields.

Jake appeared, as if by magic. Always, Peader thought, he seemed to come from nowhere. Jake was attached to him, would like to have attended him had Peader been willing, laid out his clothes, performed all the humiliating chores that were expected of slaves. Over the years Peader had discouraged him gently. Now Jake settled for helping him dismount.

He often wondered what Jake's feelings were about slavery but out of loyalty to Paul had never raised the subject. Their conversations were limited to the weather or the crops, to Peader's enquiries about the baby Jake's wife was expecting. Innocent questions – small-talk that embarrassed Peader, for he felt it belittled Jake.

Today Jake seemed agitated, talked more than usual, and Peader got the impression he was trying to delay him entering the house. Yet when he asked if everything was all right Jake said it was.

'Nothing wrong, is there?' asked Peader. 'You're not sick, your wife and the children are all fine?' They were all fine. 'Then I'll go in.'

Still Jake lingered. Something ailed him, Peader thought, but he mustn't probe. Jake if he wanted to would tell him in his own time.

On the ride back from the fields he had been thinking as he always was about Charlotte, the coming war and their future, and the decision he had reached, his reason for returning early. After washing and changing, and when Charlotte had woken from her nap he would tell her. Tell her that although it was against his judgment, against all his principles, he would stay on in the South. Stay with her to protect her. He didn't have to fight – no one could make him do that.

Charlotte, he had come to realise, was unbalanced. Maybe losing the child had caused it. The reason didn't matter. His beloved little wife was, as they'd say at home, slightly wanting in the head. She had to be, for only an obstinate child or a foolish person could ignore danger, could blind their eyes to the signs, the warnings. Only a woman sick in the head could make light of John Brown's war on slavery in the Appalachians . . . his seizing of the armoury at Harper's Ferry, waging his abolitionist war from the engine-house of the armoury. He was a fanatic, a brave one, some said but callous for sacrificing his sons. But his trial and execution had brought the anti-slavers to boiling point. These weren't Peader's opinions, intuitions, guesses – they were facts – reported in all the papers. And yet Charlotte couldn't see what was coming.

It was then, in December after John Brown's execution, that he first suspected Charlotte of being unbalanced. It explained so many things, apart from her refusal to leave Annilaun – the change in her attitude towards him, her moods. God knows he didn't expect life to be as it was when they first married. But passing time and familiaity couldn't be responsible for some of her behaviour. His poor little love was unbalanced. He'd cherish and protect her, moider her no more about the coming war, about going North, not even about leaving Annilaun. He would do everything to keep her happy.

At this time in the afternoon the house was always quiet. Servants would be dozing in the kitchen before preparations began for the evening meal. Charlotte would be resting. Paul, too, if he was home would be taking a nap. Quietly he went up the stairs and made for the room in which he now slept. Passing Charlotte's door he heard a grunt-like noise and sounds of moaning. Charlotte was having a bad dream, a nightmare. When they were first married she had bad dreams frequently. She'd babble incoherently, make strange noises and wake screaming. He'd hold her in his arms, soothing and comforting, allaying her fears.

He didn't know she still had nightmares, he hadn't slept in her room for so long. Poor Charlotte, he must waken and comfort her. Without making a sound he opened the door and saw Charlotte and Paul, naked, her legs twined round his waist. His first thought was how grotesque they looked. More grotesque than animals mating. Animals wore their pelts, were recognisable. You would be hard put to give a name to this tangle of flesh and limbs. Frantically they moved together like a horse and rider in a race. Shame filled him as he realised he was observing them and as quietly as he had come into the room, so he left it.

He was cold, shivering with hurt and shock. Flashes of thoughts went through his mind. He must leave. Go now. Never look either Paul or Charlotte in the face again. Jake must have known. Every servant in the house must know. Jake had tried to delay him. Poor Jake. How long had it been going on?

He poured cold water from the jug into the basin and splashed his face, refreshing himself, then resumed his thinking. It had been going on a long time. Probably from the beginning. Certainly from when Charlotte began making excuses for not leaving Annilaun. And the baby – whose was that?

He felt no anger, only shame and bewilderment. Ashamed of his naiveté. His acceptance of Paul's generosity at face value. Ashamed that the servants would have laughed and nudged each other each time he passed. He had no desire to confront Paul, to have it out with Charlotte. Piecing together the events of the previous years it was clear who her preference had been for, but why hadn't she told him she had made a mistake. That she didn't love him. He would have gone. All through the years he had excused her behaviour. Even when by all standards it became intolerable, thinking she was deranged. Didn't she know anything about him? Didn't she know that he wouldn't have stood in the way of her happiness?

If he was truly principled he would go from the house the way he had arrived, with nothing. The clothes he had accumulated, the money he had earned should all be left behind. But principles were one thing, making his way to New York penniless and without a change of clothes was another.

He would go now. Paul and Charlotte would sleep for a long time, he was sure. He packed only what was necessary, leaving behind various things, silver-backed brushes, a watch, a ring, presents from Charlotte. He'd ride to town, stay at an inn, write to Jacques . . .

There was no sound from the bedroom where Peader supposed Paul and Charlotte were sleeping now. But when he opened the front door, again as if by magic, Jake was there with Peader's horse.

'I'm going away Jake,' he said. 'Tomorrow you go to town and bring the horse back.'

Jake nodded.

'Goodbye,' Peader said. 'God bless you.'

Jake for the first time ever caught hold of his hand and squeezed it.

'Goodbye, Master,' he said, and his eyes looked with pity at Peader.

Arriving in New York Peader went to a hotel he knew. Assuming they would have a room, he had given the address to Jacques when he wrote and hoped a letter would be waiting for him. There was a room and a letter from Jacques – but with disappointing news, for his friend had had to leave town the previous day. However, in the meantime Peader was to make Jacques' house his. Staten Island would be lovely at this time of the year.

Reading the letter, Peader felt a great sense of loss. He had taken it for granted that Jacques would be at hand. He was suddenly overwhelmed with loneliness. Everyone in the hotel, in the street were strangers. He hadn't forgotten Katy or Jamsie, he even remembered their address. He'd love to see them again but he'd neglected them. Would he be welcome after such a long absence? What was he thinking of – of course he would – they'd welcome him as he would them, no matter how long they had been parted. He'd lived too long in the South, spent too much time amongst Paul and his kind. Forgotten the warm-heartedness of Katy and Jamsie. If they were still in New York, still in Mulberry Street, he'd be welcome. He would write a note to them and then call.

Chapter Eight

Charlotte slept after the lovemaking. When she woke, Paul was gone and Manty was standing by the bed looking agitated. 'What is it? What's the matter?' Charlotte asked, yawning and stretching.

'Master Peader's gone away.' Manty began to cry.

'Gone where? Stop that mumbling. Stop it at once Manty, do you hear me? That's better.' Charlotte sat up. 'Now tell me what all this is about.'

Manty told her how Jake had tried to delay Peader entering the house. How he had failed and following Peader at a distance had seen him open the bedroom door.

'Oh, my God!' Charlotte leapt out of bed. 'Go, go away,' she shooed Manty out of the room. 'He saw us, Peader saw me and Paul.' She talked aloud as she put on a peignoir. 'I wouldn't have wished that for the world,' she continued talking as she went to Peader's room. 'Poor Peader, I'm so sorry. I never meant that to happen.'

At first sight of the room her heart rose – it was undisturbed. On his dressing table, on his bedside table his possessions lay. But when she looked more closely she saw that other things were missing – the clothes he called his comfortable ones, the few books he had brought from Ireland. She sat on his bed, covered her face with her hands and cried.

It was there Paul found her. He sat down and put his arm round her. 'It was bound to happen sooner or later,' he said.

'But not the way it did,' she sobbed. 'Not like that, that was horrible. Poor Peader – he didn't deserve that. I'm so ashamed. You never really knew him. You can't imagine what an effect witnessing what he did would have had on him.'

'Charlotte, darling, I'm sorry too that he witnessed it, but he did and all your self-recriminations won't alter the fact. It was a horrid messy thing for him to see. But don't dwell on it and don't be too hypocritical –you didn't love him, you wanted him gone; well, now he is. It's for the best. Had he stayed, who knows how he would have fared when war comes. He wouldn't have fought on our side. He was always

311

sympathetic to the negroes. A suspicious planter might have made short work of him. Would you rather that?'

Unhesitatingly Charlotte replied, 'Yes, I would. I'd rather him dead than alive knowing I betrayed him. It will break his heart and he'll die from that.'

'Sentimental rubbish,' said Paul. 'Men have died from time to time, and worms have eaten them, but not for love.'

'What on earth do you mean?' asked Charlotte, who was beginning to get over her shock and grief, her mind starting to consider her own predicament.

'I'm just telling you that Peader will get over it. Men do. Good, you've stopped crying. What are you going to do now that you have no husband? What will be your future?' Any lingering shame and guilt was quickly banished from Charlotte's mind by Paul's question. Maybe he would throw her out. Perhaps he had decided to marry someone. Thank God she had Charles and Australia up her sleeve. And for the time being that's where she'd keep them. Not say a word until she found out his intentions.

'My future?' she said. 'I don't understand. My future – what do you mean?'

'Come now, Charlotte, you know perfectly well what I mean. Peader's gone – he'll never return, we both know that and so you're to all intents and purposes a single woman. You could walk away from here tomorrow. I want to know, that's all.'

'I don't want to go away from here, ever. Would you make me do that?'

'I might,' said Paul. 'On the other hand I might not. I've got used to you about the place.'

'Thank you,' said Charlotte. 'You could say the same about Manty or Jake.'

'Good, I've riled you. Banished your gloom. I like you angry. Humility doesn't become you – and never fools me.'

'You are the most horrible man I've ever known.'

'You love me for it, though.'

'I do not – I hate you.'

He attempted to kiss her and she pretended not to want the kiss but eventually allowed it and eventually responded. Paul kissed her a second time then stood up and said, 'I couldn't marry you even if I wanted to. But I want you to stay. For always, will you?'

'For always,' said Charlotte. 'For always and forever and ever I'll love you.'

Katy didn't dream of Peader again, though he was now seldom far from her thoughts. Sometimes she considered herself deranged for dwelling on a man she hadn't seen for years, and sometimes she was plagued by guilt for deliberately excluding Jamsie from her mind. And asked herself why was she doing it? Why had the change come so suddenly about. Once she wondered was Jamsie dead. Had he died the night she dreamt about Peader? Only snatches of the dream remained, but one was very clear – the dark man who in the dream, she remembered, had taught her how to love. The dark man she knew was Jamsie, but in the dream she didn't know who he was. All memory of him had vanished. Maybe that had been the sign, the message that he was dead.

'No,' she said aloud. 'No, he isn't dead. That wasn't why I dreamt about Peader or the dark man or woke with bitterness in my heart against Jamsie. It was the drunken men singing in the street, the man who sang the other song. Jamsie isn't dead. If he was, it's full of sorrow I'd be. What happened is that I came to my senses. I saw myself for a fool. I've been deluding myself for years with the hope of him coming back. Well, he's not. He deserted me. And if filling my head with thoughts of Peader, remembering when we were young and what might have been, gives me ease what harm is there in it?' And so she thought about him. His tenderness when they were courting. His goodness and kindness. His generosity during the Hunger. His visit to New York, how wonderful that was. And the present he had left, the money that had set up the laundry. Without the laundrying she and the children would have become destitute long ago. Why wouldn't she think about him! And so she did, and the more she did the more his presence became closer so that when his note arrived saying he was coming to visit it seemed the most natural thing in the world.

Eagerly she waited for him. When he embraced her she clung to him and began to cry. 'Oh Peader,' she cried. 'Oh Peader, I'm that glad to see you. I've thought about you so much. I needed you. The terrible thing that's happened.' She was conscious of the warmth of his body, the strength of it, the comfort of being held.

'Katy,' he said, 'what ails you? What is it – Jamsie, the children, nothing's happened to them?'

She left his arms and wiped her eyes. 'The children are all right, thank God. It's Jamsie, he's . . .'

'Not Jamsie, he isn't . . .'

'No, he isn't,' said Katy. 'He's not dead, he deserted me.' She broke down again and incoherently told him all that had happened. 'I waited and waited, for years I've waited and he never came. I prayed and hoped. I wrote and he never answered the letters. He went – he went just when we were getting on our feet. Do you remember the money you left – it got me a lock-up shop and decent rooms. We were very happy I thought, and then he went.'

'I'm so sorry, Katy. You didn't deserve that.' The sympathy and concern in his voice was like balm. He put an arm round her and led her to a chair. 'Sit down, I'll make you a drink and then tell me all about it.' She was crying softly now and watched him move about the room looking for the tea, where to get the water. He walked softly, gracefully, didn't clatter things and eventually had a kettle boiling. He was a handsome, kind, beautiful man. She noticed everything about him, even that his clothes were not so fine as on his last visit and she liked that better.

He placed her shaking hands round the mug of tea and sat beside her. 'To think you've been alone and suffering all these years and I never knew. Why didn't you write and tell me? What happened about the shop?'

She told him, and then she told him about working for the doctor. That now Bridget and Thomas were earning they managed.

'You're a great woman,' he said admiringly. 'Many a one with your burden would have given up long ago. But listen to me – whatever happened, Jamsie wouldn't have deserted you. There has to be an explanation. Maybe he had an accident, maybe . . .'

'He's not dead if that's what you're thinking. I know that. In my heart I know that.' Her voice was bitter.

He watched her while she talked. She had changed. When last he saw her, she was a girl. He always remembered her as a girl. A girl with flossy golden hair and a round smiling face. Her face wasn't so rounded any more nor her hair like golden floss. She was a woman now. A sad beautiful woman. He found himself comparing her with Charlotte. With Charlotte's soft prettiness, her white soft skin and small smooth hands, dressed in her brightly coloured gowns. Like a doll. But like a doll's the smile was painted on.

'Listen, Katy,' he said, taking the mug from her hands, putting it on the floor then holding her two hands in his. He wanted to raise them to his lips and kiss them. Her hands were reddened and rough, the skin chapped. He wanted to cover them with kisses and tell her they were beautiful. He wanted to hold and comfort her, make everything right for her. And he thought how wise Jacques was when he had said, 'Katy is the woman you should have married.' 'Listen, Katy,' he said again,

314

'don't think too badly of Jamsie. He loved you. I know he had a failing for the drink, but he loved you and his children. Don't give up hope too soon.' While he spoke one thing, he longed to say another. To say, 'You've waited long enough. Come back with me, I'm going to Ireland. Come back and be my wife in the sight of God.'

His voice, his presence had calmed Katy and she was enveloped in a lovely warm feeling. It was so good to have someone she could talk to, someone who was concerned, someone to hold her hands and look at her with admiration. 'I've stopped hoping and waiting. I've put Jamsie out of my mind. Whatever happens to me now, I'm on my own. No more dreams, no more living happily ever after when he comes back. That's finished. Gone. We won't talk about it any more. I'm so glad you're here. We'll just enjoy that, wait'll you see the children. Wait'll you see how they've grown.'

'I doubt if they'll know me,' said Peader and let go her hands.

'You were sent, God sent you today. I feel as if you've never been away. Sitting here, just the two of us it's like long ago. We had great times, didn't we Peader?' Her face was flushed, her eyes shone reflecting her mood of joy. For a moment Peader caught a glimpse of the young Katy. The Katy whom he had loved so desperately. Whose loss had driven him to long lonely years in Dublin. And he asked himself why had he let Jamsie steal her from him. He should have stopped him, killed him. If he had his hands on him now he would squeeze the life out of him for the suffering he had caused Katy.

But even while these thoughts were uppermost in his mind he knew the lie to them. He wasn't the killing kind. If this minute Jamsie walked through the door reason would override anger. He'd be doing the peacemaker. Looking for explanations and excuses. He avoided confrontations. He had avoided confronting Paul. Another man would have dragged him from the bedroom and flogged or shot him. Was he really such a tolerant, liberal, peaceable man – or did he use words and ideas for a way out of unpleasant situations? How did anyone ever know the truth about themselves? Of only one thing was he sure – he always lost the moment. For now his instinct was telling him – take Katy in your arms, hold her close, tell her you love her, that you never stopped. 'Let me take care of you. I'll make you happy.' He said nothing. But after glancing at the clock Katy did. 'They'll be in in a minute and ravenous. You'll have a bit of dinner with us?'

He didn't feel he could face anyone else, he wanted to be by himself and think about Katy. He refused, lying that he had an appointment.

'Well, have another cup of tea, then,' she offered.

315

He accepted that and while they drank the tea she asked questions about Charlotte and Catherine, and was there any news of Master Charles. He told her they were well, that Charles was prospering in Australia and that it was almost certain Jamsie's brother Johnny had been executed in India.

'You'd have heard that through Miss Catherine,' she said and went on, 'I can't pretend great sorrow, he'll have got what he deserved. He it was that let his own flesh and blood, poor Padraig, be transported for his crime. I'll shed no tears for him.'

She asked if he remembered Eileen and Mary. He remembered – but not which was which. She explained and told him Eileen had gone out of her life and that Mary was married and had a baby expected soon, please God. ' 'Tis seldom we talk about the child that's expected, but Mary did let slip that if God blesses her with a son, he'll be called Seamus.' She laughed. 'Seamus Jaeger – what do you think of that for a name?'

'There'll be stranger name combinations still as one race marries another,' said Peader. 'But yourself – how are you finding America now?'

'In my circumstances,' said Katy, 'it's not easy to judge. When I'm down I seek comfort in my memories,' and silently she added, like I do about you. 'At home I do think everything would be grand. No roasting sun or perishing cold. Memories, longings – dreams that's all they are, for I knew the other side of Ireland, too. I'm here now and the children are American. Their memories have been made in America. So it's here I'll stay until I die.

'Ask any of the women,' she went on, 'they'll tell you the same thing. For years they've kept themselves going with dreams. When the children grew up they'd all go back home. They'd save for the day. Only, when the children do grow up, they're Americans. Ireland means little to them, or to very few. Try telling them about the Hunger, and they look at you blankly. Bridget not only gives you the look but also says her piece, "Ah, Mom, not that old stuff again." ' She imitated Bridget's accent and they both laughed.

She kept talking to delay him. Having a man in the house was so pleasant. A man you knew so well, a man you felt close to, even closer of late. She enjoyed pouring his tea, touching him accidentally, looking at him. She had forgotten how handsome he was, what a fine man he was.

When at last she stopped talking, Peader said he'd have to go. 'Where are you staying and for how long?' she asked.

In a hotel for the present; he wasn't sure how long he'd stay. She wanted to see him again, but wouldn't ask straight out so used the children as an excuse. 'It's a pity you'll miss the children.'

'That can be remedied if you ask me to supper tomorrow evening.'

'Then I'm asking you.' She smiled at him in what she wasn't aware was a flirtatious manner.

'Then I accept,' he said in a light-hearted way.

'Be careful as you go,' she said. 'It's a rough neighbourhood.' They stood close to each other. She longed for him to hold her. He longed to do likewise, but neither made a move. 'So then,' she said, going to the door, 'I'll see you tomorrow,' and they parted.

Bridget was in bad humour. Katy knew the minute she came in. Her humours were back this while, for Bridget was becoming impatient with Terence. After all this time she received no more than a kiss on the cheek and as for marriage, any time she hinted at it Terence said No, not for a while – and hoped she was keeping the secret from her mother. Lately she had spoken to Mrs Kelly: 'Isn't it unnatural, not even a proper kiss?'

'You don't know how lucky you are,' Mrs Kelly replied. 'A gentleman, that's what you have in Terence McCabe. Not like some of them that's going now. Men that would be taking liberties already. You be thankful, my girl. You've got a God-fearing man who'll take you to the altar as pure as the day you were christened. Respect for you, that's what it is.'

'Well, maybe you're right,' Bridget agreed reluctantly. 'But why, if he's that respectful, doesn't he want my mother to know?'

'That I couldn't tell you,' Mrs Kelly admitted. 'And you'd be as well not to ask, not to push him, if you know what I mean. Don't annoy him.'

Bridget wouldn't annoy him – she had already learnt that particular lesson. Once, not long ago on a warm Sunday when Mrs Kelly's parlour was stifling, Bridget had suggested a walk. 'No,' said Terence. She sidled up to him, touched his face, began stroking it and pleaded, 'Please Terence, oh please.'

He had caught hold of her hand, holding it so tightly it hurt, removed it from his face and glared at her. At that moment she thought how horrible his eyes were, how frightening. 'Don't,' he said, letting go her hand. 'Don't annoy me, don't ever annoy me. And don't try your tricks, them cheap tricks on me.'

She was shocked, frightened, so frightened she wanted to run from the room and keep running until she reached home. All she had done

317

was touch his face and say please. But terrified though she was, and desperate to escape from this stifling room and Terence's glowering face, she knew instinctively that he would prevent her, hurt her. He wasn't to be annoyed and he wasn't to be questioned.

Mrs Kelly had then brought in tea and stayed to chat for a while. Bridget calmed down and for the remainder of the afternoon Terence was his usual self. By the time she was leaving, Bridget had rationalised his behaviour. He liked his own way, he must make the decisions. Well, most men were like that. You had to learn how to manage them. And his eyes weren't horrible – that was her imagination. Annoyance that she couldn't coax him – she liked her own way, too.

After speaking to Mrs Kelly she was more consoled that he had spurned her touch. Respect, as Mrs Kelly said. He couldn't trust himself. But she still wished he would soon talk to her mother. She couldn't wait to have her own home and all the things Terence promised her. Every evening a black humour fell on her when she came home. She felt that somehow it was her mother's fault that made Terence delay arranging their marriage.

'I had a grand surprise – you'll never guess who came to see me, after all these years.'

'Who?' asked Bridget.

'Your Uncle Peader.'

'He's not my uncle,' Bridget said, taking off her hat and putting it in a large paper bag she used for a hat-box.

'He's coming to supper tomorrow evening. He wants to see you all.'

'Meat loaf – ugh, not again. I won't be here, I'm working late. And afterwards I'm going to Teresa's, she's a cousin coming from Ireland. I told you.'

'You did,' said Katy, 'but you could cancel it.'

'I can't.'

'It's your uncle – you haven't seen him this long time.'

'Whose fault is that and I don't like meat loaf – not the way you make it, with too much bread in it.'

'I don't like it either – but it's cheap and filling. Eat it or leave it, there's nothing else.' God grant me patience, Katy said to herself. When she's in these humours I dread her crossing the door. I'd miss her few shillings but sometimes I wish she'd find a man and get married. 'If you explained to Teresa she'd understand.'

'No,' said Bridget. Riling her mother gave her satisfaction for the moment. Afterwards she might be sorry, but nowadays would never admit it. Everything that was wrong in her life she considered to be her mother's fault. Still living in Mulberry Street: if she hadn't given up the housekeeper's job by now they would be living somewhere else. All the penny-pinching – more than was necessary so that Mary Kate could be a teacher. Her mother would die in the attempt to see her in College. And her mother stood in the way of her marriage. Why, she couldn't fathom – but it was her mother's fault for sure. And if the truth was known it was her fault her father ran away. Who could blame him, with her always laying down the law. And now she was going on about the famine.

'You wouldn't take that attitude if you knew what he did for us during the famine. He saved our lives. Maybe you could leave your friends early just to say hello before he goes.'

'Maybe,' said Bridget.

Thomas said, 'Sure Mom, I'd love to see Uncle Peader. I'll come straight home.'

'Don't let me down, promise me now.'

Thomas promised. Thomas, she knew, would promise you the moon to be agreeable. If something or someone else attracted him tomorrow his word would be forgotten. She could only rely on Danny and Mary Kate being home for supper.

A man who had a fruit and vegetable stall in the street saw Peader and Katy come down to the door. He noted the stranger and how he was dressed. It was the first bit of news he had for Kelly.

Kelly passed it on to Terence. 'If he comes again,' said Terry, 'tell your man to have him followed. I want to know who he is, where he lives, everything.'

He was elated. Wait long enough and you found what you wanted. He'd always had his suspicions about Katy's housekeeping job. The stranger was probably the doctor. A bit more to go on and he'd tell Bridget he was ready to see her mother.

'Don't change your luck.'

'Luck!' said Jamsie. 'I'm beginning to doubt it ever attended me. What could we lose by going to Pikes Peak. Gold is coming out there by the ton. Haven't you noticed we've got this place nearly to ourselves now? They've left in their thousands.'

'Jasus, you're a terrible man for the prate. Dig more and talk less.'

He applied himself to the digging but kept talking. 'Where's this Pikes Peak?'

319

'At the foot of the Rockies.'

'Where's the name from?'

'How the hell would I know? A scout, a soldier, a trapper – it'll be called after someone like that. Now will you shut up and keep digging.'

Jamsie lay awake for most of the night thinking about Pikes Peak. Could he talk Mike into leaving California and going to the Rockies – and if not, could he go alone? It was all very well going on about luck but didn't you have to take it where you found it. And you weren't finding it here. Mike was easy, Jamsie didn't think Mike really cared if he found gold or not. Mike liked the life, working for himself. He could see Mike ending his days here. If he struck lucky, drinking himself to death and if he didn't, something else would get him. A knife in the back or belly over a senseless quarrel, a rattler which deep in its lair was disturbed by the vibrations a man's walking made.

The difference between him and Mike was that Mike had nothing to go back for. And he had a wife and family, please God. Lately he had thought more of Katy than he had for years. He wanted to go home, he didn't want to end his days like Mike. Before he fell asleep he had made up his mind that one week more would he give, one week from tomorrow – and then he would set off for Pikes Peak with or without Mike.

On the second day of the week which was the same day Peader discovered Paul and Charlotte together, Jamsie struck gold. He and Mike had moved to another location, a digging deserted by a miner in the rush for Pikes Peak. They'd trudged since dawn up and down to the river with their diggings in the cradle and by midday were exhausted. They rested, drank the bottles of cold tea, chewed tough meat in the meagre shade cast by a skinny outcrop. Overhead, a buzzard circled. The bird gave Jamsie the shivers. Though he knew they scavenged all dead flesh, in his imagination he always saw a man mortally wounded but conscious, watching the buzzard circling, knowing his end was near, knowing the bird knew that, too. It was an end Jamsie frequently envisaged for himself. He loathed the creatures.

Once when he'd said this to Mike, the big man had laughed. 'Poor bastards, they have to live, too. Maybe God felt like you about them.'

Jamsie was never sure how to take Mike. Like the way he dismissed the loss of his wife. Didn't he really mind? If he went home and found Katy gone with another man he'd find them and kill them.

'When you're not prating you're sleeping or daydreaming. Up,' said Mike, 'the siesta's over. I feel them vibrations, they're coming from you, tingling up my arms and legs. It's your luck – can't you feel it? Isn't it telling you to get back there and dig deep?'

'I feel nothing, only tired,' said Jamsie.

They carried down a cradle and rocked it, then another and another. Jamsie's hand was bleeding; the water washed the blood into the gravel, ore and sand, it clung in places like rubies.

'Jesus, Jesus Christ!' Mike was screaming. 'Jesus man, look at that. We've found it. Look, man, look! Chunks of it, lumps of it! Gold! I told you, didn't I? I felt your vibrations. Whoopee!' He shouted and flung his hat in the air.

Jamsie looked at Mike in astonished disbelief and then at the ore left in the cradle, threaded with ribbons of gold. 'It's a lot,' he said and his voice was quaking. 'Dust is all I've seen before – what'll we do with it?'

'First of all, say nothing to anyone. I think this is a big haul and we're only at the beginning of it. Man,' Mike said, throwing his arms round Jamsie, 'we're going to be rich.'

They'd hit a seam. For the rest of the day they brought out lumps, nuggets and gold-studded lumps of ore.

'How much do you think is there?' Jamsie asked Mike when they were back in the shack.

'Hard to say, the price fluctuates – but eighteen, maybe twenty. Thousands, of course!'

Jamsie could feel the madness Mike had described take hold of him. He was rich. He could go out tonight and buy up the bar, buy up the women. There was one he had often fancied. A dark, plump girl with dimples who wore a red dress. It was so long since he'd had a woman. Only one, only one since Katy. On the railroad. He never knew her name, he couldn't remember what she looked like. The girl in the red dress had sized him up. He knew. Knew her thoughts. Not bad-looking – but no money. In the mining towns you got nothing without money. He had money now.

As if reading his mind Mike said, 'Is the madness at you already?'

'I wouldn't mind a celebration, we've earned it.'

'We have but not yet. Before giving the game away we'll register the claim. The stories are true about claim-jumping, men being murdered before they register. Keep a silent tongue and behave as if nothing had happened.'

It was a terrible anti-climax. All the years, the disappointments, the back-breaking work and he couldn't go out and celebrate. Once upon a time, he thought, he'd have ignored such caution as Mike advised. But Mike knew the ropes. He'd abide by them.

The next day, while Mike went to register the claim and have the gold assayed, Jamsie dug alone. An idea was forming in his mind. He hated California, mining and everything that went with it: the girl in the red dress and her likes wouldn't give you the time of day without seeing the colour of your money. He had come to find gold and he'd found it. He was going home.

' 'Tis signed and sealed and tonight we'll eat steak and drink whiskey. Me oul son didn't I say you'd bring me luck.'

'How much was it worth?'

'Nineteen thousand dollars – nine and a half each – and that's without today's diggings.'

'Nine and a half thousand dollars! Jesus, it's a fortune.'

'A drop in the ocean compared to what's coming.'

'I'm going home,' said Jamsie.

'Of course you are.'

'I mean now, tomorrow.'

'You can't – you've got a goldmine with millions to come out of it!'

'Still, I'm going tomorrow with my share. That's the way I am. That's how I do things.'

'Well I remember – a dollar seventy-five to take you to California. But this is different. There's a fortune here – you can't walk out on that. It's the excitement. It affects men in different ways.'

'I'm serious, Mike. Do what you like – if there's more to come for me you'll see to it.'

'But why, Jamsie?' Mike asked when he saw that Jamsie's mind was made up.

'Because I know myself. The first thing I thought about when I knew we had money was her in the red dress. One taste of her and money to splash around and I'd be done for. I know what I'm like. I'd finish up like you the first time – with one hand as long as another.'

Mike pleaded, 'Give it a week, get used to the idea of having gold then decide. Ah, don't go. You're like my own son. I'd trust you with my life.'

'Don't make it hard for me, Mike. I've never known a man I liked or trusted as much, either. Jasus, you'll have me crying in a minute. Mike, I've two sons, daughters and a wife. I could pass them children in the street and not know them. And Katy – well gold or no gold maybe she won't have me. I was a bastard. Ah, sure you know all about it and you know what I'm trying to say. All right?'

'All right,' said Mike. 'Maybe you're doing the right thing. In any

322

case, the mine's as much yours as mine and half of what comes out of it.'
They shook hands on that.

Chapter Nine

Mary Kate when she heard who was coming to supper said, 'Oh no, we can't have him – he owns slaves.'

'He does not,' said Katy, not over-concerned by Mary Kate's remark. For though her head was filled with ideas of what was right and wrong she was a kind, well-mannered child who wouldn't dream of saying anything to hurt or offend a person.

As Bridget wouldn't be home she'd cook meat loaf again. The others hardly noticed what they ate unless one got a smaller serving than another. There was none of the nervousness about her that she had felt when Peader first came long ago. No embarrassment about the shabbiness of the room. Only joy that someone she knew so well, someone she was so at home with, someone who brought joy into her life was coming.

Thomas kept his promise and came home not long before Peader arrived. After the introductions and Peader's surprised exclamations at how much they had grown, how much they had changed, there was an awkward silence which Katy tried to fill with reminiscences of Kilgoran. She could have killed Mary Kate for sitting like a dummy. She had wanted to show her off. Bridget would have had plenty to say, she thought and again attempting to get a conversation going she said to Peader, 'I think it was you put the idea of hats into Bridget's head.'

'Me?' said Peader, looking puzzled.

'When you came to see us years ago you brought her a model shop full of hats and bonnets, d'ye not remember?'

'To tell you the truth I do not,' he said.

Mary Kate said, 'Bridget's a great mimic,' and Katy thought, Thank God she's found her tongue.

'She tells us stories about the customers. You'd die laughing to hear them. They're nearly all Irish who've got on. And they put on the talk – trying to be American. They come in looking for a special bonnet or hat. Bridget takes them off. They're all genteel to begin with – until they can find nothing to suit them. They're nearly all fat and their topknots and buns padded and pinned. The shop's very small and they get in a state and look a sight. Sweating and the hair coming undone, the accents slipping and the brogue coming out.' Mary Kate started laughing and couldn't stop. Tears poured down her cheeks. 'I'm thinking,' she said when she regained control, 'I'm thinking about Mrs Ryan,' and off she went into another kink of laughing. 'One day, after trying on hundreds of hats, Madame Renée brought another which fell down over Mrs Ryan's face, and she shouted out, ' "Is it me arse or me head you were trying to fit." '

Everyone laughed and Peader said Mary Kate wasn't behind the door when it came to mimicry. Katy added that it was far from milliners Mrs Ryan had been reared. The ice was broken and now you couldn't stop the talking.

Thomas admitted to liking working at the docks. He loved the sea. He'd like to be a sailor. And Katy thought how little you knew your children. Never had she known about his liking for the sea. Now Danny, yes Danny and the river and the books from David. The suppers they'd had in Gramercy Park . . . Stop it, she told herself – stop comparing the past to the present. Listen to Thomas. Stop wool-gathering.

'I remember on the ship watching the sailors climbing the ropes. Up and up they went, so fast as if it was easy. One fellow was quicker than all the others.'

'You couldn't remember much,' said Katy, 'half an hour was all we were allowed up and 'twas years ago.' She had an uneasy feeling.

'I do remember it. The sailor's name was Larry – he got drowned, thrown over the side. He was going to marry Eileen.'

'Thomas – you're making things up.'

'I'm not,' said Thomas. 'I remember him. Eileen used to cry about him and the two of you were always talking.'

'Well,' Katy had to admit, 'part of it is true. Larry was going to marry Eileen. But he drowned, that's all.'

Thomas shrugged. 'I'm not sure about the rest, maybe I imagined that.'

Thank God for that, Katy thought. All the years, all the times she had tried to protect her children's innocence. Careful when and where she spoke. Never realising how much they overheard. Not that it would matter now, not with Thomas anyway. He was a man. All the same she was glad he didn't seem to know about Terence McCabe's part in Larry's death. That was something too from the past that was better left buried.

There was another revelation. Danny was interested in Ireland, past and present. Katy listened mesmerised as he talked to Peader. Danny who, like the others seemed to go into a trance when she recalled the Hunger, evictions, bad landlords and all the injustice, was now talking about the Corn Laws, Daniel O'Connell, the Young Irelanders and the Fenians. And had anyone asked her what Danny read she'd have said unhesitatingly – books about whales and the sea.

Peader was promising to send him pamphlets and periodicals, keep him up to date about Ireland.

Katy saw Danny's rapt expression. You, she thought, that hardly saw the sky over it, that wrapped up in Ireland. You, that were an infant in my arms on the quayside in Kinsale when Father Bolger tried to imprint on Thomas' mind why we had to leave our home. An infant – and it's you, not him, that has the interest.

Such an evening it was. So much talk, so much good humour, so easy were the children with Peader, so lovely was it when her eyes met his and smiled.

Peader brought up the question of slavery and his abomination of it so that Mary Kate was able to voice her similar views. Katy felt proud of her. How much she knew. How she could converse with Peader about the coming election and Abraham Lincoln's chances of becoming President. She wished the evening would never end.

But all too soon Thomas became fidgety and made an excuse for leaving. Danny asked if he could go down and play and Mary Kate remembered a book she wanted to borrow from a friend.

And they were alone and suddenly Katy felt shy and couldn't think what to talk about to break the sudden silence. Peader spoke first, telling her what a lovely family she had. What a wonderful job she had made of rearing them on her own. And she remembered that she hadn't asked if he and Charlotte had children. He told her they had lost one and she said she was very sorry. There was another silence before he spoke again.

'Katy,' he asked, 'I was wondering do you ever go out?'

'I do,' she said, 'for my messages, to the Chapel, to Mary's.'

'I mean outside the neighbourhood.'

'Not for years. I did when I worked and years ago me, Eileen and Mary sometimes went up town. The laughs we used to have looking in the shop windows, planning what we'd buy when we got rich in America.' She smiled as she spoke.

'And what did you plan to buy?' he asked.

'A fine bed which I bought – much good did it do me. And there was a chain with an amber stone – I had my heart set on that.'

Knowing Jamsie and his plamais he could guess why the necklace would have appealed to her. It was the sort of thing Jamsie would have said. 'Katy, your eyes are the colour of amber.' They were too, he was always aware of their unusual beautiful colour back in the days when he was courting her, but could never have brought himself to comment on them.

He had only asked if she ever left the neighbourhood for the sake of something to say. Now, he thought – why not take her out of it? Without considering the whys and wherefores he asked, 'Will we go somewhere for the day?'

'I couldn't. I have too much to do.'

'One day – could you not manage that?'

One whole day away from the laundrying, cooking and cleaning, never mind that she'd have to do them on the double, one whole day with nothing to do in Peader's company.

'Wouldn't you like to?' Peader prompted, knowing she was weighing up the idea.

'If I could manage it I'd love to. Where would we go?'

Not knowing New York well Peader couldn't immediately think of anywhere. Then he remembered Jacques on Staten Island and his open invitation. 'I have a friend, I mentioned him before, Jacques Demart. He has a house on Staten Island – we could take the ferry there.'

'That's where the ship stopped when we were coming in. I was that frightened they'd find something wrong with us. Staten Island, I have always wanted to go there. Once Jamsie and I talked about visiting it.'

'Well, will you come then?'

'I will.'

'That's great. We'll go the day after tomorrow. I'll come for you at ten o'clock.'

'No, don't do that. Don't come when I'm here on my own. The neighbours would talk. New York or Kilgoran it's all the same. I'll meet you at Canal Street.'

'You will come? You're not just agreeing to get rid of me?'

Indignantly Katy replied, 'If I wanted to get rid of you, sure don't I know you well enough to be straight.'

He kissed her cheek. 'Don't come down, I know my way.'

It was still light and there were boys and youths in the street. Peader saw Danny playing with a ball, but Danny didn't see him, nor he a youth who detached himself from the group and followed him, getting a cab as he did to his hotel. There the youth got into talk with a porter, a young fellow who'd once lived in the neighbourhood.

Money from the supply for expenses provided by Kelly changed hands and the next day, Terence knew Katy's visitor was Irish, from Virginia and could afford to stay in a hotel. Not the doctor, then. A relation? Somehow he didn't think so. He'd fish from Bridget on Sunday. In the meantime, whenever that one put her foot outside the door she'd be dogged.

She altered the dress she had worn to David's for supper, the one that was the colour of a nutmeg. Perhaps, she thought, it's too dressy for daytime but there was nothing else. It was definitely too heavy for the time of year, she'd be roasted. She was surprised to find when she tried it on that the waist and bust were tight. God knows it's not from all the feeding or lack of exercise. Like a skeleton I should be, she thought as she pondered how to alter it. Age, that's what it was, it didn't always leave you withered – sometimes you fell into flesh. But all these gloomy thoughts she'd banish. She felt young again, alive, thrilled and excited, like a young girl preparing to meet her lover.

She let out the side seams and carefully cutting off a pocket and sewing the welt so it wouldn't be noticed that once it had been an opening, she inserted a gusset under each arm – and the dress fitted. She was pleased with how she looked.

Before they left for school she told Mary Kate and Danny she'd be out at lunchtime, that she was going to Staten Island with Peader. Their lunch would be left out and there'd be something for Thomas too, for she never knew from day to day if Thomas might tire of the docks and come in early.

Like an excited girl she set off to meet Peader. She met none of the neighbours, for the good living wouldn't be back from daily Mass, and those tied down with babies, or drunk the night before wouldn't be about yet. She was glad – there'd have been talk and curiosity as to where she was going on a weekday all dressed up. The man with the fruit barrow let her get to the corner before having her followed.

Although she was in plenty of time she wanted to hurry. To start the wonderful day. To see Peader again. There'd be so much to talk about. She felt marvellous and happy and smiled at anyone who glanced in her direction.

Peader watched her approach and wondered how he had ever let her go. She was so beautiful, so good, so wholesome. Such an air about her, the way she walked, held her head. A queenly woman.

She saw him and her heart raced. It was like long ago and she going to meet him. Did her heart race then, really, did she feel this excited? Or was time making the memory so. Anyway, what did it matter. They were going for a day out, they'd have a gorgeous time.

They said hello at the same time, then were flustered and tongue-tied until Peader regained his composure. 'We'll get a cab to the ferry,' he said decisively.

Katy couldn't look enough to see enough. She wanted this day imprinted on her memory forever. Her head turned from side to side looking at people, at buildings, then back to Peader.

She was cooler now, with the breeze coming off the water fanning her cheeks. The ferry was crowded so she and Peader stood close together. She was conscious of the fact that his body was touching hers and felt a guilty sense of pleasure.

They disembarked and without thinking, she took his arm and he pressed it to his side. Her head was light from the sun and her happiness. She was going to his friend's house. It would be nice to sit in a garden, move into the shade, have tea, but she hoped they wouldn't stay too long. She wanted part, most of this day to be spent alone with Peader.

They arrived at the house. It was such an imposing house, Katy thought, and hoped the friend wouldn't be too grand, and she in her heavyweight dress and with rough red hands.

A black woman opened the door. Peader said who he was and the woman beamed and asked them in. Mr Demart, she told them, was away in Europe, but she had instructions that Mr Daly was always to be made welcome. 'Always,' she said. 'For years and years I've waited for Mr Daly and his wife to come.'

She showed them into the drawing room and said she'd bring refreshments. She came back with a tray of tea and a pitcher of lime juice, and said that today she had planned to visit a relation who was sick. If she made lunch would it be all right for her go?

'Of course,' Peader said. 'We shouldn't have come unexpectedly. Please don't bother to cook anything, something cold will do fine.'

'Has Jacques got a wife?' Katy asked. Peader said no, he'd never married.

While they drank Peader became very serious-looking, reminding Katy of how he looked when he talked about politics. She hoped he wouldn't.

'Your Thomas is a fine lad.'

Thank God, Katy said to herself, he can talk all he likes about the children.

'I'm glad he has a liking for the sea. You should encourage him to be a sailor.'

'Why?' asked a puzzled Katy.

'Do you read the papers?'

'I used to, the papers and books, too.' She thought about the library in Gramercy Park. 'Why do you ask?'

'There's going to be a war between the North and South and the young men . . .'

'Peader Daly, not another word,' she said and put her hand across his lips. 'Not a single word.' She saw the back of her hand, the coarse red skin. Her fingers were rough and the palm calloused, also the fingers that were laid across Peader's mouth. He'd be aware of them. She would remove them. But before she could, Peader had caught hold of her wrist and touched the hand himself while still keeping hold of it, then he kissed each finger in turn and the red roughened back.

It made her want to cry, the tenderness of what he had done. 'I love your hands,' he said. 'They're beautiful hands.'

The maid came then and took away the tray, reminding them that their lunch was laid out and she was going now. She wouldn't be back until evening, she added.

'Will we go in the garden?' asked Katy, just for the sake of something to say. She didn't want to move from beside Peader on the sofa. She was overcome with a tiredness that was pleasant.

'First I want to give you something, a little present,' and he took from his pocket a flat wrapped package.

'For me?'

'For you, open it.'

Inside the paper was a red velvet box and inside the box on a mount of white satin shone a gold chain with an amber stone hanging from its centre.

She gasped. Apart from her wedding ring she had never owned a piece of jewellery. Never expected to. Knew hardly anyone who did. You looked at jewellery in shop windows and that only since she had come to New York. She took it out: the chain felt heavy in her hands, smooth, satiny-smooth and not cold like you'd expect.

'It's so beautiful. It's gorgeous. It's like the one I saw, the one I told you about and you remembered and bought this.' She studied it and was silent – then she said in a startled voice, 'But Peader, it must have cost a fortune. I couldn't take it – it wouldn't be right. Married women can't take presents like that.'

'Pretend for today you're not married. Pretend it's long ago before either of us were and put it on for me please, Katy.'

She was dreaming again. All this was a lovely dream, this room with its soft chairs and sofas, the smell of roses coming in through the open window, Peader leaning close to her, so close she could see herself in his eyes. 'I'll pretend,' she whispered. 'For today I'll pretend we're not married.'

'I love you, Katy. I've always loved you.'

'Ah no, Peader, don't say that. We were pretending but only about the necklace, don't spoil it.' But as she spoke the chain was slipping from her hands which were trembling, and she couldn't look away from Peader, though reason told her she should. Told her she should get up from the sofa, break this spell that was casting itself about her. Making her want to believe that she and Peader loved each other. He was so close, he was so lovely, she was so starved of love, of kindness, of affection. 'Peader,' she said, 'oh Peader,' and her arms went round him and he kissed her and she responded with all the longing that had been with her through the days and nights of her desertion.

Without speaking a word they rose and with their arms around each other, sometimes stopping to kiss they went through the strange house opening doors, climbing stairs until they found a room with a bed in it.

Partly-undressed they lay and made love. And when it was finished, fleetingly she thought of the sin she had committed before putting it out of her mind. She couldn't connect sin with something so wonderful, not now, not at this moment when she felt so loved, so beautiful, so young, so happy.

And then she felt hungry and said so. 'She said there was food, the black woman. Will we have some?'

Her hair had come undone, and Peader ran his hands through it. 'Have you no soul? Food, after such a feast,' he said and kissed her lips tenderly.

'Food,' she said, pushing him away and making to get out of the bed.

'No. Stay there, lie against the pillows, like that.' He piled pillows behind her and arranged her hair round her. 'Stay there and don't move and I'll bring the food to you.'

When he went she took off the rest of her clothes and then rearranged herself against the pillows.

He brought back a tray with cold chicken and tomatoes, strawberries, cream and wine. 'A feast,' he said, and he poured the wine and sat on the bed and fed her titbits and dangled strawberries over her mouth, touching her lips, teasing her with the fruit.

331

'Katy,' he said, when the food and wine was finished. 'We have to talk, there's so much I want to say.'

'No, no talking, no saying anything, not now. Come back to me, come back to bed.' She was lightheaded with wine and happiness, and still hungry for him.

He turned his back on her and stripped, sat on the bed before taking off his drawers and manoeuvred himself under the sheet so his nakedness wasn't completely exposed and she smiled at his modesty. He lay down and she bent over him studying his face, his skin that was no longer so fair – a golden brown now from all the years of sun. She fingered it, tracing his features, and she heard Bridget's voice, 'He has eyes like a cat.' They were green, truly green eyes. 'I love you,' she said. 'Maybe I always have. Maybe . . .'

He pulled her onto him and crushed her mouth with his. And their loving took a long, long time and she never wanted it to end. They slept in each other's arms.

She woke and was alone. Startled, she sat up for a moment, not knowing where she was. As she remembered, Peader came into the room fully dressed. She clutched the sheet, pulling it up to cover her breasts.

He sat on the bed. 'Will you come again tomorrow?' His fingers stroked her shoulder.

'Not tomorrow. I couldn't come two days in a row, it wouldn't be fair on the children.'

'Will you come again, Katy?'

Unhesitatingly she said, 'Yes.'

'Thursday at the same time and the same place?'

'Yes,' she said, holding up her face for his kiss, then she saw on the dressing table the ormolu clock and the time. 'Sacred Heart of Jesus, Danny will have been home this long time.' Frantically, she pulled on her own clothes. 'By the time we get the ferry and then a cab to Canal Street, it'll be all hours. I must hurry, Peader.'

On the ferry they leant close to each other and held hands. She was torn in two, not wanting to leave him but desperately worried about Danny. In the cab Peader said, 'Katy, this has been the most wonderful day of my life. I love you, please come again on Thursday.'

'I'll come,' she promised.

She rushed all the way home, soaked in sweat and with a stitch in her side from the rushing. The kitchen was empty, the three plates in the wire meat-safe untouched. Where were they? Something had happened to Danny and Mary Kate. All sorts of dreadful visions came before her mind: Danny dragged out of the river again, his body in the morgue, Mary Kate there waiting for her to come. She had him dead and buried and then heard his voice and Mary Kate's and them running up the stairs. The guilt and fears left her heart.

'Where were you? What did you do for food?'

'We bought some with the money Uncle Peader gave us.'

'And Mary Kate let me go to her friends. You look nice Mom, real pretty.'

'God bless you,' Katy said and ruffled his hair. 'You can eat what's there as well.'

They were home safe and she relaxed, changed her dress, hung it up carefully for Thursday. She looked in the mirror: she appeared different, softer-looking, prettier. Even Danny had noticed that.

'I'll lie down for a few minutes.' Her body glowed as she relived the hours spent making love to Peader, wishing they hadn't ended, longing for Thursday when she'd be in his arms once more. The years had fallen from her, she was young again. She stretched, and felt how supple she was and all because she loved and was loved.

She dozed, the voices of the children preventing her from falling into a deeper sleep. Mary Kate was saying, 'I told my teacher about Uncle Peader.'

'What did she say?' Danny asked.

'That it's a sin against God to keep slaves, and those who do will never see Heaven.'

Katy was now wide awake. She had been drowsily thinking of the house, the garden with mignonette, and roses, the smell of them drifting into the room where she and Peader lay. She was thinking of all that when Mary Kate began talking about sin. Oh God, why was it a sin? It wasn't fair. It hadn't harmed anyone. Her lovely day was ruined. The wine turned sour in her stomach. It wasn't fair. It wasn't a sin. But she knew it was. Knew she would have to confess it.

Once before, Peader had been the cause of her Confession. The priest, poor Father Bolger, had been lenient then. It was only a small sin, not like today's. That was it – she couldn't see him again. Today, it had just happened. When she set out there was no intention in her mind of committing a sin. Not even when they went to the house. But on Thursday it would be deliberate. She wouldn't go. No, definitely not. Or if she did go, not to the house. She'd go only as far as Canal Street. It wouldn't be fair not to say goodbye. Yes, she'd go to the street – there could be no harm in that.

★

She went to Canal Street on Thursday. He was waiting. The minute she saw him she knew that sin or no sin she was going all the way to Staten Island. And afterwards, after he went home she would attend to her sin.

They had the house to themselves again. This time they knew where the bedroom was and went straight to it. They made love and slept, ate and loved and slept again. Peader woke while Katy was still sleeping. Looking at her, it was as if all the years with Charlotte had never been, all the hurt and humiliations. Katy had never turned him down for Jamsie. She was his, his wife. Her hair was spread on the pillow. He saw the shadows and lines about her eyes and loved her all the more for them. They had wasted so much of their lives, so much love. They had been meant for each other. Would have had each other had he been more courageous. Well, he was now. Katy had given him that during their few days.

Katy stirred, opened her eyes and smiled at him. 'Hello,' she said, and reached for his hand.

'Katy,' he said, 'have you ever wanted to go back home?'

'Many a time, didn't I tell you the other night. But it's too late now.'

'It's never too late to do what you really want – what your heart dictates. We could go, go now, me and you together.'

She sat up, forgetting about her bare breasts.

'Go away – me and you!'

'Yes,' said Peader. 'I'll take you home. We'll go home to Ireland.'

'But we can't do that. We're both married – there's Charlotte, Jamsie.' She looked at him as if he had lost his mind.

'But Katy, Jamsie's deserted you. You said so yourself. You've put him from your mind – you told me so. And Charlotte's in love with Paul. I've left her.'

'It's spoiled,' whispered Katy. 'You spoiled the lovely dream. It could have lasted maybe for a long time. The dream is gone now. Everything is real again.'

'Oh Katy, love.' He sat on the bed. 'Katy, it wasn't a dream, it was real. For me it was real. I thought it was for you as well. I love you, Katy. Don't talk about dreams. Jamsie's gone. You put him out of your mind.'

'It was a lie. I told you lies. I thought it was true. I put Jamsie out of my mind, only he wouldn't leave my heart. I didn't know that. Not until now. Not until you spoke, until you asked me to go away with you. Can you understand that? You came at the wrong time. Oh no,' she said shaking her head, 'I didn't mean that. I'm glad you came. I'm glad we loved each other. We were sorely hurt and needed each other. But if you'd come six weeks, six months ago or if you came in six months' time it couldn't have happened. Jamsie's still here,' she touched her breast. 'He'll always be there. For a while I let myself think he wasn't. But when you asked me to go I knew the truth.'

'I know what you're trying to say but I don't understand. Our time here. You loved me then, you told me you loved me.'

'I do too, part of me will always love you, always has. You can love more than one man. I know that. But always one more than another. It's different. Like magic. I don't know why it should be. Maybe it's their smell, their taste, I don't know. Maybe it's true that God made one man for every woman. And He made Jamsie for me.'

He wanted to lay his head on her breast and cry and ask, 'Then what about me? Who did God make for me?' Instead he asked, 'But supposing Jamsie's dead.'

'He isn't. I know he isn't.'

'But just supposing – then would you take another man?'

'How, when Jamsie's still alive, can I answer that? Maybe if the man God makes for you dies, He has a second choice for you. Only then would you know.'

'Katy, Katy O'Donnell.' He called her by her maiden name. 'I love you so much. God must also make a woman for a man and He made you for me. I'd love and cherish you and your children. I'd do anything for you.'

She held out her arms. 'You're sore-hearted and in need of comfort. Come back into the bed with me. We'll make our farewell. I've sinned with you and will again for the last time. And God Who knows everything will know why.'

'Where will you go now?' she asked when they were finally parting.

'To Ireland. There's a ship in ten days. I'll never leave it again. Promise that you'll write one way or the other.'

'I will,' she promised. 'But you'll have to first, so I know where you are. Go now, and God bless you and I'll always remember this time and be grateful you made me a woman again.' Then she walked quickly away from him, her eyes blinded with tears.

Terence had careful note of all the meetings and partings, Peader's name and the hotel. He was waiting for Peader's next move, then he'd make his.

For several days Katy was sustained by the memory of her time with

335

Peader. She'd keep remembering things she had meant to say to him, questions she wanted to ask – now it was too late. And she wondered how he had spent the time waiting for his passage. Was he lonely – did he miss her?

But gradually the demands of the children and her work were eroding the memory of her stolen days of pleasure. The heat was oppressive, there were thunderstorms of such violence she feared the wrath of God and remembered she still had not made her Confession.

Sometimes, watching Thomas when he was unawares she thought of Peader's warning about war, and that Thomas should become a sailor. She supposed he meant – be a sailor, or he may be made into a soldier. But Thomas she knew would follow a drum if someone beat it. She'd let life take its course.

Chapter Ten

Jamsie arrived in New York on the day Peader sailed for Ireland. His plan to place the gold in Katy's lap had misfired. Taking Mike's advice that to travel with so much money was inviting trouble he had instead a banker's draft, and carried only a few hundred dollars.

He took a cab to Cow Lane. Hoping as he went that none of the children would be in the street, see him and run to tell Katy. He wanted to surprise her. To see her face. Then he remembered how long he had been gone – the children were grown up, they would be unlikely to recognise him.

His heart almost stopped when the cab pulled up. Where was the laundry? The lock-up shop was full of food. Katy was dead. Katy had gone away. He'd find her. Only please God, don't let her be dead. 'Who are you?' he asked belligerently of a man in the shop weighing up packets of tea.

'I might ask the same of you,' replied the man calmly.

'This was ours. It was a laundry. I'm Jamsie O'Hara, where's my wife?'

'Not here, I can tell you. She's been gone this long time.'

Jamsie grabbed hold of the man, a small person, almost lifting him off his feet. 'In the name of Jesus will you tell me where she is!'

'You're strangling me.'

'I'm sorry,' Jamsie said, releasing his hold. 'Where is she?'

'Gone back to Mulberry Street,' said the man, smoothing his ruffled clothes.

He ran all the way, bumping into the stalls, oblivious of the gossiping women on the steps who stared after him, almost knocking over the dirty ragged children. He ran to the house where they had first lived. The sight and smell of it struck him like a blow. Well, wait until he told Katy they'd move out, buy a house, start a business. He concentrated on all he could promise her. It calmed his nerves, his fear of the reception he might get. He saw no one in the hall or on the stairs.

He knocked on the door. From the room he could hear many voices. He knocked again and in a little while the door opened and Katy stood

337

there. Only it was Katy from long ago – a young girl, a beautiful young girl. 'Bridget,' he said, his voice a whisper. 'Bridget, it's me.'

'Dad, oh Dad!' she screamed and flung her arms round him. 'It's Dad,' she kept yelling, 'Look, it's Dad!'

'Let me in,' he was saying. 'Let me come in, love.'

Katy stood with a saucepan in her hand as if paralysed. She could hear his voice in between Bridget's joyful cries. Jamsie was home, he'd come back! Danny shook her, Mary Kate took the pot from her hand. 'Mom,' she said, 'go to him!'

She wiped her hands down each side of her apron and began walking to the door. He let go of Bridget and came to her. 'Oh Katy, aghoille mo croide, oh Katy girl I've missed you so.' He threw his arms round her and kissed her. But it wasn't how he'd imagined the meeting would be. Always he had thought of it being just the two of them. Not this crowd of young men and women hovering round them. Making him shy and embarrassed so that he let go of Katy.

And it wasn't how she had dreamed he would come, either. She would have been alone when his knock came – his knock to trick her and she would have opened the door to him. Been the first one to see him, embrace him, kiss him, their tears mingling as she told him how much she loved him, how she had waited, knowing that no matter how long it took he would return.

All that must wait until they were alone, in bed. In bed, what bed? There was nowhere for him to sleep.

'Say hello to your father,' Katy said, disengaging herself from his arms. 'Commere to your father, Danny.'

'I wouldn't have known you son, shake hands. And Mary Kate – you're a great girl, an O'Hara, isn't she Katy.' Thomas was the last to be greeted by his father. He stood as tall as him. Thomas remembered him vividly. Remembered him leaving, telling him to mind his mammy. He was delighted to see him but a tinge of regret was there also. He adored Katy, he hadn't minded her very well, but he had stayed. He knew that now for a long time she'd have eyes for no one except his father.

And Katy was watching Jamsie. He hadn't changed. Hadn't aged a day. The grey that she had mourned in his hair was no greyer, his face was very brown and because of that his eyes seemed a brighter blue.

When the excitement calmed she asked, 'Where were you this long time?'

'Everywhere,' he said.

'You never answered my letters,' said Bridget.

'Didn't I? Sure, I always meant to. But your mother will tell you I'm not much of a hand with the pen. Isn't that so, Katy?'

' 'Tis so,' she said. Bridget had a puss on her. God forbid she should start a contention over the letters. There was time enough for that. What mattered now was he was home.

'I was,' she said, 'dishing up when you came. Make room for your father at the table.' They sat, squashed because of the extra person. Mary Kate and Danny were shy of him, Thomas taciturn and Bridget vying with Katy for his attention.

And all the while he was wanting Katy alone. Katy in bed. Katy sitting with him when he told her about his fortune, not surrounded by this crowd of strangers. He'd get used to them. All these tall young men and women, all these Americans and them his own children. He couldn't get over it.

And the young one, Mary Kate, when she did come out of her shell capping every story he told. She knew everything about Indians and covered wagons, rattlesnakes and buffaloes. God, wasn't it awful that children ever grew up. His little babies that he could spellbind with stories, dance on his lap, ready as the meal progressed to contradict and cross-hackle.

He could hold their attention if he told about the gold – that would silence them. But he wouldn't. That was his business and Katy's only.

Katy's mind was working on sleeping arrangements. If Bridget would agree she and Mary Kate could go to Mary's for the night – then tomorrow she'd think of something else. In all the times she had imagined Jamsie's homecoming, never had she foreseen these difficulties. Time in her imaginings had stopped still. The children forever fixed at the age they were when he went away.

'Thomas,' said Jamsie, 'you and I will go out and celebrate.' Thomas said yes, and sadly Katy thought, some things never change. And Bridget was indignant at the suggestion of sleeping over at Mary's. 'It's disgraceful,' she said.

'Not half the disgrace of your father having nowhere to sleep.'

'We live like pigs,' Bridget retorted.

'May God soon send you a man to keep you in comfort then,' Katy replied with a calmness that hid her raging heart, her need to tell Bridget what she thought of her, her disappointment that on this his first night home, after all the years, all her long lonely nights, Jamsie couldn't have stayed from the saloon.

Eventually, Bridget went with Mary Kate to Mary's and Danny was left with his mother.

'Why couldn't we have all stayed in, like when Uncle Peader came to supper or at the doctor's?'

'Because your father's not like Peader or Doctor Purcell.'

'Why not?' asked Danny.

'He's not, that's why.'

'I wish he hadn't come. We were doing fine without him.'

'I wasn't, Danny, and don't you ever say that again. You'll get used to each other, he's your father and he loves you. You'll have great times together.'

To her delight he hadn't drunk too much nor stayed too long. Thomas was more at ease with him now and for a while they chatted, ate sandwiches and the coffee Katy had made. Danny sat beside her listening to the two men, his father and Thomas talking. Thomas with sorrow about the sailing ships that were being replaced by steamships. Jamsie commenting that America was moving fast, everything changing, machines to do the jobs; in factories and fields, work that would have needed twenty men done by one with a machine.

Katy sent Danny to bed and soon afterwards Thomas followed him. Jamsie sighed with relief. 'I thought I'd never get you to myself. 'Tis you're the beautiful woman – in all my travels I never came across your equal.'

She believed every word he said. In a sack, pregnant in a sack, if she hadn't a hair on her head, a tooth in her head he would still find the words to make her believe she was a woman who was desired. It was part of his magic. More important than knowing where he had been, why he hadn't written, why he stayed away so long.

'Katy,' he said, in a confidential whisper. 'I've something to tell you, for your ears only. Not even the children must know for the time being. Katy, girl, get up from there and come to bed with your poor lost husband and I'll tell you the secret.'

'The Lord knows you haven't changed one bit. Ever the same thing on your mind.'

'Yerra woman would you want me different?'

'I would not, indeed.'

It was as if he had never been away. They knew each other's bodies as they knew their own. Everything took a long, lovely lingering time. This was more than a joining of their bodies. It was a holy thing, a coming together of their very being, of their souls. It was the magic. The reason for being alive, the reason she could forgive Jamsie anything. He was the man God had made for her, the other part of her.

After their love-making, with her head on his shoulder and his arm holding her to him as she held babies he told her his secret. 'We're rich,' he said, 'I found gold. 'Tis in the bank – seven thousand dollars. You'll have a house and a shop. How's that?'

'You're trying to get round me again. It's your first night home, I'd let you without the lies.'

'You're a terrible woman – here am I laying a fortune in your lap and you're making a liar of me.'

'Shh,' she said, 'the children will hear your secret.'

'That's right, mock me now, you were ever so.'

And she smiled in the darkness at how often they'd argued in bed. Him going sulky. If he hadn't a penny it was grand to have him beside her. 'Go on then,' she said. 'Tell me all about it.'

He did and she was convinced and delirious with joy. Wanting to go out first thing in the morning and begin changing their life. 'No,' he said. 'I've got sense now, we'll wait and watch and make the right moves, but by Christmas we'll be out of here.'

She saw the sense of it. 'Yes,' she said, 'we'll wait, but something we'll have to do is fix sleeping arrangements for the boys. That we'll do first thing.'

He kissed her goodnight, they shifted to their comfortable sleeping positions, he with his back to her, her thighs tucked under his, fitting together like a long and a short spoon and soon were sound asleep.

Terence McCabe had all he wanted to know and a bonus – Katy's husband was home. On the next Sunday in Kelly's he was more demonstrative towards Bridget. Holding her hands and kissing her cheek. And announcing that they were to be married soon.

She almost fainted with emotion. This called for more of his attention. He laid her on the sofa and with shaking fingers undid the top button of her dress. When she had recovered enough he said, 'When you go home tell your mother and father. 'Tis not a secret any more.'

She daren't ask him why. Maybe, she thought, he had been waiting for her father to come. But her father might never have come. Still, that's what it had to be. Terence knew everything and everyone – he could have found out her father's movements,

She had him to herself again in the morning when the children were gone. She waited on him, making more tea, milking and sugaring it, stirring it before handing it to him. He talked about the places he had been, the things he had seen, about Mike and the snakes. But never once did he mention why he had stayed away so long, why he hadn't written. And she didn't ask. For the present she was content to have him home.

'Did Mike stay on?'

'He did. There's more gold. We're partners. We could finish up millionaires.'

She laughed at the idea.

'That's the truth,' he said.

'Oh, I believe you. I'm laughing because yesterday I didn't know where today's dinner was coming from and now we're talking about millionaires.'

'It was hard for you?'

'Most of the time. For a while I had a good job.' She told him about housekeeping for David and a lie as to why she had left. And remembered she hadn't mentioned Peader's visit and did with her back to him in case something might show on her face. She also remembered that the necklace must be hidden until one day when she would pretend that Eileen had sent it.

'How was Peader – still the gentleman planter? Begor, his time is running out, I can tell you. Before long he'll wish he'd never set foot in the South.'

'He's left, he's gone back to Ireland. That's why he came to see us, to say goodbye.'

'And was she with him, Miss Charlotte herself?'

'They've parted.'

'What's that you said? Why don't you sit down, sit where I can look at you while you're talking to me.'

'I will in a minute. I said they've parted. She's with Paul, the man who owns the plantation.'

'I'm not surprised. Peader didn't have what it takes to keep a woman. All the same I'm sorry. It must be a terrible thing for a man to lose his wife.'

'Very sad,' said Katy as she came and sat where he could see her. And she thought – if only you knew. Thank God we haven't the power to see into another's mind. You'd kill me. And yet she didn't regret the days spent with Peader. She would never regret them – only the false hopes she had raised in him. And because she couldn't regret them she couldn't confess them.

They had both been rejected, herself and Peader. They were hurt and lonely people and had comforted each other. She couldn't believe that was a sin. Though maybe one day in the future, when she was dying, if God gave her time and a priest to hand, she might then.

He took her back to bed and they stayed there until lunchtime. 'What'll I do about the washing?' she asked, yawning and stretching, not wanting to stir.

'Send it back – you're out of business, we're rich.'

And for the first time the money became real to her. 'Imagine – I could do that! Take it back, say – sorry, I'm not taking in laundry any more. But I won't. They'll be wanting their clean clothes.'

'You're not to touch it. I didn't come all the way from California to find you over a tub.'

'Ah, Jamsie.'

'No,' he said.

'Well then, I'll tell you what I'll do. There's a woman down the street who'd be glad of the money – I'll get her to do it.'

'Do that, then dress yourself up, we're going out – up town and I'll buy you whatever you want.'

Katy found a decent lodging for Danny and Thomas, explaining to the motherly Irishwoman that it would only be for a little while. They were going to buy a house, and the boys would come home to eat. 'But for the sake of decency, now that my husband's home they have to sleep somewhere else.'

Once they were fixed comfortably she set out to enjoy spending some of Jamsie's fortune. She bought new beds and bedding, clothes for the boys and Mary Kate. Visited Mary and Günter and brought them presents, and one for Kathleen and her new brother Seamus, too. Never in her life had she had so much leisure or money – it was like living in a fairy tale.

Walking through the streets holding Jamsie's arm, her purse full of money, she was able to buy steak and chops, good food, food she could cook quickly. Was all this real, or was it only a lovely dream, a lovely fairy story which in a minute would vanish? When convinced that it was real she thanked God for the blessings He was showering on her.

Chapter Eleven

Bridget waited a few days before telling her news. Terence didn't expect word from her parents before Sunday. She had the rest of the week . . .

On the Friday, as Katy dipped fillets of haddock into salted flour and waited for the pan to heat, Bridget came and stood before her. 'I'm courting, Mom.'

Mary Kate and Danny sniggered. 'Pay no attention to them, love. And who are you courting, someone we know? Did you hear that, Jamsie? Bridget's courting.' Katy was all smiles. In her own happiness she was happy for everyone. Especially her lovely Bridget. The bad humour she'd been in, she should have known, suspected there was a man behind it.

'I don't think so,' said Bridget. 'His name's Terence.'

'Terence,' said Katy, putting two fillets into the spitting fat. 'Isn't that a nice name. You'll bring him round, of course. You'd like to meet Bridget's young man, Jamsie.'

'Of course I would,' said Jamsie. 'We'll have to know who's walking Bridget out.'

Katy with a knife loosened the fish that had begun sticking to the pan. 'What's Terence's other name? I might know his mother.'

'McCabe, Terence McCabe.'

Katy poked furiously at the haddock; the fat spat and burned her hand. She ignored the searing pain. There was more than one Terence McCabe in New York. Please God there were dozens of Terence McCabes.

'He's a bit older than me.'

Katy's heart shrivelled like the fish in the pan. 'He hasn't got red hair?'

'Kind of,' said Bridget.

'What does he do for a living?' Please God, let him be a fireman, a policeman, an idler – let him be anything or anyone except him.

'He's rich, he owns property – things like that.'

'You're to have nothing to do with him. Nothing – you're never to see him again!'

'Mom – what's got into you all of a sudden? You know nothing about him! What do you mean, I'm not to see him?'

'Never mind what I mean – you're not, that's all.'

Bridget screamed, 'I hate you. I knew you'd be like this. I knew it.'

'Bridget,' Jamsie called. 'Don't talk to your mother like that.'

The pan overheated and caught fire, Bridget ran crying from the room. The room was full of smoke. Thomas covered the pan with the tin lid of a bucket and Katy sat down with her head in her hands and moaned like a wounded creature.

Jamsie gave Mary Kate some money. 'Take Danny out and buy some fruit, go for a walk.' Then he came to Katy, knelt in front of her and asked, 'What is it? What happened? One minute you were delighted and the next . . .'

'It's him. Didn't you hear the name? Him from the ship – Terence McCabe, God blast him and he wants Bridget. Oh Jamsie, 'tis him.'

'Stop crying. Thomas, make your mother a cup of tea. Come on now, Katy. Tell me about it.'

'Tell you?' she said, raising her head. 'What is there to tell that you don't already know? You're to find out where he lives, do you hear me. Find him and tell him. Find him and tell him to keep away from Bridget.'

'Ah, listen Katy. All that happened a long time ago. And in any case, there was no proof. Mary Callinan and the women's gossip – that was all. He was very young – maybe he's a decent man now.'

'Decent? He's evil, he was always so. Did you never look him in the face. He's mixed up in everything. You've been away, you don't know. How d'ye think he got his money? Ask anyone! You're to go and tell him to leave Bridget alone.'

He wouldn't, she knew it. Not a week back and he was letting her down on this above all. His own daughter and that – *thing*. Him with his evil influence. Spoiling the homecoming. Making her think badly of Jamsie already.

'What did he do, Mom?' Thomas asked. Katy told him. 'But like Dad said – was it proved?'

'Oh, not you Tom, not you too. Don't you make me out to be mad.'

'I didn't mean like that – 'tis only you can't go laying down the law if you're not certain. And what about Bridget, if she really likes him.'

'But Thomas, forget about the ship, Eileen, Larry. You know what he's like now. He put us out of Cow Lane. He'd hang his own mother if they paid him.'

Thomas shrugged. 'I suppose you could say he's a businessman.'

345

'Look, all you're doing is making things worse. Go out will you, leave me with your father.' When he was gone Katy said, 'Jamsie, you've got to do something. I'm right about Terence McCabe. You mustn't let him have Bridget – he'll destroy her.'

'Aghoille, aren't you being hasty? You have them married already. All right,' he said, raising a hand when he saw she was about to flare up again. 'I'll talk to Bridget and see what comes of that. I'm going out now for half an hour.'

Much good that would do, Katy thought, he might as well talk to the wall. Once Bridget was set on something, more than talk would be needed to change her mind. And Jamsie – what was the matter with him? 'Nothing was ever proved', indeed. But he knew well the girl was raped and at the time knew the culprit and the thing he'd said then –that Terence didn't like girls but that didn't mean he had no need for them. And he'd let that man marry his daughter.

She vented her anger on the pots and pans, banging and rattling them. Scraping out the burned fish, plunging the frying pan into hot water with washing soda, only then noticing the burn on her arm. Furious with Thomas, Thomas all of a sudden defending businessmen.

Bridget went straight from the house to Kelly's, where in floods of tears she demanded to see Terence. He wasn't there. Didn't she know, Mrs Kelly asked, he was busy with the Election coming up in November. 'But he'll be in later, so sit down you and rest. Will I bring in your jewellery box?'

'Yes,' said Bridget and consoled herself with her rings and bracelets until Terence returned.

'Me and your mother fell out a long time ago – on the ship coming over. We had words about the bunk spaces. Your mother's the fierce woman – she gave me a tongue-lashing. Though at the time maybe I deserved it. I've seen her a few times since and she never let on. And then there was the place in Cow Lane – but sure there was nothing personal in it. An investment, that's all it was. Your mother's a hard woman, unforgiving. Do you see now why I wanted it kept secret till your father came home?'

'You knew, then?'

'I know everything. You go home now and do no more rowing. She'll come round. We'll be married before the Election. I'll swim the neighbourhood in whiskey and beer. There'll be more handouts for them that's in the need before our wedding. And in return the party won't be forgotten and when Lincoln's in, neither will Terence

McCabe.' He kissed her cheek. 'You'll go home in a cab tonight – no more secrets.'

Where was she, Katy kept wondering as she watched the clock. It was nearly midnight. Never had she been out till this hour. Something must have happened to her. She was dead in a dark alley.

'She's asleep in Mary's,' Jamsie had reassured her.

'Well, why don't you make sure? She knew about the room for Thomas and Danny – that she didn't have to go to Mary's.'

'She forgot, that's all.'

'Put my mind at ease and go round.'

'And drag them out of their sleep? That man's a baker – up at daybreak.'

'Shh, listen, the footsteps, d'ye hear them? Thank God 'tis her. Talk to her the minute she comes in.'

'We were worried about you. It's very late.'

'Sorry, Dad.' She avoided looking at Katy. 'I'm tired, I'm going to bed.'

'Not yet. Sit down, love. I want to talk to you about this young man. He was on the ship. I remember him well.'

'And?' said Bridget.

'Don't be impertinent – what I'm saying is for your own good.'

'She put you up to it, didn't she? She's jealous – she turned you against me. She hates me. I was the one who had to do everything. Run here, run there, mind Danny. And now she wants to spoil it for me and Terence. Well, she won't – she won't. We're getting married. Before Christmas we're getting married.'

'Oh no,' said Katy. 'I'll stop that. He'll never put a ring on your finger. Not him, never. I'd rather see you carried down them stairs in your coffin than marry him. I'll tell you a thing or two that'll make you change your mind about Terence McCabe.'

'I know everything. He told me. He told me about the ship. I love him. I'm going to marry him, I am, I am,' she cried.

'Go to your bed, Bridget,' said Jamsie. 'Go on, go now and no more talk. Not tonight. Go now like a good child.' When she went he said to Katy, 'And let us do the same. The poor child – you were hard on her.'

'Hard on her? I'm brokenhearted for her. I'd die if she had anything to do with him. Why won't you believe me – he'll destroy her. She's my child. My little girl, my baby. He doesn't love her. He couldn't love anyone. He's not a man – he's – oh God I don't know, he's like something out of Hell. I think he wants her because she's mine. I

347

don't understand his reasoning unless it's to punish me.'

'Ah, for the Lord's sake, Katy, now you do sound mad. Creatures out of Hell and punishing you. So he's not the man you'd have picked for Bridget. Your mother wouldn't have picked me, either. But isn't it likely he just loves Bridget because she's a beauty?'

'How little you know him. I know things inside me. When you were away and people said you were dead – I knew you weren't. And don't laugh – it's not anything to laugh at.'

'Ah, love, what can I do for you. How can I help you?'

'By going to see him and putting a stop to the business, that's how.'

He said he would, but she knew he'd find an excuse, put it on the long finger. Well, in that case she'd go herself. She lay awake half the night planning how to handle Terence McCabe. Bridget was too young for him, she'd say. They'd known each other no time. To marry so soon wouldn't be wise. And if he didn't agree, then she'd remind him of the girl who was raped, Larry's drowning and threaten to tell Bridget. If that didn't work she'd bring the priest on him, so she would.

It was morning and Jamsie brought her a cup of tea in bed. 'I let you sleep on. They've all gone – and this came for you, it's from San Francisco. Who do you know there?'

'No one,' she said, not even curious, for her mind was already thinking about Bridget and Terence McCabe. But after opening it her expression changed. She smiled and said, 'Jamsie, it's from Eileen! Oh, isn't that the grand thing, listen and I'll read it.'

No. 5, Goldcrest Mansions

Dear Katy,

At long last a letter. What do you think of the fancy address? All mine, or will be when it's paid for.

Me and the girls – five of us are in business. Paddy was a let-down in more ways than one. He developed a roving eye and it wasn't roving in my direction so I said to myself, 'Eileen O'Flaherty, you'll never see forty again: you've a head on you – use it. You've earned money and saved money – what do you need a man for?' So I threw him over – and off I went to San Francisco. Me and the girls do entertaining and so far the men and the money keep rolling in.

I often think about you and Jamsie and hope he didn't stay away too long. I guess Bridget's real grown up and beautiful. Did Mary marry the baker? And if so, I wonder if they ever got round to doing it. Though by the time Mary finished the rosary the poor man would be past it.

I'd love you to write and tell me all the news. Every single thing that's happened since I went away. Remember me to everyone and in your prayers. Your true friend

Eileen

'Thank God she got sense at last,' said Katy when she finished the letter.

'You know the sort of entertaining she'll be doing?'

'I'm not a fool altogether. But married she might have been if it hadn't been for him. That letter came for a purpose. Eileen would have had a presentiment of my trouble. She wrote to give me heart in what I have to do.'

'And what's that?' asked Jamsie.

'I'll tell you when it's done. Commere,' she said, 'sit down,' and she patted the bed. 'I'm sorry it happened like this to spoil your homecoming. It would have been grand without this trouble. We'd be making our plans for the new house and our little business. And talking of our hopes and remembering home, instead of having our hearts scalded.'

'It might all blow over. After all, weren't you promised to Peader and didn't that blow over.'

'Peader,' she said. 'You reminded me of something he told me about your brother Johnny. He's dead, the Lord have mercy on him.' And she told him why and where he'd died.

'The Lord have mercy on him, he had a quick end. I wonder if he ever gave a thought to poor Padraig.'

'I wouldn't say Johnny ever gave a thought to anyone but himself.' And in saying it she thought about Bridget, how over the years she had changed, become self-centred and the same thought occurred to her about Jamsie. Wasn't it the same lack in him that kept him away for all the years. There was the O'Hara drop in them.

Then she thought: God forgive me for being such a bad-minded woman. It's the evil influence of that creature affecting my mind. Isn't Bridget my child, a lovely soft innocent girl with a girl's careless whims toward her mother and her head turned by him. And thoughtless too is Jamsie, but not an ounce of badness in him. Get up out of the bed and put an end to this thing that's bringing disharmony into your home.

'Are you going out?' asked Jamsie, when she was washed and dressed.

'I'm going for my messages and I'll call in to Mary's.'

'Right, so. I'll ramble out myself later.'

As if it was of no consequence she introduced Terence's name into her conversation with Mary and before they'd finished their cups of tea she knew where he was to be found.

'He has an office nowadays. Before, you saw him in Kelly's or did your business with Kelly as the go-between. Now it's an office and two hours a day he's there – in the mornings. Ten till twelve. It does be crowded, I believe, with them that want favours. He's a great Party man. People speak highly of him.'

'Them that gets his favours,' Katy said. No doubt Mary had been at the receiving end, for Kathleen had found a teaching job easy to come by, she thought. She told Mary about the letter from Eileen.

'So she got to San Francisco – and did she become a great singer?' Mary asked, with her usual impatience to know the end of a story.

'She didn't and she didn't marry Paddy. He was no good – you were right. But she's happy and very comfortable – in the hotel business.'

'Isn't that great. I'm glad for her and no loss she suffered – she's well rid of him. And yourself – you're content to have Jamsie home. I used to pray for you. You're a marvellous woman, Katy and God will bless you.'

Mary was good and kind, had been a help through all the years. And Katy wished she could open her heart to her, tell her about Bridget and Terence, her intention to confront him, to put an end to his marriage plans. But Mary wouldn't understand. Mary would only see the great match, the fool Katy was for going against it. She was a kind, fat, comfort-loving woman with no doubts. As sure of her place in Heaven as she was of her next meal.

Katy said she'd better not stay too long, Jamsie wouldn't like being left. And Mary agreed. 'Will Mary Kate stay on at school now?' she asked as Katy was leaving.

'She will,' said Katy, and no more. But as soon as Jamsie gave the word she'd tell Mary about their good fortune and about Peader and Charlotte. The information would keep her going for months.

There were two rooms, one was crowded. Katy recognised some of the people waiting. Some sat silent. Others talked about what had brought them here. Landlords who wouldn't do repairs, broken fire escapes, rats in the rooms, holes on the stairs. It was time something was done. Time the man on the next floor was evicted. He had a pig in the room.

350

Katy concentrated on what she would say and wished Jamsie was with her. Wished Jamsie had taken this in his own hands. Wished that Terence McCabe was struck down dead before she had to look on his face, argue, fight, beg if necessary to keep Bridget from him.

He hadn't expected her to come so soon. 'Mrs O'Hara,' he said and held out his hand. She ignored it. He didn't care. She was here, she'd come to defeat and humiliate him again – so she thought. 'Sit down,' he said. She did because her legs were shaking. 'Well now, what can I do for you?' From force of habit his voice was pleasing, his manner implying, 'I'm here to help you. You're one of us, we look after our own.'

'You're to leave Bridget alone.'

'I'm going to marry Bridget.' The statement begged the question. 'What are you going to do about it?'

'I won't let you. Bridget is only a child. You're too old for her. You've known her no time.'

'She didn't tell you? We've been seeing each other this long while.' He wanted her rattled. He watched her face, the realisation on it of Bridget's deception. He wanted her threatening.

'It was you,' she said. 'It was you with the flowers. You laid a trap for her. From the time she was a child.'

'I was courting her. A few flowers – I waited until she was a woman.'

'You,' she said. 'You and flowers and courting – what would you know about things like that. Well, you won't have her. I'll see to that. I'll stop you. I'll put an end to it. You'll never have my child. I'd rather see her dead. You won't have her.'

'I will,' he said, and Katy wanted to lift the heavy brass ink-well and crash it into his face.

'I will,' he repeated, 'and you can't stop me.'

'Oh, I can. I can so. Is your memory so short you've forgotten the ship, the girl, the girl who bit the man that raped her, your sore finger and the sailor, Larry, who was thrown overboard – blamed for what you did? Do you think any woman would marry you, would touch you, breathe the same air as you when they knew that. Do you?'

'You know nothing about me.'

'Nothing? I was there. I saw the girl. I saw your hand. I saw Larry going over the side.'

He let her talk. Let her believe she had him. 'Don't tell me I know nothing. I was there. I saw you rob and cheat. I know you. And I'll see that Bridget knows about you. If you ever as much as talk to her, look at her, I'll let her know what you are.'

351

He heard her deep sigh. Satisfaction. Victory. He let her think she had won. Let her rise from the chair, turn her back and then very quietly he said, 'And if you do, I'll tell your husband about Staten Island – times, days, dates. And I'll tell Bridget everything else is lies. You've made it all up to cover your own guilt. Who do you think she'll believe? The ship was years ago – Peader Daly was last week. You've gone a queer colour, would you like a glass of water, Mrs O'Hara?'

Katy prayed, oh please God don't let me collapse, don't let me faint, leave me the strength to get out of here. She began to walk to the door. He let her almost reach it then he spoke. 'And another thing, Mrs O'Hara – this is going to be a big happy, Catholic family wedding. I've already spoken to the priest. You'll be there, Mrs O'Hara.'

She went around in a daze and not one of the children nor Jamsie noticed. Bridget came and went. No more was said about her courting –Katy knew she was biding her time. Mary Kate, Danny and Thomas weren't interested and Jamsie thought it had blown over.

Katy contemplated it all the time, thinking about nothing else. Wondering what should she do, what could she do. Shouldn't she leave it – let Bridget get her desserts. She hated Bridget. The sly cunningness of her. All this time deceiving her behind her back, seeing him. Then she was sorry for her, loved her, pitied her for being inveigled by him. Her head turned. Her lovely girl, her lovely daughter. But at the root of all her mind-searching lay her guilt, her sin for which God was now punishing her. Had she not sinned with Peader, she could have stopped Terence. Shown him to Bridget for what he was. She could still do it. Tell Bridget, sacrifice her happiness and Jamsie's, for she never doubted but that Terence would fulfil his threat. Wasn't that what she must do? Wasn't Bridget's future – her whole life – more important than what was left of hers or Jamsie's. And her courage would rise and she'd believe that she would right this terrible wrong that was being done to her daughter.

And then the doubts set in again. Supposing she told Bridget – and Bridget confronted Terence, then he told Jamsie about Staten Island and told Bridget, too, then convinced her the stories of the sailor and the ship were lies. Lies to cover her mother's guilt, which accidentally he had discovered. Who would Bridget believe? She remembered Thomas' reaction. 'You've no proof, Mom.' Wasn't Bridget already infatuated, sure to discount what she told her. And then there was Jamsie. There would be no doubt in his mind but that Terence told the truth.

352

Bridget would marry him. And Jamsie, if he didn't kill her, would go away again and this time never come back. What a price God was exacting for her few hours of pleasure. And all the while her mind went its tortured way she cleaned the house and cooked the food. Went for her messages, went to bed with Jamsie and made love: and listened to his plans as to how the gold should be spent. No one noticed that she said less, laughed less, ate less. No one asked if she was tired or sick, or what ailed her. And so one night in bed when everyone else slept she knew there was no more she could do. She didn't want Jamsie to leave or kill her. She didn't want it known that she'd lain with Peader. Bridget was a woman, older by years than she had been when she married. She had tried and failed to protect her. Bridget must go her own way. And she must protect herself and Mary Kate and Danny. They still needed her. And protect Jamsie and keep him with her.

No one noticed when the weight lifted from her and she knew she had made the right decision.

Chapter Twelve

The announcement of Bridget's wedding coincided with the choosing of the new house and a shop fitted as a proper laundry. The house had two rooms and a kitchen and three bedrooms and a yard where one day Katy would grow flowers.

Mary congratulated Katy on Jamsie's good fortune, on Bridget's grand match and on the baby Katy was expecting the following April. Katy imagined she saw a fleeting smile in Mary's eyes when she told her the month. As much as to say, 'He lost no time.' But the thought was in her own guilty mind.

The wedding was the biggest one the parish had ever known. Crowds gathered outside to call down blessings on the parties as they arrived. The church was packed with the local tradesmen, saloon keepers and politicians and Mr and Mrs Ryan were there and Katy, as the mother of the bride, was sitting in front of them. Not allowing herself to cry when they were married. Thinking of Bridget as a baby, a little girl, looking at her as a radiant bride, her veil thrown back and the October sunlight shining on her glorious hair. And silently she prayed for God never to bless them with a child, never to allow hers and Jamsie's blood to flow and mingle with a child of his.

Bridget, happy and tired after the day's celebrations waited for Terence to come to her. 'Terence, you can come in now, I'm ready for bed.' In the bathroom, Terence drank rum from his hip flask and his sweating hands dulled the flask's silver cover. 'Terence,' Bridget called again. He came out of the room.

She was standing before the mirror brushing her hair. It draped her shoulders like a golden cloud. He could see the front and back of her, the white satin nightgown draping her body, the froth of lace at her neck. He was reminded of the flowers, the lilies with which he had once wanted to fill his room. And remembered his first encounter with lilies. Years ago he had taken one from a Protestant grave and stared in fascination at it. He had never seen anything like it, anything that felt

354

like it when he touched its petals. He took it home and his mother shouted for him to take it away. Lilies were for funerals, for the funerals of the gentry – lilies were unlucky. In the lean-to where the pig slept he went with his lily and when eventually he tired of looking and touching and smelling it he tore it into pieces and threw it in the pig's trough. Bridget was like a lily, his lily, in his room for him to do with as he wished.

She turned from the mirror and smiled shyly, half-invitingly. 'Do you like it?' she asked. 'Madame Renée made it for a wedding present. It's satin,' her hands smoothed the stuff. 'It feels gorgeous.' Then she went to him, her arms held out. 'Oh Terence,' she said, putting her arms round him. 'Oh Terence, I love you.' Awkwardly he embraced her, his hands on the white satin, his fingers sliding over it.

'Terence,' Bridget whispered and pressed her body close to his. 'Kiss me, Terence.' She brought his head down until his lips were on hers. And inside himself the frenzy began.

His hands were grasping the folds of satin, and he wanted as he had torn the shift from the girl on the ship to tear the nightdress from Bridget's body, throw her on the bed, subdue her struggles, gag her screams, bury himself inside her and find release from the frenzied madness that possessed him.

Bridget began to struggle, her hands pushing at him, moving her mouth, pulling it away from him. 'You hurt me.' Her fingers went to her lips. 'You hurt me, look I'm bleeding,' she said. Her eyes were frightened. 'You didn't mean it, I know that, only you shouldn't have kissed me so hard.' She smiled her forgiveness. 'Will we go to bed?' she asked, reaching out a hand.

It was leaving him, the frenzy, subsiding, the desire to beat her into submission. His mind was clearing, he could think again. And he thought, she's my wife. She has to submit. I can do with her what I like.

'Come on,' she said, 'you must be awful tired.' She talked to him as if he were a child. She took his hand and led him to the bed. He lay beside her. 'I'll turn off the light,' she said and pulled the hanging cord which extinguished the gas. They lay in silence for a while. Then she said, 'You can kiss me again if you like,' and she whispered, 'I love you. I'm glad you're my husband. I'm that proud of you.'

He listened and was gratified. She moved nearer to him. He could hear the swish of the satin. Her arms went round him and he was aroused. Her nightgown and his nightshirt were in the way of what he wanted to do. Clumsily he struggled with the clothes. He ejaculated before the nightdress was halfway up her legs. He rolled off her and turned away.

355

Bridget felt the moistness on her clothes and thought of the beautiful nightie being ruined. Suddenly she was no longer happy or excited. She wasn't sure of what should have happened between her and Terence. Maybe this was all. The damp patch was drying, it felt stiff as if starched. She didn't like what had happened. Her mouth was hurting, her sore lip throbbing. She thought of her mother and father asleep now in bed. Her eyes filled with tears and she wished she was at home lying beside Mary Kate.

During the night Terence woke her. He was on top of her and her nightdress was above her waist. Frantically he moved on her until she felt a dampness spill on to her thighs. Again he left her and again he said nothing. 'Terence,' she said. 'Terence, say something, speak to me.' He ignored her. She longed for it to be daylight. In the morning, she told herself, everything would be all right. In the daytime Terence would leave her alone.

When next she woke Terence was up and dressed. He came and sat on the bed. She loved him, she told herself. She hadn't liked what had happened. Perhaps no one did, perhaps that was why no one spoke about it. But it was how God had made it to be, so that a woman and man could have children. She would get used to it. It must be the same for everyone. It must have been the same for her mother and father, too.

Terence was bending close to her, his voice low and threatening. 'You're to tell no one. No one, do you hear?'

She didn't understand what he was talking about and was afraid to ask for an explanation.

'Don't you,' he said, 'ever mention what went on between us last night, to no one. Not to the priest, your mother, to no one.'

'But I wouldn't, Terence. I wouldn't say a word. You don't. You don't talk about that.'

'If you do I'll kill you.' She believed him. She was terrified. He looked like a madman. 'And don't start crying. I can't bear crying.'

'No, I won't. I wasn't. I won't.'

'Good,' he said. 'Stay in bed, have a sleep. I'll be back in an hour. I'll take you out and buy you something for your jewellery box.'

As the weeks passed she was tempted to ask Maura who had a young married cousin, if she could find out what did happen with a man and his wife in bed. But always when she almost asked she remembered Terence's threat to kill her, his voice, his eyes when he made the threat and she remained silent.

On the first of April, 1861, Katy had another son and she called him Sean. Everyone said he was the image of Jamsie. Katy said he looked like himself and Jamsie said he was their Golden Boy.

Bridget came to visit and she and Katy talked of everything except her marriage. She looked well. Katy hoped she was happy.

For her as her pregnancy had progressed a peace had descended on her and she had come to think that life was like the sea. Sometimes so beautiful and breathtaking you thanked God for letting you live. And you prayed for it to remain so, for the calm stillness to stay. For you to float along from one day to the next. For peace to be with you and yours. But like the sea you never knew from where or when the change might come and your hopes be dashed like the white crested waves dashing against the shore. And you waited and watched and prayed. Sometimes it was only a little storm which passed quickly – sometimes a tempest that raged for a long time.

And she prayed, and again after her safe delivery: 'Please God, let it be like this for a while more. Let me and Jamsie see them reared. Let the waves be gentle for poor Thomas and poor Bridget and for all those I love. Let it stay like this for a while more.'

Epilogue

The American Civil War began the week after Katy's son was born. Thomas, caught up in the recruiting drive, joined the army. Katy was distraught. His going diminished the pleasure she had found in their recent good fortune. Only the baby received her full attention. But even as she nursed him, Thomas was seldom far from her thoughts. Thomas would be killed. God would punish her transgression by taking his life. She raged and grieved and prayed and wished she had taken Peader's advice and encouraged him to go to sea.

But as time passed and rage and grief ran its course she found acceptance and picked up the threads of her life. A young Irish girl now helped her in the new house and laundry. She planted flowers and a lilac tree in the yard, sent Thomas parcels, wrote him letters and prayed that by the time the lilac tree bore flowers the war would be over and Thomas safely home.

Jamsie, determined never to work under anyone again, bought a horse and cart and told himself that one day he would be the biggest carrier in New York. However, his gold mine ran out but not before he had acquired another horse and cart.

Mary Kate went to College. On Miss Cook's advice, Katy set her heart on Danny becoming a doctor. Already, Miss Cook pointed out, children of immigrants were qualifying in the professions. Danny was clever enough to do likewise. Please God, Katy prayed and wished he was less interested in the news from Ireland which Peader, now a teacher in Dublin, sent him regularly.

Mary Kate qualified and got a teaching job in Brooklyn. Bridget lived in a big house with servants to which Katy, though invited, never went. Bridget came home to visit occasionally. She brought presents for her father and the baby. Her husband was never mentioned. Each time she left Katy cried for the closeness that had once been theirs and now no longer existed.

Three years after the war began, Terence McCabe was killed. He had long ago given up his attempts to make love to Bridget. When he needed a woman he went to a brothel. Choosing one far enough from his own

358

locality where he was sure of not being recognised. Leaving it one night he was attacked, stabbed and robbed. He died almost instantly but not before he remembered Hell and its eternal fire. He had a big funeral to which Katy wouldn't go. Only her fear for Thomas' life stopped her rejoicing that he had lost his.

After ostensibly mourning Terence for a year but privately congratulating herself on the fortune she had inherited, Bridget opened a fashionable milliners on Broadway.

Sometimes, looking at Sean, Katy thought she saw in him a resemblance to Peader and she remembered her days on Staten Island and that Thomas was still at the war. God might yet exact His price. And she prayed more fervently than ever for his safety. Yet still she could not confess her sin for she could not regret it.

A month before the war finished Bridget came on one of her usual visits. Amongst her gifts was one for Katy. 'Please,' she said, 'accept this one. It's a long time ago since you let me give you a present.' Katy took the gift – a book of poetry, Walt Whitman's *Leaves of Grass*. 'I remember when you worked for Dr Purcell you mentioned it.'

'Fancy you remembering that,' said Katy, trying to sound brusque for fear she would cry.

'I remember lots of things,' said Bridget, and before leaving kissed Katy's cheek.

Thomas came home. And as she had so many times in her life and especially for Thomas, Katy made an Act of Thanksgiving and then another for her lovely family, for Jamsie, for the life that had been given to them in America and for the signs of peace between her and Bridget.